Honeymoon

From Mugs and Saucers
to Moonlit Waters

W K WAITE-GRACIE

INTRODUCTION

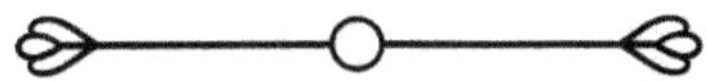

W Katherine Waite-Gracie, the international best-selling author of *The Mugs & Saucers Café*, is back with the 4th book in The Maggie Ashberry Series, and it's hotter than ever! Just when you think Maggie and Billy couldn't spice things up more, they do, and they manage to do so multiple times and ways while traveling around the beautiful island of Jamaica in The Emerald Pearl. With more delicious encounters than you can count, you'll find yourself smiling happily and breathing heavily, wondering where this insatiable couple will end up next. Travel around Jamaica with one of the sweetest and spiciest couples and drift away into Katherine's sensual fairy tale fantasy world of Maggie Ashberry.

MAGGIE ASHBERRY – Honeymoon – Playlist

Reggae music on the radio
Feels So Right – Alabama
Hey Baby – Bruce Channel
All Of Me – John Legend
Patience – Guns N' Roses
Free Fallin' – Tom Petty
Heart Like Mine – Blue Rodeo
Possession – Sarah Mclachlan
Rose-Coloured Glasses – Blue Rodeo
To Love Somebody – Blue Rodeo
Emmylou – First Aid Kit
Kiss You All Over – Exile
Misty Blue – Dorothy Moore
Sugar Sugar – The Archies
I Can't Help Myself – The Four Tops
Rock Me Gently – Andy Kim
Heart Of Gold – Neil Young
Harvest Moon – Neil Young
Old Man – Neil Young
Interstate Love Song – Stone Temple Pilots
Crash Into Me – Dave Matthews Band
Stereo – The Watchmen
Knockin' On Heaven's Door – Guns N' Roses
One Week – Barenaked Ladies
Runaway Train – Soul Asylum
Boombastic – Shaggy
6345789 – Wilson Pickett
My Girl – The Temptations
Georgia On My Mind – Ray Charles
You've Really Got A Hold On Me – The Miracles
What I Say – Ray Charles
You're The First, The Last, My Everything – Barry White

Ain't No Sunshine – Bill Withers
Beautiful Brown Eyes – Solomon Burke
He'll Have To Go – Solomon Burke
Goodbye Baby, Baby Goodbye – Solomon Burke
Bring It On Home – Sam Cooke
Nothing Can Change This Love – Sam Cooke
You Send Me – Sam Cooke
Lovable – Sam Cooke
I've Been Loving You Too Long – Otis Redding
Cry To Me – Solomon Burke
Moondance – Van Morrison
Just Breathe – Pearl Jam
Wondering Why – The Red Clay Strays
Into The Mystic – Van Morrison
Coconut – Harry Nilsson
Somethin' Bout A Boat – Jimmy Buffett
Here With Me – Dido
Sunshine – Nazareth
Listen To Your Heart – Roxette
Angel – Aerosmith
With Or Without You – U2
Forever Young – Rod Stewart
Fall In Deep – BLOW
Do You Remember – Jarryd James
Play The Part – Two Feet
Put It On Me – Matt Maeson
On Our Knees – Konoba (featuring R.O)
The Fault Lines – David O'Dowda
Apocalypse – Cigarettes After Sex
Looking Too Closely – Fink
Santa Claus Is Back In Town – Elvis Presley

TABLE OF CONTENTS

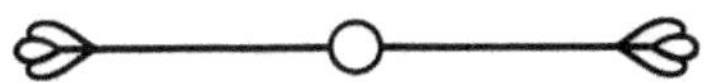

CHAPTER 1

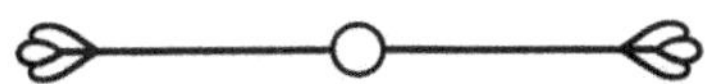

Maggie sat on the edge of the bed as they kissed, Billy leaning forward over her. She moved to the side, their lips unlocking as she stood up. Billy looked at her with some confusion, and she gave him a sultry stare, her emerald green eyes flashing with hunger. She pushed him back onto the bed, lifted her wedding dress and pulled her lacy peach coloured underwear down, letting them fall to the floor, keeping her garter belt in place. She grinned at him, then undid his pants, and pulled them off him. Billy's boxers were already showing signs of great excitement. She leaned over him and kissed his mouth, deeply, pressing into him forcefully, then, she undid his shirt buttons, and looking into his deep blue eyes intensely, pulled his shirt open and ran her tongue from the top of his boxers all the way up to his mouth, in one long wet lick, the hair that was free, falling in ringlets, cascading down over his tanned muscular body. When she got to his mouth, she bit his lower lip, giving it a little tug, still staring into his eyes. Billy's deep blue eyes flashed cheekily and she moved down again, pulling him free from his boxers, watching him spring out, and continuing her seductive gaze. She held the base of his hard dick and leaned down, licking all around the top, then from the base to the tip, her hand running up to meet her mouth. Sliding her hand back down, she took him into her mouth, slowly, wrapping her tongue all around him as she moved up and down, with deep, wet slides. A few more caramel curls freeing themselves from her bun, tickling his skin softly.

"Ohhh, Gawd!" Billy growled. Maggie moved slowly away from his body and licked the end of him once more. She moved back up his body, kissing her way over his skin as she encouraged him to move up all the way onto the bed. Raising her dress again, she climbed on top of him and slid right down. With a mutual moan, Billy grabbed her legs and she slid her hips back and forth, slowly, in small circles, up and down his lap. "Maag, you're *so* hot," he called out. She let her body fall forward to kiss his mouth. He reached up and ran his hands back into her curls, holding her face as their tongues found each other and started lashing. Maggie's hips still grinding back and forth and around and around. Billy grabbed her hips and squeezed, kissing her raised neck. "Mag, you're driving me crazy!" Billy groaned looking into her eyes. She stared back, still not saying a word. Sitting up straight, she lifted her body up and down, riding him harder. "Awww," he moaned happily, and she became more aroused. "Maggie, talk to me," he growled, helping her rise, up and down with his hands, her white dress spread out all around her over his strong body. She looked into his eyes again.

"Tell me what you want Billy." She felt his hips thrust forward as he watched her moving up and down. She raised her hands, unleashed her long loosely pulled up hair, letting it fall over her shoulders, her curls bouncing on her breasts with electricity. Her eyes were deep, and seductive. Her head tilting to one side, mouth open, eyes closed, and she continued to bounce up and down. Billy's legs moved longingly, with elation, his back arching with pleasure and his growing desire to pound her.

"Just talk to me Mag," he said, groaning deeply. She dropped down, hands on either side of him on the bed, grinding in circles again, looking into his eyes.

"Billy, you make me so hot," she breathed, and she felt his hips moving deeper, holding her legs tight. "You feel so big," she whispered, and he looked into her eyes again, and she saw that dark animal instinct behind the blue that made her crazy. "I want you to play rough with me Billy," she told him with a velvety purr, and suddenly he was grabbing her, and with purpose and strength, he flipped them over, so he was above her. Then he grabbed Maggie again and flipped her over onto her front, pulled her dress back up and spread her legs. "Billy!" she cried, and his face was in her hair, growling, biting her ear, her shoulders, sucking her neck and then, he pushed himself inside of her, hard, holding her hands above her head and he continued gliding in and out with force.

"Talk to me Mag," he growled in her ear, his body heavy and hot on top of hers.

"Don't stop Billy," she said, so quietly, her body writhing under his. "Oh God, harder Billy!" He let go of her hands and she felt him leave her body. She was almost crying with the intense erotic vibrations and excitement coursing through her as he pulled her up to all fours, grabbing onto her hips and pounding himself back inside her.

"Owwww!" she cried with aching delight, her head dropping, bracing herself.

"Maggie!" he yelled.

"Ohhh..." she moaned, and he moved faster, pulling her into him as he hit harder. She knew he was close, and she was so turned on but knew she wouldn't finish like this. "Billy, lay on top of me again," she said, and she slid her legs back down to lay flat, Billy following her down and still moving in and out.

"What do you want?" he breathed.

"Touch me while you move inside of me." Billy's hand slid under her hip to her abdomen, then down to her center with an arousing growl.

"Oh my God Mag, you're so wet," breathing into her ear as he spoke, and she felt herself starting to let go.

"Billy, I'm so close." His glides quickened again, his fingers rubbing her clit with pressure.

"Maggie, I'm going to cum!" he called out, and she reached down and held his hand. "Ahhhh..." he moaned, and Maggie inhaled deeply and breathed out, long and slow.

"Ohhh, Billy," she moaned, moving her body into his fingers as her legs started to vibrate. Both of their bodies shaking forcefully as they finished. Billy landed on her, wrapped in her hair, both breathing hard and fast. He rose up a little and she turned over to face him. With their chests rising and falling quickly, they grinned at one another before Billy leaned in. Grabbing each other's faces and kissing fiercely, then Billy held her face and looked at her.

"Mag, you are so effing hot!" he told her with a devilishly cheeky grin.

"Billy, I could do this with you all night long." Maggie lifted her head and kissed him hard. "You drive me wild, Lover!" she said.

"I bet the boat was rocking," Billy added with a chuckle. Maggie laughed and kissed him again. Her skin was still tingling, and both continued to experience random shivers throughout their bodies. "Well, Mrs. Stanton," Billy said with enthusiasm, "That was...mmm...WOW! Damn fine!" Maggie grinned at him.

"Why yes it was Mr. Ashberry." Both laughing and kissing again.

"And we *have* been at it all night, Beautiful!" Billy told her looking at the clock with a big grin.

"So, do you think that was enough to consummate things?" she asked him with a smiley sweet look. Billy squeezed her closer to him, then with his head falling back he yelled,

"NEVA!" and rolled around the bed with her, kissing her neck, Maggie giggling, then stopping on top of her and looking at her lovingly, his lips pressed against hers, Maggie's hands in his hair, they held one another close.

"I love being on your boat for our honeymoon Babe, but there's one problem." Billy looked at her with some concern, "There's no room service," Maggie added.

"Well, everything is all hooked up Mag, I could be your room service. What would you like?" he flashed his cheeky Billy grin at her.

"Oh, but Mr. Stanton, I don't have any money to pay for your services," she replied, smiling seductively at him.

"I think we could come up with some sort of arrangement," he answered, winking at her. "Coffee, Babe?" he asked, finally climbing out of bed. She watched him with bemused satisfaction. His body was still strong and beautiful. He had always been very active. In his youth, he was in cadets, played baseball, football, was on a hockey team, and in dance classes his parents made him take for years, all of which had kept him fit and healthy. Then he became even more fit in his years in the military, before honorable discharge, and he continued to keep himself in shape over the years. Maggie never grew bored of taking any chance she got to check him out. His body was still taught and muscular. His hair still thick and dark, the odd fleck of grey mixed in, adding to his rugged beauty. Maggie was still quite fit too. She had grown up a hardworking farm girl, and was strong, doing a lot of the work herself for years, especially when her parents became ill, and she was left to care for them and run the farm. She had ridden horses her whole life and had great strength and beautiful posture. She walked every day, did yoga almost every day and a number of months ago, she had started teaching a belly dancing class with her friend Carla. She swam regularly and rode her favourite stallion, Black Beauty, a couple times a week. Her legs and core muscles were very strong, and she was quite flexible. Also, the amazing, very active sex life they shared definitely added to their fitness as well.

"Those are some sweet cheeks you got Lover!" she said as Billy left the room. He turned his head and grinned at her.

"Thank ya Ma'am," he replied, then proceeded out to the front quarters of the catamaran. She hadn't really had a chance to take in the cozy beauty of the boat yet. It really was lovely, all pine wood interior, with cozy little cubbies, and cute little round windows. She noticed their luggage under a long desk like shelf on the outside wall of the bedroom, along with her shower gifts. She decided to get up, grabbing her red satin 'Mrs.' housecoat and went out to find Billy. She walked past a closed door with a sign on it. One half read 'Gulls' the other said 'Buoys'. She giggled to herself thinking, *Cute, corny Billy.* The front half of the boat was pretty much a wall of windows, and Maggie looked out onto the crystal waters of St. Ann's Jamaica with a smile. The sun shining across it, creating millions of sparkling, dancing diamonds on the surface. Along one windowed wall, ran a long-curved cushioned bench couch with a table in front of it, little book nooks, lanterns, and odds and ends here and there. A 6-step staircase going up to the outer deck, then along the other side there was a comfy chair with another little shelf behind it, a little apartment sized fridge, sink, stove, and L-shaped countertop. The coffee maker was burbling and working away, and Maggie walked up the steps to have a better look at the beach. She was now under a little roof, where the outside table and bench seats were, and above was where the steering console was located. She sat down and looked out over the water, the sun and a smile on her face.

"Hello Beautiful," came Billy's deep voice. Maggie looked at him and grinned. He was in his matching 'Mr.' housecoat.

"Hello Handsome," she replied.

"Coffee's almost ready, Mag," he told her. She stood up, giving him a kiss as she passed him, and gave his sweet cheeks a squeeze.

"Okay, I'll be back." She made her way to the washroom. It was super cute and again, the walls were finished with pine wood. It wasn't very big, but there was a sink, a few cupboards, a shower in the corner, and another little round window above the toilet.

"Looks like all our stuff is already here Mag," Billy informed her as she came up on deck with their coffee. "And look Babe," he said grinning, waiting for Maggie to put the mugs down, then holding her hand and pulling her to the back of the boat. There, attached to the railing was a long banner, in every colour, reading 'JUST MARRIED'. The two of them grinned at each other, then pulled one another close, gazing dreamily into each other's eyes and kissing a long deep kiss. They sat down and enjoyed their coffee in the warm sun, Maggie's legs across Billy's lap.

"So, what's the plan Billy?" she asked him curiously.

"What do you mean Babe?" he replied.

"Where do we go from here?" she asked. He had taken another sip of coffee, put it down and rubbed her leg, smiling at her warmly.

"Well, it's another one of your birthday surprises Babe," he answered, winking cheekily at her.

"Goodness, there's been a lot of those!" she laughed, leaning forward and kissing his cheek.

"Well, unless you'd rather not." He stopped for a moment, smiling hopefully before going on. "Carla, Frankie and I have worked things out so that you and I can drift around on the Emerald Pearl for the next month or so Babe!" Maggie was at a loss for words.

"Really?" she said, grinning, but not too sure about the plan. "Like, live on the boat? For a whole month?" she asked him. He chuckled and nodded.

"Yes Mag, just you and me and wherever we want to go." He leaned towards her, his hand running farther up her leg, the other holding her face gently, and he kissed her softly. Looking into her eyes and grinning he asked, "So, what do you think Beautiful. Wanna be my first mate?" Maggie grinned, leaned closer and rubbed her nose with his.

"I've said it before, gorgeous Lover of mine, I'll gladly go wherever you go." Billy looked so pleased and pulled her face close with both hands and gave her a big kiss.

"So, Frankie's staying at the house, and he's even going to keep your bookshop going for you Mag," he said happily. "We talked about bringing Bo and Bill but thought it would make it harder for us to do what we want, when we want." Maggie looked a little sad suddenly, already missing her old kitty. Billy quickly added, "We could always make arrangements to have them later on Mag, if you'd like." And he kissed her on the nose. She snuggled up under his chin, her head on his chest and wrapped her arms around him. He wrapped his over top of hers and held her close. "I love you," he said softly. She grinned again and squeezed him.

"And I love you." After they snuggled for a little while, Maggie was wondering about something else. "But, what about our second week at Sunshine Villa?" she asked.

"Oh, all the Cabiners are staying in it for the week. That was all part of the plan too Mag. They're coming down later to see us off." Maggie put her head back down and rested it on his shoulder. "We'll have to go and grab some groceries and figure out where you want to visit first."

Billy went back inside and came out a minute later with some maps and papers and a pencil. He laid them out on the table for him and Maggie to look at. "Okay, Mag, I'm thinking it might be nice to follow the coast and make our way around Jamaica completely. Then, if we have time, we could do the Caribbean route too, and eventually make our way back here." Tracing his finger along the route on the map as he spoke, then he looked up at her and smiled. Maggie grinned at him.

"That sounds amazing." She leaned against him and looked up into his twinkling eyes.

"Mag, I'm so excited to do this trip with you!" Billy reached out and held her cheek, kissing her warmly. Maggie reached up and held his hand, smiling as she kissed him back.

"When's everyone coming?" she asked as he kissed her forehead.

"Around 4:00 I think, Babe. We should probably grab our groceries soon." She was sliding her hand under his robe now and looking at him with deep eyes.

"Ok Billy... let's get going." Maggie grinned at him as he jumped a little at her hand moving down between his legs. He kissed her, long and hard, then for a change, it was Billy who said,

"We better get going Mag." Maggie looked surprised. "Not that I wouldn't rather have you sit on my lap!" he added with a wink. Maggie smiled hungrily as she kissed him again, pushing her lips firmly against his.

"Mmm, ok Billy..." and they kept kissing. The two of them grinning. Maggie looked into his eyes and saw his smiling back. "Well, let's go before I jump your bones then Mr. Ashberry!" Billy's head fell back as he chuckled at her, grabbing at her as she left the seat, and they made their way below deck. They dressed, and kissed, and kissed and dressed, then kissed some more. Finally stepping up onto the dock and heading up the beach to the road.

"There's a grocer just down the street, Mag." He pointed as they walked hand in hand, through the happy hustle and bustle of tourists. After a few minutes they reached a store called Dolphin Market and went inside. It was quite large, and they seemed to carry both local and international foods. Maggie grabbed a cart and she and Billy started off with some produce, then grabbed some cheese and eggs, bacon and a couple different kinds of cold cuts. As Maggie pushed the cart, Billy moved up close behind her, wrapped around her with his hands on top of hers, Maggie giggling as he kissed her neck.

"Billy!" she exclaimed laughing. He kissed her again, then walked along beside her, giving her butt the odd squeeze, or rubbing her shoulders as they walked the aisles. They got a few different condiments, rice, bread, milk, coffee and juice, bottled water and of course a case of club soda, stopping at the liquor aisle so Billy could grab some Red Stripe.

"Should we get some snack foods, Mag?" he asked, holding a bag of chips in his hands already.

"Sure Babe, whatever you like," she answered, and Billy tossed 2 bags into the cart. They paid for their groceries, then taking their bags, made their way back to the beach and onto the boat. After they put everything away, Billy came up behind Maggie and wrapped his arms around her, nestling his face against her neck.

"Mmmm, you smell delicious, Babe!" he said, taking a deep breath. Goosebumps running up Maggie's arms.

"What time is it Billy?" she asked hopefully. She felt him turn, then he answered in her ear, sending more goosebumps up her neck.

"Almost 4:00." She turned in his arms and kissed him.

"Oh, that's too bad." She grinned. He pulled her tight and kissed her hard, holding her head in his hands. As they were kissing, they heard voices and the loudest one yelling,

"Hey Mr. and Mrs. Dude, you guys decent?" They grinned at each other and headed up to the deck. All 17 of their friends were on the dock grinning at them.

"Hey Mags! Sweet Cheeks!" Carla hollered, waving and smiling. Becky next to her holding a huge basket.

"We brought you two a going away gift!" Becky said, walking towards the boat and handing Billy the basket.

"Wow, you guys, look at all that. Thank you!" Maggie said, checking it out and smiling at them all. She could see snacks, some little bottles of champagne, jars of pickles, jams, spreads, all kinds of goodies.

"Oh, and take the CD player too," Becky added as Justin handed it and a CD carrier to Maggie.

"Yuh two coming up here for hugs or we hafta come aboard?" Alvita asked, grinning at them. Delroy reached out his hand for Maggie and she climbed out of the boat, Billy right behind her, and as Delroy hugged Maggie, Alvita hugged Billy. They were passed between friends, hug after hug, with lots of big smiles and happy sails.

"Oh, it's been so great seeing you all again!" Maggie said, tearing up as she let go of Tina and Bridget, the three of them in one big hug.

"Ya, thanks again for coming everyone!" Billy called out grinning.

"Carla, you'll check in on Frankie for me?" Maggie asked, going over and giving her and Stu one more hug.

"You betcha, Mags!" she replied with a nod.

"You two stay safe, alright?" Stu said to them, shaking Billy's hand.

"We'll get a hold of you in a month before we head home, Carla," Billy called out from the boat. Carla smiled and waved.

"Bon voyage!" Delroy announced.

"Bye!" "Have fun!" "Don't forget your sea legs!" "Enjoy yourselves!" All their friends shouted out randomly.

"Don't forget to leave the boat once in a while, you two!" Jon added, chuckling. Everyone smiling and wishing them well as Maggie climbed back down onto the boat. Billy and Delroy untied it then looked at one another.

"Be safe my bredren. Happy sails. Bless." he told Billy, and they hugged and patted each other's backs. Billy hopped back down onto the boat, walked up to the cockpit and started the Emerald Pearl up. Maggie went up and stood with him, both waving to the many hands waving back at them from the dock, and off they went, into the turquoise waters of their honeymoon.

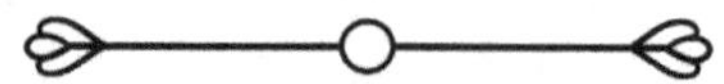

CHAPTER 2

They headed down towards Kingston first, hoping to port in the harbor for dinner. They moored at the Royal Jamaica Yacht Club, reported their cargo, showed their passports and all the paperwork Billy had ready for their travels, then left the mooring area to go grab a bite to eat. Maggie and Billy could feel the history as they walked through the streets of old and new architecture of the now quiet fishing village. Noticing plaques and statues with folklore and stories here and there, along with many fishing boats and little market vendors, with locals shopping for the best catches of the day. They found a tiki bar, with a plaque on the wall of the kitchens stating that 'Port Royal, was known as the wickedest city on earth. Beware marauding pirates, daring naval conquests with their looting riches, destruction and devastation.'

"Rrr, better watch out me pretty!" Billy said from right behind Maggie, snuggling up close and giving her ass a little squeeze. "Wouldn't want anything wicked to happen to you." She turned to smile at him, he grinned and gave her a wink. They were taken to their seats where they sat by the water and enjoyed the first dinner of their honeymoon, looking around at the beauty of their surroundings, just as the sun was setting. The menus were fun and keeping with the pirate theme had skulls and crossbones, ships and sword images on them. Both Maggie and Billy ordered fish and chips. Maggie had an ice-cold Ting and Billy had a drink called The Kingston. After they paid their bill, they walked along the beach for a little while, the nightlife starting to kick off. It wasn't too much more lively, loud or busy here then it had been in St. Ann, but there were a number of places that seemed to jump into life as the sun went down. Maggie and Billy were soon lured into dancing at one of the bars they passed on their way back to the boat.

Every bar seemed to be playing reggae music, lively and happy people dancing everywhere. They danced together for an hour, smiling and laughing and snuggling happily, before they decided to call it a night. They climbed back onto the Emerald Pearl and locked up for the night.

"Hey, Billy?" Maggie called while she was in the bedroom changing out of her day clothes.

"Ya, Babe," he answered from the living area.

"Who named this boat?" She heard him chuckle.

"I did." Maggie hung her dress up on one of the many hooks along the wooden wall.

"When did you name it?" she asked, finding her green teddy from her girl's night presents and slipping it on.

"Almost 13 years ago, Babe," he answered, his voice sounding closer now.

"And why did you name it that?" she asked, grinning as she had already guessed what the answer might be. The bedroom door opened all the way, and Maggie turned to see Billy standing there grinning,

"It's named after you of course Mag, *my* Emerald Pearl." And as his eyes traced over her body, Billy gave a little growl and walked right up to her. "Wow, Mag, that's pretty nice!" he swooned, running his hands all over her. She grinned as she watched the excitement in his eyes.

"Oh, this old thing?" she answered, teasingly. He was already bent down kissing her neck, his arms around her and squeezing her ass.

"Mag, let's christen every port!" he said, not even coming back up, still kissing her neck, and squeezing her tight. She was holding onto him now too, her head back as she felt shivers running through her body.

"Mmmm, okay Lover!" she crooned. Billy lifted her off the floor and threw them both onto the bed, leaning over her and looking her up and down again, his eyes twinkling hungrily.

"You look beautiful," he said, leaning down and kissing her neck again, Maggie softly ran her hands all over his back. Billy's face moving down to kiss the tops of her breasts and down between them, then he looked up into her eyes, a small smile playing around the corner of his mouth and twinkling in his eyes.

"What are you up to Billy?" she asked, suddenly feeling more excited by him.

"Hmm, just thinking, I wish we had some ice cubes." She grinned at him.

"Oh, well, we'll have to save that for another night, my Lover." Billy continued kissing his way around her chest and back up her neck. Then he got off the bed and stood up, undressing, and watching Maggie. Her eyes happily soaking him in. She wasn't wearing anything except the teddy. She hadn't got that far before he came into the bedroom. Billy climbed back onto the bed and as he bent down and kissed her mouth deeply, she felt his hand running along the inside of her legs and up into her center, where his fingers played and pushed and caressed her. He was back to kissing and now sucking on her neck. Maggie felt very pleased and taken care of. "Billy, I need you," she whispered, and she heard him inhale deeply, kissing her mouth again, fingering her as he slid his tongue into her mouth. Maggie grabbed his body and pulled him towards her, kissing his shoulder and neck, her hunger for him escalating. Billy used his legs to spread Maggie's, then before he entered, he held one of her breasts in his hand, massaging it slowly, leaning down and taking as much of it as he could into his mouth, he sucked and licked hungrily. "Billy!" she called out, "I want you so bad..." she moaned, and he released her from his mouth, and she felt the tip of him enter her. He slid in a little, then back out, teasing her, watching her body moving on the bed, her hands pulling at him. Now they were staring at each other.

"Tell me what you want Mag," he said to her.

"I want you inside me, long and slow." And as she spoke the words, he did just that. "God, that's so hot Billy," she moaned, her head falling to one side, Billy moving in very slow, deep glides in and out of her wet body. Billy's eyes were closed, his face raised slightly as he tried to keep from moving faster.

"Ohhh, you feel good," he moaned, Maggie's legs wrapped around him. Billy bent down and kissed her, their tongues sliding together, the tips flicking slowly. Billy's movements started to become faster.

"No... slow." Billy moaned, finding it so hard not to attack her.

"Mag, this is so hot, I'm not going to last." She held his face and looked into his eyes again. With their gaze deep, she pumped her hips around his slow movements, watching with delight, his arousal, and the intensity in his eyes. "Mag!" he growled, and she felt the electricity growing.

"Don't stop Billy... I'm almost there." Their tongues reaching out and licking each other's. "Mmm. A little faster Billy," she breathed, still looking into one another's eyes. His thrusts became faster and harder. "Billy, I'm so close!" He slowed down again, dropping his face down to her neck and sucking gently. Maggie's eyes now rolling back, Billy's tempo quickening.

"Mag, I'm going to explode!" he breathed in her ear.

"Me too! Don't, stop, sucking!" And with a huge exhale, her body shook, Billy raising his head back up and sliding harder, moving steadily, instantly groaning with satisfaction.

"Ahhhh, gaaawd!" releasing from his lips, Maggie felt his body thrusting involuntarily into her as he finished. Then looking into each other's eyes again and grinning, Maggie running her fingers along the side of his face and into his hair Billy kissed her passionately. "It just keeps getting hotter Mag!" he told her between kisses. She grinned and kissed him harder.

"I know. Deeper and deeper, Lover," she purred back at him. "Wait until I get some of my other gifts out Babe!" she said, smiling at him. Billy's eyebrow raised and he grinned.

"Oh?" he said, "what sort of gifts?" her grin growing broader.

"You'll just have to wait and see." Smiling he kissed her again, half on her, half on the bed, laying with her. They held each other, running their hands over each other's bodies, sleepily. Maggie drifting off, feeling Billy's chest rising and falling, his warm breath on her skin, and a smile on her face.

* * * *

The next day, they enjoyed their coffee on deck, then dressed and decided to go to the beach, known as Lime Cay. Packing themselves some water and snacks they made their way to the marina to find someone to take them. They waited for a boat to ferry them to the islet, which took about 35 minutes, dropping them off at the woodsy sandy shores along with a few other visitors. The boat would head back to Port Royal 3 hours later. It was quiet and peaceful and the lovebirds felt like they were on their very own deserted island. With no amenities, no attractions except the glorious islet itself, it was a lovely way to relax and spend some time alone in the sand. They found a spot where no one else seemed to be and peeled off their clothes enjoying a skinny dip together before heading back to where they were to meet up with the others. Some had gone snorkeling while others seemed to just enjoy relaxing in the sun.

Once they were all in the boat, they sped off back to Port Royal feeling peacefully blissful. Maggie and Billy walked a bit and found a place to have lunch.

"It's just so beautiful here, Billy," Maggie said smiling, looking around in awe. Billy didn't answer, but when she looked back at him after a moment of silence, she saw he was looking at *her*, smiling.

"Ya, isn't it?!" he replied, and she grinned at him, leaning in close to give him a soft kiss. Billy inhaled deeply, kissing her cheek as they moved apart. They ate light and enjoyed cold drinks, sitting in the shade, feet wrapped under the table.

"Have you been here before, Babe?" Maggie asked, Billy still ogling her.

"Hmm? Um, yes actually, well, not *here*, but in Kingston." She took a drink of her club soda. "Only a couple of times though," he added, now looking out at the water. She felt like there was a story there, but something told her she did not want to know it. "Hey Mag, did you know Port Royal sank? Ya, there was an earthquake and most of it ended up at the bottom of the sea." Maggie grinned at him,

"Huh!" she responded with interest, and he grinned at her.

"Should we start our walk back, Beautiful?" he asked. Maggie nodded at him. They couldn't stop smiling at each other and when they both stood up, they were instantly wrapped in one another's arms, kissing. "Let's go Babe," he said, holding her hand as they left. They walked for most of the day, and by the time they got back to the Emerald, the sun was setting, so they went to the end of the dock and sat with their feet over the edge, Billy's arm around Maggie, Maggie's head against his shoulder, and relaxed as they watched the last of the glowing orb sink into the Caribbean Sea.

Surprisingly, they didn't attack each other when they boarded the boat. Well, actually, having walked beaches all day and both being in their mid-40s, it wasn't that surprising. But it was for Maggie and Billy. They were just *that* tired. They snuggled up together in bed and talked about their day. They had planned to move on to Port Esquivel the next day, and after they talked for a little longer, they soon drifted off to sleep.

CHAPTER 3

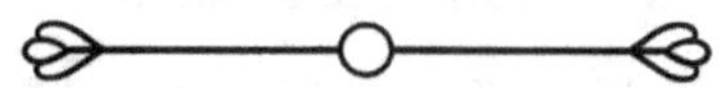

Maggie sat up in the cockpit with Billy as he navigated his way around the coast and headed for Port Esquivel. The water was fairly still, and they didn't see too many other boats out. They discovered why there weren't many boats out in the water with them when they headed into port, along with more than a dozen other boats waiting to do the same.

"Hey Mag, you know, we could always drop anchor and stay out in the sea tonight," Billy suggested to her. Maggie smiled.

"Sure Babe, that's fine with me." He nodded and redirected the boat, changing course before moving into the lineup. Billy turned the radio on and listened to the weather, then checking their coordinates and navigating them to a lovely spot nestled in an alcove, he turned the engine off and dropped anchor off the bow, then lowered the sails. They were about 50 feet from land, the waves gently rocking the boat as they floated in the alcove.

"Ok Mag, here's home sweet home for the night," Billy announced as Maggie walked over to him with a smile.

"Mmm, I like this, Billy. It's like we're the only two people in the world." Billy pulled her close and smiled down at her.

"And what would the last two people on Earth do, if they found themselves all alone, in the Caribbean Sea?" he asked, kissing her softly. Maggie grinned at him mischievously, then answered,

"Play rummy?" Billy chuckled, his eyes crinkled happily, kissing her again.

"Sure Mag, that's what we'll call it." They sat on the deck bench, snuggled up and just breathing in the sea air. It was still early, and the sun was high in the sky and getting very hot. They were tempted to go for a swim, but Billy informed Maggie of the southern Jamaican crocodiles, so they decided to go into the cabin out of the sun instead. They changed out of their clothes and put on their matching red robes. Billy went over and turned the little transistor radio on and found a station that came in, it was reggae of course, and he turned it down so they could just hear it in the background.

"So, Mag, what else did you get from your girls' night?" he asked her, smiling. She grinned broadly at him.

"Oh, well, lots of goodies. Say, speaking of goodies, where is our gift basket?" She got up to look around.

"Oh, I'm not sure, Babe," Billy answered looking around. "Oh, there Mag!" He pointed to it under the end counter of the kitchen.

"Let's see what we've got," she said, sitting on the floor and pulling things out. Billy came over and sat with her.

"Where's all your gifts from the girls, Mag?" he asked again.

"Oh, right, I'll be right back," she told him, getting up and going down the hall to the bedroom. After a moment she came back out with the box from Alvita. "Well, I'll save a few of the gifts for other moments for us, but this is a fun box!" she said putting it down on the floor between them. Billy opened the lid and looked inside, his face breaking into a huge smirk.

"Oh, ok, wow!" he said, and she laughed at him looking a little embarrassed as he pulled out the feathers, and vibrators and held them up looking at Maggie.

"Ya, crazy, eh?" she said grinning. "Keep looking Babe." He dove back in, now pulling out the tantric sex book and the whip.

"Mag, who gave you this stuff?" He was looking back into the box with a smile. Maggie laughed again.

"That would be your dear friend Alvita." Billy looked up quickly, with surprise.

"Wow, no wonder those two are always smiling!" he said, chuckling. "Oooh, what's this?" he asked, pulling out the oil and body cream set.

"Mmm, yes, that's one of the things I was excited about too, Lover." Billy started reading their labels.

"Hmm, think this stuff works?" he asked her, his eyes twinkling at her.

"Well, there's only one way to find out!" she answered, her eyes dancing as she looked back at him. "Oh, there's a game and some dice in there too Billy." she added, and he looked back into the box and found them.

"Anti-Climaxing?" he read, aloud. Maggie moved over to sit next to him as he opened the game up. There were two sets of cards, a timer, dice, two game pieces and a game board. "I say we play a boardgame Mag!" Billy smiled at her with devilish delight in his eyes.

"Oh, you do, do you?" she giggled. "Okay, as always, I'll do whatever you like my gorgeous Lover." He grabbed her and kissed her hard.

"Mmm, it makes me crazy when you say that Mag." They grabbed some pillows off the couch and sat on them on the floor, then Maggie read the rules.

"Okay, pretty straight forward. We take turns rolling the dice, moving, and doing what it says to do on the board. There are first half cards for each of us, then we go to the next level and use the *extreme* rated cards, and we try to make it to the final space in the second level." Billy was grinning again.

"And how do you *win*, Mag?" he asked, winking at her. Maggie looked back at the instructions.

"It says the object of the game is not to orgasm. The first to orgasm has to roll this extra dice, giving the amount of how many minutes they have to do whatever their partner wants." She looked up at him grinning too. "Okay, we need props. Lets see, it says we need alcohol, check, and us, check." Billy opened the game board.

"Okay, play ball!" he said enthusiastically. Maggie laughed, then Billy rolled a four and handed Maggie the die, she rolled a three so Billy went first.

"One, two, three." he counted moving his player, landing on "toast a drink." Maggie passed him one of the small bottles of champagne and the corkscrew from their gift basket. She grabbed two glasses and Billy poured half a glass in each.

"To us!" Billy said.

"To the fun we're about to have." Maggie said, their glasses clinking, Billy smirking as they had a drink, then gave each other a little kiss. "Remember, orgasm not!" Maggie said grinning. She picked up the dice and rolled and landed on a 'Passion' card, so she picked one up and saw that the card had a picture of a man with his shirt off and a woman standing behind him licking his back. Billy smiled and looked at Maggie, she smiled back. *This was going to be a challenging game if they played by the rules* she thought. The look on Billy's face told her he was thinking the same thing. Flipping the 5-minute timer, she crawled the distance between them and resting on her knees, moving behind him, she softly pulled his robe down his back, her hands running down his arms as she bent down and licked the nape of his neck, then ran her tongue down and across his shoulder blades, down his spine, around his lower back then kissing straight back up. She did this a number of times, moving her tongue back up to the top of his neck. He gave a shudder just as she kissed his ear and by his cheek, and she grinned thinking she might just win this game. She moved back to her spot across the board game from him on their floor pillows. He pulled his robe back up and stared at her, that cheeky twinkle in his eye. He rolled the dice still looking at her, then

"7" placing him on 'Passion'. He grinned hungrily at Maggie, picking up a card. Billy looked at the card and chuckled.

"Oh, Mag!" he said grinning. He moved across the floor towards her. Still grinning, he moved behind her, and softly with the back of his hand, moved her hair off her neck and shoulders, moving his face towards her neck.

"Shit!" she said, and Billy chuckled, his face moving against her neck, hearing him growling, Maggie already trying not to lose it. And there they were! His hot, soft, wet, well Maggie practiced, lips on her neck. *Keep it together Maggie* she thought to herself as he kissed her softly and slowly. She was looking at the timer. It was still half full. *At least he's not on my favourite side,* she thought. Then she felt Billy moving to the other side of her body, pulling her hair back and kissing the other side of her neck, his lips pressing deeply and breathing heavily. Maggie's chest was moving rapidly now, her breathing also becoming heavy, Billy very much growling now as he kissed her. Maggie pulled herself back and saw that time was up. Billy smiled at her then went back to his pillow. Maggie felt drugged.

"You alright, Mag?" he laughed.

"Mmm, very alright Babe!" she answered, smiling. "Here we go," she said, dropping the dice. "5" sitting her player next to Billy's on another 'Passion'. She was feeling pretty aroused and looking forward to following the next card's illustrated instructions. When she saw it she looked straight up at Billy with a big grin. She flipped the timer. "Oh, Billy, watch out, here I come!" Maggie moved towards him, again behind him, moving his arm to drape around her as she snuggled against his side and ran her hand down his pelvis, over the top of his thigh and grabbed between his legs over his boxers. She softly moved her open palm up and down over his now very firm package. She slid her hand as far down between his legs as she could reach and made sure to rub all the way back up to the very tip, then grasping as much of him as she could, stroking him a few times, and returning to running her hand over him.

"Mag." His voice was deep, and she looked and saw the timer was done.

"Want me to keep going?" she asked, slipping her hand back and sitting up again. He stared at her intensely. She handed him the dice and smiled. He rolled. This time he landed on 'drink', so they both had some champagne. "How're you doing, Lover?" she asked him, picking up the dice again. "Don't worry, we're almost at 2nd level!" she added, and they smiled at each other excitedly. She landed on a picture of hands held up, palms out. Checking the rules, it meant waiting for your partner before moving to the next level, and Billy was back to grinning at Maggie as he rolled. His picture was a man nibbling on a woman's breasts, through her shirt. Timer set, he spoke,

"This might be tricky for both of us." He kneeled in front of her, grabbed her hips, bending his face down, and started softly biting her breasts and nipples. It seemed like a long 5 minutes, a good 5 minutes, but they managed to do the action without either of them climaxing. "Ok Mag, ready for extreme rated?" She shook her head but smiled, a huge smile. And right off the bat, Maggie landed on an x rated passion card. She picked one up and looked, put it on her chest like it might bite, grabbed her champagne and took a big mouthful, then flipped the timer. Billy looked at her with a funny grin, then she watched his face become more serious and intensely aroused, as she stood up, pulled her black panties down, dropped her robe, then proceeded to lay down next to him on the floor, face up. She ran her hand down her body and in between her legs, closing her eyes, she continued to rub and finger herself, her other arm above her head on the floor, caramel curls spread out all around her face. She thought she might be self-conscious at first, but it was actually very erotic, and she had to reign herself back in. She

felt Billy kiss her mouth and she opened her eyes. He mouthed, "Timer."
Then kissed her again. "I don't know how much longer I can play this
Mag!" And he gave her a Billy smirk. She sat up and pulled her robe back
over her shoulders and grinned devilishly.

"Your turn Lover." He rolled, looked at his card and gave a long
intake of air. Maggie started the timer.

"Ooooh. Good luck, Mag!" She felt a shiver go through her. He
crawled towards her, held her and laid her down, resting her head on a
pillow. Billy pulled back her robe and began kissing and licking and
sucking her breasts. "Ohh, God!" she moaned, her hands sliding up into
his hair. "Billy, this is so intense!" she breathed, which only made his
movement more passionate. She wanted to pull him on top of her, but
the need to win was still strong. "Timer." she breathed, looking to her
side. Billy looked up at her from her chest and she grinned down at him.

"I like this game, Mag." he said, eyes flashing.

"Mmm, me too!" she cooed back. Maggie landed on another 'x
rated' and picked it up smiling, then looked at the card and looked back
up at Billy, shaking her head slightly.

"We're not going to make it, Lover!" she told him, putting the card
down. She let her robe fall off again and crawled over to Billy, grabbing
a small pillow for his head. She flipped the timer and said,

"Are you ready?" Then, she pulled off his robe, and got him to lay
down. She proceeded to climb onto his face and fall forward, her face
between his legs. A position she had not done in a very long time, but
something that was proving to be quite enjoyable, and effective, well not
for the game, but seemed to make both Maggie and Billy very happy.
The timer ran out, Maggie rolled off Billy and sat up. She was vibrating.
Billy looked at her like someone had just taken his favourite toy out of
his hands. They didn't speak, Billy just picked up the dice and rolled. He
landed on switch places with your partner, which put him on 'x rated.'

"Oh, Mag, think we'll last?" They were only three and four spaces from the finish. He grinned so big when he saw the picture.

"I think I've won, Babe!" he declared, putting the card back down, and flipping the timer. Neither one had their robe on now, and Billy moved purposefully towards Maggie, pressing his body up close behind her, sitting tall on his knees, and pulling Maggie up to do the same, he grabbed one of her breasts with one hand and with the other reached down to fondle her very wet and ready center. Her head fell back onto his body, and she reached one hand up behind her to wrap around his head, then he started kissing her neck.

"Ohhh..." Maggie moaned, Billy rubbing in circles right where she was aching for him to, squeezing her breasts, pinching her nipples, and pulling a little. "Billy, mmm Billy." She was so close. Then, time up. He was still in the same position but now stretched around a little to be able to kiss her mouth, and they could hardly stop.

"Wow, okay, just a few more spaces." he said as they moved back to their spots to sit. Maggie took a drink, then rolled, her hopefully last roll before any explosions. She reached the last space. The instructions read, if you land here first, you get to pick how you would like to orgasm, also making sure to fulfill your partner's orgasm. Maggie grinned broadly. "Hmm, what else is on these cards?" she wondered aloud, having a look. She looked around, then got up and went down the hall, coming back with a big towel and laying it down on the table. Maggie sat on the end and beckoned Billy over, where she kept herself perched on the edge, laid her upper body down, and invited Billy closer, placing her feet on his shoulders, his hands on her breasts, and sliding her hand down to guide him in. "Ahhh!" she cried as he slid in and moved back and forth, squeezing her breasts, Maggie's hands on his hands. "Billy, you feel amazing." she moaned.

"Mag, oh my gawd!" he was moving so fast, hitting her hard.

"Oh, Oh, Oh, Billy!" she cried with each hit.

"Ohh, I'm going to cummm." He groaned, and she pulled him forward slightly with her feet.

"Oh, God, Billy, don't stop, ohhh." Their bodies were shaking together, Billy still banging into her, Maggie cumming, with joyful cries. Billy's head fell back, finishing right after her. He was huffing and puffing with a smile.

"Oh... my... God, that was way better than Twister!" Billy said, and Maggie burst out laughing. He pulled her up to sit and they embraced and kissed, smiling and laughing, as their hands ran all over each other's backs. Although it was just a dirty sex game, the prolonged act of continuously stopping at the brink of release was incredibly intimate and vulnerable. It had brought them closer together. They were very lovey with one another and couldn't help but touch each other often.

After they tidied up the gifts and put their robes back on, they decided to make something to eat. They hadn't really planned on it tonight, thinking they'd be on land and able to find a restaurant, but had enough groceries to happily fill their bellies. They sat out on deck after dinner and enjoyed the beautiful sea air wrapped in each other's arms again. At one point, Maggie went back in and grabbed the open champagne, and they shared another half glass as they watched the sun setting. It was still warm, and very lovely, with the breeze off the water, the moonlight sparkling across the gentle waves. Billy stood up and held out his hand for Maggie. She took it and he pulled her up, into his arms and started dancing them around. Grinning up at him, Billy's eyes stared deeply into Maggie's. "Feels So Right" was what he started singing, pulling her close and wrapping his arms around her, dancing slowly. His deep sexy voice, in her ear, gave her shivers, as she held him tight, her eyes closed and smiling. She hugged him as they moved together, and one of Billy's hands slid up her back and into her hair to hold her head lovingly. Then he spun them around, doing an old time swing dance with her as they sang and laughed to "Hey Baby".

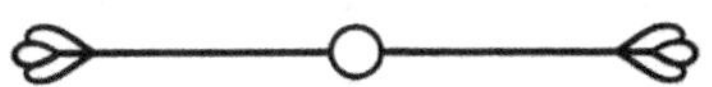

CHAPTER 4

"Coffee's ready, Billy." Maggie called towards the bedroom the next morning.

"Ok, be there in a minute." he answered, and she poured them both a cup. Billy came out and stood behind her, wrapping his arms around her and hugging her tight. "Loving this only us time, Mag." he said, kissing her neck.

"Mmm, me too Lover of mine." she replied, with pleasure. She turned in his arms and reached up to wrap hers around his shoulders, Billy leaning forward and kissing her lips lovingly.

"Are we going to shore today, my Love?" he asked, looking at her with a twinkle in his eyes.

"Doesn't matter to me Billy." He grinned, then took her hand and kissed it. She grabbed his coffee and handed it to him, then took hers and they went outside to enjoy the sunshine.

"You know Mag, I was thinking, maybe we should just pass by Port Esquivel and go straight on to Port Kaiser. Esquivel is very industrial, and in St. Elizabeth, there's a whole street of shops where we can stock up on supplies before we head up towards Lucea." She sipped at her coffee and smiled at him.

"Alrighty, Captain my Captain." she replied, and he grinned at her.

"Hey, that gives me an idea Mag!" he leaned over, holding her face and kissing her pressingly.

"Ohh?" she said when he pulled away.

"Mmhmm." he said, winking at her, but not telling her his plan. They sat quietly, enjoying their coffee and the beautiful scenery. Maggie reached out her hand and put it on his leg, Billy looked at her, his eyes smiling. She leaned over and kissed him, the two pressing together for a long time, then smiling at one another as they pulled apart.

"Well, going on to Kaiser sounds like a good plan to me, Billy." He finished his coffee and stood up.

"Ok, I'm going to check on a couple things, then we'll head towards Port Kaiser." She watched him walk away, and sat thinking about how much she loved him, and how lucky she was to have him.

"What can I do to help, Lover?" she asked, getting up.

"Hmm, well you can help me do a check before we move on, Babe." he suggested, smiling happily. They put their mugs in the sink and sat down with the maps at the table before checking the boat. "Okay, we should be there in time for dinner Mag, then we could shop in the morning if you like?" Maggie nodded her agreement. "Alright, all hands on deck." he said grinning at her, Maggie knowing he was being cheeky. She kissed him, then walked ahead of him up onto the deck. "Right, let's check the sails Mag, first the mainsail." He pointed towards it. Maggie followed him up towards the mainsail, where it was clipped in its protective cover. "You can start unclipping those, Mag." Billy said as he started on one end, meeting Maggie in the middle. "Alright Babe, now, back down." She followed him. Billy reached up to pull on a rope. "This is the mast Mag." he told her, patting the large vertical pole, "and this is the boom." he said, patting another one running horizontally with the sail rolled up on it.

"Okay, mast, boom, got it." Maggie repeated, and he gave her a little kiss and grinned at her.

"Now, this rope is the halyard, and we have to untie it to release the sail." Billy undid the rope and showed Maggie how the halyard moved the sail up and down, to adjust it. "Ok Mag, follow me to the helm." And they walked to the cockpit. "See this, Mag?" he pointed to a gauge.

"This shows what direction and speed the wind is traveling, which is how we know which way to line up the sail and the bow in order to catch the wind." Maggie gave Billy a kiss and he smiled at her. "With me so far, Babe?" he asked, and she nodded.

"Think so, my Lover." And she watched the dial on the gauge as Billy left to pull the anchor up, then returned and started the engine, and slowly moved the boat out into the open water. The gauge changed and Billy corrected it to point in the right direction for the wind, of which there wasn't a lot of. Billy showed her how you had to put the mainsail line in the winch, then crank the winch handle and raise the sail. She watched, loving seeing him doing one of the things he obviously enjoyed doing. His arm muscles contracted as he worked, and the sail slowly rose higher. "Wanna give it a go, Mag?" he asked her, smiling.

"Sure!" she said, walking closer and giving it a shot, surprised at how much strength was needed to do it.

"Almost there," he said looking up at the mast. "Okay Mag, perfect. Now we release the topping lift so the sail is free to catch the wind." And he switched something at the helm and used another crank. "Now we check our direction and follow our path to the next port." She sat in the chair next to him in the cockpit.

"What are those?" she asked, pointing to red dots on the screen.

"Rocks, Babe." he said, looking back up.

"Oh, that's handy then isn't it?" she said, smiling at him. He chuckled and smiled back at her.

"Yep." Billy got up and released something else.

"What's that do, Billy?" she asked, going over to watch.

"Just giving it a little more belly." he answered, and she looked at him funny. He pointed to the sail, "Watch." Maggie looked up and saw the sail bow a little more, thinking *oh, it does look like a belly.* "We'll have to put the jib up too Mag, there's not much wind right now." Billy showed her which handle to crank to pull the jib up. Billy sat down and turned the engine off. "We're only moving at about five knots Mag, so it'll probably be a couple hours before we get there." She sat down next to him and looked out at the water all around them, a huge smile spreading across her face.

"No rush is there? It's beautiful up here Billy." she said, closing her eyes for a moment and enjoying the sun on her face. When she opened them, he was smiling at her.

"*You're* beautiful, Mag." he replied, his eyes deep and bright in the sun.

"Thanks for the lesson, gorgeous Lover." He winked at her.

"You'll be all set to do it yourself next time, Mag." he answered, and she laughed.

"Ya, maybe in a few more next times, Billy." After a bit, she went down below and made them some lunch and brought it up with some cold drinks.

"Thanks Babe." he said, taking his sandwich from her and gladly starting to eat. "The wind has picked up, so, looks like we'll be there in about 40 more minutes." he informed her, looking at all the dials and gauges. The water was so blue and beautiful, and they both relaxed and enjoyed the rest of the journey. As they came close to Port Kaiser around 2:00, Billy hopped on the radio and made sure they had clearance to approach. As always, upon arrival, they showed all their paperwork, passports, cruising license, etc., paid to stay for the night, then they made their way to where they were told to moor the boat for the night. Billy and Maggie both lowered the sails, Maggie lowered the jib as it was smaller and easier for her, then they clipped the cover back in place on the mainsail and tied the rope holding the halyard in place. Billy showed Maggie how to tie a boat knot, which she thought was pretty cool, and soon became her favourite boat helper job.

Stepping onto the dock, Billy held out his hand for Maggie and they smiled at one another.

"So, where to Babe?" Billy asked, kissing her while pulling her in. Maggie's body landing against his. She kissed him and grinned.

"Back on the boat." she said, giving him another kiss. Billy turned back towards the boat and said,

"Ok, let's go!" Maggie laughed as he turned back towards her, taking her hand and walking up the dock together. They found a visitors main building and looked for information on the area, the closest restaurant to them, called Grapes 'n' Bunches was about a ten minute drive from the port. They grabbed a cab and with arms wrapped around each other in the back seat, they looked out their windows and soaked up their adventure.

"Wah gwaan Billay?" came a happy voice as they walked into Grapes 'n' Bunches. Both Billy and Maggie looked around to find the man who spoke.

"Jo!?" Billy said, seeing an older man behind the bar waving at him. Billy held Maggie's hand and they walked over to the bar where the two men shook hands, Billy saying, "Bless up!" and the man answering with a big smile,

"Greetings!" he said, then looking at Maggie and smiling, he added, "Now, who yuh gyal Billay?" Billy beamed, introducing them.

"Mag, this is Jo, Jo this is my Maggie." The man put his hand over his heart with a pat, shaking his head a little.

"No, Billay, nuh Maggay?" Billy grinned at her as Jo took her hand to shake it, then put his other hand on top. "Maggay, such a pleasure!" And he patted her hand a couple of times before letting go, still smiling, shaking his head again at Billy. "Wuh brings yuh to di Grapes my bredren?" Billy wrapped his arm around Maggie's lower back, both of them grinning.

"Well, I'm a married man now Jo." Jo clapped his hands together, came out from behind the bar and he and Billy linked hands, pulled each other in and hugged, then he did the same, with Maggie.

"Bout time my bredren, congratulations. Aw long yuh here?" Maggie and Billy sat down on the bar stools.

"Just passing through, Jo. How long have *you* been here?" Jo thought for a moment. "Bin bout two years now, Billay. Say, wuh can I get yuh two?" looking at Maggie.

"Club soda and lime, please." she answered.

"Ok gyal, rum an ginger or Red Stripe, Billay?" Billy smiled.

"I'll take a Red Stripe, thanks Jo." The man turned to get their drinks, Maggie looked around at the restaurant. It was small, and very colourful, painted a mix of pinks, yellow's and greens. There were a few other people at tables, talking and laughing. "We're going to go out to the patio Jo." Billy said, Maggie following him out to a covered table. Billy pulled a blue lawn chair out for Maggie and she sat down.

"Alright, Mag?" he asked, with a big smile on his face. She smiled back.

"Of course. So, I take it you've been here too eh Babe?" He nodded.

"A long time ago Mag, not at the Grapes though. Jo used to work at a bar further west." Jo came out smiling, carrying their drinks. "How's your family Jo?" Billy asked, taking his drink. Jo sat in another chair with them.

"Oh, yuh know, dee same as always. Missy gone tuh college inna dee states Billay!" and Billy sat down his beer.

"No, she hasn't?" Jo nodded his head.

"She's gonna be a docta, Billay!"

"Wow, Jo, that's amazing! You and Cedella must be so proud?" Jo nodded again, beaming.

"Oh yea, we suh proud of our wee baby gyal. Have yuh seen

Taniyah yet Billay?" Jo asked, Billy suddenly looked slightly uncomfortable.

"No, haven't run into her Jo. Where is she living now?"

"She inna Manchesta." Billy didn't say anything but reached out his hand across the table to hold Maggie's and his eyes crinkled as he looked at her. A young woman came out and asked them what they wanted to eat.

"Oh, Billay, have dee jerk fish!" Jo suggested, "its dat good Billay!" he added. The woman smiled and nodded.

"Yea, it a favourite." The woman told them, so Billy and Maggie decided to give it a try. Jo went back in with the young woman and left the two lovebirds alone. As soon as they went in Maggie grinned at Billy mischievously.

"Taniyah an old girlfriend, Babe?" she asked him. Billy shifted in his chair.

"Well, ya, sort of Mag. Went out a dozen times." She grinned at him, knowing there was definitely more to the story. He looked into her eyes and grinned back. "She was pretty sweet on me Mag, we had our fun, but..." and he stopped.

"Billy?" she said, trying to bring him back. He shook his head slightly, his face showing some strain.

"Mag, it was so long ago, I was such a different person, and I really wasn't happy. I filled my time with work and music and a handful of friendships here in Jamaica, but as corny as it sounds, I only ever wanted you." She grinned again and squeezed his hand.

"Aw, Billy, you're too sweet." He looked seriously at her, locking eyes.

"Maggie, I really mean that. A day didn't go by that I didn't think of you or miss you or wonder about you." Maggie was always so pleasantly surprised at how she could continue to love him more and more. The two of them leaned forward across the table and kissed.

"I don't know if I completely believe your story Babe, but I like your sappy ending." He opened his mouth to speak, then closed it again. "No worries Lover, we've got each other now." she assured him, and he grinned at her. Their server came out with their meals and asked if they needed anything else. Happy with what they had, they thanked her and started on their fish. It was beautifully cooked and came with rice and peas and a side order of delicious tangy coleslaw with onions and raisins, carrots and coconut. Jo brought them out another drink each.

"On dee house." he told them and went back in.

"Billy, this is delicious!" Maggie said, enjoying another bite. He grinned at her, taking a swig of beer.

"Ya, people always said the food here was good, Mag." They sat and talked for a bit after they finished their meal before heading back in and saying goodbye to Jo.

"Yuh come back anytime Billay and Maggay!" he said happily as he and Billy hugged again.

"Bless, to you and Cedella and the rest of your family, Jo." Billy added as they shook hands.

"Bye." Maggie said smiling, thanking their server as they left.

"Feel like walking, Babe?" Billy asked as they left the restaurant. It was kind of overcast, but just big white clouds, and the temperature was lower than it had been the day before. A nice day to take a long walk. "Probably an hour back to the port, but we could always get a cab if we wanted." he added.

"Walking sounds good." she answered. So, hand in hand, they headed back. Billy pointed out a few places to Maggie, they talked about the people, the trees, the yummy food they just ate, stopping once in a while to kiss and hug. They ended up walking the whole way back, taking them about an hour and a half with all their stopping and exploring. Maggie got to see so many interesting things, and she loved discovering more puzzle pieces to Billy's life.

Walking back down the dock and to the boat, they both gladly sat on the long couch together after their long adventure.

"Mmm, that was nice Mag." Billy said, pulling her over so she was leaning against him on the couch and putting his arms around her. She put hers on top and snuggled him close.

"Yes, lovely." she said, closing her eyes and smiling.

"Time for a nap." Billy said, and she laughed.

"Yes, for sure." The two of them resting happily in each other's arms. They did end up sleeping for an hour.

"Billy." she said, not sure if he was awake.

"Mmm?" he answered sleepily.

"You awake my Lover?" He hugged her tightly.

"Nope." he answered.

"Kay." she grinned, and they laid with each other for a little longer.

"So, what are we going to do tonight, Mag?" he asked her, breaking the silence.

"Mmm, let's just do this Billy." she said, very content in his arms.

After a bit, Billy laced his fingers with hers and started rubbing her hands and playing with her fingers, looking at her ring, then holding her hands in his.

"Say Mag, did you say you kept some gifts for another night?" She grinned and giggled a little.

"Mmm, so I did." she replied. He was quiet for a minute, still playing with her hands.

"So, when were you thinking of getting them out?" he asked and she laughed, turning over to face him on the couch. She grinned at him, and he grinned back.

"Well, actually, now that you mention it, I was thinking...tonight Billy." He chuckled and held her face, gently pulling her close and kissed her softly.

"Mmm, I love you Mag." he whispered to her, their eyes opening as they pulled away.

"I love you." she said back, pushing herself up. "Well, you saw some of the things in the box Billy, anything in there, interest you?" One of his eyebrows raised with a cheeky grin.

"Why don't we have a look again." he said sitting up next to her, kissing her again, then the two of them walked to the bedroom to open the box. They sat on the bed with it and took turns reaching in. Billy held up the fuzzy handcuffs.

"Well, we already know these will be fun." Maggie laughed, thinking of their scarf romps, then pulling out the feathers and body oils.

"How about these, Lover?" she asked and without answering Billy pinned her down playfully and kissed her, Maggie laughing.

"Ok, give me 10 minutes, Billy." she told him sitting back up, and pushing Billy off the bed. He looked at her with his dark blue eyes, almost pleading with her.

"Oh Mag, 10 whole minutes?" he asked.

"Yes, Lover." she replied with a grin and got up and marched him out, squeezing his sweet cheeks on the way. She followed him out and headed into the washroom for a couple minutes, then back to the bedroom, looking for the black and red lace bodysuit she'd been gifted at her stagette. It was so beautiful. Red satin under layer, covered in black lace. It was a corset style, doing up with laces at the back, lace around the tops of the bust, and the bottom coming down about 2 inches over the tops of her legs, with a wide frill of black lace along the bottom edge, making it possible to leave the fact that she wasn't wearing panties, a lovely surprise. She moved the box off the bed, turned the little lamp on, throwing a pink scarf over it so the room looked a little more romantic. Then she found her hair clip, twisted her curls up, letting some fall onto her shoulders, and clipped it into place. She got the little set of oils out and the handcuffs and feathers and sat them on the end table. Walking over to her dresser and rolling on her vanilla and lavender, then opening the door a crack and calling out.

"Oh, Lover." she said in a throaty voice.

"Ready for me, Beautiful?" he asked with eagerness, and she backed away from the door, sitting on the edge of the desk with her legs crossed waiting. In seconds the door swung open all the way and when Billy's eyes found her, she laughed with amusement. His eyes twinkling, a smile playing around them as he grinned at her.

"Wow!" he breathed. "Damn, you look hot Mag!" he proclaimed walking towards her. She bounced her crossed leg up and down a little, and played with one of her curls, her head down slightly as she looked up at him with bedroom eyes. "Come'ere Mag!" he said, grabbing her hands and pulling her up, so he could get a better look at her. His eyes traced every inch of her with a smile. "Okay, well, I'm good Babe, thanks." he said, turning and walking away.

"Billy!" She laughed, and he ran back and picked her up off the floor, Maggie wrapping her arms and legs around him, holding his face and kissing him deeply. He moved them to the door, where he used her body to close it, then pressed her against it, still kissing deeply. Between kisses, he said,

"Mag, seriously," more kissing, "that is effing hot!" kissing her again.

"Mmm, Billy, I love when you're this turned on," she breathed, her chin lifting as he kissed her neck passionately. His heavy breathing in her ear making her crazy.

"You smell so good, Mag," he said as he moved from one side of her neck to the other.

"Billy," she said.

"Mmm..." he responded, still kissing her, now down to the tops of her breasts.

"Let's play," she told him, and he stopped kissing her to look into her eyes.

"Play?" he asked, going back to kissing her.

"Put me down!" she said, with authority. Billy looked at her, then seeing the intensity in her eyes, slid her body down to the floor. Maggie turned them around and pushed him against the door. Billy grinned.

"Mmm, I like it when you take charge, Mag." She grinned back. She kissed him hard, then backed away.

"Take your clothes off!" she said finding her way back to the bed and sitting on the edge, watching hungrily as he pulled off his T-shirt, then his shorts and boxers. Then, with one finger she beckoned him to her and looking like a hungry wolf he obeyed. He grabbed her face and kissed her when he came close. They kissed for a few minutes, deeply and intensely, then Maggie held her hand against his chest and pushed him back a little.

"On the bed, Lover!" She ordered him, and as he sat and slid back, Maggie crawled onto the bed and grabbed the handcuffs. Billy's eyes flashed as he watched her. She sat them next to his body, then crawled over him and straddled him, leaning over him and making her way up to his face and bending forward to kiss his mouth. She reached for his hands, running hers up his arms and stretching them above his head, she grabbed the handcuffs, and they smiled at each other as Maggie cuffed him to the head of the bed. She grabbed the bag of oils and found the one called Golden Arrow. She rolled the oil over her palms, then moved down his body and took his rising cock into both her hands, softly twisting and stroking the oils over him with her warm hands. Billy's eyes closed and his body rose.

"Aww," he groaned with pleasure. She stroked with one hand up and down, from base to tip, then started to massage his legs, slowly and deeply, bending down and kissing along the way, then running her hands up his sides as she kissed from his pelvis to his stomach, up to his chest and licking over each of his nipples and then sucking his neck and ear lobes. Billy making "Mmm" sounds the whole time, his hips moving with hunger. They looked into each other's eyes, and Maggie held his face, her hands in his hair and kissed him, tongues sliding, kissing deeper and deeper. "Mag!" he breathed as she sat back up and moved down, sliding herself up over his very hard dick a few times, then raising herself and sitting down on top of him, both groaning with pleasure as she felt him inside of her. She had her hands on his stomach as she rocked her hips back and forth, making the odd half circle, then back and forth again. She was moving her hips so sensually and deeply. Her chin lifted as she started to move a little faster and harder.

"You feel so good," Billy moaned, and she looked back into his eyes. He was watching her so intensely.

"Tell me what you want, Billy," she breathed, a seductive grin on her face as she moved in circles again, now moaning herself.

"You're so sexy." He moaned again. Maggie sensually grinding. "Don't stop," he said, his body in ecstasy, his hands pulling against the cuffs. Maggie leaned forward and kissed his chest, licking across his nipples, nibbling gently, rocking her hips slowly and deeply.

"Do you want me to ride you harder, Lover?" she asked, and he looked at her with fire in his eyes.

"God yes!" he answered. She sat up keeping their gaze locked.

"Watch me," she told him, and he was more than happy to. She lifted herself up, then slid back down, pushing her hips into him deeply, then holding his body with her hands she started bouncing up and down, fast and hard.

"Oh my God!" Billy growled. "Mag, uncuff me!" he begged. She grinned at him.

"Keep watching, Lover," she said, still lifting and dropping in rhythm. Billy could hardly stand it.

"Mag, I'm going to explode!" he groaned. Maggie riding faster still, Billy's body writhing with pleasure. "Oh, Mag!" he yelled, she kept going and he looked into her eyes again. "Grind me," he said so deeply she felt her skin tingle and she started sliding forwards and backwards again, circling, then back and forth. "Mag!" Billy yelled, and she felt his body tighten and his hips move forward hard. "Ahhh, my God!" he yelled, Maggie falling forward, still rocking gently, Billy's breath heavy and quick, smiling at her as she kissed him. "Ok, seriously Mag, let me out of these!" he said with a definite growl. She reached up and uncuffed him and he wrapped his arms around her and kissed her hard. He flipped them so he was on top and started to make very soft gentle glides inside of her. Pressing close to her and kissing her neck. Billy's hands sliding up behind her and holding her shoulders. Maggie loved when he did that. Feeling his magnificent power. It made her feel so safe and complete somehow, and she loved that he'd been the only person who ever did it. Maggie let her head fall back, her mouth opening slightly, eyes closed in pure bliss, as Billy lifted her body slightly and kissed her neck and chest. Billy still sliding ever so slightly. Maggie felt like she was melting in his hands. Lifting her up so he was sitting on his knees and Maggie on his lap, Billy slid his hands up the front of her body and held her breasts. Maggie leaned down and kissed him, sliding her tongue around his a few times, then deeply kissing him.

"Ohhh," Maggie moaned with pleasure as he squeezed and played with her breasts. Maggie's hands in his hair, all over his head, and she started to gently grind again.

"Mmm," they both groaned together, kissing harder, Maggie holding him to her body tightly now as Billy slid his hands down to squeeze her ass and hips.

"Tell me what to do," Billy whispered. Maggie tingled.

"I want you to suck on my breasts while I grind your big dick," she told him looking deep into his eyes. Pulling her corset down and freeing her, she heard him growl with delight as he started licking her nipples, then reaching up and holding her breasts again, squeezing and fondling lightly, sucking and kissing them, long wet licks. Maggie grinding with sheer elation. "You're so hard," she whispered, still grinding, Billy's licking becoming more vigorous. "Ohhh!" she cried, achingly close to cumming. "Billy, Oh God," she moaned, moving in deep slow wide sweeps. "Don't stop, Billy!" she cried, sliding harder now. "Ah, ah, ahh." Maggie grabbed Billy's shoulders to flatten herself against him. "Kiss my neck," she said to him, hardly able to speak.

"I want to feel you cum," he breathed looking up at her before sucking all over her neck. Billy reached for the oils and found the one that read Joyous Occasions. Maggie watched as he took the top off, then started rolling the oil over her nipples. Feeling so turned on, her nipples growing harder, the sensation of the oil heightening her already greatly aroused body, Billy softly and teasingly pulling her closer and closer to release before dropping the bottle.

"Mmmm," Maggie moaned blissfully, grinding quicker, pulling him tight. "Ohhh, oooh, Billy," her words hardly audible as she came, slowing down her hips slightly, then, grasping each other tightly, they pressed into one another, kissing hard. Billy's hands in her hair, caressing her neck and up the back of her head, Maggie running hers all over his shoulders and shoulder blades.

"Mag!" he said, their kissing slowing. "You're absolutely delicious," he told her.

"Mmm, you are..." and her body shivered, "scrumptious." They grinned before kissing again.

As they laid side by side, chests heaving, smiling through heavy breathing, Billy reached between them and held her hand. Their fingers interlocking as their hearts continued to race.

"That was gooood!" Maggie said with a long exhale.

"Mag, with you, it's always good!" he answered and turned to face her, Maggie looked at him and smiled. He pressed his lips to hers and kissed a long-pressured kiss. "Mag, you are the best effing sex I've ever had!" Billy told her, kissing her again, Maggie smiled, held his cheek with one hand and looked into his eyes.

"You are by far the tastiest Lover I've ever known, Billy." He kissed her hard, his arms wrapping around her tight, both running their hands over each other's backs, squeezing each other's ass's, and kissing passionately.

"Mmm, you are simply the best," he breathed, staring into her brightly shining green eyes.

CHAPTER 5

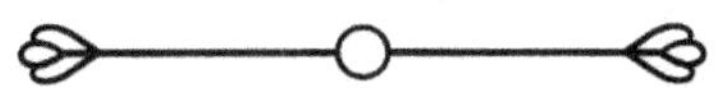

"**M**orning, Lover," Maggie breathed in Billy's ear, the two spooning, as she wrapped her arm around him and then kissed down his neck and shoulder blades.

"Mmm, morning, Beautiful," he replied, his body moving back happily against hers. She ran her hand down his arm, down his hip and the top of his leg, then back up again, still kissing his back. They snuggled up and started their day feeling very lovey.

"You putting the coffee on, Lover?" Maggie called as Billy left the bed.

"Course my Love," he called back. She smiled and closed her eyes again. *I could get used to this,* she thought happily. Getting up and getting dressed in one of her long light dresses, then using the washroom before joining Billy up top with their coffee.

"So, shop and move on, Mag?" he asked as she sat down next to him. He put his arm around her shoulder.

"You bet, Babe," she answered, taking a sip of coffee. They chatted in the morning sun for some time, deciding to eat somewhere in Santa Cruz while they were out shopping.

They walked to the main marina and called a taxi, then sat and waited in the shade. It was very sunny and already quite hot.

"How far is the strip, Billy?" Maggie asked as they climbed into the cab.

"Wah Gwaan," the cabby said as they shut the doors.

"Nagwan," Billy responded smiling.

"Weh yuh deh head?" the driver asked.

"Santa, bless, Boss," Billy answered.

"Yuh get it!" The man replied and he started the meter.

"How far, Boss?" Billy asked him.

"Bout 45," he answered, then turned on his music and off they went.

"So, what's Santa Cruz like?" Maggie asked, excited to see all the people and shops.

"Busy, Babe!" he laughed. "Lots of cars and people, and a lot of shops." He smiled at her. She looked back out her window, enjoying the rock faces and all the different trees. So many she'd never seen before.

"Are we leaving today?" she asked Billy, kissing his cheek, and smiling.

"Not sure Babe, depends on when we get back, I guess." he answered, holding her face and kissing her softly. "Might be able to drop anchor again, then we wouldn't have to pay to stay moored another night," he added, thinking out loud more than answering.

"Yuh two marry?" asked the driver, looking in the rear-view mirror with a grin.

"Yes, almost a week ago," Billy answered with a smile.

"Yaah, what a lovely couple," he said, nodding. Maggie smiled at him too, Billy looked at her and grinned. "Wi will be bout 10 more minutes," he added, smiling again in the mirror.

"Thank you!" Billy said.

The driver let them out in a KFC parking lot at the start of the strip, which Maggie thought was very strange to see, being so far from home.

"Bless op!" the cabby called out the window, driving off.

"Ok Mag, here we go." They took each other's hand and started down the road. It was very busy, and they passed many people and many colourful stores, most painted yellow. They started the day just going into places of interest. It was very hot, and they stopped halfway through the day for some cold drinks and a rest in the shade before moving on. Maggie bought a few more dresses, some tank tops and shorts, Billy grabbed a couple more pairs of shorts and a few more button-down T-shirts. Then they found a patty place, known for being the best, and ate them as they walked along. There were many clothing stores, a few stores that literally had everything, markets all over the place, pharmacies and doctors' offices, gas stations, liquor stores, and some fast-food chains. It was quite an experience for Maggie, and she loved every second of it with Billy by her side. After they enjoyed a few places, and grabbed a few gifts to take back home, they headed through the ever growing crowd, into one of the grocery stores to stock up on supplies for the trek around the western coast of Jamaica, towards Port of Lucea. They spent a lot of time in the Santa Cruz Market, buying lots of fruits and vegetables. Maggie asked Billy lots of questions about so many things she'd never seen before. Every spot they stopped, they chatted happily to the vendors, constantly being offered the many things being sold, being coaxed into a few new things and bargaining prices in good spirits. After they had spent most of the day wandering, they finally hailed a cab around 3:00 to head back to the boat. It took a bit longer, as they inched their way through Santa Cruz's afternoon traffic, before moving a little faster on the open road. They arrived back at the dock near 5:00 and got everything on board. The two wrapping their arms around each other and kissing, standing on the top deck together.

"Well, that was a fun day, Lover!" Maggie said, smiling at him.

"Yes, it was, thanks Babe." He smiled and kissed her again. "I'm going to go let the office know we're heading out, Babe." She nodded. While Billy was gone, Maggie started getting organized and putting things away. By the time he got back the sun was getting lower in the sky and on its way to setting. Billy went up to the cockpit, Maggie followed and watched as he started the boat up and checked all his gauges, flipping switches and checking the screen for their path out. Then he got up and walked out to the mast.

"Let me know when it's lined up, Babe," Billy called, waiting to raise the mainsail.

"Ok. About 10 more degrees," she told him. Billy unclipped the sail, undid the rope on the halyard, then came back and started cranking the sail up. He hopped back into his seat and moved them out.

"There's a nice wind tonight, Mag, we might make it to Negril if it keeps up." She smiled at his happiness in the captain's chair.

"Excellent, Captain," she said grinning at him, Billy's eyes dancing as he smiled back. The sun was setting, and the wind was picking up enough that Billy shut down the engine. The boat had two, but he often just ran The Emerald Pearl with one. He kept a close watch on the screen, navigating the rocks, and Maggie smiled at the freedom she felt sitting next to him on the open water.

"I love you, Mr. Ashberry!" she said grinning broadly at him after an hour of sailing. Billy grinned at her; his eyes crinkled cheekily.

"And I love you, Mrs. Stanton," She got down from her seat and stood next to him, wrapping her arms around him, and kissing his cheek so he could keep watch. They were headed north, northwest now and the sun was dipping into the water off the starboard side.

"Hungry, my Lover?" Maggie asked, still standing next to him.

"Ya, a bit Mag," he answered.

"Ya, me too. I'll get us something." She gave him another kiss on the cheek and headed below to fix them a snack. Maggie washed some grapes, cut up some pineapple, mango and avocado. She sliced up some cheese and some salami and poured some little veggie crackers into a bowl. She put everything on a tray, then grabbed a couple waters for them and took them up. Billy had lit the lantern that hung above their chairs, and the glow and smell brought a comforting feeling to her heart, reminding her of days spent cottaging and camping with friends in her youth.

"Hey Mag…" he greeted her, "…think we'll drop anchor in about half an hour, putting us just below the Black River." She sat down with the tray, handed Billy his water and nodded.

"Okay, sounds great," she replied, smiling.

"Looks good Mag, thanks." Billy took a few things off the plates and popped them into his mouth. They enjoyed their snack and not long after Billy headed closer to land, hoping to find a good spot to stay for the night. The wind had died down a bit, which would be good for them now that they were stopping, and they had a little northern land jutting out, sheltering them as Billy went to the deck and dropped the anchor for the night. He came back up and checked everything before they lowered the sail. "Ok Babe, home for the night," he told her, pulling her close and kissing her.

The two brought out a big lantern and sat it on the deck table. Billy had made himself some kind of coconut rum drink and Maggie was drinking some sparkling water that she had added a lime wedge to. Billy found a deck of cards and they played rummy together, laughing and talking in the lamp light. He told Maggie a few more stories of when he had lived there, Maggie smiling broadly at him, loving these moments together, Billy sharing more pieces of himself with her. He had gone fishing with some locals once, when he had first arrived, and they thought it would be funny to break in the newb.

"We went out in two small motorboats just before sunset, about eight of us, myself, the only one not from Jamaica. We went pretty far out too!" he chuckled. "They told me it was the best time for catching Snapper." Billy shook his head, laughing at himself. "So, they got me to move to the front of the boat with my rod and they all jumped into the other boat, along with the motor from the boat I was still in." Maggie's eyes grew big, listening. "Then I heard their motor rev and turned to see them booting it back in the dark. So, there I was, no light, no motor, no clue!" Maggie's hand was on her mouth now as she listened intently.

"Billy, what did you do?" she asked, concerned, and Billy reached out his hand and patted hers, chuckling again.

"I sat there Mag." He laughed. "I just sat there. I had no way of getting back unless I wanted to swim. After what felt like hours, I heard a motor approaching. It was someone in a similar boat, shining a light towards me." Maggie didn't know why it was so funny, but she smiled at Billy as he told his story.

"'Wah yuh ah duh out here?' came a man's voice, and the boat bumped up against the side of mine, a rope landing next to my feet. The man, laughing at my worried face. 'Yuh let dem get the betta of yuh mon!' he said, laughing heartily. 'Here, tie dis rope to di front.' He told me, so I did, climbed into his boat and we pulled the empty, motorless one back. Well, when I got out of the boat, I thanked him and offered to buy him a drink, he laughed again and told me to follow him. We walked right up to The Robinsons Rockhouse, where he worked for his father at the time." Maggie smiled again.

"Delroy?" she asked, and Billy nodded.

"Yes, Delroy. That's how I met him. His cousins, some of the goofs who took me out fishing, were laughing and bragging about the silly white military boy they left out in the boat In Swallow Hole and he came and got me." Maggie shook her head, dealing out another round for them.

"Wow, thank goodness eh Babe?" She laughed a little too. Billy smiled, nodding back.

"For sure. I was lucky it happened though. After that Del took me under his wing. He's only about 13 years older than me, but he's always felt like an uncle to me Mag, and he and Alvita were already married, and she adopted me as her own the second she met me. They took me in, eventually letting me stay in the old family house I called my shack. I found whatever work I could, soon starting my own little fix it business, then playing in their bar a couple times a week and after a couple years, I bought my boat." Billy grinned, lost in thought. "Wow, feels like a lifetime ago, Babe." She smiled at him as he laid down the last of his cards. "Rummy!" he called out, Maggie slapped down her cards.

"Ah, come on, not again?!" she said half mad half teasingly, Billy laughing. "Hey Billy, it's not technically a port, but we've dropped anchor..." she looked at him seductively, Billy chuckled and grinned at her.

"So, a christening is in order I believe?" he said, sliding towards her on the bench. He grabbed her, Maggie giggling as he kissed her neck.

"I believe so, Captain," she answered.

* * * *

"Hoist up the sail, Mag," Billy called out, as he finished pulling up the anchor.

"Yes Captain!" she said, grinning at him and watched as he made his way back up to the helm.

"I could really get used to that, Mag!" he told her, giving her a kiss on the neck as she worked. He sat down in his spot and started the engine, turning the boat towards the northwest again, so they could continue past Negril and make their way up to Port Lucea. "Should be there just after lunch, Mag," he told her, smiling as he watched her lock the main sail in place and sit down next to him. "The wind is moving between 9 and 10 knots," he said looking at the gauges. Billy set their course and turned the engine off.

"Mmm, what a beautiful morning, Lover," Maggie said, smiling out at the water, then looking lovingly back at Billy. He winked at her and grinned.

"Beautiful," he agreed, still smiling at her. The morning was perfect for a sail and they both enjoyed looking out over the Caribbean together, coasting in The Emerald Pearl.

"Remember all your birthday surprises, Mag?" Billy said after they'd both been sitting quietly for a bit. Smiling as she answered.

"Yes, of course, lovely surprises." His deep eyes twinkled.

"Well, I never said they were done, did I?" he asked, grinning. She sat up straighter in her chair and grinned at him. Looking down at the screen, she noticed they had changed direction from what Billy had originally mapped out.

"Where are we going, Lover?" she asked excitedly. He didn't say anything and just kept grinning. They could make out the shore now and Maggie's breath was taken away, heading for the greenest, most lush mountains, and trees and bushes dense with the odd fleck of tropical colour. Cream-coloured buildings, like little mansions, were spread out through the greenery, with a long pier jutting out towards them. Billy moved past it and over to a mooring zone. He had switched the engine off as they drew closer, and Maggie started to drop the sail. He guided them in with ease, and they went through the usual formalities before disembarking. Billy also made arrangements for the boat to have a maintenance check and paid for them to fill the tanks. Maggie could feel her mouth hanging open slightly and closed it smiling. When she turned her head to look at Billy he was staring at her with a big, hopeful smile on his face.

"What do you say Mrs. Stanton, wanna spend a week here with Mr. Ashberry?" Maggie jumped up into his arms, wrapping her arms around his shoulders and kissing him hard. Billy chuckled as he wrapped his arms around her, to catch and hold her.

"Billy, this is amazing!" He grinned,

"Let's go check in, then we'll come back for our luggage." Taking each other's hand they walked towards the main house. They went up to the front desk, where a few women were working at computers.

"Aftanoon," said one of the women as they reached the counter.

"Hello," Maggie said, Billy nodding at her.

"Reservation for Mr. and Mrs. Stanton," he told her, and she looked back down at the computer and started typing.

"Aw, yea, di 'oneymoon suite. Congratulations!" She smiled at them, then moved around at her station, gathering some things up, and handed them their room keys, a pamphlet, instructions on how to get to the house, with what was included in the package for the week, which was a lot. They thanked her and went back out to pack up their suitcases to take to the house with them.

Once they were back in the bedroom of the boat, Maggie ran at Billy again as he stood near the bed, knocking the two of them onto it, Maggie sitting on top of him and kissing his whole face. He laughed as she finished with a big kiss on his nose. Billy held her face and looked up at her grinning.

"Let's get packed, Billy!" Maggie said, climbing off excitedly and grabbing her suitcase. Billy chuckled and got up from the bed to pack his things.

As they approached their honeymoon oasis, Maggie became more and more awe struck looking at its overwhelming beauty. There was a house nestled within the dense green foliage that stretched behind it and up the mountains, their view overlooking the Caribbean Sea. Hidden by nature, they stepped under the covered entrance and Billy unlocked the door, pushing it open. He put the suitcases just inside the door then turned around and walked towards Maggie, who was grinning from ear to ear. Then, without warning he scooped her up, Maggie laughed gleefully, and as Billy walked inside he closed the door with his foot as he carried her into their home for the next 6 days. Maggie wrapped her arms around his neck and looked at him with her big Maggie smile. He smiled back at her, and Maggie, holding his face tenderly, kissed him, slow and lovingly, her hands gently moving into his hair.

"Mmm," he responded, as she pressed her lips to his more firmly, pulling his face tight to hers. The room was so nice. There was a huge four poster bed, with white tulling hanging down from each corner, and Billy laid Maggie down on it, leaning over her and continuing their deep sensual kiss. The two moving up further on the bed together, their kiss becoming deeper. The energy between them growing, the kiss breathy, moist, and warm and their lips moved more passionately, pressing firmly together. Maggie's hands running through Billy's hair, Billy holding her body with one hand and running the other up her leg, then her hip, then holding the side of her face and into her hair at the nape of her neck. Maggie held his body close with her leg bent and wrapped around his body, Billy's hand running back down her body and squeezing her ass. "Mmm, Mag," he breathed between kisses. Maggie smiled, still kissing him deeply. Their kiss became slow and even deeper, their tongues sliding playfully together, then becoming firmer and more intensely determined. Maggie was trying to pull Billy's shirt off, fumbling with the buttons, their kisses becoming more urgent, frantically releasing each other from their clothes and grabbing at each other's bodies with a heated need to attack one another. Billy's strong arms lifted Maggie to the center of the bed and he laid on top of her as she traced her hands over his back and ass and back up to his neck and into his hair. Billy squeezed one of her breasts as he kissed her neck.

"I need you now!" Maggie moaned, and Billy's mouth was back on hers, his tongue sliding in again, Maggie's mouth opening as her tongue circled around his and she spread her legs, wrapping one around him again, feeling the powerful, insatiable push of his strong glide inside her very ready body. "Awe," she moaned as he slid with pure determination, growling with each glide.

"So good," he groaned, kissing her neck, Maggie's hands clawing and pulling his strong body deeper and closer against her soft naked skin. "Mag," he breathed in her ear and her whole body gave a shudder.

"Oh God, Billy," she breathed back. He groaned with pleasure, his rhythm quickening. She was squeezing his ass with one hand, the other hand still running through his hair. "Ohhh!" she cried with pleasure as he slid a little harder now. "Mmm..." he was back to sucking and kissing her neck.

"You smell delicious," he added.

"Billy...don't...stop..." she cried, her chest rising as she began to climax.

"Oh gawd!" Billy announced as he became more aroused at her closeness to finishing.

"Billy," she moaned, wrapping her legs tightly around him and he hit harder and faster now.

"Mag." She felt his body tighten then release. Still kissing her neck, his lips hot and wet, Maggie's eyes started to roll back as she let herself go, grinning with satisfaction, her body contracting as she fully climaxed. Kissing frantically again, their bodies still moving slowly together, pulling each other as tight as they could, their skin wet and hot pressed together as one. They held onto one another, breathing heavily together, their hearts racing, not letting go and absorbing the delicious feeling of the moment for as long as they could, then laying on their backs and resting for a few minutes.

"Wow!" Maggie called as she rolled out of bed and walked to the bathroom. She was looking at the enclosed toilet room and the open L-cove with a long double sink, big stand-up glass shower and within a few more steps, a soaker tub on the balcony facing the sea. She was walking towards it as she called out, "Billy, you gotta come check this out!" Both, still naked, Billy walked towards the sound of her voice and found her out on the balcony already sitting in the tub. Laughing, his eyes crinkled with a smile, he leaned down and kissed her.

"You're too funny, Mag!" he told her, looking out at the water. "These views are amazing aren't they Babe?" he said standing next to the tub. Maggie giggled,

"Mmhmm, great view!" she agreed, and Billy looked back to see her giving him a once over.

"Mag!" he laughed. She climbed out of the tub and stood beside him, wrapping her arm around him.

"Absolutely gorgeous, Lover!" she answered as he hugged her. "Let's go see the rest of it, Billy," she said, grabbing his hand and pulling him along, back inside. There was a small grassy yard outside the entrance, and inside, a couch and tv opposite the bed where there was access to a small dining table and chairs on the balcony, which stretched the whole water side of the house and around the corner. Out the bathroom was access to the balcony where the soaker tub was and lounge chairs facing the sea. Down below, using the entrance was their own private infinity pool, high above the green bushes and trees, making it look like it was part of the Caribbean. Steps walking down into the pool and lounge chairs around the edge.

"Let's go for a swim," Billy said, walking up behind Maggie and hugging her.

"Sounds good," she answered. They grabbed their robes and went out to the pool, walking down together. The sun shining above, the aquamarine waters of the Caribbean stretching out in front of them. Both swimming around a little then making their way back to one another and embracing. Maggie grinned at Billy and kissed him.

"This is a beautiful surprise, Billy. Wow, just wow!" she told him, and he smiled at her happily.

"I'm glad you like it, my Love," he replied, kissing her and hugging her tight. "I know we're enjoying the boat, but how could we have a honeymoon without some pampering?" he said grinning and winking at her. "Speaking of which, horseback riding on the beach tomorrow, then we have massages booked for the day after, my beautiful wife." His eyes grinning lovingly as he called her his wife. "Then the second last night we have a sunset cruise booked." Maggie's eyes grew with excitement.

"What about the other days?" she asked, grinning. Billy's eyes twinkled mischievously.

"Well now, I just don't know what we'll do, Mag." And they were kissing deeply, their wet bodies wrapped lovingly.

"Where do we go for dinner, Lover?" she asked him, kissing his lips softly, looking into each other's eyes dreamily.

"Here Mag, we have our own chef." Maggie's head moved back looking at him with surprise.

"Our *own* chef?" He grinned and nodded, kissing her, running his hand gently over her forehead and back to hold her head and kissed her again. Maggie's hands trailing water over his shoulders.

"Well, that's amazing!" She kissed him again, a little harder now, both lingering more now.

"Mag?" kiss, kiss.

"Mmm?" kiss.

"What should we eat?" Maggie grinned, remaining quiet for a moment.

"Oh, for dinner?" she said coyly. Billy smiled.

"Yes, Babe," he replied, and she kissed him again, shrugging.

"Why don't we go in and figure it out?" she suggested. They walked back out of the pool together and put their robes on. Once back inside, they took their pamphlet out to the balcony and sat together.

"I actually had to let them know what we would like to eat when I booked it Mag, so we'll just have to let them know when we'd like dinner." Maggie grinned.

"Fancy, Billy!" she laughed. "Okay, well let's let them know we are ready to eat." She grinned again. Billy called the front desk and they told him dinner would take about an hour, and someone would be up with drinks and appetizers in about 15 minutes. The two love birds sat in the balcony lounge chairs while they waited, hands reaching out and holding on as they relaxed together. Then they heard someone knock on the front door and Billy got up and answered, still in his red satin 'Mr.' robe. A man came in with a tray and walked to the table on the balcony. Maggie got up and waited, smiling, as he set things out, then Maggie and Billy thanked him.

"Dinner will be 30 minutes," he told them, and they heard the door close as he left.

"Beautiful," Billy said, pulling Maggie's chair out for her.

"Thank you, Lover of mine," she said sitting down. There were 2 salads, with sides of a few choices of dressing, fresh bread and butter and a charcuterie board with cheese, olives and meats. There was also a small pitcher of ice water, and each of them had an umbrella'd, peachy coloured cocktail that appeared to be carbonated. Billy picked his drink up and raised it, Maggie did the same.

"To my beautiful bride!" he said, smiling broadly.

"My gorgeous husband!" she added, clinking their glasses, both taking a sip.

"Mmm, that's yummy, Babe," she said, noticing Billy's eyes smile at her.

"It's champagne and peach juice, Mag." She grinned.

"Mmm, delicious." Their feet soon tangled together under the table as they sat and took their time snacking and staring out at the water.

Soon their dinner arrived, and it smelled absolutely delicious. It was pan-roasted chicken with grapes and garlic and rosemary, served with wild rice, and it was so yummy.

"This is so tasty!" Billy said, Maggie taking another bite and nodding. They ate so much and wished they hadn't, but it was just so good.

"Oh, my goodness, I'm so full!" Maggie said as they went and laid in the lounge chairs.

"I ate way too much, Mag!" Billy said, both laughing at each other.

"Let's not move for the rest of the night!" Maggie decided, and Billy nodded his agreement.

CHAPTER 6

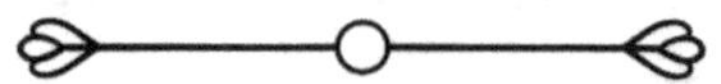

"Good morning, Beautiful." Maggie smiled, her eyes still closed, feeling Billy's body hugging up behind her, his face in her hair by her ear.

"Morning, Lover," she said back, holding his arm and rubbing it. "What time is our ride?" she asked, still keeping her eyes closed, feeling happy-sleepy.

"Couple hours, Babe," he said, nuzzling a little closer. As he did, she suddenly felt him strong and firm between her legs, as he spooned her tighter.

"Why Mr. Ashberry, are you happy to see me?" she asked, grinning.

"Oh Mrs. Stanton, I'm *always* happy to see *you!*" And he pushed himself a little further between her legs.

"Mmmm," she said happily, pushing her body against his a little more and placing her top leg over top of his. Maggie reached back and held his leg, sliding her hand back and grabbing his firm ass, and Billy reached over her body, and slid his hands gently over her breasts. Rubbing softly up and down, her nipples growing harder with each tender brush of his strong hands.

"Your skin is so soft," he told her "Mmm, and you smell so good Mag," he breathed, licking up and down her neck, still massaging her. Maggie moved her hips and slid herself along his body, breathing heavily and becoming very aroused.

"I love feeling your strong body pressed against mine," she breathed and reached up and ran her fingers through the hair on the back of his head. Billy's face moving around her neck, kissing, and breathing deeply as he slid inside her already very wet center, Maggie letting out a long low moan. He moved slowly, squeezing and fondling her as he kissed her neck. Maggie grabbing him tightly and pulling her body into his with every push he made. "Ohhh!" she breathed as she grinded him and he continued to slide, in and out. "God, Billy," she moaned, and his hand was now reaching down between the front of her legs, running his fingers along her wetness, fondling between her legs and rubbing her as he continued to move in and out of her body slowly.

"You feel so good, Maggie." he breathed in her ear pushing deeper inside her, Maggie moving her leg back a little more, so he could push deeper still. She wanted to kiss him so bad. She was almost crying with pleasure.

"God, you feel good," she moaned slowly, grinding in deeper circles, Billy squeezing and pulling on her nipples and sucking her neck as their bodies pumped together. "Harder Billy!" she cried out and he held her abdomen and slid all the way in and out, pressing against her body hard. "Ah!" she cried.

"Maggie," he growled, both of them reaching new levels together. There were no boundaries, just hunger and trust. They were one and enjoying the same vibrations without anything but pure pleasure, and just like that, so quickly they were both moaning and crying out.

"Owe, God Billy, harder, harder... oh my God!" She was bouncing off his body as he held her chest, holding her body as close to his as he could, Maggie's head against his shoulder.

"Oh Mag! Oh God Mag!" And with a hard thrust, sending her body forward, they moaned together.

"God, Oh God!" she cried, feeling her whole-body shake. Billy pulled her close, spooning them again, and she turned her head to kiss him, Billy lifting his to reach her, holding her face, their tongues stretching out. It wasn't enough, she moved off of him and turned around so they could face each other and kiss deeply.

"Mmm." They were both moaning as they kissed, holding one another tight.

"My God I love waking up with you, you beautiful sexy woman!" he said grinning at her. Maggie grabbed his ass and squeezed.

"And oh, how I love waking up with you, Sweet Cheeks." She pulled him close and kissed him hard.

"Mmm, Mag, you are heavenly." And back to kissing, their lips pressed hard and moving against one another firmly, holding each other's body like they might disappear if they didn't.

"Billy, you are a wonderful man," Maggie said, tracing her fingers over his chest and over his shoulders. Looking up at him lovingly, brushing his beautiful salt and pepper hair off his face, and holding his cheek, kissing him gently. She smiled looking at every detail of his face. He was so handsome, and his eyes were so kind, and such a deep blue, and very mischievous, too. She loved the way they twinkled when he looked at her. Feeling his arms wrapped around her, breathing in his natural, spicy, woodsy scent, she felt intoxicated, and safely embraced, and like the luckiest and most beautiful woman on Earth. She was still looking at him, his eyes closed enjoying her fingers running softly over his skin. He could smell her vanilla scented skin, the hint of lavender in her curls, and he inhaled deeply, running his fingers up and down her spine, feeling her body quiver slightly and pulling her a little tighter. He opened his eyes and held her face in his hand, his thumb gently tracing over her cheek, then over her lips, leaning in and pressing his warm soft lips to hers, their lips almost lazily kissing, with such love and tenderness, peering into one another's eyes and smiling.

"Maggie, I love you with every breath I take." He kissed her again, still holding her face, keeping their lips pressed together. "You taught me what true love was almost 30 years ago, and I am thankful everyday that we found each other again." Maggie was almost crying.

"God, I love you, Billy," she said, holding his face and kissing him back. "I'm not complete without you," she whispered, and he smiled at her, and softly kissed the end of her nose. Then she nestled into his body, and he wrapped his strong arms around her, and she felt like she was home. "Never let go!" she said, and he hugged her tighter still.

* * * *

"Ready, Babe?" Billy called from the balcony.

"Yes, be right there," she called back. Maggie was so excited to go for a ride, especially on a beach with Billy. They walked along the beach a little way and headed down to a corner of the cove where a man was waiting with 3 horses.

"Mornin," he said, smiling at them.

"Good morning," Maggie responded, grinning happily. She was already next to the horses and patting them.

"Yuh bin horseback riding before?" he asked them. They nodded, and Billy stood next to Maggie, his hand rubbing her back.

"Maggie grew up with horses," he told the man.

"Oh good, good." He smiled. "Call me 'enry!" Maggie and Billy introduced themselves. "Ok we will take di horses down di beach inna di wata, den back tuh di beach tuh dis spot." Then Henry pulled himself up onto his horse, which he was riding bareback. Henry then proceeded to introduce the horses. "Dis is Suga, Lightning an I with Patty," he told them with a big smile. Maggie claimed Lightning as Billy stepped closer to Sugar.

"You alright, Billy?" she asked him, smiling so big her cheeks were almost hurting. He grinned at her, soaking up her joy and kissed her.

"Sure am, Babe." Maggie turned and in one fluid movement mounted her horse. She bent forward and hugged him, patting his head and neck. Billy was on his horse now too, feeling much more comfortable than he would have, before Maggie started giving him lessons.

"Ok, wi ready?" Henry called leading them. Billy smiled and waved, then nodded his head for Maggie to go next. He was more than happy to watch her riding. He loved watching Maggie ride Black Beauty back home. Billy already thought she was the most beautiful woman, but what happened to her when she sat on a horse was magical. The happiness and joy, and freedom bursting from within her. Her posture and effortless elegance, like she and the creature were one, was breathtaking. They trotted along the edge of the water, surrounded by green hills on one side and bright beautiful blue water on the other. Then as they neared the end of the beach Henry turned and led them right into the sea. The horses moved happily, as they walked deeper, until Maggie's legs were under the water up above her knees, the water splashing against her, the sun shining bright above them. She turned back to look at Billy who was smiling too.

"Beautiful, Babe!" he said, winking at her. Maggie thought, he looked awfully sexy astride his steed, the beauty of Jamaica surrounding him. They rode through the water for a good half an hour or so, slowly making their way up to the beach opposite their starting point, then another 20 minutes later they were back where they started. Henry smiled at them as they jumped down from their horses.

"Tank yuh!" he said as they went over to say goodbye and to thank him. Maggie talked to her horse and patted him before they left. Hand in hand, Maggie still smiling broadly, they walked along the beach together. Then Maggie stopped and looked up at Billy.

"Thanks Lover, that was so wonderful," she told him. He held her face and smiled, his eyes twinkling as he kissed her. Maggie's hands reaching up and holding his arms, kissing him back.

"So glad you enjoyed yourself, Mag," he said, grinning at her. "It *was* pretty neat wasn't it," he added. They stood kissing on the beach, dreamily gazing at one another before heading to their beach house for lunch, which was brought in shortly after they arrived back.

Sitting at their balcony table, they enjoyed patties, jerk chicken salad, coco bread, mango, jackfruit, and guava. Each of them had a cold Ting, relaxing in the lounge chairs, hand in hand.

"That was a lovely morning, Billy," Maggie said, eyes closed, lying in her coral bikini, soaking up the sun.

"Mmm, keeps getting lovelier too, Babe," he said, and she looked at him grinning at her cheekily and giggled.

"Oh Billy, in the words of Carla, don't you ever get enough?" she asked, laughing.

"Not as long as I'm with you, Beautiful," he answered.

"Excellent!" she said, with a giggle. "Wouldn't want it any other way." And now she was eating him up with her eyes as he lay in his swimsuit, his skin very brown now from the sun, his strong body glistening slightly with sweat. "Mmm, I could eat you up, Lover!" she told him.

"Is that a promise, Mag?" She grinned.

"Could be." Billy chuckled.

"So, what's on the agenda for the afternoon?" Maggie asked, feeling quite content to stay put.

"Whatever you wish, my Love," he answered, his eyes closed, lazing happily too.

After a long swim and some more lounging next to the pool, Maggie and Billy decided to go back inside. It was getting very hot out in the sun and the air-conditioned room above was calling to them. They still had a couple hours before dinner, and nothing else planned until their massages the next morning.

"How do you think Frankie's getting on with Bo and Bill?" Maggie asked as she and Billy laid on the bed together, just in their housecoats.

"I'm sure he's just fine, Mag. Probably really enjoying his own place for a change," he answered rolling over to look at her, his dark blue eyes grinning cheekily. She turned her head to look back at him.

"Well, hello handsome husband!" she said, smiling broadly at him, feeling his body and growing excitement pressed against her hip.

"Hello, beautiful wife." He ran his hand across her stomach, then reached around to her lower back and pulled her body closer to his. Billy undid her robe belt, then slid his hand under her housecoat and across her hip. Maggie grinned, and turned to face him, holding his face and gazing at him. She moved his hair away from his cheek, and ran her hand down his neck, Billy's hand sliding back to squeeze her bottom as Maggie kissed his lips softly. Now, both holding each other's faces and kissing gently. Their bodies, pulling together. As their hands gently stroked each other's faces, and fingers ran through each other's hair, they continued to softly kiss one another's lips, and cheeks, so tenderly. Maggie's mouth slightly parted as Billy kissed each of her lips, one at a time, then the end of her nose, then both back to pressing their lips together, a little harder now and holding the backs of each other's heads. Billy ran his tongue along her lips, then, pushing slowly into her mouth he found her tongue, the tips touching playfully, then circling, then their kisses became deeper, their breathing heavier. Maggie undid Billy's belt and moved his housecoat off his shoulders, her hand trailing across his chest and back up into his hair.

"Mag," he breathed between kisses. Her chin rising as he kissed her neck.

"Mmm?" she purred.

"Do you have any fantasies?" Maggie's eyes opened, and she lifted his face. Looking at him whimsically, Billy grinned as he saw a flash of fire within her deep emerald eyes.

"Fantasies?" she asked playfully, Billy back to kissing her neck softly.

"Mmhmm," he growled.

"Um, never really thought about it." She was still making contented noises as he continued to kiss her neck. "We've done so many things together Billy, I've never had to think about wanting more." He looked up and grinned at her. "What about you?" she asked him, his eyes intense as he held her head and kissed her hard.

"Mm, well definitely not lacking for pleasure Mag, but I did like it when you took charge," he said, his tongue sliding into her mouth again, then kissing her and looking at her again, he chuckled slightly at another memory. "And when we did it on the porch!" he added, pulling her tight, his tongue back in and sliding more frantically now. Frenching each other deeply, holding tighter and tighter before pulling away again.

"Mmm, yes, that *was* exciting!" she breathed back. Billy was pulling her robe off her, kissing her shoulder and neck.

"I liked it when you were forceful, Billy. Gawd that turned me on!" she said feeling more aroused just talking about it. "But I get so turned on when we take our time too. Oh, and, I love when we talk to each other," she added, now kissing him passionately and pulling his robe right off.

"Damn Mag..." he growled, both clawing at each other, "...talking works for me too!" and now their tongues were circling each other quickly and purposefully, their mouths open more and kissing harder.

"Talk to me, Billy," Maggie breathed.

"You're so hot, Maggie," he told her, her hand sliding down and grabbing his ass and squeezing hard.

"I want you so bad, Billy," she groaned, their hands all over each other.

"I want you to lick me all over," he moaned, and she began licking down his neck, under his chin and down his chest, kissing and licking each of his nipples and down his stomach, her body sliding down his sensually. "Mmm, Maag," he growled as she neared his navel. She licked in a circle around it, her hands caressing and squeezing his body as she continued down kissing and licking each of his hips, letting her lips trail, open, across his warm skin. Moving his body flat she moved further down unto the bed and licked and kissed up the inside of each leg, then she found her way to his hard eager dick, held him with a soft caressing grip and ran her tongue around his balls. "Mmm," he moaned, his body moving gently. Maggie licked her way up, in wide wet circles, still holding and softly rubbing him as she licked right to the end with a kiss, before making her way back up his body with her tongue. Before she could kiss him again, Billy flipped her, and he was on all fours, looking down at her with hunger. He leaned his face down to her and stretched his tongue out, Maggie's meeting his and they flicked the ends together erotically, then kissed so deeply. Breathing words between kissing.

"Tell me... what you... want," Billy whispered, kissing Maggie's neck again. Maggie's body writhing and squirming with desire.

"Mmm, my neck Billy." And he was kissing her so deeply, his lips so hot and wet on her skin. Still on all fours above her, Maggie reached out her hand and started to fondle his balls as he sucked on her neck. "Ohh," she moaned. Billy growled with pleasure.

"Mag, I want to taste you!" his voice was so deep in her ear. "And I want you to taste me," he added, kissing her mouth again. They looked into each other's eyes for a moment, as they kissed, before he pulled them over onto their sides. Then he made his way down, so his head was at the opposite end of the bed and with his hands, he spread her legs. She felt his tongue running up the tops of her legs, then licking her center with an intense hunger.

"Ooooh, Billy!" she cried, moving her face towards his body and licking him; almost drooling as she moved her mouth over him, her tongue wrapping around him as she moved him in and out of her mouth, Billy's tongue flicking her sweet spot expertly.

"Mmm..." he growled, Maggie becoming wetter with every sound he made, and she licked enthusiastically. He could feel her legs trembling, running his hand between, holding the bottom of her ass and sliding a finger inside her.

"Aaah," she cried, licking and sliding faster along his very hard cock. Her legs were shaking intensely, and Billy kept licking, his tongue strong and keeping rhythm, Maggie hardly able to stand it, becoming more and more animal-like, sucking and gliding with such zestfulness. Both of them kept going, ravaging, almost aggressively licking and sucking and sliding, until they were both so close. Maggie's hand stroked him as she continued to take the end of him into her mouth. Her body vibrating and Billy felt her cumming. Her head falling back, still stroking Billy.

"Mmmm," he groaned, still licking her center, as she came, then she slid him back into her mouth and moved from tip to base a few more times. "Oh God," he groaned. "Oh God!" Billy held her body tight as he came. Maggie held him in her hand with fast strokes, as her tongue licked, sliding around the tip, enjoying his release, his body shuddering. He quickly moved back up her body and pulled her on top of him, grabbing one another and kissing intensely, tongues licking and tangled again. Both growling with satisfaction.

"Mmm, you're delicious," Billy said. Maggie pulled him tight and kissed him hard.

"Billy," she moaned as he kissed her with deep pressure. "You taste so good," she whispered between deep kisses, making Billy kiss her harder still.

"You make me so hot!" he growled, and he flipped them back over and she felt him push himself inside her.

"Oh, Billy!" she cried out with surprised delight. "God, you're so hard!" she yelled, and he slid with powerful thrusts, Maggie's hands reaching above her to hold onto the headboard.

"Maag," he moaned, moving faster and faster.

"Ah, Ah, Ah!" she cried with each impact of their bodies. Then he stopped, his hips still moving as he slid out of her, flipped her and pulled her up to all fours, sliding in quickly and back to thrusting hard and fast, holding her hips with his big hands, pulling her against him tight. "Oh... my... God!" Maggie yelled, Billy's body hitting hers harder.

"Mag, oh, Mag." And he pushed hard, slowing down, but smacking against her, Maggie's head dropping to the bed, her knees bending as Billy pushed inside her, not sliding anymore, but grinding into her.

"Ohhhh, Billy..." she moaned, and his hands were under her squeezing her dangling breasts. Billy's body now draped over hers, groaning his satisfied pleasure. Both breathing heavily. Then he pulled out and she rolled to her back, Billy laying on top of her and kissing her. Holding her face, their bodies wet with sweat, pressing together, Maggie's hands above her, as she panted happily. Billy stopped kissing her and looked at her.

"Well, that was effing awesome!" he said huskily. Maggie giggled.

"Let's do it again!" she said grinning, holding his body and kissing him. Billy laughing as he kissed her back.

"Better give me a few minutes, Love," he told her and they both grinned, Billy rolling to lay beside her, his leg and arm over her body, kissing her shoulder. Maggie ran her fingers along his arm.

"Hope you ordered deli sandwiches for tonight Lover!" she added, and they both laughed, relaxing and breathing deeply.

'KNOCK KNOCK' at the door maybe 10 minutes after their escapade.

"I'll just be a moment!" Billy called out, Maggie got up and ran for the bathroom. Billy grabbed his robe and headed for the door. She heard the two men talking as the food was taken to the balcony, waited until she heard Billy say thank you and the door close, before coming back out. "Mmm, come here you!" Billy growled, pulling Maggie close and kissing her passionately. Maggie's body almost went completely jelly-like as he held her. "Hungry, Beautiful?" he asked, the two walking to the table hand in hand.

"Always," she answered, smiling at him seductively. They sat down together and ate, smiling flirtatiously with each glance. Tonight was corn soup, rice and peas, festival, fried plantain chips and a plate of stamp and go. They also enjoyed ginger beer together, something else that was new to Maggie, which she found was surprisingly good too. "Goodness, this is yummy!" Maggie said, licking her fingers. Billy grinned at her and gave her a wink.

"I know something yummier," he said, and she grinned back, feeling her cheeks flush slightly. They called room service for coffee which they took to their spots in the lounge chairs on the balcony and enjoyed, while they let dinner settle. There was a lovely breeze tonight, and they laid quite comfortably watching the sunset, reaching out and holding hands after their coffee.

"Wow, I'm exhausted, Babe," Billy said lazily after they laid there quietly for a time. Maggie laughed slightly.

"Me too, Lover." She grinned at him as he turned his face to look at her. "Shall we snuggle up, gorgeous man?" she suggested, hardly able to move. Billy nodded and they helped each other up, hugging and looking deeply into each other's eyes.

"Have I told you yet today how much I love you, Beautiful?" Billy asked, moving the curls from her face.

"Hmm, not sure, better tell me again, just in case," she teased.

"Damn, I love you!" he said, and she felt her body tingle, as his lips gently touched hers, softly running his hands into her hair and cradling her head, then looking at her with a smile.

"I love you so much, Billy," she said back. They rubbed their noses together.

"Come on Babe, let's get ready for bed." Billy slid his hand across her lower back, and they walked back inside.

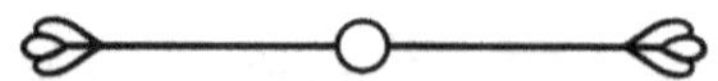

CHAPTER 7

Maggie woke up to yet another beautiful sunny morning. She turned her head and saw Billy still sleeping, his beautiful, tanned body stretched out beside her. She was tempted to run her tongue from top to bottom but, resisting, she decided to use the washroom and jump in the shower before he woke up. The shower felt so lovely, and after she cleaned her body and hair, she stood under the water letting it rain down as she closed her eyes and enjoyed the moment. She turned off the tap and wrapped her towel around her body, then threw her hair forward, letting it fall down in front of her so she could squeeze the water out and squish up her curls. Then flinging it back behind her again, she opened the glass door and stepped out. She grinned as she saw Billy sitting up in bed watching her with a smile.

"We should definitely get a glass shower for the house, Mag," he told her with a cheeky grin. She grinned back and walked over to him, climbing onto the bed and kneeling next to him.

"Good morning, Lover," she said. Billy wrapped his arm around her, and she leaned in to kiss him.

"Morning, Beautiful," he replied, giving her another kiss. "You smell good enough to eat, Mag," he told her, kissing her neck and making her giggle. She kissed his nose, then tried to get up and he pulled her down, Maggie falling onto his lap and looking up at him smiling. She pulled herself back up, they kissed again, then she got off the bed.

"What do we wear for our massages, Billy?" she asked as she went to the counter and put on her oils and deodorant.

"Not sure Babe, think we strip down anyway, so, probably doesn't matter." She looked at him in the mirror, watching him as he climbed out of bed, very much enjoying his thick, strong naked body.

"Wow, looking extra manly this morning, my Lover," she said, grinning at him as her eyes scanned his body and stopped between his legs. He winked and walked up to her and grabbed her, pulling her tight.

"Must be the scenery, Mag." With twinkling eyes, they kissed each other with smiles, before Billy used the washroom then headed for the shower.

Maggie wore her turquoise dress, so it would be easy to slip out of, Billy in shorts and a T-shirt, and they headed down to the beach where a gazebo, and two tables, were set up. Two masseurs waited for them.

"Mr. and Mrs. Stanton, good mornin," greeted the two women. Both Billy and Maggie smiled and said good morning. "Wi will let yuh both take yuh things off den yuh may lie down on the tables with a towel ova yuh lower halves." And they both walked towards a table where they had oils and stones waiting for them. Billy and Maggie grinned, kissed and stripped down, then climbed onto the massage tables and waited. The women asked each of them if there was anything specifically bothering them, then began their 90 minute massages. They laid there in heaven, listening to the waves rolling up onto the beach, feeling the light warm breeze on their skin as the two women worked their magic.

"How you doing, Mag?" Billy asked, sounding very relaxed.

"Mmm, this is wonderful," she answered. "How about you, Babe?" she asked him.

"Ya. Goood," he answered sleepily. The women started to add drops of scented oils now, massaging them in, then placing warm rocks in specific spots on their backs. As the rocks cooled, they removed them and finished the second half of their session.

"That was glorious!" Maggie announced as she and Billy walked back to their place wrapped tightly.

"Yes, it was," Billy agreed, still sounding very sleepy.

"You sound like you could use a nap, Lover." Billy opened the door, let Maggie walk in and followed her.

"Actually, that sounds like a good plan," he replied, smiling at her.

"A real nap, Lover?" she asked, grinning at him.

"Well, maybe," he grinned back.

"I was thinking about going for a swim Billy, I'll wake you up when I come back if you like?" And she flashed him a big Maggie smile. He pulled her over closer and kissed her.

"Promise?" he asked, and Maggie nodded, still smiling.

Loving the feeling of breaking the surface of the water and feeling it totally envelope her body when she dove in, Maggie stayed under and swam the length of the pool, then surfaced in the shallow end. Letting her head fall back and running her hands over her hair. She took a deep breath in and dove under again, swimming to the other side and holding the wall of the deep end. With her feet, she pushed herself off the wall, floating on her back and drifted around the pool, relaxing. She did a couple more lengths, then walked up the stairs, grabbing her towel and drying off. She decided to sit in a lounge chair for a few minutes, letting the sun dry her a little more, before going back in. She thought a nap sounded pretty good too and coaxed herself off the chair and headed upstairs. Billy had fallen asleep, sprawled on his back, right in the middle of the bed. She hung her wet things in the shower, then pulled her robe over her shoulders as she walked towards the bed and laid down next to Billy, spooning herself against his side, resting her head on his arm. He moved slightly, holding her cozily, but stayed asleep. Maggie soon drifted off as well.

They woke up sometime late that afternoon. Billy's arms wrapped around her, Maggie smiling as she snuggled up to him, listening to his breathing and the beat of his heart, breathing in his scent, and feeling safe and loved.

"Wonder what time it is?" Maggie said, breaking the silence. Billy pulled her closer and held her tight. "You ok, my Lover?" she asked, looking up at him. He smiled at her, his eyes twinkling.

"Never better," he answered, and Maggie stretched up, held the side of his face, and kissed his warm lips.

"Feel like a bath?" Maggie asked, still looking up at him. He kissed her softly, his nose brushing hers.

"Mmm, that sounds nice, Mag." He smiled at her squeezing her tight.

"Ok, Babe, I'll get it ready for us." Sitting up, hopping off the bed, Maggie went out to the balcony and started to fill the tub.

"I'm missing music, Mag," Billy told her, getting up and walking out to the balcony and standing against the railing.

"Ya, me too," she replied, standing next to him. The sun was getting lower in the sky, and the water was very still.

"I'm going to go grab my guitar while you're filling the tub," he told her, and she watched him walk away. By the time he was back, Maggie was in the big soaker tub already.

"Hello, Beautiful," he winked, standing next to her, stripping off his clothes and climbing in from the other side. Lifting her legs and placing them on his as he usually did and running his hands along them. Both letting their heads rest on the tub with their eyes closed. They massaged each other's feet as they laid there peacefully. It was lovely having a bath outside, and the view was absolutely beautiful from the balcony.

"I stopped at the main house and asked for a light dinner for us, Mag," Billy told her after they had laid there for a little while.

"Ok Babe, sounds good," she replied, smiling at him. They closed their eyes and relaxed in the warm water, listening to the distant sound of the waves, and the light rustle of the warm wind moving through the plants and trees.

"Heaven!" Maggie purred with a smile, running her hands up Billy's feet and legs, her eyes still closed, her head still resting back enjoying the whole experience.

"Ya mon!" Billy replied, sitting up and running his hands right up to the tops of Maggie's legs, pulling her close to him with a grin. Maggie giggled, then grinned her Maggie grin and leaned forward to kiss him.

Smirking flirtatiously at one another and kissing once more.

"We might want to get dressed soon, Babe," Billy suggested, giving her another kiss.

"Mmm, let's just live in the bathtub, Billy." She watched him climb out, then accepted the towel he wrapped around her as she stood up and held her while she stepped out.

"Thank you, gorgeous lover." Maggie gave him another kiss then led the way to the bedroom where they put their cotton hotel robes on, waiting on the balcony.

* * * *

"Smells delicious," Billy said, pulling Maggie's chair out for her and running his hand across her back as she sat down. Billy sat across from her and lifted the lid on the tray. Fish in a coconut run-down sauce, vegetables and a side of herbed rice pilaf. Maggie put a spoonful of rice onto each of their plates, then Billy scooped some sauce up and poured it on top.

"This is tasty," she said, taking a second bite.

"Mmhmm," came the sound from Billy as he continued eating. They didn't fill up too much and sat with their feet wrapped together under the table, watching the sunset. They finished with coffee and gizzada tarts, which were super yummy. Room service came and cleared the table for them, bringing water, a bottle of sparkling water for Maggie and a Red Stripe for Billy. The two lovebirds sat in their lounge chairs and watched the last of the sun melting into the Caribbean.

They snuggled up together in bed, both still feeling very relaxed and sleepy. Billy sang "All Of Me" as he played with her curls. Maggie's voice joined in and she harmonized quietly. Billy ran his hand up and down her back gently. She looked up watching him sing happily, his eyes closed. He grinned at her as they finished singing, then softly brushed her cheek, his thumb on her lips, his eyes twinkling as he looked into hers and Maggie smiled back at him. He lifted her chin and leaned his face closer; she could feel his warm breath on her face, her lips breaking apart ever so slightly, as he touched hers, kissing her so gently. His hand ran along her face and into her hair and holding her lovingly, he kissed her over and over, as they looked into each other's eyes and he whispered, "Mag..." kissing her again. "*You* are my everything." He breathed deeply, and she reached her hand up and held his face, kissing his lips gently and smiling at him. They fell asleep holding each other.

* * * *

Maggie woke up to the sound of Billy's guitar. She grinned to herself, as she heard him singing "Patience". Rolling out of bed, grabbing her robe and walking to the balcony, Maggie looked down and saw Billy sitting by the pool. She slid her arms into her robe and pulled the red satin up over her shoulders. She continued to listen happily as he played "Free Fallin'" then grinning nostalgically as he played and sang "Heart Like Mine". Maggie sang along as she did her robe up and walked out and down to the pool, kissing the top of his head, and running her hand along his shoulder as she sat next to him on the lounge chair. He grinned at her.

"Morning, Beautiful," he said, leaning towards her and giving her a kiss.

"Morning, Cute Guitar Guy," she said back. Billy smiled at her and chuckled. "I don't know how I forgot, but I used to call you that when we first met," she added with a dreamy look on her face.

"Oh?" Billy chuckled again before going on. "Well, I used to call you 'Damn Yummy' when we first met." He replied with a goofy grin. "And that was before I tasted you and knew how true it was." Maggie giggled and bumped softly against him.

"You make me blush, Lover," Maggie cooed lovingly.

"Sleep well, my Love?" he asked, both still leaning forward, and giving each other little pecks.

"Always do, in your arms, Billy." They grinned. "Nice way to wake up," she added, sitting up straight again. He grinned at her.

"Ya, feels good to play again." He started strumming random chords. "How about you sing me a song, Mag." Billy looked at her, his eyes dark and cheeky. She laughed at his persuasive expression, ready to tell him it wasn't going to work, but it was already working.

"K, what?" she asked, grinning broadly at him. He shrugged, smiling at her.

"Whatever you like, Damn Yummy." Maggie laughed, then thought for a moment. With a gentle smile at Billy, she started to sing "Possession", her hands over her heart, pulling the words and the notes from deep within, her eyes closed as her voice grew stronger. Her head tilted down slightly she looked up at him with a sultry stare, locking her bright green eyes with his dark beautiful blues. Billy strummed quietly, listening to her. He smiled as her eyes closed again, her hands beating in time, her body rocking gently back and forth, looking at him again, belting out the last few lines, her heart bursting as she stared at him. As soon as she finished, Billy sat his guitar down on the lounge chair, stood up and pulled her up into his arms, kissing her so hard, almost taking *Maggie's* breath away. He held her head with one hand, the other running all over the back of her body. Maggie held his arms as he continued to kiss her purposefully. Their pulses quickening, breathing growing deeper, kisses becoming more intense, holding each other's faces, and pulling each other in. Both of them were just in their robes. Standing, caressing, by the pool, the morning sun warm on their skin. Tongues deeply intertwined and bodies pressed tight together.

"That was sexy, Babe!" Billy's eyes lustful as he spoke. "God, I want you so bad right now!" he breathed as they continued to squeeze and caress each other. Billy pulled away from her, letting his cotton robe drop, then sitting down on top of it, he pulled her down onto his lap. Maggie wrapped her arms around his neck, and they were locked in deep kisses again. Their hands up and down each other's backs and in each other's hair, growling with hunger for one another. Billy's legs were crossed, and Maggie's legs stretched around to the back of his body. Kissing frantically, tongues lashing, Maggie pressing her breasts tightly against his chest and Billy's hands sliding down to massage her ass, noticing she had nothing on, under her housecoat. She lifted herself slightly, feeling his hard cock rising. Then he slid his hands under her and lifted her up again, placing her right on top and pushing down on her hips as she slid down. Their heads falling back, their mouths open releasing delighted "Aww's" as she moved back and forth. Sliding steadily back and forth, Billy's hands up and down her thighs and lifting her body. He started to move her faster and she slid her tongue along his ear, whispering,

"Slowww, Billy." She heard him groan achingly as she slid forwards and backwards along his legs, taking him in with long slow wet glides. He kissed her neck as her head fell back again, holding his shoulders so she could pull herself back and forth. "Ohhh, Billy," she moaned, and he squeezed her hips and thighs. Billy was growling deeply now, and she knew he wanted to move faster. As he tried moving her up and down, more quickly, she repeated, with a throaty purr,

"Mmm. Slow." He started sucking her neck, with hot deep, tonguey kisses, Maggie becoming more aroused and rocking deeper, sweeping and grinding slowly, holding him tight.

"Mag, I can't stand it!" he groaned.

"Almost there, delicious Lover," she whispered, and he was biting her shoulders and her neck, licking her neck and throat hungrily, then as she cried out with pleasure, he threw caution to the wind and lifted her body up and down, bouncing her off of his lap.

"Maag!" he growled, and she held tight letting him move her.

"Billy!" she cried, and she felt he was close. He was kissing her neck again, shivers running through her body.

"Mag, Mag, Mag," he groaned as he came, Maggie still bouncing as she continued her quivering release, Billy switching to her favourite side and sucking her neck deeply as she gave a small cry and her body shuddered.

"Oh, my God Billy," she whispered, their hands holding each other's faces and kissing each other hard again.

"Mmm, Mag," he smiled, looking at her with a hungry grin.

"Wow!" she added, grinning back. She gave him a long loving kiss, then looked at him grinning again. "Thanks for the ride, Tiger!" she said, Billy's head fell back with a deep chuckle, his eyes cheekily twinkling.

"Mmm, my pleasure," he replied. Then she stood up, walked to the edge of the pool and dove right in. As she surfaced, she saw Billy standing on the edge, grinning at her.

"Come on, big boy!" she called out to him, and he chuckled again. He stayed put, watching her with a smile. She dove under and swam around again, resurfaced and looked up at him still watching her contentedly. "Oh Lover, I need you," she pleaded, her eyelashes fluttering, water dripping down her face. He couldn't refuse and dove in next to her. Maggie giggled with surprise as Billy swam towards her, grabbing her body and pulling them both straight under. They looked at each other under the water, then watched one another as they rose back up, arms wrapping around one another, Maggie laughing, Billy pulling her tight and kissing her. Each of them had one hand out to wade water and move towards the wall where they grabbed on, kissing again. Moving along to a spot where they could stand so they could run their hands all over each other's wet bodies. Slowly trailing their hands, scooping water up and letting it trickle down one another's bodies, kissing slowly, and deeply. Maggie wrapped her legs around Billy's strong core, and he pulled her tight. Kissing passionately and dipping in and out of the water. "Mmm" They both moaned, bound so tightly, heart, body, and soul. Holding Maggie's face and looking at her, he kissed her again, pulling her snug, Billy's hands moving in her hair, between smiles and kisses. Staring dreamily into each other's eyes, grinning as they soaked in the details they loved in one another. Maggie noticed the grey in Billy's hair around his ears. The silvery-grey threads seemed to have multiplied over the last couple years and were stretching well up and over the crown of his head. She tenderly ran her fingers across his face and into his hair. Beaming at him with her big Maggie smile, thinking he was quite a sexy, delicious silver fox and how glad she was that he was hers. Billy moved Maggie's hair off her shoulders and smiled.

"You've got some beautiful silver highlights happening, Mag," His eyes twinkling with love for her. "Like moonlight woven right into your curls." She grinned at him, appreciating his deep desire for her, and loving how much they loved each other, after so long, and through all the aging changes as they entered this stage of their lives. They grinned and took one another's hand and walked out of the pool, lounging in the sun to dry off. Deciding to go up and order brunch, carrying their robes, Billy chased Maggie up while she giggled, then tackled her onto the bed, both laughing and rolling about and kissing.

"Want to spend the rest of our lives together, Mag?" he asked, and she grinned.

"More than I love cheesecake!" she answered, and he laughed and kissed her face all over.

"Wow, that is something!" he exclaimed, and Maggie held his face and kissed him hard. Billy got up and ordered their food, and they grabbed clean robes and sat on the balcony to wait.

"So, nothing planned for today, my Love?" Maggie asked, their fingers playing and stroking as they laid side by side.

"Nope, just you, me and nothing to do." He grinned at her and winked.

"Perfect," she said, closing her eyes again.

* * * *

Brunch was beautiful. Hot Jamaican porridge, roasted pumpkin and yams, fried plantain and banana fritters, saltfish fritters, and mangos, pineapple, papayas, oranges, bananas and passionfruit. They each had an icy fruit smoothie too and enjoyed a fresh pot of coffee. They sat smiling and flirtatiously bantering as they enjoyed their brunch, knowing they had all day to eat each other up.

"Feel like a walk on the beach, my Love?" Billy asked, stretching his arm across the table to hold Maggie's hand.

"That would be lovely," her eyes lighting up as she answered, sliding her foot along his. Grinning, and sliding his other foot so hers was nestled between both of his. Billy poured them each another coffee, and they sipped away, happy and content, looking at each other and out at the white sand stretching in a huge arc from below their balcony, bright aquamarine water glistening in the early sun, beautiful, lush green trees, palms, and mountains surrounding them, and a sky so blue it went on forever. Eventually, they went in and changed into their swimsuits, Billy throwing on a button down T-shirt, Maggie in her coral dress. They packed a bag with some drinks, towels and a blanket, then kissing, and grinning, hand in hand they left their oasis to walk the beach. Soon carrying their shoes, feet pressing into the sand, both in and out of the water as they walked, letting the waves wash over both of them as they chatted and hugged, laughed and kissed, stopping once in a while to hold one another, looking out at the water or kissing and grinning, eventually finding themselves at the very end of the cove, quite a distance from the resort houses. Standing looking out, they watched the waves washing up onto a 4-foot wide tip of beach. Side by side, still hand in hand, Billy turned to her, running his hands up her arms and into her hair, she reached up instinctually, and held his wrists, as he leaned closer and kissed her, both instantly feeling the hunger. As their kisses grew more intense, so did their hunger. Billy pulled the blanket out of their bag and laid it down on the sand, dropping the bag at one corner and their shoes on the opposite to hold it in place. Then he stood back up in front of Maggie and undid the front of her dress, staring into her eyes as he took his time with each button, until reaching the bottom. Maggie's breathing became quick as she looked at him with lust and desire, and she reached out and undid the buttons on his shirt, both grinning slightly, their eyes sparkling. Sliding her straps down her arms softly, Maggie shuddered, and Billy leaned down and kissed one shoulder, then kissed up the side of her neck, moving her curls away with his hand as he kissed up to her ear, then did the same thing on the other side, this time up to her mouth. Shivers went right through Maggie's whole body. Then, holding her straps as he slid them down, he moved his body down hers, letting her step out of her dress. He laid it down beside him, then looked up at Maggie, still kneeling on the blanket. He held the back of her legs and kissed up the front of them. Maggie looked down at him, holding his face in her hands as he drew closer to her center. He nibbled between her legs, over her bikini bottom, still looking up at her. Then he pulled them off her and as she stepped out of them, he held her legs apart and his tongue found its way into her center. Her hands in his hair as he began working his magic, licking long swipes, curling his tongue, and flicking, then circling pointedly. The sound of the water and the wind matching the ebb and flow happening throughout her body as he massaged her with his strong hands and licked her luscious middle making her wetter and hungrier for his body by the second. Then holding Maggie's hands, he sat down, pulling her down towards him, so that he was laying on the blanket, out of the sand. Maggie smiled, looking deep into his eyes as she lay on top of him, feeling the water just hitting the bottoms of their feet. Billy smiled at her as she moved her face closer and started kissing him. Her lips soft and gentle on his, the sound of the waves in the background. Her body quivered as he ran his fingers up the top of her legs, over her ass and the small of her back, and all the way to her neck. She felt him smile as they kissed when he felt her body shiver. Rolling them onto their sides, Billy's arm still under Maggie's body, the other meeting it to undo her Bikini top. She felt it tighten for a moment before he set her free, then his hand was sliding to the front of her body, cupping her breasts and slowly, deeply, squeezing as he kissed her mouth with more pressure.

"I want you to touch yourself," he told her with a deep growl. She felt her pulse quicken as Billy started pinching and pulling at her nipples.

"Ow!" she cried, tantalized, and he kissed her harder.

"Mag, you're so hot," he breathed deeply. Maggie slid her hand down between her legs and with two fingers started sliding and rubbing, her thighs squeezing together, Billy's hands squeezing her breasts harder and his kisses pressing deeper, sliding his tongue in her mouth. "You taste so good," he whispered, and with her mouth opening slightly, he slid his tongue in again and circled around hers, growling as he reached down and held her hand, feeling Maggie touch herself, his hand sliding lower between her legs and sliding a finger inside of her. Now, kissing with wide wet kisses, Maggie rubbing harder, Billy's finger curling and pressing as deep as he could, pulsing inside of her.

"Ohhh," Maggie moaned, and Billy kissed her neck, licking, wet wide licks with his hot tongue.

"I wanna watch you cum," he groaned, sucking her neck. She looked straight into his eyes, and pushed him flat on the blanket, Billy growled a little and grinned at her. Then, Maggie held his hands by his sides as she hungrily licked her way down his body, letting go of his hands to pull his bathing suit down and with one wet, tonguey open mouth, she took him in, with such aggression and enthusiasm, licking like she was competing in a contest for hottest blow job. Billy was sure she'd win. "Oh God!" he yelled out as she used her hand to stroke, still sliding her mouth up and down, then moving her hand and mouth in opposite directions, still licking wildly. "Mag!" he groaned with deep satisfaction, hardly able to contain himself. Trying to pull her back up, she looked up at him, still licking the tip, Billy's body writhing explosively now. He coaxed her towards him, Maggie kissing her way up his body, their eyes still locked. As their bodies became level with one another, they were quickly wrapping their arms and legs around each other and kissing with a frantic desire. With the water splashing up their legs, Billy moved her onto her stomach laying his body on top of hers. Maggie moaned happily, loving the feeling of his weight on her body. Then she felt one hand slide down her front between her legs and his fingers rubbing into her wet center. He was breathing heavily into her ear. "Help me touch you," he told her.

"I want you inside me," she moaned back.

"Together," he whispered, and she reached down to hold his hand, but he moved hers into her center and slid his hand over hers so he could feel her touching herself. "Oh God, Mag." And she felt him sliding himself between her legs now as she rubbed and wiggled around her's and Billy's hands.

"Billy!" she cried as he pushed his way into her body, his body moving up and down her back. "Mmmm..." came the aroused sounds from Maggie. Billy pulled them up, so Maggie was on all fours, but she didn't stop there. She pushed right back so Billy was kneeling, and she could sit with her back against his front, on his lap. Billy reached around and fondled her breasts as she began to bounce up and down. "Ohh, Ohh," she moaned, her head falling back onto his, Billy holding her waist as she rode long hard glides onto his lap, over and over. His hands grabbing and squeezing, now pulling and pinching her hard nipples, Maggie crying out. "Owe, oh Billy, don't stop." She started bouncing faster.

"Mag!" he yelled, Maggie was steadily bouncing, moaning blissfully, then bending forward slightly, she moved in a deep circle, grinding up and down his lap, placing her hands down onto the blanket, and Billy grabbed her hips and started pulling her body down into his. Her breasts swinging, Billy sliding faster and harder. "Maaag...." his voice trailed off and she felt his hips gyrating and pushing deep.

"Don't stop..." she moaned, pushing her hips back and grinding him again.

"Mag, I'm... oh my God!" he yelled, and he burst within her. Flipping her over onto her back and sliding in while he was still hard, Maggie's body squeezing him tight as he leaned down and started sucking her neck, one hand squeezing her breast and pushing himself deep so she could continue grinding.

"Oh, Billy..." she almost whimpered as her body gave way to pleasure, shuddering with the breeze that was dancing off the water, along with the climax and release their bodies had created together. Billy was still sucking and licking her neck, and Maggie could hardly let him go, still holding him tight inside of her, her hands grabbing his ass and squeezing her fingers and digging her nails into his taut skin, her hips still circling as she came again. "Oh my God!" she moaned, feeling her body contract, release and relax, and as Billy felt her melting, he moved his face to hers and kissed her mouth. She ran her hands over his back, feeling his strength and holding him tight.

"Mag," he breathed, looking at her, then kissing her again, suddenly noticing the water lapping over their toes as they grinned.

"Billy!" she said, with some urgency. "There's a boat!" She was looking past him. Billy rolled over onto the blanket next to her and looked where she was pointing.

"Here, Mag," he said, handing her bikini to her and grabbing his bathing suit, pulling it back on quickly. She pulled her bottoms on, then as she slipped her arms through her straps, Billy did it up for her at the back. They smiled at each other as he sat back down next to her, and he held her face and kissed her again. Maggie, feeling relieved they didn't get caught with a slight feeling of excitement at coming so close. The boat was passing by but would have definitely had a good show had the two of them been any longer.

"Think they saw us?" she asked Billy, and he grinned.

"Could be, Mag," he answered with a chuckle. After they watched it carry on Maggie stood up.

"Wanna join me for a swim, before we head back, Lover?" she asked, smiling at him, and walking towards the edge.

"Of course," he told her, standing up and walking towards Maggie. The water was deep and there was a sudden drop at this point off the island. They dove into the crystal depths, rising back up and treading water then they swam out a little farther. Maggie dove under a few times, letting her head fall back so her hair was off her face. Billy dove under and she soon felt him rising up under her, sitting on his shoulders, pushing her out of the water Maggie jumped off, diving in, then resurfacing and laughing as she saw him grinning at her, reaching out his hand to pull her back in. The two swam for a little longer, then made their way back to grab their things and walked back along the beach, hand in hand.

Billy stopped her before they started up the beach to their oasis. He wrapped his arms around her waist and pulled her close, grinning and leaning down to kiss her.

"Mmm, you are one fine woman, Mrs. Stanton!" he said, his eyes cheekily twinkling. Maggie smiled back, sliding her free hand around his neck, and pulling him back down to kiss him.

"Mr. Ashberry, you rock my world!" He chuckled and kissed her again before they finished their walk and went inside.

"Hey Babe, will you call for dinner while I jump in the shower?" Billy asked.

"Only if I get to watch," she answered with a saucy grin. Billy ran at her and picked her up, Maggie giggling as he kissed her neck.

"Ok, but if you watch, you have to join me!" he told her, placing her back down and kissing her hard. Maggie giggled again and gave his ass a squeeze.

"You're on!" she answered, and Billy kissed her neck.

"Mmm"-ing his enjoyment, Maggie giggling again.

Maggie called for dinner, and they told her it would be about an hour, asking if she wanted appetizers, but she said, no thank you, they would be fine waiting the hour. Then, hanging up, sitting on the bed, she turned to watch Billy in the shower with a grin on her face. He was singing something as he moved under the water and her heart filled with love as she listened and watched. The glass was fairly steamed up, but she could see the water pouring down over his perfect beautiful manliness, watching it cascade from his head to his feet, moving his hands all over himself to clean his body. She enjoyed the show with hungry satisfaction. Maggie knew every inch of his body. Had long since memorized his beauty and strength, loving each and every inch more with time. His broad shoulders and strong, powerful, muscular arms. His thickened body, still firm and his abs still toned. His legs, muscular and solid. Incredible core strength and stamina. His skin, so dark and tanned and defined. His strong, gentle, experienced, delightfully large hands. His beautiful, kind, patient heart. And... his substantial package, and sweet cheeks. All stirring things up within her as she watched him hungrily. The shower door opened a crack, and he peaked out.

"Hey Beautiful, deal was, you watch, you join!" She grinned and shook her head slightly.

"Mmm, no, I quite like the view from back here, Lover of mine." He chuckled and closed the door again. She watched, feeling herself squirming a bit, starting to change her mind. Waiting as long as she could, Maggie pulled her clean robe off as she walked towards the shower, hanging it next to the door. Billy turned with a grin when he heard her and pulled her under the water and held her close to him.

"Mmm, I'm glad to see you!" he told her and kissed her, then grinned again. "I wondered how long I'd have to linger to get you in here." Maggie laughed and slapped him flirtatiously.

"Not long apparently," she replied. Billy's hands sliding down over her wet bottom and grabbing on, pulling their hips together. Maggie reached back and did the same. They looked deeply at one another, water running down their faces, as they moved closer. Maggie, tasting the water as her lips parted, their noses almost touching, their lips meeting and pressing together, both inhaling deeply. Their heads in and out of the water as they kissed, still squeezing, and massaging one another. Pressing and moving against each other, together. As their kissing grew deeper and slower, they swayed together, the water still falling down over their increasingly hot bodies.

"Mmm" along with growls and purrs, as they soaked each other in. Billy ran one hand right down to the bottom of one of Maggie's perky cheeks, then slid his hand over her hip to the back of her thigh and pulled it up. Rubbing it along his leg and squeezing, bringing her a little closer and opening her up against him where she moved sensually. Billy moved back against the wall, still pulling and squeezing Maggie's leg, lifting slightly up and down, Maggie pressing and sliding her hips against him.

"Mmm," she moaned as his hips started moving too. Still deeply kissing, Maggie's hand running up Billy's neck and into his hair, pushing him harder against the wall, her leg sliding down so Billy could run his hands all over her. Maggie slid one hand down Billy's body, between his legs, then grasped him, feeling him growing at her touch, their breathing growing faster. Billy turned them and pressed Maggie against the wall, held her hands up above her head and kissed her hard. Frenching her slowly, pushing his body hard against hers, then back, then hard again. Holding her hands now in just one of his, the other hand slid down Maggie's face and neck, continuing down her body, squeezing and pinching along the way, right down to the top of her leg. As he slid his tongue into her mouth he slid his finger along her center. He played and rubbed, still holding her hands above her head. Maggie's body writhing, with pleasure and enjoyment. Then she felt Billy's raised readiness as he slid between her legs, almost lifting her off the floor pushing himself deep within her tight, hot body.

"Ohhh!" Maggie cried out, Billy's hands holding hers above her head still, sliding slowly, deeply. Their faces close, mouths open, breathing hard and heavy.

"Damn, Maggie," he groaned, sliding so slow, Maggie was in ecstasy.

"Billy..." she moaned back, hearing each other's breathing, growing more aroused. Maggie's body, tight against the wall and Billy pushing deeply, Maggie pressing and circling her hips each time. He had picked up the pace slightly, but was still making long deliberate glides in and out. "Oh. Oohh," Maggie's voice a whimper, her chest rising with elation at his fantastically purposeful movements. "Billy, you feel amazing," she whispered.

"Ohh, Maag," he growled back, lifting her up, her arms dropping down to hold his shoulders, her legs wrapping around his waist.

"Mmm," they both groaned as he quickened his rhythm, lifting her body up and down with each glide, Maggie close to squealing her delight, Billy groaning with such emotional and physical pleasure. As Maggie lifted her chest and chin, Billy's face dropped to suck her neck, kissing deep wet kisses.

"Oh, my gawd!" she yelled, and he was pressing them against the wall harder now, Maggie's legs holding him tight.

"Mag, Oh God, Mag," he said with each glide.

"Billy, I'm.... Oooooh..." she moaned, grinding deeply and squeezing him tight.

"Maggeee!" bursting from his lips, then his body bursting, cumming and exploding into hers. Shuddering uncontrollably as he came, both grinning and kissing, Maggie still wrapped around Billy. As her legs slid back down his body, she pulled his face closer, kissing him slowly and deeply, her hands running up into his hair and neck. Billy's hands holding her body tightly against his, still pushing against her body, pressed against the shower wall.

"Billy, that was..." and he grinned at her.

"Damn fine, Mag!" he chuckled. Maggie pulled him in again and kissed him long and hard, pressing her body close as they wrapped their arms around each other and moving back under the water.

Hardly able to pull themselves apart, they stepped out of the shower. Both grabbing towels and drying off, grinning at each other as they watched with satisfaction. Then, just wearing their housecoats they went out to the balcony to lounge and wait for dinner, hands outstretched and holding on.

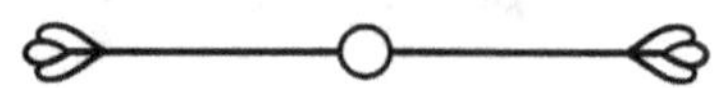

CHAPTER 8

"Last full day, my Love," Billy breathed, wrapping his arms around Maggie as she stood at the sink rinsing off her toothbrush. She looked up into the mirror and smiled at him, then turned in his arms to face him.

"It's been so lovely," she told him, kissing a few times, grinning at each other again. "Should we spend the day laying on the beach, Lover?" she asked, pulling him tight and looking up at him adoringly.

"Sounds great, Mag." Billy grinned and leaned down to give her another kiss.

"I'll call and ask them to pack us a picnic lunch," Maggie said, walking over to the phone and sitting down on the edge of the bed, watching his fine ass with a smile as Billy walked out to the balcony to finish his coffee. After she hung up, she joined him. He was standing at the railing looking out at the Caribbean and as Maggie stood beside him, he wrapped his arm around her and pulled her close. Maggie rested her head against him, and he rested his head on hers. They watched as the waves rolled up onto the white sand below. They saw Henry out with a few people on horses, walking them into the water. There was a lovely gentle breeze this morning, and although it was already very hot, the breeze made it quite lovely.

"What time is our cruise, Babe?" Maggie asked, her hand running over Billy's back, his moving up and down her hip and waist softly.

"It's a dinner cruise, so we should be there by 4:30-ish. We'll be out for the sunset," he answered, looking down at her. "Mmm, my beautiful Mag," he said, smiling at her.

****

Their picnic arrived about 40 minutes later, and they changed into their swimsuits, grabbed towels and a blanket, their picnic basket and headed down to the beach. They were the only ones there and were quite content, feeling like they were the only two on the planet. Maggie laid on her stomach for a while, warming her back and legs up, Billy sitting watching the waves. Then she turned over onto her side and looked at him. The gentle breeze blowing his hair softly, the sun giving his body a bronze glow.

"You're a hottie, Lover of mine!" she said, smiling at him. He chuckled, then looked down at her.

"Thanks Babe. Not too bad yourself!" He winked at her then bent down to give her a kiss. "Think I'm going to go for a swim, Mag. Care to join me?" he asked her, standing up.

"Hmm, I don't know," she answered playfully, Billy stretching out his hand to take hers and helping her up. Before she could stand up straight, he picked her up, almost over his shoulder and ran for the water.

"Billy!" she squealed with laughter, and she felt the water splash up onto her legs before Billy put her down again, grinning at her and walking deeper before diving under. She waited for him to surface, and he laughed at her attempt to be grumpy at him when he looked back at her. She swam out to meet him and he pulled her close and gave her a big kiss. They swam together for a bit, then Maggie went back in, just far enough to sit on the sand, with most of her body still in the water and watched Billy swimming for quite some time. He swam closer, then he walked towards her and leaned over her in the water, grinning cheekily and kissing her. Maggie grinned back, giving him a once over and taking a deep breath in.

"Why Mr. Ashberry, you do stir up a fire within me." He chuckled sitting down next to her in the waves.

"Why do you think I'm not getting out yet, Beautiful?" he said grinning. "Watching you moving back and forth in the waves, got me all riled-up, Babe!" Maggie laughed and bumped into him playfully.

"Think we'll still get this turned on in another 25 years?" she asked, and he was leaning over her again and kissing her deeply, his hand holding her head, the waves rolling over top of them. Still holding her he looked at her and grinned.

"Damn straight we will!" he answered, and then he was instantly kissing her again. "Just might move a little slower," he added with a twinkle in his eye.

"Mmm, that's alright with me, Lover," she said, smiling back and pressing her lips tightly against his. Standing over her, Billy reached out his hands to Maggie, and she hopped up with a big smile. With a little hug and double butt squeeze, they walked hand in hand.

They sat down on the blanket across from each other smiling. Billy opened their basket, and they had a look at their last lunch in their little paradise. Patties, coco bread, sliced fruit, cheese, Ting, and bottled water. Drying in the sun, chatting, and laughing they enjoyed their lunch on their nearly private beach. They saw a few more people as the afternoon progressed, but not many, and after laying about for another hour, they decided to pack up and get ready for their dinner cruise. They both showered, managing to behave themselves, then got dressed with only a few stops along the way for quick make out sessions. Billy put on his white linen button T-shirt and Maggie wore a short white dress with bright blue mandala designs on it. Both in their sandals and ready to go by 4:30.

"My oh my, you look handsome!" Maggie told Billy as she ran her hands over his chest and up his neck, reaching up to kiss him.

"Mmm, how bout I take you on a cruise right here, Babe!" he said, his hand sliding down and grabbing her ass. She grinned at him playfully, turning to rubber. His eyes twinkled, their hands linked as always as they left for the evening and joined the others.

The boat had a glass bottom, which allowed them to see the beautiful coral reefs below. The colourful fish and marine life swimming under them were absolutely beautiful. They saw a few turtles sitting up sunning on some rocks, and relaxed and chatted with the sound of reggae playing softly in the background. The company of a few other couples made it a pleasant experience and they had a good time sharing a meal together. Then as they drank cocktails and coffee, they watched the sunset, people cozied up to one another. Billy and Maggie stood at the railing with their arms wrapped around one another.

* * * *

"That was nice, Babe," he said, opening the door up for them, arriving back in the dark; sun and beach tired and ready to snuggle up together for the night. They cuddled on the bed, Maggie's body nestled along Billy's side, her head on his chest as his hand ran softly over her back, playing with her curls, kissing her forehead every so often. As they laid there, Billy started singing "Rose-Coloured Glasses". Maggie grinned and snuggled into him a little tighter and sang along with him, singing the harmony, falling more in love with him with each note they sang together. Oh, how she loved this man she could now call husband. Almost three decades of waiting, and her dreams had come true. She drifted off somewhere in the middle of "To Love Somebody" still smiling as she felt his voice resonating deep within, holding him tight and breathing him in.

* * * *

Packing up, double checking they had everything, grabbing his guitar, they left for the main building to check out.

"Tank yuh for staying wid us. Wi hope yuh enjoyed yuh time here!" said the woman at the front desk, as they handed in their keys and paid for the boat maintenance and fuel.

"Yes, we did, thank you," replied Billy. Maggie was smiling and nodding.

"Yes, so beautiful, thank you!" she added, and they picked up their things and headed back to the Emerald Pearl. Walking down the dock, both quietly soaking up the last images of this beautiful cove they'd shared in their Caribbean paradise. Billy climbed into the boat first, taking their luggage as Maggie passed it to him. Maggie untied the rope, then reaching his hand up, Billy helped Maggie down, and as her feet landed he pulled her tight and kissed her.

"Love you, my Mag," he told her, his eyes twinkling. "Thank you for a beautiful week," he said between his kisses.

"I love you more each day, my Billy," she added, holding his face, and kissing him, their bodies rocking together.

"Mmm," a sound of contentment coming from Billy as he hugged her tight.

"Guess we better move on, Captain," she said, and Billy grinned at her.

"You know what to do first mate!" he answered playfully, and they smiled at each other as they hoisted the sails, started the engine, and drifted out into the Caribbean Sea, away from their honeymoon cove.

Their coordinates were set to make their way around the western tip and head to the Port of Lucea. A voyage of about 4 hours without setbacks. They would have liked to have stopped sooner, but there were no private boat ports until Lucea. Billy was sitting at the helm when Maggie came up from grabbing them some water.

"Thanks, Babe," he said, taking the bottle she handed him and smiling.

"Feels good to be back on the water, Lover," she thought aloud, with a soft grin.

"Yes, it does," he agreed, smiling broader. He sat quietly for a moment, still smiling. "You really like it, Mag?" he asked hopefully, and Maggie was nodding, smiling as she answered.

"Mmhmm, I do more than I thought I would. I'm loving moving through the water with you!" He chuckled, joy twinkling in his eyes. She stood up from her seat and walked in front of him, leaning to the side so he could watch as needed, but leaning in close enough to give him a pressing kiss. She snuggled up to his side, and Billy wrapped one arm around her as they slowly lost sight of the cove and pressed further west into the beautiful turquoise waters. The sky and water going on forever, bright white clouds seemingly dipping down into the water becoming one with their reflection. Moving from westward, passing through Little Bay, Billy directed them more northwest, making their way north past Negril.

They decided to drop anchor for lunch and went down below out of the sun and made something to eat together. Billy grabbed eggs and fried some up, Maggie sliced some cheese and grabbed some bread from the freezer along with the mayonnaise. Waiting until the eggs were just about finished before toasting the bread. They grabbed sparkling water and went to the table to eat their fried egg sandwiches. Within minutes their feet were snuggled up together under the table. Making eyes at each other and grinning.

"How are you doing, Beautiful?" Billy asked before taking a drink.

"Perfect, Lover, how about you?" He leaned forward over the table and Maggie met him halfway.

"Never better, Sexy!" Their lips locked. As they pulled away, they were grinning again, and soon back to eating lunch. Billy sat back with his drink, having finished his sandwich. Maggie soon did the same. They lounged for longer than they had planned but were in no rush to leave their lovely spot in the sea.

The wind started to pick up as they moved through Long Bay and pushed them north at about 23 knots.

"We're making excellent time, Mag," Billy told her as she sat back in her seat next to his captain's chair. "Probably be docked by 4:00," he added, looking at the cockpit. White sands, rock faces, and green rolling mountains in the distance, all stretching along the Emerald Pearl's starboard side. A stunning blanket of forever blues, and pure white fluffy clouds dancing along the horizon port side. As they drifted into the cove, Billy started up the engine, while Maggie dropped the sails. He pulled into the docking area and Maggie hopped out of the boat and tied it up. Then back onto the boat to cover the mainsail while Billy gathered up their paperwork, licenses, and passports. Ready to go they went and registered with the port operative's office and paid for one night. It wasn't very busy, and Billy's organization of documents made things quick for them. After they left the office, they walked along the beach for a look at Lucea. Almost completely, surrounded by the cove, surrounded by many green hills, homes and resorts, they stood staring, and tried to soak it all in. It was like nothing Maggie had ever seen. Like being in a place from a fictional fantasy story. They headed back towards the marina after walking for a good half hour. Soon back on the boat, they got themselves ready to go somewhere for dinner, locking up and walking hand in hand up the dock eager to enjoy yet another paradise on earth. Maggie hugged Billy, then grinned at him.

"You're looking pretty gorgeous again tonight, Lover!" she said. Billy's eyes smiled as he chuckled and grinned at her.

"Thanks, Babe," he answered, holding her face, and kissing her.

"You look absolutely Beautiful!" he said, as their lips broke apart. She smiled and he pulled her in for another kiss, Maggie holding onto his wrists gently. As they let go, they held hands. Then, noticing a few parked taxis, they headed over to them.

"The nearest restaurant, please," Billy said and he reached for the door handle. The driver nodded.

"Ok, yuh get it!" their cabby replied. Billy opened the door for Maggie to climb in first. The trip was a short one, just over 10 minutes when their driver pulled up in front of the big, round, open patio style, thatched roofed restaurant. The views facing the gorgeous Caribbean. Tiny islands, green trees, and fauna, all set in the small cove. Maggie and Billy climbed out of the cab amazed. They stopped and held each other grinning and Maggie leaned against Billy, his hands holding her arms and squeezing her in for a long kiss.

"This is so nice," Maggie said as they were shown to their seats. Both looking around at the restaurant. It was a little fancier decor than some they'd enjoyed on their trip so far. With the walls completely open, allowing a lovely breeze to weave through the many tables, which were all pretty well spread out from one another. Long yellow tablecloths hanging over the tables, green cloth napkins, and multi-coloured glass vases sat in the middle of each table with tea lights inside. It was very nice. They were taken to a table for two near the back of the open water facing side. A waiter came over to fill their glasses with water when they sat down and asked what they'd like to drink. A moment later, another took their orders. There were only a few empty tables left closer to Maggie and Billy, and looking around a bit, Maggie noticed the other customers seemed to be mostly couples as well, with a few tables that had multiple people. Maggie slid her chair closer to Billy's so they were sitting next to each other and could both look out at the view and the restaurant. The sun was setting, and the restaurant was lit mostly by candles on the tables and hanging yellow and red lanterns scattered all around the edge of the circular roof and up into the center. The bar on the other side of the patio also had little lights running across it. Making the whole scene very romantic. Maggie and Billy ordered a steak and seafood platter that they shared. Snuggled together, sandals off, as they played footsies under the table. They gazed into each other's eyes throughout the meal, sweet little kisses every so often and lots of smiles back and forth.

"Dessert?" The waiter asked when he brought them another drink. Before Billy could answer, Maggie did.

"Not yet, thank you." The man nodded. "No hurry!" she added, and he nodded again, and left them. Billy looked at Maggie and she grinned mischievously at him. He kissed her, then sat up with a surprised smirk as he felt her hand run down the inside of his thigh. Nose to nose he whispered,

"Mag!" and she grinned again, her hand moving between his legs and gently caressing him. He gave a little jump, hitting the bottom of the table with a clang. A woman looked over at them but turned back quickly. Maggie used her other hand to pick up her drink and take a sip, trying to look innocent, while undoing his shorts at the same time and reaching into his boxers and grasping his steadily stiffening cock. Then she took one of the cloth napkins off the table and draped it over her hand in Billy's lap. "Mag," he whispered again. His eyes flashed excitedly. She was already stroking him under the table as he said her name. The waiter came back and handed them the dessert menu. Billy took it quickly and opened it up in front of himself on the table, hardly suppressing a little moan. Maggie grinned as Billy held the table with one hand, the other held the menu, trying to show as little reaction as he could as the waiter left them. "My God, Mag!" he breathed, and she steadily and slowly stroked up and down. Billy's head falling back slightly, holding the table firmly, Maggie leaned close and gave his ear lobe a little nibble and whispered,

"Faster?" He didn't answer, just shook his head slightly and she grinned, keeping the rhythm steady. She felt the tip become wet and teased the end of him with a few very soft rubs before she slid her hand up and down with full strokes. Then she started to stroke a little faster, stroking the end very lightly, then back to moving up and down.

"Mmm," Billy moaned as quietly as he could. "Maag!" he whispered, looking at her with intensity.

"Should I stop?" she asked, grinning at him. The restaurant was quite busy now, and Maggie was finding it very difficult not to just ignore them all and jump right onto Billy's lap.

"Don't stop Mag. Oh God!" he groaned in her ear, and she knew he was about to blow. He hit the table suddenly, almost tipping their drinks and held his breath, his other hand down near Maggie's hip, his fingers under her bottom, holding on tight as his body convulsed. An older couple not too far from them looked over at the sound of the slam. Maggie grinned sweetly at them, they looked at her, then at Billy and back at Maggie, then went back to eating their meal. She was now sliding her hand quickly and cupping the tip with each stroke. "Mmmm," he groaned, Maggie keeping the speed quick. Billy, hardly able to keep it together, as he whispered. "Faster," and she sped up her strokes. Billy reached down and grasped her hand in his, holding hers a little tighter and moving their hands together faster as he finished with a muffled moan and deep exhale. Feeling hot, wetness bursting over their hands. Suddenly super sensitive, Billy held her hand still and looked at her like he was going to eat her up right there. The waiter was on his way back, Maggie's free hand reached out for her drink, and she smiled at him.

"Have you decided on dessert?" he asked, Maggie grinned slightly, stifling a naughty giggle.

"Um, I think we'll just take the check, please." He nodded and walked away. Billy and Maggie's heads leaning towards one another.

"Mag, that was crazy!" he told her, grabbing the other napkin and fixing himself up. She heard him zip up and grinned cheekily at him.

"Good crazy, Lover?" He growled at her and kissed her. "You said you liked when we did it on the porch, so I figured you might like…" She grinned and softly pressed her mouth to his ear as she continued. "..a public…seeing to." Maggie felt Billy shudder and he looked at her and growled. She felt her insides bubbling up, sending shivers through her.

"Just going to use the lady's room," she told him, and off she walked. She looked back and saw him watching her, shaking his head with a surprised smile. When she came back, he went to the washroom too, then they paid the bill and left. Billy's hands were all over her as they walked the beach. Stopping and holding her and kissing her intensely, slipping her the tongue and squeezing her ass. She couldn't stop grinning, and Billy couldn't stop caressing her.

"Damn Mag, I can't believe *you* did that!" he said, embracing her again.

"Mmm, it was rather naughty of me, wasn't it Lover of mine?!" she responded, a seductive gleam in her bright green eyes. Billy pulled her up to his body quickly and kissed her hard.

"Yes. It was Mag," he whispered with a sensual moan in her ear and kissed her again, Maggie feeling goosebumps run up her body.

"Not sure we'll be allowed back though! I think they knew something was going on." She laughed, and Billy chuckled. "Good dessert," she added, and he threw his head back with a deep chuckle.

"Best dessert!" he exclaimed, kissing her again.

They made their way over to a phone booth and called for a cab. While they waited, they were all over each other. Almost eating each other up. A taxi pulled in and rolled down the window. Billy asked the driver to take them back to the port, and they climbed in, sliding up close to one another in the back seat. Instantly locked in a deep kissing embrace. With one arm wrapped around her, Billy whispered in Maggie's ear,

"Naughty or Nice, Beautiful?" Maggie's chest rose with a deep inhale, her pulse speeding up, Billy's other hand running up her leg, over the front of her body and into her hair. After a short drive, the cabby stopped the car.

"We here," he announced and Billy, still looking at Maggie intensely, pulled his wallet out and paid their driver. Climbing out of the car, and moving towards the tree line near the marina, Billy walked Maggie backwards and against a tree, kissing her intensely, and sliding his hand down to grab one of her breasts.

"Mmm," Maggie moaned excitedly, holding him tight. Billy let go, grabbed her hand, and started walking them towards the dock. Stopping to hold her face and kiss her deeply every few feet. Their hands moving quickly over each other's backs. Billy stepped onto the boat first, then reached up and held Maggie's waist, helping her down, her body sliding down his, kissing him as her feet touched the floor. Breathing heavy and fast, Maggie quickly undid the buttons on Billy's shirt, Billy's hands in her hair, holding her head, as they kissed passionately, moving towards the cabin door. Billy stopped to take the keys out of his pocket, Maggie's hands still moving all over his body, kissing his neck, and breathing in his ear. He opened the door and walked down the stairs, holding out his hand for Maggie. She walked down to his open arms, the two embracing quickly and tightly, frantically kissing again. Billy's hands were pulling Maggie's dress up and sliding down the back of her underwear as Maggie slipped her hands under his shirt and pulled it down off his shoulders, letting it drop to the floor. He was squeezing her ass and pulling their bodies together tightly. Maggie ran her fingers through his hair and pulled his face closer, bringing his lips against hers with urgency.

Suddenly, Billy picked Maggie up, holding her tight as she wrapped her legs around his waist, her arms wrapped around his neck and shoulders, kissing deep and hard. Billy walked towards the bedroom and sat down on the bed. Maggie was still wrapped around him, holding his face, and sliding her tongue in sensual circles around his.

"Mmm, Mag," he said with a moan, looking at her hungrily. "That trick of yours was good foreplay." His hands were holding her face. Both feeding off of each other's arousal, the passion between them becoming more intense with every breath. Maggie stopped kissing him and looked into his eyes, a sultry hunger igniting deep within.

"Let's take our time, Lover," she whispered as she stared at him. Her hands, trailing and massaging over his warm tanned skin. Running across his shoulders slowly and up his neck into his hair. Billy's head falling back slightly, his eyes closed, his lips parted as Maggie softly kissed his cheek, taking her time to kiss his whole face softly, then so gently, she ran the tip of her tongue across his bottom lip, then kissed his lips softly, her hands still running through his hair. Billy's hands were under her dress again, caressing her back while he enjoyed her tender touch. "I want you so bad," she breathed, and she felt Billy's breath quicken. "And I want it to last," she breathed the words slowly, sucking his tongue, and holding his face tight. Billy moved himself, and Maggie, back further on the bed, resting his body against the headboard. Maggie looked into his eyes again and she saw them crinkle into a grin. Then she felt his hands holding her dress and sliding it up her body. She held her arms up so he could pull it off her. Billy held her body, under her arms and leaned down to kiss her chest, Maggie's head fell back as he softly kissed up her neck, and chin and then her lips. Sliding his hands back and undoing her bra, Maggie held him tight and kissed him hard again. They were in such a tight embrace; their skin becoming one.

"You smell amazing," he told her as they kissed each other's faces and necks. Maggie let her straps slide down her arms and dropped her bra on the bed. Billy's hands reaching for her breasts and slowly, pressing and massaging them, Maggie's hands were back in Billy's hair.

"Mmm," she moaned quietly, with a smile, and she reached down and undid his zipper, pressing her knees into the bed, her body rising off of Billy's lap. "Take them off," she spoke. They stared into each other's eyes, and he wiggled out of his shorts and boxers. His hands trailing and squeezing all over her body, and Maggie climbed off, took her underwear off and climbed back onto his lap.

"Ohhh God," he said in a deep husky whisper, as Maggie sat down and took him into her body. She bent her face down and kissed his shoulder, with slow, open mouth kisses all the way up his neck, then finding his ear she sucked on the lobe. Licking and sucking hungrily.

"Mmm," she purred, kissing his neck again. "You taste delicious," she breathed. Billy pulled her up so she was still kneeling over him, her body up higher, and holding her ass he brought her close again, his tongue finding her breasts and licking, wet, hot and hungry licks over both. "Ohh!" she cried as Billy started sucking, his tongue playing and flicking. "Ohhh gawd!" Maggie was crying with delight, moving her wet center over the tip of him, causing Billy to lick with more vigor. "Ohhhh!" Maggie was dripping with pleasure and needed them to become one again. She slid down, slowly, letting him push her body down, hard.

"Aww!" they both groaned as she moved up and down a few times, as slowly as possible, both of them aching for more.

"Damn, Maggie," he moaned, kissing her neck as she continued to ride him, slowly. She was now pressing into him, rocking and grinding slowly and deeply, her hips sweeping seductively, like a provocative dance. Both kissing everywhere they could get to, holding each other tight.

"Help me," she whispered, and Billy's strong hands held her hips, his fingers grasping her ass as he moved her up and down, Maggie still sliding as slowly as possible. "Oh my God!" she cried out.

"You're driving me crazy!" he growled at her.

"You feel so good, Billy!" she breathed. They continued the slow rise and fall. She was so turned on, so wet, and so completely entranced by their bodies moving with such patient erotic pleasure together.

"Mag!" he yelled, wanting to speed up. She started to grind him again, kissing one another hungrily, holding each other's faces and opening their mouths more, kissing deeply. "Mmm," Billy growled as she started speeding up her movements, pushing harder, feeling him deeper. Then, when he couldn't stand it any longer, he grabbed her and flipped her down onto her back and started sliding quicker.

"Oh Billy…" she moaned, her arms stretching above her head, searching for something to hold as he slid faster and harder.

"Mag, I'm so close," he told her, looking into each other's eyes again, both becoming more eager now. Her hands running all over his body, grabbing his ass and squeezing hard.

"Slow," she breathed so quietly. "Ooooh…" Billy's glides became slow and long, and Maggie cried with pleasure. His unhurried, steady, and deliberate movement in and out of her, making them both crazy.

"Mmmm. You feel sooo damn good," he growled deeply, looking at her with lustful pleasure.

"Don't stop, Billy," Maggie begged, her body rising and falling, writhing on the bed with aching satisfaction. Billy continued to slide slowly, bending down, he kissed her mouth with warm, slow pressure.

"Maaag!" he yelled out and he pushed suddenly, deeply, holding himself inside her. Maggie held him tightly and moved her hips as he released, his body shaking. Still within, he kissed her again, moving his lips down to her neck, sucking as Maggie continued to grind her hips into his. He slid one hand down and squeezed her breast while he kissed and sucked her neck. Maggie's eyes started to roll back.

"Mmmm," she moaned, her body quivering now, Billy breathing heavier, kissing near her ear.

"Oh, Mag," he whispered, and she felt herself climbing, so close. Her body holding him inside her so tight. "Cum for me," he growled with a deep whisper, Maggie's body rising and writhing.

"Say my name," she breathed. Still kissing her neck, feeling his lips hot and wet on her skin, he pushed himself deeper as she circled her hips against his.

"Mmmm, Maggie," he whispered. She felt her body shudder. "Maggie," he growled, becoming aroused again. He slid his hands under her body and wrapped them up over her shoulders, his mouth still on her neck, licking and sucking. "Maggie," he breathed. His body moving into hers again.

"Ohhhh, Billy," she groaned, her head falling back.

"Let me feel you cum!" his deep sexy growl vibrating through her, and she was moaning, aching as her body tried to let go. "Mag. Oh. Gawd. Maggie!" Billy was sucking her neck, his body shaking with the power of her climax and that was it. Shuddering from head to toe, tingling and quivers within every cell, her legs moving and squeezing together, she came, exploding with blissful, wild abandon.

"Ahhh!" she cried out, her legs shaking and her body vibrating, and Billy held her tight. Maggie reached up and held his face, trembling, kissing him steadily and slowly. "Mmm," she was still releasing, her body still quivering. Still pushing together, kissing deeply, Maggie shuddering, and Billy kissed down her neck again, Maggie lifting her chin slightly, delighting at his touch.

"Damn, I'd do you all night if I could!" he told her, looking at her fiercely. Maggie grinned at him and kissed him again.

"I'd gladly let you!" she answered, hardly able to speak. Billy grinned back. Arms wrapped around each other, they rolled to their sides and kissed and kissed. Hands and arms back to running over one another's backs and holding each other tight.

"You are so sexy, Mag!" he said as they snuggled up together. Maggie smiled to herself. He made her feel sexy. His hunger and desire for her, and his deep love for her, made her feel confident, beautiful, and attractive.

"Billy, you light my fire, Lover!" Billy lifted her face and looked into her eyes.

"Forever, Maggie," he said to her, kissing her lips tenderly. They held each other for so long. Caressing one another softly, listening to each other breathing. Laying together in complete, safe, satisfied, blissful comfort.

"Billy?" Maggie said after ages of quiet.

"Ya, Babe," he asked softly.

"Well, I was just wondering something." He looked at her, wondering if something was wrong.

"What is it, Mag?" She was quiet for a moment, then, trying to suppress a grin she looked into his eyes and said,

"Are you ready for more yet?" She smiled at him. He breathed a sigh of relief, and in true Billy fashion, chuckled, eyes twinkling and scooped her up, kissing her neck and making her giggle.

"Mmm, Mag, don't you ever get enough?" he asked jokingly. The two laughing and kissing, legs and arms wrapped around one another, the beginnings of another round of love making close at hand.

Hours after they had arrived back on the boat, they pulled themselves from bed, put on their matching housecoats and put the kettle on. Maggie leaned against Billy at the counter, arms around each other, kissing and grinning while they waited for the water to boil. After they made themselves tea, they took their hot mugs over to the couch and snuggled up, sipping, and talking. Planning all the places they still wanted to visit over the next 2 weeks. A drive and stay in Negril, long walks on the beaches of Lucea, snorkeling in Montego Bay, the Luminescent Lagoon in Falmouth, the Green Grotto Caves not far from Runaway Bay, freshwater pools and falls in Ocho Rios, and stopping to visit with the Robinson's at the end of their travels.

"Ready for bed, Babe?" Billy asked, long after their tea was gone. She was snuggled against him and didn't want to move.

"Yes," she answered, not moving.

"Come on, Mag," he said, getting up and pulling her up with him. Walking hand in hand, they did what they needed to do before bed, then climbed in, cuddled up under the sheets and drifted off to sleep.

CHAPTER 9

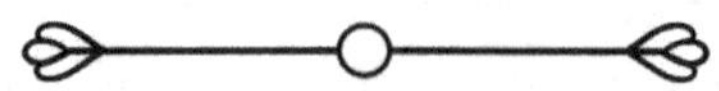

Water pouring over her, steam rising all around her, singing "Emmylou", Maggie's voice echoed in the tiny shower as she cleaned her body. Rinsing the conditioner out of her hair, feeling tired but incredibly happy from the late-night love making, she turned off the water and reached for her towel, her hand moving around and finding the hook, empty. Not able to find her towel, Maggie pulled the curtain back and jumped slightly.

"Looking for this, Beautiful?" Billy asked, standing in the doorway with her towel in his hands.

"Morning, handsome Lover," she said, grinning at him. Her heart racing a little from the surprising break in her solitude.

"Good morning!" he responded, smiling back, his eyes tracing over her wet body. She held out her hand for the towel, Billy grinned.

"Yes, I *was* looking for that," she answered, noticing he wasn't moving. "But if you like..." she stepped out of the shower onto the mat and watched his eyes trace over her body. "*You* could help me," she said, her head tilted down slightly, her emerald eyes looking up at him seductively. Billy walked towards her and wrapped the towel right around her, pulling her closer. "Will you dry me please?" she asked, reaching her arms up around his shoulders. Billy grinned at her, his eyes dancing cheekily.

"Mmhmm," he answered, and she felt his hands patting and rubbing her shoulders and back, moving the towel down and around her body, then down to her bottom. She looked right into his eyes, feeling her heart beating faster. Billy was now crouching down, drying the tops of her legs, then back up over her bottom, looking up her body. He leaned forward and kissed her stomach, standing back up again, kissing her chest and shoulders. Then, draping the towel around her back, he pulled it tightly around her to the front of her body, and started to dry her hips, her stomach, and her breasts, which didn't last long. A few pats, his hands let go of the towel and he was holding her face as he leaned down, looking deep into her eyes and pressing his lips firmly against hers.

"You smell delicious, Mag," he told her, grinning at her, then kissing her again.

"Take me to bed Captain, or lose me forever!" she begged, and he scooped her up and carried her like a rescued damsel in distress. Maggie kissed his neck and nibbled his ear as he carried her to the bed and laid her down gently. Then off came his housecoat. "Wow!" she said, smiling and looking down at his body. "Why Mr. Ashberry…" she added, waving her hand in front of herself like she was fanning off. "My my my, you are such a big, strong man!" He grinned as he lunged for her, growling at her, Maggie giggling as she backed up on the bed and he climbed towards her.

"How ever did you board my ship, madam?" he asked playfully. "That is strictly forbidden, and you shall be tried as a stowaway." Maggie tried to look concerned.

"Oh, please Captain, you wouldn't persecute *a woman*, would you?" she asked, blinking her eyelashes, and laying back, moving her body seductively. Billy smiled broadly at her and leaning over her with fire in his eyes he answered,

"It *is* standard procedure, madame." Maggie was now running her hands gently over her body, looking up at him intensely.

"Well, if I have to be punished, best get on with it," she answered, grinning. Billy made a deep growling sound, sweeping his hands and arms under her body and pulling her up towards him. "Oh!" she cried with surprise. "Captain, you're so rough!" Billy dropped her down, flat on her back and straddled her. "Oh!" she cried out again, casting a devious grin. "I like it rough," she whispered and in the middle of kissing her chest he sat back up, a gleam in his deep blue eyes. He slid off the bed and pulled her body to the edge. Maggie's heart was racing with anticipation. Letting her legs drop over the side of the bed, Billy leaning down and licking his way up one of her thighs, then down and back up the other, pulling her legs apart quickly, he leaned back down and pressed his face into her warm center sliding his tongue right inside of her. "Aww," she moaned. He slid his tongue in and out, nibbling and sucking, then licking again, pushing firmly around her clit. His hands under her body, squeezing her ass, hard, as his tongue played the center of her body expertly. Finding her magic spot, Maggie's legs started shaking. "Oh Captain, my Captain!" she moaned, Billy's tongue pressing harder. Then, licking all around her hips, kissing and sucking around her legs, he stood up and pressed himself against her at the edge of the bed. Reaching forward to grab and squeeze her breasts very firmly, pulling and pinching roughly. "Aww!" she cried, and he pulled her up to sit, pulled her body tight and picked her up, standing up straight, turning and pushing her up against the wall. "Oh!" Maggie cried out as Billy licked and nibbled at her body, pressing her body firmly against the wall. Holding her body with his, Maggie's legs around his waist, he held her hands above her head and kissed her hard.

"It's about to get rougher!" he growled at her. Maggie's pulse quickened, as he sucked her neck, then grabbed her ass and pushed himself in fast and hard.

"Owe!" she cried out, grabbing onto his body and holding him tight. Her body hitting the wall with each hard thrust he made. She could feel his muscles working hard, the sheer power in his body, the deep growling groans he made hitting his body persistently and unyieldingly into hers. She was so turned on by the incredible animal instinct that had been so aggressively awakened within him, yet knowing and trusting she was completely safe in his arms. "Oh. Oh. Oh!" she was almost screaming out now. Holding her hands against the wall again as he continued to pound her. Driving deeply and purposefully.

"Ahhhh!" he groaned.

"Billy!" she cried out and they were kissing, and licking each other's faces, making hungry moaning sounds, almost eating each other. "I want to ride you," she breathed, and he bit and sucked her neck, holding her up and turning towards the bed again. He sat down on the edge of the bed, both still frantically attacking each other. Maggie straddled him, and she began to bounce up and down, hard and fast. Billy's hands on the bed, either side of his body, his head back, mouth open. Maggie pinched his nipples, pulling and twisting as she bounced, Billy growling with lustful pleasure. She slid her hands up and held his shoulders, her head falling back, crying out long, whimpering moans of delight as she slid up and down, up and down, up and...

"Ohhhh God, Billy!" she yelled, and he grabbed her hips and kept her body going. Growling again as he kissed her neck.

"Don't stop, Mag!" he breathed, in a low groan. "God you're so hot!" he called out and she was cumming.

"Oooooh, Billy," Maggie smiled as she said his name, every part of her body tingling now. He held her closer and pushed shorter thrusts inside her, fast and hard.

"Maag..." he moaned, and she felt his body shudder, his hips moving sporadically as they wrapped their arms tight around one another, kissing deeply and hungrily. "Hot Damn!" Billy said, kissing her hard again. "Shit Mag, that was crazy!" He looked at her, still with animal hunger in his eyes. She could still feel her body squeezing him tight inside. She held his face and kissed him hard and long.

"Mmmm," she moaned, pressing her lips firmly against his. "Mmm, Lover," she said, looking into his eyes again. They both grinned and kissed. Moving themselves up onto the bed, lying next to one another, facing each other, and caressing, grinning as they kissed and stared into each other's eyes. Every so often Billy's body shuddering again.

"Wow!" he'd say and kiss her hard.

"Intense!" she breathed, her fingers running into his hair and holding his face, kissing him softly. Billy's hand holding the back of her head, his eyes smiling at her. "Do I have to disembark, Captain?" she asked meekly. Billy chuckled.

"God no! Can't do *that* with just any stowaway!" and they both laughed.

While Billy showered, Maggie threw on her housecoat and went to the kitchen to make breakfast. She grabbed some bananas and eggs and found some flour and baking soda in the cupboard, grabbed a can of club soda, and made pancakes. While the pancakes were cooking, she sliced up some apples, mangos and bananas, tossed them together in a bowl and put them on the table. They didn't have any syrup, but she grabbed the jam and found some cinnamon and brown sugar and set them out on the table too. The coffee was just about finished brewing as she heard Billy turn the shower off and watched him walk out of the washroom with his towel wrapped around his waist.

"Well, you are a handsome beast!" she purred at him, Billy grinned at her and walked over to kiss her.

"You're glowing, Beautiful," he informed her, kissing her neck and then smiling at her again. "Just like when you've ridden your Stallion!" he added with a wink. Maggie giggled. Then with a very sultry gaze,

"I have an amaaazing Lover!" she replied, pulling him in for another kiss. "Hungry, Stallion?" she asked, grinning, then turning to the counter she poured them each a cup of coffee.

"Always," was his response, along with a smiley wink. They took their cups over to the table and sat them down. "Need any help, Mag?" he asked her, she shook her head and smiled, walking over with the plate of pancakes.

"No, all set, thanks." She sat down with him at the table.

"Mmm, these are good, Mag," Billy said, taking another bite of pancake.

"Good," she replied, grabbing her coffee and having a big sip.

"So, what's the plan, Babe?" he asked, having a drink then another bite of his breakfast.

"Well, I think we might need to go shopping again," Maggie answered, and he nodded.

"Ok... Then we can come back and get naked again?" he stated hopefully. Maggie grinned and laughed.

"Mmhmm. Definitely," she answered. Then added, "but I think you should indulge me with a strip tease Lover!" Billy's eyebrow raised, and a little grin played around the corner of his mouth as he responded.

"Oh?" She smiled her big smile at him and nodded slowly.

"Oh yes and sing to me while you get naked." Billy's head fell back with a hearty chuckle.

"For you Mag, anything!" They leaned towards each other and kissed, smiling, and finishing their meal.

Grabbing a taxi, they headed a short distance to a grocery store called Sharry's, arriving close to lunch time. They found the store mildly busy and meandered lazily around the isles. Stocking up on more condiments, groceries, lots of fruit and veggies, more sparkling water, and a case of ginger ale.

"Hey Billy, we should grab some more cheese too," Maggie called from one end of an aisle, Billy pushing the cart in the opposite direction, while Maggie went back to grab some pasta and sauce. They had asked their cabby to stick around, and once they paid for their groceries, they loaded up the car and headed back to the boat.

"Thank you," Billy said, closing the trunk and waving at the driver.

"Bless!" he called out and drove off.

They had a lot to carry but managed to do it in one trip, both putting things away, singing while they worked, their hands trailing across each other's bodies when they were near enough. Then they grabbed drinks and went up to sit in the late afternoon breeze. Maggie's legs on Billy's, his hands on her legs, taking a swig of his beer and grinning at her.

"Hello, Beautiful," he said, winking at her and she smiled at him.

"Hello, Handsome," she said back.

They had plans to go to Negril the next day, maybe stay a night somewhere there, then come back to the boat and sail on to Montego.

"I'll have to go to the office and pay for a couple more nights, Mag," he told her, taking another drink.

"Ok Billy. Think I'll grab a quick shower while you're gone." His eyes filled with mischief as he looked at her.

She was already out of the shower and wearing her peach-coloured, lacy, satin camisole and matching panties, when he got back. The room was glowing warmly, with just a lantern lit. Maggie was sitting and waiting on a big blanket on the table. As Billy descended the stairs and locked the door he turned and saw her and stopped dead.

"Mag!" he exclaimed, whistling at her, a huge grin spreading across his face. His eyes dancing as he walked towards her.

"Dinner's ready!" she announced, and he laughed.

"Mmmm. Watch out, here I come!" he said, leaning down to kiss her. Holding his shirt as she kissed him back, Maggie put her hands on his chest and held him back.

"So, what will you be singing for your strip tease, Gorgeous?" she asked him. Billy chuckled.

"Oh, you were serious eh, Babe?" he asked, grinning.

"You betcha!" she answered, looking at him eagerly, twisting her finger into a loose curl falling down the side of her face, a hungry smile playing in her eyes.

"Alright," he said, still chuckling. He backed up a few feet and as he turned around, she called out.

"Nice view!" He laughed. "Well, come on Lover!" she coaxed.

"Okay, just thinking of a song. Can't rush talent, Babe." Maggie laughed and then watched as he started moving to the beat in his head and then started singing "Kiss You All Over". She giggled, but from the depths of her heart, with sweet, bemused laughter. He sang the first part of the song, dancing around for her, Maggie smiling and moving her body and dancing along, soaking it up. Then he started to undo his shirt, playfully, Maggie keeping in beat with her hand on her lap, and grinning broadly at him. He pulled his shirt down off his shoulders and slid it back and forth across his back, then pulling it right off with one hand, up over his head, swinging it in circles, he let it fly towards Maggie. She whistled and yelled her satisfaction as she caught it, clapping and laughing. Billy undid his shorts, pulled down the zipper and opened them up slightly, winking and grinning at Maggie, spinning on the spot, and then shook his hips. Maggie grinned, filled with love, enjoying his comfort level, his playfulness, and openness with her, as well as his strong beautiful body. Watching eagerly as he started to pull them down, still singing, moving more provocatively now, shorts dropping to the floor and turning back to face her, dancing towards her. She grinned and moved to the song and as he drew close enough, she playfully pushed him back and he danced away, pulling down one side of his boxers, and turning his head back to grin at her.

"Take them off!" she yelled, both of them laughing again. Dancing out of his boxers, singing and wiggling his hips, moving in low circles, he looked at her with hunger. "Ya! Sweet Cheeks!" she yelled, Billy danced his way back up and turned to dance back towards her. He pulled Maggie off the table and danced her around the boat. She was singing with him now, and their dance became more of a skin-to-skin grinding, sweeping movement together. Billy danced them over to where Maggie had put the CD player and pressed play. "Misty Blue" started playing, and they moved back out to the center of the floor, and she let him lead her in a seductive sensual dance. Her body, almost like a rag doll, her hands running over his naked body tenderly. Billy slid the straps of her camisole down her arms, then back up and pulled it over her head, letting it drop to the floor. Supporting her lower back with one hand, the other cradling her head he swept her into a dip and up again, kissing her mouth gently, then continuing to rock them sensually. Their movements became slower and closer, their faces up close, almost nose to nose, looking deeply into each other's eyes. Maggie's lips breaking apart, Billy slid his tongue across his lips lightly and she could feel the heat and energy building between them as he moved in, his breath on her face, then pressing his lips against hers, she felt her heart thumping faster. Hearing him inhale and finding herself even more tantalized. She shivered with pleasure as his fingers trailed up her back, her fingers moving through his hair and pulling his face closer to kiss him deeply. One of his hands now holding the top of her bottom, the other moving up her back and into her hair, holding her head as he kissed her more pressingly, slow warm loving kisses.

"Mmm," she moaned softly, holding him tight. He backed her up towards the table, she felt the softness of the comforter draped over it against the back of her legs. Billy held her face and their eyes met. Then, as he grabbed her panties at each of her hips and slid them down her body, he kissed straight down between her breasts, then kissed his way back up, his hands running up her arms and neck and holding her face again, looking into her eyes and smiling before picking her up and sitting her down on the table. Maggie pulled him tight, her hands running all over his back then down to grab his sweet cheeks and pulled him closer. He looked at her again, and between kisses he quietly said,

"I love you Mag..." more kisses, "...You're all I've ever wanted..." another soft kiss, still cradling her face gently in his big hands. "I want to kiss *you* all over," he whispered to her, Maggie smiled, and her hands were up, holding his wrists as he continued to kiss her tenderly. Then he softly began kissing her face, down to her chin and neck, ever so gently. He kissed down her shoulders and across her chest, down each arm and each of her hands, looking at her lovingly, and holding her face again, kissing her mouth, then moving down to kneel, he kissed all around and all over her breasts, over her stomach, down around her navel and into her center and down her legs, right to each of her knees, kissing down her legs and the tops of her feet, before standing up again and moving his body against hers.

"Billy," she whispered as he held her face again. "I love you." Maggie closed her eyes as his lips found hers, now their tongues sliding slowly together, holding one another tight. She wrapped her legs around him and pulled herself closer to the edge. Billy was very ready and pressing himself against her. Holding those sweet cheeks again, Maggie was squeezing and pulling him inside of her.

"Ahhh," he groaned, her legs holding him tight. Continuing to kiss her slowly and deeply, his hands in her hair, gently holding on as he moved his body back and forth, Billy moved in long patient glides. Maggie softly rubbed her hands all around his back and into his hair, their bodies pressed tightly together, hardly moving apart now, just pushing into one another in a slow dance.

"Mmm, Billy," she breathed as he kissed her neck, her head falling back as she pulled his body deeply into hers. They were moving as one together. A wave of push and pull, skin to skin, ebbing and flowing so subtly, so connected and enveloped in their love and appetite for each other. Their energy, stronger and fiercer than their movements. Breathing each other in so deeply and completely as they kissed.

"I love you," he told her, and they hugged and caressed tenderly, Billy hardly moving out of her body, rocking them together, back, and forth.

"I love you, Billy," she whispered in his ear as they kissed one another's faces and necks, then mouths again. They danced together for so long, the electricity and affection building and building. Billy held her body so her head could fall back, and he kissed down her throat and down her chest. Their bodies still moving slow and deep, then Billy kissed his way back up, Maggie holding his face as their eyes met. Watching each other's subtle movements together, their mouths open slightly, hearing one another's low heavy breathing, all adding fuel to their fire.

"Mag," she saw his lips *mouth* her name. Looking at her intensely, then Billy's head dropped back, his mouth opening with pleasure, Maggie kissed his neck and chin and he looked at her again, his eyes dark and soulful. Their movements becoming a little quicker now, back to kissing slowly and deeply and pulling one another tighter still. Billy held Maggie's face and looked into her eyes again.

"I want us to cum together," he whispered, and Maggie shuddered.

"Billy..." she breathed, and his eyes closed.

"Talk to me, Mag." He looked into her eyes again, hungrily.

"Keep looking at me," she told him, kissing him then holding his face, keeping their deep gaze. "I love you, Billy," she whispered.

"Mag, I'm so close," his body pushing harder now.

"Tell me what you like," she whispered.

"Mmm, I love your body," he moaned, and Maggie's body quivered.

"I love when you say my name, Billy," and he pushed deep and hard now. Their bodies became tighter still as they moved deeper and deeper into one another.

"Maggie, you feel amazing." And his hands were holding her hips as he moved faster.

"Ohh, Billy, I don't ever want you to stop." Maggie pulled him in and out, using her legs while he pulled her body tighter against him.

"You're so deep!" she cried. The intensity, escalating.

"I love the way you make me feel," he groaned. Maggie's breathing was getting faster now.

"Oh God, Billy," she moaned, her hands holding his body so tight, moving her hips back and forth with his.

"Mag, Oh God, Mag!" he was moaning so deeply. "I want to feel you cum with me." Sliding faster, still short movements but hard and quick.

"Kiss my neck!" she cried out. "I'm close, Billy." Billy's lips, hot and pressing against her skin. "Oh gawd," she moaned.

"Ahh. Maaag…" he let out a long growling groan as she felt him exploding inside of her, kissing her neck again, Maggie now squeezing him so tightly with her legs. "Cum, Mag," he breathed in her ear. His lips trailing, kissing, pressing against her skin, his breath heavy on her neck.

"Oh, oh, ohhhh," her body shaking, "Billy!" she yelled, and she fell forward against him breathing heavily, her chest rising and falling quickly. Billy lifted and held her face and kissed her hard. Their bodies, still moving slowly together. "Mmm," she moaned with extreme satisfaction. Still holding her face, he looked into her dreamy emerald, green eyes, his deep dark blue eyes smiling back at her.

"That was another level, Mag!" he said, kissing her softly. "Did you feel it?" he asked, the two of them still looking deeply into one another's souls. Maggie's eyes glistening, she smiled at him, held his face, and kissed him.

"Yes, my God, Billy, it felt like we were both inside of one another's bodies. Like our hearts were pounding as one," she answered, kissing him again, looking up at him euphorically. Kissing and stopping to look at one another again, then Billy held her away slightly, to look at her whole face, with such love, his eyes grinning.

"I felt our souls dancing, Mag," he told her, kissing her longer, pressing their faces together, hands in each other's hair. Still holding tight, Billy stood up straight and helped Maggie down. They kissed again then went to the bedroom to grab T-shirts and undies. As Maggie walked towards the door, Billy grabbed her hand and pulled her back. Hugging her tight, he kissed her long and hard, lips unlocking and smiling at each other.

"How is it you always look so beautiful, Maggie? Especially after we make love," he asked, smiling at her warmly.

"Mmm, Lover, how is it you always know what to say to make me weak in the knees?" Grinning at each other, then embracing and kissing deeply, hugging, and squeezing one another tight.

"Hey Babe, want a deli sandwich?" Billy asked, walking hand in hand to the kitchen.

"You know it, Sweet Cheeks!" she answered, grinning at him, and she walked over and took the big comforter off the table. Billy winked at her before she turned to walk away.

"Mag, you want salami?" Billy asked as she headed into the bedroom.

"Already had mine, Lover!" she replied, and she heard Billy chuckle and grinned to herself. Leaving the blanket on the bedroom desk and walking back out to the kitchen, she made her way over to Billy. She moved up behind him and hugged him while he made their sandwiches.

Then she grabbed them both a cold drink and some napkins, and they went up to the top deck to enjoy each other and their meal. After they ate, they got dressed and packed overnight bags. They were taking a taxi to The Sandals resort in Negril for the night, then spending the day there before heading back out on the Emerald Pearl.

"Ready, Mag?" Billy called from the deck. Maggie smiled as she walked up the steps to meet him.

"All set," she answered, their hands touching and trailing as he walked past her and locked up the boat. A taxi was waiting in the marina parking lot, and they climbed in and snuggled up together, watching the beautiful scenery go by. About 45 minutes later they arrived at the resort.

"Thanks, boss," Billy said, paying their driver and following Maggie out of the cab.

"Wow!" Maggie gasped, looking at the building. "This place is huge!" She felt Billy's hand on her lower back, and they walked into the main entrance, where they were greeted and helped with their bags as they made their way to the front desk to check in.

"Enjoy your stay Mr. and Mrs. Stanton," the woman at the desk said, handing them their room cards. Maggie saw Billy's eyes twinkle, knowing how much he loved hearing 'Mrs. Stanton', and she ran her hand along his back grinning up at him.

"This way," said the man with their bags and he led them towards a hallway, branching out to a wing facing the beach. "Room 11," he said, stopping and waiting for Billy to open the door, then leading them in and sitting their bags down. "If you need anything, please feel free to call the front desk." Billy thanked him, and as soon as the door shut, he scooped Maggie up and she squealed with delight, holding his face, and kissing him. Sliding her down, they walked towards their private patio doors and stepped out to their own pool and patio, with beach access.

"This is Beautiful!" Maggie said, turning to face him, Billy holding her hand and smiling at her.

"*You're* beautiful!" he told her grinning and Maggie stretched up onto her tip toes and kissed him. Then of course she had to check their room out, and Billy watched her eyes light up as she looked around. They decided to have a quick swim before they got dressed and went to the dining room for a late dinner.

"That's a nice dress. Is it new, Mag?" Billy said, smiling from across the table at her.

"Thanks, Handsome, yes it is." She smiled back at him warmly. Maggie was always so pleasantly grateful at how attentive he was. The dress was white with bright blue flowers, a short, off the shoulder dress, that was light and comfy. She had pulled her hair up into a high ponytail, her curls full and falling down her back. Billy was still staring at her smiling, and she felt his foot running along her leg and saw his eyes twinkle cheekily at her. "You going to make it through dinner, Lover?" she asked teasingly. He chuckled and reached out his hand to hold hers. As they sat gazing at one another, out on a beautiful open patio on the beach, their waiter came over with their drinks. Maggie ordered a Pina Colada; Billy ordered a Bob Marley. Raising his colourful drink, Billy said,

"Here's to forever, Babe." Maggie grinned and tapped her glass to his.

"Forever, Lover!" she said, taking a sip. For dinner, Maggie enjoyed a delicious grilled chicken and vegetable alfredo, and Billy dove into the surf and turf. Then they ordered coffee and shared a piece of warm Jamaican fruit cake, feeding each other, their feet playfully touching under the table. After they finished Billy took her hand and they walked together down the beach, soon walking with an arm wrapped around one another, quietly soaking in their surroundings as the night grew darker, the colourful lights all along the resorts on the 7-mile beach adding a magical glow as far as they could see. They walked for a while then headed back towards their resort where lively rhythmic music was being played on steel drums and guitars, a multitude of voices singing. They watched elaborately dressed feathered dancers, others hanging from hoops, contortionists flying from one hoop to another, and fire eaters lighting up the darkness. As they drew closer, they noticed tables set up with bartenders, and a crowd of happy people dancing together in the center of it all. Billy grabbed Maggie's hand and led her towards the group of dancers, pulling her close and kissing her. They laughed and danced together, absorbed in the vibrant energy of everyone around them. Billy led her in a samba and salsa, Maggie's big smile filling him up, his eyes twinkling happily at her enjoyment. Then dancing apart, Maggie smiling from ear to ear, both soaking up the music happily, they continued to move their bodies to the beat. Billy went and got them drinks, and Maggie waited near one of the tall tables watching and enjoying herself.

"Care to dance?" she heard, and a man stepped closer towards her and held her arm. He was already pulling her out to the center, holding her closer and moving his body against hers. She politely tried to decline, but he held her tighter, moving her deeper into the crowd and holding her tight. "You are very sexy!" he said, still holding onto her and dancing.

"I'd rather not dance," she told him, trying to pull away, but he didn't listen. It was so loud; she knew Billy wouldn't hear her if she called for him. People didn't even notice she wasn't enjoying herself. The man pulled her tighter, dancing his body into hers, Maggie trying to pull away, as he pulled her farther away from everyone.

"Really, I don't want to dance!" she repeated, but he held on, his hands becoming a little too friendly. "Let me go!" Maggie urged. Then, suddenly, Billy was next to her looking at the stranger.

"You alright?" Billy asked, looking at Maggie. The man smiled at him.

"We're dancing, brother!" he told him and started to move away with Maggie again.

"I don't think so," Billy said, stopping him from moving. The man's smile faltered, but he pulled Maggie closer and started dancing with her again. "I said, I don't think so!" Billy repeated, sounding quite angry. "I think my wife would like you to let go of her, *brother!*" he added, standing up a little taller and moving closer to the man, who now had a slightly worried look on his face.

"Alright, alright, just having some fun, aren't we?" The stranger smiled at Maggie and finally let go. Turning and walking away, muttering something to himself. Billy wrapped an arm around Maggie, and she looked up at him with relief.

"Are you okay, Mag?" he asked. Maggie nodded at him. She wrapped her arms around him, and he held her tight, kissing her lips, then looking at her with concern. She smiled at him and held him tight again, Billy's arms embracing her completely.

"My hero!" she said, not letting go. Billy hugged her tight and Maggie's nervous system settled. They started dancing again, staying close together. Maggie was rattled but relaxed a bit as they watched a group of people play limbo, and some of the professional dancers joined in with the visitors, smiling and teaching people some fun moves. After another twenty minutes or so, Billy pulled her tight.

"Should we head back, Mag?" he asked, and she nodded and took his hand. Making their way through the crowd and back to their room.

"Well, that was interesting," she said as they walked into the foyer of the resort. Noticing a sign reading 'Carnival Night' as they headed towards their hallway.

"Loved being out dancing with you, Babe. Sorry you got stuck with that idiot. Sorry I didn't get there sooner." He ran his hand over her back and snuggled her.

"Well, luckily I've got a personal bodyguard," she replied, smiling at him. "Thank you! And yes, it was fun to go dancing. The entertainment was pretty cool too," Maggie added as Billy opened the door and let her walk in first. They made their way over to the bed and flopped down, lying next to each other. Their hands moving towards each other and grasping. After a few minutes Maggie sat up and leaned over Billy. She looked down at him and smiled, reaching out a hand and softly sweeping it across his cheek and into his hair.

"You are such a beautiful man. Inside and out," she said to him, leaning down and rubbing her nose against his. He smiled at her and held her face as she leaned a little closer and kissed his mouth, slowly. Maggie sat up and looked at Billy fondly. "Feel like a bath?" she asked him, and his eyes twinkled.

"With you? Always!" he answered, sitting up with a smile. They walked to the bathroom together, their hands, as always, touching one another lovingly. Maggie walked over to the tub and put the plug in and turned on the water. Billy walked over and turned the big light off and found a little lamp sitting on the far counter and turned that on instead. It gave a soft warm glow to the room. Maggie sat on the edge of the tub watching the water rising. She added some of her oils and grabbed her coconut body wash, setting everything on the chair beside the bathtub. Then she turned the tap off. Billy reached out, helping her up, gently taking Maggie's face in his hands. His fingers stretched up into her hair as he moved his face closer and kissed her lips softly. Maggie reached towards his chest, sliding her hands up his body and started to undo the buttons on his shirt, looking up into his eyes. Billy grinned, slid his hands down her body and held the back of her hips. She slowly pulled his shirt down his arms, trailing her fingers and giving his body a few loving squeezes, dropping his shirt behind him. He reached up and pulled her dress down her arms. All the way down to the top of her legs, and then let it drop to the floor. She reached behind her back and undid her bra letting that drop too. Billy grinned at her desirously, and Maggie watched with fondness as he slid his shorts and boxers off, their eyes twinkling at one another as she slid her underwear off too and stepped out of them. Both knew this wasn't going to be one of their regular chatty baths. Maggie and Billy had their best talks in the tub and bathed together often. Sometimes they ate in the tub, sharing a snack or meal on a tray between them, filling each other in on their day, planning things together or just reminiscing about old times. They always shared lots of kisses, sometimes snuggled up together, and laying in one another's arms. They usually gave each other a foot rub, and quite often bathed one another. Maggie and Billy climbed into the tub and slid down into the water, leaning towards one another. Maggie had her legs bent, over top of Billy's, his, stretched out on either side of her. His hands gently reached up and slid along her neck, moving up and cradling her head as he kissed her mouth. With short, soft, kisses, they smiled at each other. Maggie held his wrists as he pulled her in closer and kissed her, long and hard, warm water dripping down their arms.

"I've missed our baths, Babe," he said, kissing the end of her nose.

"Mmm, me too," she breathed, smiling at him affectionately. She gave him another kiss, then smiled and said, "Turn around, Lover." Billy smirked at her. He turned the opposite way, then moved his body back towards her. Maggie wrapped herself around him, hugging him tight, stretching her arms right around the front of his body. "Love you!" she said, Billy's hands holding her arms.

"Love you with a never-ending fire, Mag," he replied, pulling her tight. She hugged him once more then sat up and reached for the coconut body wash. Dribbling some over his shoulders, setting it aside and rubbing her hands all around his back. She rubbed his shoulders, and neck, slowly and lovingly. Cupping her hands and scooping warm water up and pouring it over his body. Sliding her hands over his beautiful, tanned skin. Over the front of his shoulders and all over his chest, her hands wet and soapy, slipping sensually across his skin. Her wet naked body pressing up against his back. Maggie nestled her face close to his ear and exhaled deeply. She felt Billy shiver as he snuggled back, and she kissed his cheek and hugged him. Maggie leaned back, then she motioned for him to slide down and he did, resting his head on her chest, so she could wash his hair for him. Billy's eyes closed, a peaceful look on his face as Maggie cupped the water with her hands and let it fall over his head, massaging her fingers gently over his scalp, then holding the bottom of his head and massaging it under the water. Bathing each other brought them such a deep intimacy. Their connection, growing stronger all the time. She kissed his forehead, and he looked up at her and smiled. He sat up and held his head back, using his hands to move the water back. Then Billy turned back around and reached for her face, pulling her close, smiling at her with love, and kissing her deeply. He gestured for Maggie to turn around, and she did the same as he did, moving back towards him. Her hair still in a ponytail, he moved it to one side and leaned down to kiss her shoulder. Then a little further up, another kiss, over her neck, soft, warm kisses up to her cheek. Maggie's head tilted as her body quivered. Billy wrapped his arms right around her, hugging her close. She felt him breathing her in, as his face nestled against her neck. Billy grabbed the body wash and dripped some over her shoulders. Then his strong hands were massaging her and sliding over her back, up her neck and back to her shoulders. Then scooping up big handfuls of warm water and pouring it over her. Maggie's body moved gently with the water. Billy's hands sliding over the front of her body, down her chest and pulling her a little closer. He dipped his hands into the water and massaged her breasts.

"Mmm," Maggie moaned, her body moving into his as her heart beat faster. Squeezing and rubbing methodically, his mouth close to her ear, his breathing making her even more turned on. Still massaging, his fingers started to pull and pinch, twisting and squeezing, Maggie squirming with pleasure against his body. She reached her hand down between her legs and started to caress herself. With the other hand, she reached around behind her back and started to fondle and lightly grasp him, making small strokes.

"Damn you're hot!" he breathed in a husky whisper, and he squeezed and pinched and pulled a little harder.

"Oh!" Maggie cried out as Billy concentrated on pinching and pulling both her nipples, and started breathily, growlingly kissing her neck, making Maggie crazier, her legs moving and squeezing together. "You drive me wild," she breathed, Billy's fingers faster and more delicious by the second, his fingers like magic, playing her body into climax. "Billy...don't...stop," she moaned slowly, feeling herself close to cumming. "I'm... ohhh..." she breathed deeply. "Ooooh!" she let out a long-delighted moan. Turning her face and kissing his mouth, one arm around the back of his neck as his hands slid all over the front of her body.

"Mmmm," through kisses, they both made deep loving sounds as they pressed their lips together, their tongues sliding in and out sensually. Billy's hands still caressing the front of her body, squeezing, and sliding all over her. Maggie turned her body all the way over and straddled him. They both wrapped their arms around one another and grinned.

"We're not doing foot rubs tonight, are we Mag?" Billy asked, chuckling. Maggie shook her head, smiling. Billy pulled her close, holding her head and kissing her hard. Their hands now sliding all over each other's wet backs. Their breathing and kissing became faster and deeper, as they pulled one another tighter.

"Mmm," Maggie moaned, and Billy gave a little growl, his hands sliding down and grabbing her ass. They stopped and looked at each other and gave one another a knowing look. Maggie watched as Billy started to move, ready to climb out of the tub. Reaching out her hand to hold him, Billy looked at her and smiled.

"What's up, Beautiful?" he asked, running his hand down her arm.

"Just had an idea, Lover," she told him with a seductive stare. Billy sat down again and moved in close to kiss her.

"And what might that be?" he asked, pressing his lips firmly into hers, his hands brushing back a rogue curl off her cheek. She looked at him seductively, her eyes pulling him in as their hands started sliding over one another again. Kissing deeply, mouths open, holding each other so tight. Pressing into one another, kissing hard. Then Maggie pulled away, gave him a few shorter kisses, rubbed her nose on his and grinned at him. She dipped her hands down into the water and grasped him. Watching his expression and hearing him breathe with pleasure as she started to slide her hands up and down. Faces close, watching one another intensely. Warm soapy glides from base to tip.

"Maag," he breathed her name deeply. Maggie continued to stroke him with one hand, the other sliding down to fondle his balls gently. His head fell back, his breathing heavier as he contentedly made pleasurable sounds. Looking back up into her very sexy bed roomy eyes, he grasped her breasts in his hands and began squeezing them, occasionally, running his thumb over her nipples. Faces close, eyes locked, watching the pleasure deep within one another. Then Maggie gave him a long kiss. She turned around to face the other way and positioned herself on all fours. She looked behind her and saw Billy grinning salaciously. Maggie felt his hands running along her wet skin as they moved over her ass. Billy moved himself up and over Maggie, her body dipping into the water just deep enough that her breasts were hanging below the surface, the top of her body out, with Billy's hot wet body pressed up behind her. He slid his hands up her bottom, over her back and leaned forward and grabbed her breasts, moving his hips back he slid between her legs. He moved back and forth a few times, squeezing Maggie's breasts, then moved back up and held her hips.

"Oooh," Maggie moaned, feeling him slide in. Moving slowly. Long, wet glides, firmly holding her hips and moving their bodies together, rocking the water back and forth with them. The sensation of being dipped in the warm water, her breasts moving with the ebb and flow, and the cool air on her skin was quite delicious for Maggie. "Billlly," she moaned. Their bodies moving like the waves back and forth.

"You feel goood, Mag," he moaned back, continuing his slow, long glides in and out of her body. Now Billy was holding the side of the bathtub, moving deeper and harder.

"Gawwd!" Maggie moaned, her head dropping slightly. Maggie started to move back and forth, sliding him in and out. Billy handed over control and caressed her back as he watched her move, rocking her body, the water moving her gently.

"Mag," he groaned, his head back, holding her hips gently as she moved, taking him in and out at a steady pace. Maggie enjoyed the control and pleasure she was feeling. Billy enjoyed it just as much. He straightened up slightly, then held the tub again and pressed his hips forward, allowing him to slide deeper, her pace becoming faster, making shorter, quicker thrusts against him. "Damn..." he breathed, holding her hips tighter and finding it impossible to keep still. Pushing into her and pulling her tight, he moved faster and faster, hardly leaving her body now.

"Oh God, Billy," Maggie moaned; her body started to shake. Billy's body strong, his breath held as he pushed deep. "Billy!" she yelled. Billy moving fast, his breath still held. Quick, deep, thrusts. Then exhaling,

"Ahhhh," he groaned, his body moving out of his control, exploding completely. "Maag!" and Maggie felt herself shuddering. His climax, so powerful. Making her so much more aroused. She started to grind and circle her hips against him.

Billy leaned over her and pulled her up, so she was sitting on his lap. He wrapped his arms around the front of her body and held her tightly against him. Kissing her neck, he whispered in her ear,

"Mmm, God, that was good." He kissed her neck softly again. "Good idea, by the way, Mag!" he said, continuing to kiss her. Maggie enjoyed his kisses and feeling his body pressed against her back for a few minutes. Then she slid off his lap and sat down, facing him again. They looked into each other's eyes as their bodies moved closer, holding one another's faces, and kissing slowly and deeply. Squeezing and caressing each other, Maggie, still just on the brink of climax. They massaged each other, dripping the oily coconut water all over their bodies as they loved on one another, and cuddling up tight and enjoying sitting in the water together. In no hurry to leave the tub, they kissed and snuggled, stopping, and smiling once in a while, eyes twinkling at one another, trailing their hands and fingers lovingly over each other. Maggie moved her face back and smiled at him.

"Come on, Lover," she said, grinning at him with desire. Maggie stood and stepped out of the tub, grabbing each of them a towel and wrapping one around herself. She handed the other one to Billy as he stood up, and as he stepped onto the bathmat, he wrapped it around his waist. Maggie moved closer and grabbed his towel, pulling it loose. Then she started to slide it up his back, moving it back and forth, drying him off. They stared into each other's eyes as she took her time rubbing and drying his arms and shoulders. Patting and squeezing the towel over his strong muscles, knowing and loving every inch of his body as she moved the towel up and over his broad shoulders. Then back around to dry and squeeze his sweet cheeks. Billy's eyes twinkling as he kept his gaze on Maggie. She slowly dropped to the floor, kneeling at his feet as she dried his hips, then down each of his strong legs, looking up at him with her green eyes sparkling. She stood up and wrapped the towel around his waist again, Billy pulled it tight and secured it, then reached out and held her face and leaned down to kiss her lovingly. She felt his hands unwrapping her towel and he began rubbing and drying her body, pulling her close to him as he dried her lower back and down to her bottom, bending down to kiss her shoulder as he squeezed and rubbed her body. As he descended, he dropped the towel and kissed down the front of her body, licking and sucking her breasts as he squeezed them. Maggie's hands in his hair, holding on lightly as she made soft pleasurable sounds. Billy stood up and picked her up. She wrapped her legs and arms around him, smiling as he carried her to the bed, where he sat her down. Kneeling on the floor in front of her, pulling her to the edge of the mattress. He wrapped his arms around her lower back and as Maggie ran her fingers through his wet, silvery hair, he looked up at her, leaned forward and started sucking her breasts. Licking and sucking hard. Moving back and forth between each one before kissing his way down to her center. She could feel his breath between her legs, hot and strong. Billy lifted her legs over his shoulders, letting them fall down the length of his back. Then she felt his tongue licking between her legs. She heard him growl as his tongue slid down, then pushing inside and back out and up to circle and press against her clit.

"Mmm," she moaned with delight, and he licked with succulent skill. He slid his hands under her body, pulling her a little further over the edge of the bed, squeezing her ass as he flicked his tongue harder, rhythmically pushing and circling, giving her clit a little suck, still massaging her ass. Spending time stimulating her, he could soon feel her getting wetter and wetter, her body writhing. He flicked a little faster and lighter. "Mmm," she moaned again. He kept going, her body rolling into ecstasy. Then, with his tongue flat and relaxed, Billy still holding and squeezing her ass, he pressed his tongue and face against her center, and slowly moved up and down, growling his indulgent hunger, as Maggie's body moved into him with pleasure. Pressing and rocking his tongue against her, breathing heavily, his hot breath adding to the sensation. "Ohh, God, Billy," she cried, almost whimpering with joy.

"Billy...Ohhh...Yes...Yes!" she yelled, her legs shaking, her body shuddering with pleasure. He nuzzled deeply, keeping a constant rhythm, moving his face up and down against her. As he enjoyed her body, his movements became hungrier and more vigorous. Feeling her legs shaking again, Billy kept pressure with his tongue and slowed down his movements. Now backing off, then licking hard, slipping his tongue in and out a few times, then licking hard again. As he teased her, Maggie squirmed for more. "Oh God," she moaned, and he returned to full tongue pressure and slow movements up and down her center, keeping a steady rhythm. Nodding his face up and down, pressing and wiggling, over and over. Her legs were vibrating, her hands stretched out grabbing at the blanket. "Ohh...Billy...YES!" she yelled, and with ecstatic satisfaction, she came. Losing all control of her body, laughing with delight. Her eyes rolling back, her chest heaving as Billy continued to lick, sliding his tongue inside her and out again, then licking all the way up her soft, warm, wet center. Her hands were back in his hair now as he kissed her legs and her hips. His hot lips pressing and moving all around her stomach and back up and over her breasts, over her chest and then kissing and softly sucking her neck. "Mmm," Maggie purred, smiling as he breathed next to her ear again.

"Mmm, I love the way you taste, Maggie," he growled, and her body shivered again as she grabbed his face and kissed him. Pulling him up as close as she could. Their naked bodies pressed tightly as they kissed one another passionately. Billy held her face and smiled at her and kissed her again, both his hands holding her and pulling her oh so tight.

"God, I'd like to ride you all night long, Lover!" she breathed, sucking on his ear lobe.

"Maag," he moaned, grabbing her face, and frenching her deeply. They were both growling now, pulling at each other like hungry animals. Rolling around on the bed, hands caressing and squeezing all over the backs of each other's bodies. Billy rolled on top of her, his hands on either side of Maggie's body, and stretched his arms straight to look down at her. "Is that a challenge?" he asked, his eyes grinning cheekily at her. Maggie held his face in her hands and smiled, reaching her face up and kissing him deeply again. Billy scooped his arms under her and pulled her up off the bed, bending down to kiss her neck and chest. Maggie, smiling as her head fell back, lost in the fantastic tantalizing vibrations surging through her body. Rolling about again, Maggie ending up on top, she slowly and very sensuously kissed and licked her way down his neck, trailing her hands over his body, as she made her way down his chest, kissing across both his nipples, sucking and nibbling, and down the center of his stomach, holding his torso as she pressed her wet, open mouth over and down his pelvis. She softly slid her face down his rising cock, then with the tip of her tongue, licked the whole length, grinning as she felt him move and heard his breathing become heavier. As wet as she could, her tongue out and with a hungry appetite, she held him at the base with one hand, and licked up and down, all around, dripping and licking her tongue over him enthusiastically. "Gaawd, Maag," he breathed, with a low growl. She ran her tongue all the way up from the bottom of his dick, and took the tip of him into her mouth, her tongue still out, still very wet, with slow movements, licking deeply and joyously, while her hand moved up and down, matching the speed of her mouth. "Mmm," he moaned. She slid her mouth all the way down to her hand, still moving slowly, taking him in and out, her tongue working its magic, her hand sliding up and down, then in a gentle, corkscrew movement and back to rising up and down with her mouth.

"Mmm," she purred, totally enjoying his cock, lapping him up hungrily and eagerly. Keeping a steady rhythm, speeding up slightly, she slid her other hand between his legs and gently grasped his balls, moving them between her fingers, and gently massaging them.

"Maag," he whispered, and she felt his body tensing slightly. Letting go with her hands and continuing to move her mouth up and down, Maggie reached up and took her pony tail out, letting her hair cascade down over his body, adding a tickling sensation that made Billy quiver. Then holding him again and sliding her hand, with her mouth, Maggie slid her other hand under his body and grabbed one of his firm cheeks, squeezing and massaging as she continued to devour him enthusiastically. Her fingers sliding between his cheeks, pressing, and squeezing while she moved up and down on him faster and more fervently. "Mmmm," he moaned so deeply, his hands in her curls now, holding on and moving his body into her mouth. "Mag! I'm going to cum!" he said with a very turned-on groan. "Mag!...Ohh my gawd!" the words bursting from his mouth as he exploded into hers. His hips rising and falling with short quick thrusts and Maggie licked hungrily before releasing him from her mouth, still holding him firmly with her hand as his body shook, and then relaxed. She began kissing his stomach, holding his torso again as she moved her body up and against his, kissing his chest, and up his neck, pressing her lips firmly, she kissed up to his ear.

"Mmm," she whispered, licking his ear. "So good." Billy held her tight and rolled her onto her back, kissing her hard.

"Mag," he said looking at her but suddenly at a loss for words. Maggie grinned at him.

"I know. Who has time for sandwiches eh, Lover?" He chuckled, his body shuddering again. Kissing deeply, but slowly now. Their bodies pressed tight. Then Billy rolled beside her, and Maggie draped her leg over his body. They wrapped an arm around one another, and she nestled her face into his chest. He ran his fingers through her hair, playing with her curls as she traced her fingers over his warm body.

"I'll never get enough of you, Beautiful," he said softly, kissing her forehead and squeezing her tight.

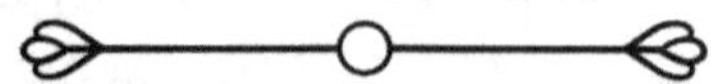

CHAPTER 10

Maggie felt Billy stretching next to her. She laid still, smiling at the new day next to the love of her life. She'd been lying there, on her back, lost in thought. A hand on her heart, the other above her head resting on her pillow, while she happily replayed the previous night's delicious intimacy shared between them. Her pulse racing thinking about how hot and animalistic they'd both been. Snuggling up to her, his hand running across her naked body under the sheet, Billy kissed her shoulder, breathing her in deeply.

"Good morning, beautiful wife," he said, pulling her close.

"Mmm, good morning, handsome husband," she replied, bringing her arm down and over his, holding him tight.

"Sleep well, Babe?" he asked, kissing her arm again.

"Mmm, always do next to you," was her contented response, and she turned to her side so they could hug one another. Looking into each other's eyes and smiling, their faces moving closer until their lips pressed softly together. Holding tight and kissing lovingly before pulling themselves apart and grinning at each other again.

"How'd you sleep, Lover?" Maggie asked, seeing a sudden twinkle in his eye.

"With pleasant dreams, Beautiful." He gave her another kiss. They laid together cuddling for a while before Billy asked,

"Beach walk?" Maggie smiled and nodded.

"For sure." Snuggling for a little longer, before Maggie got up and jumped in the shower. When she got out, Billy had a coffee ready for her, finishing his own, then jumped in the shower himself. Maggie put her bikini on, then a long light dress over top. Then she rolled her oils on and pulled half her hair up into a small clip before going out to the table by the pool to finish her coffee.

"God, you're gorgeous!" came Billy's deep voice from above her, his hand squeezing her shoulder as he walked past and sat next to her. She looked up at him, his eyes bluer than normal standing next to the water, his skin so tanned, his hair blowing softly around his strong jawline. She smiled, then leaned towards him and stretched out her hand to hold his face.

"And you, Billy, are the most beautiful man I've ever laid my eyes on." He grabbed her face and kissed her, long and pressingly. "Mmm," they both made loving noises as they kissed. Billy stood up and held out his hand for Maggie's, which she took, standing up and, still holding on, they left their hotel room and headed for breakfast. After they ate, they gathered up their things and left them at the front desk. They had to check out but would be spending most of their day walking, so the hotel said they would gladly hold their things for them. Then when they came back to get their things, they'd take a taxi back to the Emerald Pearl.

Hand in hand, sandals in their free hands, Maggie and Billy started their trek along the beautiful seven-mile beach. Listening to the waves, and the breeze. Watching the beautiful azure blue and turquoise water stretching forever, their feet softly kicking up the soft white sand as they talked and held each other, kissing and swimming, and loving the natural beauty all around them. They stopped a few times to sit in the sand. Snuggled up together and staring out into the Caribbean. They enjoyed a few pit stops along the way, water breaks and lunch at a little bar and grill. After 3 hours of walking, swimming, and basking in the sunshine, they made their way back, dreamy eyed and feeling peaceful. At one point chasing one another and laughing, Billy scooped Maggie up, her feet stretched up into the air behind her, wrapping her arms around his shoulders and kissing him with a big smile.

Getting back to the hotel around 5:00, they decided to eat dinner before grabbing a cab and heading back to the boat.

"What a lovely day, Billy," Maggie said over dinner, their feet snuggled under the table as they gazed at one another adoringly.

"Gorgeous," Billy said, winking at her. They paid the bill, picked up their luggage at the front desk and waited for their cab. Sliding into the back, Billy wrapped his arm around Maggie, and they snuggled up tight. They were exhausted. Up almost all night ravaging one another, then walking and swimming the whole day, they were very ready to climb into bed and sleep.

Maggie was almost asleep as they pulled into the marina 40 minutes later.

"Thanks, boss," Billy said, paying their driver. They climbed out of the cab, took their luggage out of the trunk and headed towards the dock. The Emerald Pearl looked even more inviting than usual. Maggie could hear her pillow calling for her. After leaving the luggage at the boat, Maggie taking care of it, Billy went to the office to let them know they were back and would be heading out in the morning. She was already in the bathroom and out of her clothes when she heard Billy locking up.

"Back, Babe," he called out and she finished drying her hands and face and putting her toothbrush back in her cup. Then she opened the door and peeked out at him.

"All yours, Lover," she told him, yawning and smiling. He moved close and pulled her in for a hug.

"I'll be in soon, Mag," he said, kissing her forehead and then going into the washroom. Maggie climbed into bed and got herself comfy, pulling the sheet up and closing her eyes. She felt Billy climb into bed next to her, and then as he wrapped his arm around her, pressing his body up against the back of hers, she snuggled closer and found herself drifting off quickly.

* * * *

Maggie felt a kiss on her cheek. Then Billy's breath near her ear, his fingers moving her hair off her face as he whispered,

"Good morning, Beautiful." She smiled, even before she opened her eyes.

"Mmm. Good morning, lover of mine." She turned her face and looked up into his deep blue eyes.

"We're heading out soon, but you can stay in bed if you like, Mag. There's a coffee here for you." And he leaned down and gave her a warm kiss. Maggie reached up a hand and softly brushed his cheek, looking into his eyes and smiling at him lovingly.

"Thank you," she said, giving him a kiss. He grinned at her then headed out of the bedroom. She laid there for a while, feeling so thankful for him, for their deep love and for the universe bringing them back together. Then stretching and sitting up, Maggie picked her coffee up, and with a smile of appreciation on her face, she took a sip. She enjoyed the first half sitting comfortably, before getting up and starting the day with some long overdue yoga stretches, then hopping in the shower for a quick wash. They were already quite a distance from the port in Lucea when she joined Billy at the helm. She wrapped her arms around him and kissed his cheek.

"Need anything, my Love?" she asked him.

"You." he answered with a cheeky grin.

"Mmm, later Sweet Cheeks." Billy chuckled.

"Want another coffee?" she asked.

"Sure Babe, thanks." And off she went, grabbing each of them a fresh cup.

"Here you go, Lover," she said, handing him his cup.

"Thanks, Babe," he took it with a smile. "So, next stop Montego Bay." Maggie sat in her chair.

"Oooh, I've always wanted to go there, Billy!" She told him excitedly.

"It's a busy place, Mag! It's where most people want to go for vacations. It *is* beautiful." Billy took a sip of coffee. "I'm looking forward to Falmouth, Babe," he added.

"Oh ya, me too," she agreed, thinking about the luminescent water they had read about. Looking out at the forever blue water surrounding them and peacefully enjoying the sound of the sails billowing in the breeze; *Heaven on earth* she thought to herself as she soaked up the beautiful views all around them. Then, looking over at Billy captaining his boat, so handsome, gentle, and confident. Feeling like she didn't really mind where she went, as long as Billy was by her side. "I love you, my Billy," she said, and he looked at her with eyes twinkling.

"And I love *you*, my Mag," he responded with a grin.

After their coffee, Maggie took their empty cups below deck with her, planning to make them some brunch. They were only about an hour from Montego Bay and had decided to drop anchor and eat before finishing their voyage. With a fresh pot of coffee brewing, Maggie finished cutting up some veggies and grating some cheese to throw into the frittata she planned to make. The bacon just starting to sizzle in the frying pan.

"Mmm, smells good, Babe," came Billy's husky voice as he walked down the stairs towards her. He gave her butt a slap. Maggie grinned to herself, then turned her head to smile at him. He kissed her cheek, moving up closely behind her and placed one hand on her hip. Then he reached out with the other hand and turned the burner off. Maggie looked up at him.

"Aren't you hungry?" she asked, puzzled. He was silent for a moment. Then snuggling up behind her, with both his hands sliding over her hips, he bent his face down and softly spoke next to her ear.

"Mmm, yes, very," he answered, making a deep hungry groaning sound in her ear. His hands sliding up the front of Maggie's body and massaging her breasts. He moved her hair off her shoulder and started kissing her neck. Deep, open mouthed, warm moist kisses, holding and squeezing her breasts again. Running his nose along her neck, he lifted her hair and started gently kissing from her shoulder blades up her neck, taking his time and trailing his lips along, breathing deeply and nuzzling his face against her skin. "I love your scent, Maggie," he breathed. She could feel his warm breath on her skin as he kissed and gently sucked his way over to the other side of her neck, his fingers trailing across her shoulders, moving her hair, and making his way back to her favourite side with his lips. Maggie's skin tingled with pleasure, and she rested her head back on Billy's body as he began to suck and kiss harder, one hand moving down to her center, stroking lightly, then pressing his fingers against her, the other massaging her breasts.

"Billy!" she gasped. Her pulse raced, as Billy's hands pulled her long skirt up with a sudden urgency, and he continued to suck her neck. Then he slid one hand down the front inside of her underwear, moving his fingers in, opening her up and slowly rubbing and pressing. Sliding back and forth just inside her marvelously inviting folds. As she became wetter, and her breathing more rapid, he slipped his middle finger inside, cupping and gently massaging. "Ohh," she moaned, her chest rising, her body pressing back, against Billy's. With him sliding his finger inside, gently moving it back and forth, bending it and playing slowly, while squeezing her breasts and kissing her neck, Maggie could hardly stand up. Closing her eyes, her mouth opened, as she reached up her free arm and slid her fingers up his neck, running them through his hair.

"You're so wet," he breathed the words deeply, making Maggie even more turned on. His hot breath on her neck as he slid his tongue over her skin made her shudder. He was making her crazy. And *that* was making Billy crazy. "Talk to me," he told her, his voice husky and commanding. His finger curled and pulsing inside her.

"Ohhh," Maggie whimpered.

"Mag..." he breathed deeply. She was squirming with pleasure. Billy found a tempo that taunted her most and beckoned her into blissful submission. She was moving her body against his hand, Billy's palm pushing against her so she could grind while he fingered her.

"Take me, Billy," she groaned. Still fingering her, with his other hand, he tugged her underwear down a little further, then he undid his shorts and freed himself, pressing against her ass and sliding between her legs.

"Mmmm," they both moaned as he slid back and forth across her warm center using her incredibly turned-on body to make himself wet. Maggie grabbed the counter and leaned forward slightly. Billy slipped his finger out and grabbed her ass, spreading her cheeks. He used his foot to move her legs apart and leaned over her body. Sliding his hands under her top he started pinching her nipples, hard, then massaging her breasts slowly, continuing to slide his hard, eager cock back and forth. Slow, wet, and deliciously arousing. Billy moved his face near her ear again.

"I wanna play rough, Mag!" he told her. Maggie became more aroused and held tight. Back to kissing and sucking her neck with aggressive hunger. "Mmm," he growled as he moved over her warm skin. Maggie was so turned on.

"Hurt me nice, Billy," she whispered back, holding tight.

"Oh God, Mag," he growled at her words, grabbing her hips tight and pushing himself inside her with brute force.

"Aaah!" she cried, her upper body lunging forward, as Billy slid in and out, pressing himself inside of her, moving his body into hers with force. The teasing and anticipation turning to barbaric arousal and unbridled, insatiable power. He pushed deeply and moved their bodies together in half circles. Slowly, still deep inside, he sucked her neck. His hands back up under her shirt, he grabbed and pulled her bra up, letting her breasts fall. He grasped them, almost savagely squeezing them, pinching and pulling and twisting her nipples. "Owe!" Maggie yelled, pressing her hips up and back as he began to move faster and harder. Billy's strong, hard body, nailing her over and over. Her head dropping, holding the sink tightly, his urgent hunger almost aggressive as he glided with such determination. The rawness, almost overwhelming; filling Maggie with rapturous pleasure.

"Maag!" he growled, sliding faster and faster, harder, and harder. "I wanna make you moan," he breathed, grunting and groaning like a hungry wolf. Her body almost lifting off the floor with each thrust he made.

"Ohhhh, God!" she ached. The words guttural and escaping her lips with sharp breaths in and out.

"Mag, I need to hear you," he begged her.

"Ohhh..." her voice, a whimpering moan. Billy's hot breath and growls next to her face sending tantalizing chills throughout her whole body. "Billy... you're...so...strong," she told him. Billy began making long, slow, glides.

"Keep talking, Mag," he urged her with another low growl.

"Mmm, God you make me so hot," she purred, both of them becoming so frantically turned on. Billy leaned down and bit her shoulder, snarling and growling as he bit all over her shoulders and her neck.

"Harder!" Maggie coaxed. "Owe. Ohh. Billy. Suck my neck," she begged. "Suck hard!" she added, and Billy growled agonizingly, as he lapped her up, sucking and licking and biting like an animal devouring his prey. His strong body hitting hard against hers with intensity and determination. The sheer animal aggression and raw power in his body was making her toes curl. Awakening a raging, primal desire within her.

"Pull my hair," she whispered. She heard him growl again as he ran his hand up her body, and up the back of her head, sliding his fingers into her hair. Then he grasped a handful of curls, and squeezing gently, he held on firmly. She started to make small circles against him as his glides became faster. "You're so powerful," Maggie's voice was velvety and slow as she spoke.

"Mmm," Billy moaned low and deep. "Gawd, you're so effing hot," he breathed, his arousal heightening. Holding her hair firmly, his upper body leaning back slightly, his aim shifting up towards her abdomen, as he made long, powerful glides, in and out.

"Oh Gawwd!" Maggie cried with an anguished sort of moan. "Oh Billy," she cried with a whimper. In and out, in and out. "Don't stop!" Sliding hard. "Mmm..." Billy, steadily hitting her body with his. She could feel his balls slapping against her center with each thrust and found it quite deliciously stimulating. "Yes Billy, ohh... yes!" she yelled out, standing up on her toes to lift her hips so he could enter deeper still. Billy suddenly grabbed her hips again, squeezing and holding tight, his excitement peaking.

"Mag...Maag...Aaaa... I'm going to cum." Hitting harder. "Aaah... I'm cumming!" he announced, his head lifted as he started making shorter, deeper, more rapid movements. "Damn!" he growled, his body convulsing and gyrating, Maggie's shaking as he continued to press her into the counter over and over. He leaned over her body again, sucking her neck, a hand squeezing her breasts, the other pressing and rubbing her clit as she pushed and rocked her hips, pressing and grinding while he was still inside her.

"Ohhhh," she moaned. "Harder," she breathed hungrily. Billy pulled and twisted her nipples as he kissed and sucked her neck.

"You make me so hot," Billy spoke low, breathing heavily into her ear, sucking her neck again. "Mmm," he moaned, kissing and sucking and licking. "Cummm... Maggie." He sucked harder now, his hands back to grabbing her breasts, grinding his body into hers and feeling her grinding sensually into him. "You're sexy as hell, Mag," he growled next to her ear, squeezing her breasts, sucking her neck deeply. Standing firm while she moved her body, grinding hard, her movements becoming quicker, rocking and sliding into him up and down, until,

"Oh God...Oh my God!" Every part of Maggie shook. Orgasm taking over her whole body. Completely consumed with fierce delight, Maggie's body tensing, her muscles contracting and squeezing him tightly inside, her body almost spasming then bursting with ecstasy, before relaxing and falling forward. Billy's arms wrapped around the front of her, catching her and draping himself over her.

"Oh my God, Mag!" he said, squeezing her tight. Breathing heavily. Maggie's body was still shaking uncontrollably. He was still growling, and she could feel his body shuddering.

"Billy," Maggie whispered, breathing heavily, almost making no sound at all. He held her tight, their bodies heaving together, the heat radiating between them. Then, feeling her relax, he slowly pulled himself from her body and turned her around. Holding her face in his hands, Billy kissed her mouth deeply. Maggie wrapped her arms around him and held him tight, kissing him back. Blissfully and greedily sucking face and pulling one another close. "Mmm," Maggie moaned as they pressed their lips together intensely. Billy held her face and looked down at her. His eyes, so blue, so dark. Smoldering.

"That was fan-fucking-tastic!" he told her, snarling and growling at her, with a cheeky grin. Grabbing her quickly and pulling her close, he kissed her hard. They pulled one another tight again and rubbed each other's backs. Making quiet little satisfied sounds as they embraced. Then they looked into each other's eyes, staring deeply for a moment, and kissed softly. They started to move away from the counter together,

Maggie's legs still shaky.

"I didn't hurt you, did I, Mag?" Billy asked, pulling her close again and looking at her seriously. Maggie slid her arms around Billy and hugged him tight. Then she looked up into his eyes, with impassioned affection behind her lusty emerald greens.

"Mmm. Hurt so good, Lover," she answered grinning at him. Billy pulled her close, his eyes grinning as he leaned down and kissed her lips ever so gently. Cradling her face in his strong hands, their lips breaking, he rubbed his nose with hers. Their eyes opened and they grinned again. Hand in hand, they turned, and Maggie giggled, thinking she probably looked like she'd just had her first horse ride.

"Sea legs," she said, and Billy chuckled. Maggie pulled her underwear back up and Billy did his shorts up again, then they made their way to the bedroom. Flopping down to lay next to one another on the bed. Their pulses still racing and their chests still rising and falling rapidly. Finding each other's hands between them, they held on, fingers linked, as they rested with happy sighs.

"Let's stay anchored for the night, Lover," Maggie said softly, breaking the silence. Billy lifted her hand and kissed it.

"As you wish, my Love," he answered, holding her hand to his chest.

"I just want to lay in bed with you all day," she added, snuggling up beside him.

"Mmm, I like that plan, Mag." And they turned their heads to face one another, grinning affectionately. "And what do you want to do with me?" he asked her, his eyes flashing with mischief. Maggie smiled at him.

"Well, if I ever walk again, perhaps... some cribbage." Billy chuckled and grabbed her, pulling her on top, then rolling them over so he was looking down at her. Still grinning, he leaned down and kissed her mouth, softly, warmly, pressing gently, then looking into her eyes again, he said,

"Damn, I love how green your eyes are when we've made love, Mag." Kissing her softly again. Maggie's hands holding his face, she looked at him with adoration as they kissed one another lovingly.

"You are a fantastic lover," she said with satisfaction, looking back into his eyes and licking the tip of his nose playfully. Billy's eyes twinkled.

"Shit, Mag! You drive me wild!" And he pressed his lips to hers passionately. His hands and arms sliding under her body and embracing her tightly. Their tongues sliding around each other as they kissed deeply. Both moaning again with pleasure, Maggie's hands sliding all over his back, grabbing his ass, then sliding up into his hair. Breaking apart and smiling at one another.

"Let's lie naked, holding on and kissing all day," Maggie suggested and Billy nodded. "Oh and eat brunch," she added with a new hunger.

"God, I love you!" Billy said, chuckling affectionately and hugging her tight.

* * * *

Back in the kitchen, in their matching robes, music playing, dancing, snuggling, kissing, and singing, Billy and Maggie got brunch going again. "Sugar Sugar," "I Can't Help Myself," and "Rock Me Gently," playing, Billy pulled Maggie close and danced her around, the two of them laughing together as he spun her and dipped her, coming back up to kiss and pull one another into a tight embrace. Maggie took the coffees up to the top deck, along with their cutlery, Billy followed with the plates, and they sat and enjoyed their meal in the sun, floating out in the Caribbean Sea.

"Best restaurant in town!" Billy proclaimed, smiling broadly at Maggie, leaning over to hold her face and kiss her softly.

"Always tastes better when we cook together, Lover," she said, grinning at him.

After they ate and washed up the dishes together, they went back up to sit in the afternoon sunshine. Maggie went back downstairs after a bit, returning a few minutes later with cold drinks, a deck of cards and the cribbage board. Billy looked at her and grinned as she sat down on the bench seat and started shuffling the cards.

"So, you really meant *crib*, eh Babe?" She grinned back at him.

"But of course," she answered. "I think I might need to take a break from anything frivolous for a bit." Billy winked at her. They played a few rounds, then snuggled up close, Billy's arms wrapped over and around Maggie, and they enjoyed the sound of the waves, and the boat gently moving in the beautiful water. Getting up and returning a few times with fresh drinks and snacks, they held each other tight watching the bright orange sun sinking down into the darkening blue sea. Softly trailing their hands over one another's arms, cuddling, and chatting, kissing softly as night fell. Billy sat up and smiled at Maggie. He held out his hand as he stood up and Maggie took it, standing up in front of him.

"Come on, Mag," he coaxed, holding her hand, and leading them back inside. He walked over to the CD player, changed the CD, then skipped ahead a few tracks. He turned and smiled at Maggie as he walked back towards her. "Heart Of Gold" started playing and Billy wrapped one hand around Maggie's waist, taking her hand in his and pulling her close. Maggie wrapped her other arm around his shoulder as he started moving them across the floor. Resting her head against his chest, Billy rested his on her head and pulled her tighter still. Then he started singing along, their bodies swaying together, back and forth, around and around. Moving as one, like a rolling wave. Maggie smiled, feeling his deep husky voice deep in her soul as he sang to her. Hugging him tight, letting him move her body with ease. Then she started to sing with him.

The song ending, "Harvest Moon" started, as they continued to dance and sing together. Billy's hand kept time on her lower back, then pulling her snug and swaying her side to side, still dancing as "Old Man" began to play. Billy's voice deeply resonating between them, filling Maggie up. Their love for music, and for each other, forever strengthening their bond. From their first mesmerizing glance right into one another's souls, the first bewitching words sung from the depths of their hearts out over their lips, and their explosively passionate first touch of skin on skin, they were hooked, instantly and forever connected. Time and space pulled them apart but brought them back again. It never ceased to amaze them how much more love and passion they continued to feel for each other. Dancing together for hours, then getting ready for bed and snuggling up together and falling asleep in one another's arms.

CHAPTER 11

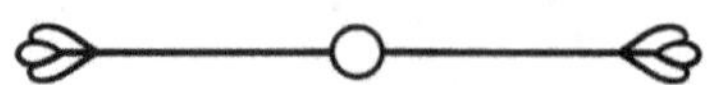

Maggie was up and showered before Billy woke up. She had the radio playing as she put the coffee on, singing along to some old 90s favourites. She walked back into the bedroom and pulled back the little curtains on the round windows, letting beams of sunshine extend into the room. Sitting down on her side of the bed and looking down at the beautiful man lying there. She smiled as her eyes traced over his dark hair, the sun catching the silvery-white threads woven throughout his wavy locks. Loving the wrinkles around his eyes and his mouth. His beautifully dark smooth skin, and thick muscular body. His broad chest rising and falling slowly as she reached out and softly placed her open palm over his heart, feeling it beating, she closed her eyes. Moving closer to his body, she inhaled his warm, spicy scent, trailing her hands over his chest and watching him lay there peacefully. Maggie leaned forward, her lips close to his, her hands sliding up his chest, up his neck, up into his hair as she softly pressed her lips to his. She kissed him gently. Then Billy's hands slid over her and he hugged her, pulling her in as he kissed her back.

"Mmm," he moaned, his hands in her hair, holding her face and smiling at her.

"Morning, Lover," Maggie said, smiling back at him.

"Morning, Beautiful," he answered, pulling her face close again and kissing her tenderly.

"Gorgeous man," she said, grinning at him. She could just hear "Interstate Love Song" starting to play as she moved down his body and pulled the sheet right off him. Her eyes were dark and provocative.

Billy's twinkling back at her, feeling her need, and growing instantly hungry for her. Then, before another thought, Maggie was kissing her way down his body, looking back up at him, her eyes becoming more seductive as she ran her tongue down. Licking and kissing down to his navel and from one hip to the other. Sliding her fingers down the sides of his body, Maggie lifted her face and looked at Billy again, her hair falling down over his stomach, she kept eye contact as she moved her curls across his abdomen, over his morning excitement, over the tops of his legs, then grinning almost deviously, she grasped him with one hand, holding him firm, still watching him as she leaned down, opened her mouth, and licked all around the tip. Very hungrily, very wet, her tongue wide and hot. Her gaze lifted intensely.

"Gawd!" he moaned, his hands holding the sheets as he watched her. Sliding her hand up and down as she continued to lick eagerly. Then Maggie straddled the bottom of his legs and slid her mouth down, slowly, salivating and licking, her head moving up and down, twisting her face slightly left and right as she kept a steady rhythm. Her hands sliding over his stomach and chest, pinching his nipples, gently dragging her nails over his skin as she licked and slid with an almost ferocious animal hunger. Billy's body writhing with pleasure. He was growling and groaning, and as she held him firmly again, her hand sliding up and down with her mouth, she looked at him. Realizing she was watching, he looked down at her. His face showing signs of blissful arousal.

"Sexy," he whispered to her, grabbing the sheets again as she moved up and down faster, her fingers fondling his balls, her other hand holding and sliding in the opposite direction from her mouth. "Oh my gawd," he groaned. Maggie kept her hand moving, speeding up a little and licking around, across, then back over and down, taking him back into her mouth. "Maggie!" he groaned, feeling his body twitching, and shaking, she continued her wet, licking tempo, making hungry enjoyable sounds as she ate him up. His hips now rocking slightly, she knew he was close and kept her indulgent feast going with succulent enjoyment. A few more quick slides and… "Maag! Ohhh my God!" Tasting him as his body started to shudder, beginning its release. She licked and gripped him just the way he liked. Recognizing his body language, she licked straight up to the tip, looking back up at him, grinning sinfully, holding him with both hands, as his body finished exploding, waiting for him to relax. "Crash Into Me," playing from the main cabin, finished with Billy's release. She held his hips and kissed his whole body. Pressing her lips firmly against his warm skin, feeling his pulse stronger and quicker, his breathing fast, kissing her way up. As she drew closer, he grabbed her and pulled her face towards his, kissing her hard, holding her face. "Damn you're good at that, Mag!" he told her, still shuddering. Maggie laid down next to him, pulling the sheet back up over his body. Billy held her tight and ran his hands over her back, into her hair, still growling with satisfaction. Maggie looked up and saw he still had a smile on his face, lying happily with his eyes closed. She snuggled up tight, breathing him in. Laying contentedly in each other's arms. "What's for breakfast, Babe?" Billy asked after a few minutes of quiet.

"I've just had mine," she answered quickly. Billy laughed suddenly with surprised amusement. She looked back up at him grinning, and he pulled her towards him, holding her face and kissing her deeply. "Not sure Lover, but the coffee's ready." He grinned at her.

"Perfect," he answered. They both sat up, Billy grabbed his robe and pulled it on. Giving Maggie another deep kiss, then heading for the washroom. Maggie went back out to get herself a coffee. "Stereo" by The Watchmen came on, and she put her cup down, turned up the volume and started singing. Then as the song became heavier, she started rocking and dancing around the room. Billy came out of the washroom, grinning broadly at her, and stood watching for a few seconds, grinning with amusement. Soon, unable to fight the urge, he started rocking with her. Both headbanging and bouncing about. As the song ended, they laughed, falling into one another. Hand in hand, "Knockin' On Heaven's Door" playing, they grabbed their coffees and sat together on the couch. Neither one could contain themselves and were both singing along. After their first cup of coffee, they got up and, without saying anything, still singing and dancing to their nostalgic 90s music, they started making breakfast together. Maggie cut up all the fruit, as it was extremely ripe and needed to be used. She made a fruit salad while Billy made French toast. Laughing again as they both tried to remember all the lyrics and sing along to "One week," setting the table, refilling their coffee cups, and sitting down to enjoy breakfast. As usual, playing footsies and grinning at each other flirtatiously as they ate. Finishing up the dishes to "Runaway Train." Billy jumped into the shower and then got dressed while Maggie went up and sat out in the sunshine. They hoisted the sails when he joined her on deck, pulled up the anchor and headed towards Montego. There was a strong wind, and Billy figured they'd make it to port in 45 minutes or so.

"Never bored of this," she told him, looking around and back at Billy. He smiled at her.

"It's pretty fantastic isn't it, Babe?" he said, and Maggie smiled back at him nodding.

It took longer than any other port they'd been to so far. Billy hadn't exaggerated when he said Montego was the place everyone wanted to go. Slowly following a number of other boats into the docking area, it took longer to dock than it had to get to Montego that morning. Billy went and registered, paid for three nights and came back to relax on deck with Maggie.

"Well, that was hectic," he said sitting next to her. He wrapped his arm around her, and she rested her head on his chest.

"So, where to, today, Lover?" Maggie asked, looking up at him.

"Wherever you like," he answered, kissing her head and resting against her. "Thinking, if you still wanted to, we'd snorkel tomorrow?" he suggested. She sat up so she could look at him.

"Sounds like a good idea. So, maybe just some wandering and a nice dinner?" Maggie suggested. Billy's eyes grinning as he looked at her.

"As you wish," he replied, and leaned in to kiss her gently.

"Ok, I'm just going to put my bathing suit on and grab a few things before we head out," Maggie said before getting up and going below deck. Billy followed and when Maggie stepped off the last step, he ran at her. She giggled with surprise and ran towards the bedroom. Just before she made it there, he wrapped his arms around her, pulled her tight and scooped her up. Squealing with laughter, the two of them flopped down on the bed, rolling about, kissing and laughing. Huffing and puffing, still grinning at one another, Billy moved close enough to brush her cheek with his hand and kiss her lips. Pressing deeply, Maggie hugged him tight.

"I love you, Billy," she told him as they pulled apart. He smiled at her as he said,

"I love you, Mag." Getting back up, Maggie walked over to her dresser and pulled out her bikini. "Oh good, I was hoping you'd pick your bikini, Babe." She turned around and saw him watching with a big grin. Shaking her head with a smile, she grabbed her long light blue, pink, and green dress to wear over top. Billy sat down on the bed, continuing to smile at her. She looked at him, tilting her head questioningly. "Don't let me stop you, Beautiful," he coaxed her. She laughed and turned around, pulling her shirt up over her head, her shorts down, then reaching back she undid her bra. Looking over her shoulder, Billy watched with affectionate enjoyment. He winked at her, and she turned back to pull her underwear down. She slipped into her bikini bottoms, then she pulled her bikini top on and did it up at the back, reached for her dress and pulled it over her head, the thin cotton fabric falling softly down her curvaceous body. Holding the straps she turned around and walked towards Billy, who was still sitting and smiling lovingly. Standing against his legs with her back to him, she looked back slightly.

"Will you help me?" she asked, holding her straps behind her neck. Billy slid his hands up her shoulder blades and took the straps in his fingers and Maggie lifted her hair off her neck. He tied it in a bow, then holding her waist, he leaned forward and kissed between her shoulder blades. Slowly, kissing then pausing, kissing again, pausing. Maggie gave a little shiver. Turning her around, he wrapped his arms around her and pulled her close. Maggie held his face as he looked up into her green eyes. "Thank you," she said softly, and she grinned as she bent down and kissed him tenderly. Her hands moving his hair back gently, cradling his face as she kissed him so lovingly. Then, smiling, still holding his face, she looked into his deep blue eyes, rubbed her nose to his and asked. "You ready, my Lover?" Billy's eyes twinkled cheekily. "Come on, Handsome," she encouraged him, reaching for his hand and pulling him up off the bed. Billy grabbed a backpack and packed a couple towels and water bottles, the boat keys, and his wallet. "All set?" she asked, as he pulled it over his shoulder. Billy nodded and let Maggie lead the way.

They disembarked from the Emerald Pearl and walked along the dock towards a brightly coloured entry gate, reminding Maggie of her younger days when she and her besties would spend a day at Canada's wonderland over their summer holidays. Leading them to a terminal and an area for shopping and dining. There were people everywhere, and Billy and Maggie held hands as they navigated through the crowd. Taxi's waiting, buses parked in a large lot and huge cruise ships on the other side of the port. Green mountains and water surrounded them. Large buildings a little further in the distance. They carried on through the shopping strip, finding souvenir shops, boutiques, clothing shops, spas and an abundance of coffee shops, and restaurants. They soon found their way to the beach, discovering it was even busier than the shopping strip. Red, yellow and blue beach umbrellas as far as the eye could see. They walked together, past all the vacationing people, taking it all in, smiling at each other, the occasional hello and some random conversations with the strangers they encountered. As the afternoon became hotter, they stopped and took a swim, then lounged on the beach for a while before walking back in the direction they came from.

"Feel like going for an early dinner, Babe?" Billy asked as they headed back.

"For sure," Maggie answered, taking in who she was with and where they were together as she looked out at the water. Mesmerized by the unbelievable aquamarine colour. Watching the many boats and ships coming and going and feeling the happy energy from the many people in the water and on the beach, looking more and more like sardines by the hour. Billy stopped them and pulled her close. Holding her head softly, he looked at her and leaned down to give her a big kiss.

"Did I tell you yet today, how beautiful you look?" he asked her with a grin. She smiled at him as he kissed her again.

"Come on, gorgeous Lover. I'm hungry," she told him, giving his butt a squeeze. He chuckled and took her hand in his again as they continued down the beach. They were almost back to the Emerald when they found a restaurant on a stationary houseboat. It was painted green and yellow and had an uncovered upper deck with tables as well as the main inside area. A little boat ferried them across a short distance to the restaurant, where they were greeted happily by a woman dressed in bright red flowered clothes. She asked if they wanted upper or lower, and they chose upper under a small canopied table out of the direct sunlight.

"What yuh would like to drink?" she asked as they sat down. Billy looked at Maggie.

"Drink drink, Mag, or bubbly?" She smiled at him.

"Hmm, drink drink. Something coconuty," she added. Billy looked back at the woman.

"A red stripe and a Caribbean delight, please." The woman nodded and left them with their menus. Billy and Maggie smiled at one another, stretching their hands towards each other across the table and holding tight.

"How're you doing, Beautiful?" he asked her.

"Perfect, Lover," she answered with a big Maggie smile. Billy looked down at the menu on the table in front of him.

"Mmm, this all sounds really good, Mag," he said, and Maggie looked down at her menu.

"Mmm, it does." Their waitress was back with their drinks.

"Ready to order?" she asked.

"Feel like lobster, Babe?" Billy asked.

"Actually, yes," she nodded. They both ordered the grilled lobster with Caesar salads and garlic baguette. The woman asked them to follow her to choose their lobsters and they picked out the two liveliest of the bunch and returned to their table. As they waited for their dinner, enjoying their drinks, the tables slowly filled up around them. Their feet stretched out and sliding together as usual. Their dinner was delicious and very filling. Maggie had another drink after they were done, which surprised both her and Billy.

"Dessert?" the woman asked, but they politely declined. After they paid, they made their way back down to the beach for a short walk, watching as the sun started to make its way into the sea with bright vivid colours filling the sky. After walking off some of their meal, watching the last of the sun setting, they walked back to the boat. They passed many bars. All of which were becoming lively, with music blasting, people dancing everywhere, and as tempted as they were to join in, they were tired and decided to go dancing the following night.

Maggie brushed her teeth and washed up, then joined Billy in bed. He was reading a mystery book and looked up and smiled at her as she pulled the sheet over herself.

"Mind if I read for a bit, Babe?" he asked her.

"Not at all, Lover," she answered with a smile. "What'cha reading?" she asked. Billy showed her the cover. It read, The Knight Club, in dark red letters.

"Still into that detective series I like. Think there's only a couple more books in the series though." He answered. Maggie fluffed up her pillow and got comfy, laying on her side and looking up at him happily. He leaned over and kissed her forehead.

"Love you, Beautiful," he said, and she closed her eyes.

"Love you, Handsome," she replied.

* * * *

Maggie and Billy laid snuggled together as the sun poured into the bedroom. Sleepily trailing their hands over one another, cozy and happily lazing in bed.

"Morning, Mrs. Stanton," Billy said, hugging her tight.

"Morning, Mr. Ashberry," she responded, snuggling her face against his chest.

"I'll go put the coffee on, Babe," Billy offered, rolling out of bed, not worrying about grabbing his robe.

"Mmm, I'll watch!" Maggie answered, and Billy turned back to see her smiling. Her head slightly lifted off her pillow, curls everywhere, and her eyes scanning him from head to toe. He left the room with a grin on his face and Maggie laid her head back down, closing her eyes and smiling to herself. A few minutes later she heard the shower turn on and lost herself in thoughts of Billy's thick strong body. His hands running over his wet soapy skin. *Mmm.* She thought pleasantly, having a few delicious memories to replay while she waited for his return. Deciding to get herself up, Maggie stretched and found her yoga mat. She took it to the main cabin and rolled it out. Standing with her feet together, she did a handful of sun salutations, flopping into ragdoll pose, then rolling herself back up. She managed a one-minute plank, then did a few rounds of downward dog to child's pose then sitting and twisting out any tension lingering in her muscles before Billy joined her.

"All yours, Beautiful," he said, smiling at her. She smiled back, a twinkle in her eye as he stood there in nothing but his towel wrapped around his waist. She moved off the mat and rolled it back up. Billy was at the counter getting his coffee and Maggie walked up behind him and kissed his back, moving from one side to the other.

"Mmm," he growled. As she walked off, Maggie grabbed his towel and took it with her. Standing at the bathroom door holding it up with a cheeky grin. Billy's head fell to the side, then he turned around and faced her with an even cheekier grin, shaking his head with a chuckle.

"Come and get it big fella!" she invited, laughing, and as Billy ran at her, Maggie shrieked excitedly, both laughing as he stopped in front of her, picked her straight up and kissed her, put her down, then walked away without his towel. When he got back to the counter he turned his head and winked at Maggie.

"Sweet cheeks!" she said, turned, walked through the door and took her turn in the washroom. Maggie decided to have a quick shower. When she finished, she joined Billy with a coffee of her own at the table. Grinning at one another flirtatiously, fingers linked and playing, they finished their coffees.

"Let's go for a late breakfast somewhere, Babe," Billy suggested.

"Sure. Snorkeling tomorrow then, Lover?" she asked.

"I was thinking that, yes. Late breakfast, maybe a walk and a swim, then dancing the night away." She smiled at him.

"Sounds great, Billy." Maggie leaned close, Billy meeting her halfway, and their lips pressed together for a sweet kiss. They made their way to the bedroom, where they both put on their bathing suits.

"We should do another load of laundry within the next couple days I think," Maggie mentioned as she reached for her coral dress. Billy walked over to her and put his hand on her shoulder.

"Hey, Babe, speaking of clothes, where's that white and blue dress of yours? You know, the short one," he asked her rather keenly. She looked up and saw him grinning cheekily.

"Umm, it's here too, why?" Maggie grabbed it and looked back at him. His eyes were still cheeky as he smiled at her.

"Just like that one on you, Babe," he answered, acting nonchalantly.

"Oh, ok Lover," was her response and she pulled it on over her bathing suit. She watched as he put on a T-shirt, turned to face her and buttoned it up. Maggie walked towards him grinning.

"You are one fine looking beast, Billy Stanton," she said with a purr. Billy chuckled and hugged her closely.

"Why thank you, you beautiful creature," he responded, then they kissed long and gently, hugging one another lovingly, then giving each other a squeeze.

Walking hand in hand, they made their way towards the main strip to find somewhere to eat. There were many places to choose from, so they picked one that wasn't too busy yet and made their way over to a table facing the sea. A waitress soon came over and asked if they'd like coffee, leaving menus on the table. They ate light, then left and spent the day wandering in and out of shops, swimming and laying on the beach in the sun, walking and swimming again before heading back to the boat. It was going on 5:30 when they jumped back onto the Emerald Pearl. Billy pulled Maggie in tightly and slid his hands down to grab her ass, giving both cheeks a firm squeeze.

"Looking forward to dancing the night away with you, beautiful wife of mine." She slid her hands down to grab his sweet cheeks and gave them a good squeeze.

"Mmm, me too, gorgeous husband." They put their things away, and Maggie took her bathing suit off and slipped into a white lace bra and undies set. Her skin looked beautifully tanned with the white lace against it. Then she pulled her white and blue dress back on. She lifted her hair off her shoulders, twisted it a couple times, then held it in place with one of her clips. Curls escaping and bouncing around her face. She reached for her locket, smiling as she held it, feeling its history of stories in her hand, then she did it up around her neck. Billy was suddenly right behind her, moving his hands softly up and down her arms and kissing the back of her neck.

"Mmm. You always smell so good," he breathed, sending shivers up and down her back. She turned and smiled at him. He had put his dusty blue button up shirt on, and his eyes were deeper and bluer than ever.

"Hello there, Handsome!" Maggie said with a big grin. Kissing for a few minutes, then they took one another's hand and left the boat.

It wasn't hard to find a place to dance. Montego seemed like the place to be if you enjoyed the nightlife. They picked a place at random and walked up to the bar. There were some seats along the counter, and they sat down next to one another. Looking around, Maggie noticed throughout the club, standing tables stationed here and there in the open patio style room surrounding a large dance floor. Billy grabbed himself a coconut water and Maggie a sparkling water with lime, and they went over to a standing table near one of the corners at the back.

"You look beautiful, my Love," Billy told her as she took her glass.

"Thanks, Gorgeous." And he winked at her with a grin. The lights dimmed and coloured lanterns lit up around the room. Lively Reggae music was playing at the hands of the DJ in another corner and smiling couples and groups of friends were filing in quickly. Soon the music and chatter were so loud Maggie and Billy could hardly hear one another.

"Just going to use the washroom," she said to Billy.

"Ok Babe, I'm going to grab another drink, want something harder?" he asked, and they both grinned saucily at each other.

"Sure Babe, surprise me," she said walking off. When she came back to him, he slid her drink over. He'd gotten her rum and vanilla schnapps and asked for a double. Billy had plans to repay her restaurant hand job favour and thought it might be easier with a stiff drink. Listening to the steady beat of the music, it didn't take long for Maggie to want to dance, and as she worked her way through her drink, her eagerness to pull Billy out onto the dance floor grew.

"Come on, Lover," she coaxed, grinning broadly at him. He happily took her hand, and they joined in with the dancing crowd. Reggae and dance music cranked up, deep bass, fast beats, and bodies pumping and jumping together. Maggie and Billy didn't stop smiling as they danced. "Boombastic" with its heavy bass, moving Maggie and Billy together like a heartbeat. The two lovers filling up with the energy all around them, joining in with the other dancers and following their moves. Dancing together, bodies close, then out apart, watching each other move on the dance floor. Billy danced up to Maggie and wrapped his hand around her waist and pulled her in close. Leaning his face to her ear, he asked,

"Having a good time, Babe?" She grinned up at him and nodded, dancing away, hands in the air, fingers stretching, hips moving wildly, smiling at him as he danced in front of her. Both lost in the beat, enjoying their night. After a few more songs, Billy pulled her tight again and asked if she wanted another drink. They danced their way to the bar and Maggie asked for a club soda. Billy got another coconut water. He leaned in close to Maggie, and cozied his face next to her ear and said,

"You're effing hot, Mag!" He slid his hand across her lower back and down to her seat. She looked at him intensely, feeling her heart race. They sat at the bar and had their drinks, hands on each other's thighs, looking enticingly at one another. Then as Maggie started to head out to dance again, Billy grabbed her hand and led her to the end of the bar and around the corner. He pressed her against the wall that led down the hallway to the rest rooms and pressed himself against her body.

"I'm going crazy watching you dance, Mag," he breathed in her ear, his hands sliding behind her and grabbing her ass and squeezing. He looked into her eyes hungrily and kissed her hard. Then, still kissing her, he slid his hand down the back of her underwear and started squeezing again.

"Billy!" she said, surprised. He let go and pulled her over to a corner behind one of the standing tables.

"Turn around, Mag," he said, and she turned to face the table. He leaned up behind her, his body pressed close to hers as he whispered in her ear, "Mag," he breathed her name so sensually. "It's time to return the favour," Billy said and kissed her ear softly. Then growling the words, he added. "It's time to make you squirm." And she felt his hand lift her short dress. His hand slid down her ass and between her legs, pressing against the soft material of her underwear. He started softly running his fingers over her center. Maggie felt herself instantly becoming wet. Billy pressed and rubbed, while Maggie tried not to completely melt on the spot. Then he slipped his hand inside her underwear, sliding between her legs again and moving back into her center.

"God, Billy," she cried suddenly. She held the table as he slid his finger inside. Breathing heavy in her ear, his tongue slipping out and licking as he moved inside her, curling and fondling. "Ohhh God," she moaned, trying to stand still.

"Do you want me to stop, Mag?" he asked, finding her sweet spot, and pulsing his finger. Her legs quivered and she shook her head slightly. People were dancing nearby, drinking, and singing. Maggie was looking towards the middle of the dance floor, while she and Billy stood on the edge of it all, playing naughty. His lips were pressed to her neck, his finger keeping the pressure and rhythm that was making her weak in the knees. "When we get back to the boat, I'm gonna do you all night, Maggie!" he said, with a deep raspy growl.

"Oh God, Billy," she moaned. She was so wet now. "I want you," she told him, and his pulse quickened.

"I want to feel you cum, right here," he breathed heavily.

"Mmmm," Maggie whimpered, holding the table firmly as her body quivered. Billy's fingers pushing and circling and fondling as he kept one curled and pulsing inside her. "Suck my neck," she begged him. Without needing any coaxing, Billy pressed his lips to her neck, kissing, licking, then sucking. His finger still working its magic and his thumb pressing and circling into her clit. Maggie's legs were shaking, as she felt the powerful release.

"Ohhh," she moaned with a smile.

"Mag," Billy spoke close and deeply, sliding his fingers all around her wetness, then cupping his hand close and warm as her body relaxed deliciously.

"Shit, Billy!" she said suddenly, gently elbowing him in the stomach. He laughed and kissed her cheek. Then he slid his hand from between her legs and let her dress fall back into place. They walked to the restrooms and parted for a few minutes. Maggie came out of the women's washroom to find Billy waiting with a grin.

"Well, two things my Lover…" she said, leaning against him.

"Mmm, and what might they be?" he asked saucily.

"First, that was yummy. And bad!" And she stretched up and gave him a deep kiss and a sexy grin. "And 2nd, that was not easy!" and she gave him a teasing smack. "Oh, a bonus though. Wasn't it fun to make me crazy in public?" His eyes twinkled, giving him away instantly. "So, that makes us even, Lover," she added with a grin. He held her face and smiled at her. Then he gave her a big kiss.

"More dancing?" he asked, taking her hand. She grinned and followed him to the dance floor where they danced, bodies close. One more drink and a few more dances, they called it a night.

They were all over each other all the way back. Walking and kissing, wrapped around one another and holding tight, they were beyond ready to eat each other up. Billy jumped onto the boat first, then held his hands up and helped Maggie down, letting her body slide down his. She felt her feet touch the floor as Billy held her face and kissed her passionately. The cool night breeze made Maggie shiver, but they both knew that only stoked her fire.

"You make me crazy, Mag," Billy breathed, kissing her ears and neck. His hands sliding up and down her arms. "You dancing tonight Mag... Damn Sexy!" he told her ravenously. Maggie shivered.

"Didn't you say you were going to do me all night long?" she asked, with a lustful stare. Billy looked into her eyes, grinned mischievously, and growled as he bent down to suck on her neck. Maggie's body shivered again. He made his way back up and kissed her mouth, holding her head in his hands. Then he looked at her again.

"I want you, bad!" he said, looking right into her eyes. Maggie felt her knees go weak. She reached up and held his hands as he kissed her deeply. Backing towards the door, still kissing, Maggie reached into his pocket for the key. Billy let go of her while she unlocked the door and led the way. Watching as Billy locked up, then turned and held her face.

"Take me!" she breathed and was surprised when he bent down and scooped her up. "Whoop!" she cried, then wrapped her arms around his neck and kissed him.

"God, you turn me on, Maggie," Billy said, kissing her again as he walked further into the boat cabin.

"Billy, you make me weak," she breathed back. He put her down and they held each other close. Then their hands started sliding all over one another.

"Tell me what you want," Billy said, kissing her neck and pulling her tight.

"Do me standing up." She felt his chest rise, and he backed them up to the bedroom door. "I want to wrap my legs right around your beautiful strong body," she said, hugging him tight. He pulled the door closed and pressed his body against hers, pushing her against the door. "Make me beg, Billy," Maggie said, almost moaning the words. Billy growled and grabbed both her breasts and started squeezing. He slid down her body and began nibbling at her nipples through her clothes. Maggie's hands running up and down his neck, into his hair. "Mmmm," she moaned quietly. "Tell me what to do," she said to him, and his eyes were suddenly looking deeply into hers.

"Take your clothes off," he commanded, aching for her. She grinned provocatively then started to slide her dress up her body, pulling it over her head and tossing it aside. He hungrily looked her up and down as she slid her hands behind her back and undid her bra. Taking her time, one at a time, she slid each strap down, holding her bra up, then as his eyes twinkled, she pulled it right off and tossed it too. She could see how hungry he was and was extremely aroused by him.

"You're so beautiful, Maggie," he said, watching her. Then she slowly slid her white underwear down her body and kicked them away with one foot.

"Now you, Lover," she told him and his eyes grinned cheekily. He undid his shirt buttons, and she watched with pure enjoyment as his chest came into view, then his broad shoulders and his strong arms as he slid his shirt down and let it fall to the floor. "Gorgeous man," she told him, one finger at her mouth as she watched him undo his shorts and pull them and his boxers down. "Mmm," she said, looking at his body hungrily. Her desire adding to his arousal. Then, with sudden rapture, they grabbed one another and kissed fiercely. Billy pushed her against the door and their hands slid over each other's bodies. She kissed down his face, down his neck and over his chest, sliding her tongue over his warm skin, then kissing back up to his mouth. Her fingers moving and squeezing through his hair. Billy's hands holding and squeezing her ass, pulling her into his body and pressing them tightly together. Then he lifted her up and Maggie wrapped her legs around him. She reached up and took her hair clip out, her curls falling down over her shoulders. Billy's face moved down her chest and sucked her breasts. Fast, wet, tongue licks, then sucking again. "Oh, Billy," she moaned, and he sucked harder.

"I want you so bad, Mag!" he growled, and she held his face as they looked at each other. Billy moved back up her body. Kissing hard, tongues sliding, Billy rocked his hips and pushed himself inside her.

"Ohhh," Maggie groaned, holding his face and looking into his eyes. He slid in and out, her body pushing against the door. Staring into one another's eyes intensely.

"God, I love your body!" Billy growled the words. Maggie's head lifting and falling back against the door.

"Billy, you feel so good," she cried.

"Mag, ride me," he whispered. She looked back down into his eyes and gave him a look. He opened the bedroom door and walked them over to the bed. Maggie still wrapped so tightly around him, kissing him passionately as he turned and sat down on the bed. Sliding off as Billy moved up towards the headboard and laid down, Maggie climbed on and straddled him, running her hands over his chest and down his stomach. She looked into his eyes again as Billy's hands trailed over her legs. Then, with his hands under her ass, she lifted herself and slid down, as slowly as she could, onto him. Both of them moaning with pleasure as she rocked back and forth, sliding and grinding, taking him in and out slowly. Watching each other as she moved.

"You're so hot," he whispered. Her hands slid up her neck and lifted her hair, still moving into him, making circles, then back and forth, taking her time and enjoying the ride. "Oh Mag, you're making me crazy," he groaned, reaching out and squeezing her breasts.

"Mmmm. Billy," she breathed, looking intensely at him again, then leaning forward and lifting herself up and down. She kissed his mouth, then sat up again and started riding him hard and fast. Billy's hands lifted her up and down as Maggie landed hard, over and over.

"Maag!" he groaned, and Maggie kept the tempo fast and hard. "Don't stop!" he told her. Maggie's breasts bouncing, her hair flying, her hands on his chest, pinching and squeezing as she rode with blissful determination.

"Billy!" she cried out. "I want you behind me," she said, urgently. He pulled her off quickly and flipped her, pulling her body onto all fours and holding her waist. "Ohh. Ohhhhh!" she cried as he glided in, sliding quickly back and forth. His breathing, one long growl.

"I'm so close, Mag," he groaned. His glides, shorter and harder.

"Billy," Maggie moaned his name. He pressed deeply, then,

"Maag!" He came. His hips thrusting hard, staying deep within her, shaking as he finished. "Damn, Mag!" he said, with frenzied release, as his body slowed to a stop. He pulled out of her and leaned over her body. "Now, how do you want to finish, Sexy?" he asked, kissing her. Maggie laid down flat on her stomach and Billy laid on top. He didn't have to ask her what she wanted. Billy slid his hand under her body and down between her legs. Rubbing and pressing, Maggie's body grinding into his fingers as he started sucking and kissing her neck. "You smell delicious, Mag," he breathed the words heavily, his breath spreading over her skin, sending shivers. "Like that, Mag?" he asked her.

"Mmm," she moaned. "Just like that," she said softly, purring with pleasure. "I want you inside me," she added, and although he had finished, he was still quite hard and easily slid back inside her body. He felt her squeeze him as he continued to rub.

"Help me," he breathed in her ear, pressing his lips to her neck. She slid her hand down to meet his, and he let her take over, his hand sliding on top so he could feel her pleasure herself. Billy moved his body into hers, feeling Maggie's body squeezing him tighter. He rocked his hips and trailed his tongue around her neck. Maggie groaning her pleasure, her body moving and squeezing. "Let me feel you cum," Billy hardly whispered the words to her.

"Mmm," she moaned. "Deeper," she told him, and he pushed harder and held firm as she grinded him, climbing her way into ecstasy. "Mmmmm," Maggie slowly moaned long and deep as her body held him tight. Then he felt her whole body shudder. "Ohh... my... God!" she groaned.

"Mag, you're so wet," he breathed, turned on by her searing satisfaction.

"Ooooh." And she shuddered again. "Billy." she breathed as he softly kissed her neck.

"Mag," He whispered back. He felt her body quiver and then relax.

"Don't leave, Billy," she said, and Billy leaned his face down and kissed her lips.

"Not going anywhere, Babe," he assured her, staying inside her, laying on her until she completely relaxed. Then Billy rolled off, his arm wrapped over her. Maggie turned enough to be able to move face to face and kiss him. Billy pulled her body in closer, so they were skin to skin as they kissed deeply and slowly. They kissed and kissed. Maggie nestled snugly to Billy, feeling safe and loved and protected in his arms.

"I love you, Billy," she told him, looking up with misty emerald eyes. With his Billy twinkle, he smiled at her, kissed her again, rubbed noses and said,

"Love you with a never-ending fire, Mag." She looked at him lovingly, their gaze held for a moment as their lips moved slowly closer, then feeling each other's warm breath on their lips, they pressed together in a long kissing embrace. They held one another for a time, snuggling and caressing softly.

CHAPTER 12

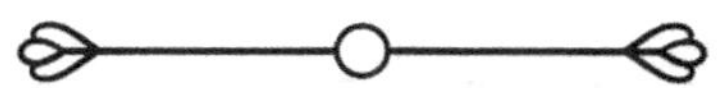

Billy awoke to the smell of coffee and breakfast. He stretched out his arms and legs, smiling contentedly to himself, then opened his eyes and looked around the room. The sun was bright and pouring in through the little round windows. Laying there for a few minutes, he then rolled out of bed and grabbed a pair of boxers and pulled them on. After using the washroom, he walked down the hall and his eyes lit up at the sight of Maggie curled up in the corner chair with a coffee and a book. Looking up and smiling, Maggie greeted him.

"Morning, Lover," she said as he walked towards her, leaned down with a grin and kissed her.

"Morning, Beautiful," he responded. He helped himself to a cup of coffee, then Maggie got up, sat her book down and joined Billy at the couch.

"Sleep well, Billy?" she asked him.

"Mmm. Very well. You, Babe?" he asked, his eyes smiling at her.

"Oh yes," she answered with a sexy grin. "Ready to eat?" she asked. Again, his eyes smiled, sexier this time. "Breakfast?" she added.

"Sure," he answered. Maggie got up and walked to the kitchen. He got up and joined her, lifting her hair and kissing her neck. She giggled as his breath tickled.

"Mmmm, smells good," he told her, not talking about breakfast. She turned and gave him a kiss, holding him tight. Then they smiled at one another and grabbed their plates. Maggie flipped omelets onto each of their plates, both of them grabbed forks and took their food back over to the couch.

"More coffee, Mag?" he asked, bringing the pot over, and pouring some into his own mug.

"Yes please," she replied, and he topped hers up too.

"So, snorkeling today, Babe?" he asked as they ate.

"For sure," Maggie answered, having another bite of her eggs. They finished breakfast and had the last of their coffees before getting changed into their bathing suits and heading out for the day. They made their way to a snorkeling site in an area known as Secrets Reef. Billy and Maggie joined a small group of four other people taking a short boat ride out to the reefs. They had a brief lesson, put on their wetsuits, masks, snorkels, and fins and jumped into the water. Billy and Maggie swam down together, only having to dive about five feet to see the beautiful coral along the bottom of the sea. Tiny brightly coloured schools of fish swimming in and around the reefs, bright electric blue, vivid yellow, orange, black, purple and lime green, silver and pink. A jellyfish majestically sweeping through the deeper water and an eel or two moving along the sand. The coral below, so many different colours and shades, sizes, and shapes. Sea urchins and plants, so strange and beautiful. It was gloriously haunting. Maggie looked back up towards the surface and found herself awestruck. A complete feeling of weightlessness. Her body felt so light and connected to the water hugging her. The clear water rippling, the sun a distant shimmering orb above the surface, the echoing silence under the sea holding her in amazed appreciation of the power and beauty engulfing her. Billy swam over to meet her, and they took each other's hands and swam to the surface. Then after a moment above water they dove back under and swam along together watching the beautiful marine life. At one point, they found themselves suddenly part of a school of Sergeant Major's. The beautiful white fish, shimmering silver in the beams of light from above. Yellow tops and five dark finger-like stripes down their backs, swimming past Maggie and Billy. They looked at each other happily, knowingly acknowledging Billy's rank as Sergeant Major and grinning in their masks. Maggie suddenly grabbed Billy's hand and pointed down near some cave like coral at two stingrays gliding through the water. It was all unbelievably beautiful. They swam and enjoyed themselves for an hour or so, then they all made their way back to the boat and were taken back to shore. Saying goodbye to the other swimmers, Maggie and Billy headed back to the Emerald Pearl to change before heading out for a late lunch.

"That was absolutely magical, Billy!" Maggie said as they came out of the bedroom together.

"Amazing!" he said, smiling at her. "I'm so glad we got to do that together, Mag," he added, wrapping his arm around her shoulder, walking out into the living room. Maggie turned and hugged him, smiling up at him. He held her face and leaned down to kiss her lips softly.

"Mmm, me too, Billy," she said, grinning at him again.

"Ok, Babe, let's go fill our bellies." They disembarked, their footsteps echoing on the wooden dock as they made their way back up to the street.

"Where to, my Lover?" Maggie asked.

"Anywhere with you, Beautiful," was his response. They found a quiet place and were shown to a table for two overlooking the sea. They both got soda water with lime and ordered jerk chicken wraps with rice and peas and Jamaican coleslaw. They sat looking out at the blue, blue water, their feet snuggled together under the table. A light breeze had started sweeping across their warm tanned bodies and they stared at one another lovingly.

"Feels like nap time, Mag," Billy said, winking cheekily at her.

"Oh ya?" she asked. "For real or is that some sort of uncrackable code?" she asked teasingly. Billy chuckled, his eyes crinkling with amusement.

"Yes, to both," he said with a big grin. They left their table and paid the bill. Walking along the street away from their boat, then heading down to the beach so they could walk back along the edge of the water together. Shoes off, hand in hand, they took their time. Their footsteps sinking into the warm white sand, waves stretching up, just inches away. They put their shoes back on and made their way back down the dock to the boat. It was close to 2:30, and after changing out of their clothes and into their robes, Maggie freshened up a bit then joined Billy in the bedroom, where he was lying down waiting for her. She sat on the edge of the bed and braided her hair, letting it fall down onto her back softly. Then she crawled up beside him and rested her head down on his chest. He wrapped his arms around her and snuggled her in close. Maggie closed her eyes, feeling very sleepy and relaxed.

"Nap first, Babe?" Billy asked. Maggie nestled in closer.

"Mmhmm," she answered contentedly. Listening to his breathing, the sound of the water hitting the boat, and being gently rocked by the waves, Maggie and Billy soon drifted off.

* * * *

"Mmmm," Maggie woke up to her own moans. Billy's tongue sliding up and down her thighs, lightly licking over her clit, circling, and sliding gently back and forth, then kissing her center deeply. "Mmm," she moaned again. Billy's tongue licking all around her center, and her legs, nibbling and kissing, sliding one finger inside as he continued kissing her body softly. Noticing Maggie waking up and enjoying her wake up call, Billy dove his face deeply between her legs, licking and sucking hungrily. As his hands spread her legs further apart, and his fingers softly opened her up, he growled voraciously,

"You taste amazing," he said looking up at her with dark eyes. Maggie's body surged with tingling electricity at his words. His mouth and tongue back to their happy work. Hearing him making enjoyable growling sounds as he licked and kissed her center was making her squirm deliciously. His nose pressing into her center, his tongue pressing and flicking her clit steadily, her legs twitching and her body shuddering as he pulled her into blissful pleasure.

"Oh God, Billy," she groaned. Billy squeezed her body with his hands while keeping the tempo she was shaking with. Her legs were vibrating. He moved his face around her center, deeply, licking and sucking adamantly, then back to circling and pressing. She reached down and tickled her fingers through his hair, then her hands grabbed the sheets beside her body as he found her sweet spot. "Ohhhh, Billy, don't stop!" She could hardly stand it. "Yes! Yes!" she was yelling, pulling the sheets tight in her hands as she came. "Ohhhhh God!" she moaned slowly as Billy finished her off with ravenous hunger. He kissed her thighs, taking his time, kissing up and around her hips, under and around her navel and across her stomach. His hands moving up to squeeze her breasts as he kissed his way up to each one, licking and sucking, kissing up to her chest and her neck. Maggie wrapped her arms and legs around his body as he looked down at her. She was still shaking.

"Mmm. Delicious," Billy breathed looking into her eyes, still possessed by the animal lust within.

"God, you're good at that!" Maggie said with deep satisfaction. Feeling totally aroused and pulling him in for a long hard kiss. One of their downfalls was that, usually in their attempts to please one another, they ended up more turned on and found themselves lost in hours of sexual play. Not really a bad thing but made it tricky to be able to have quickies. Quickies were like foreplay for them. Rolling about together on the bed, kissing and wrapped tightly. Their hands squeezing one another's asses, pulling each other tight. Billy was soon inside her. Staying right up close, deep inside her, moving in short thrusts, growling his pleasure and holding her so tight. He pressed in and out, hardly moving. Their bodies pressing hard and circling against one another. "Mmm. Gawd you feel good," Maggie whispered, licking his ear and neck as she spoke.

"Awww," Billy's growls becoming deeper and longer. Rolling over, Maggie on top, Billy still holding her body tight so she could only grind deeply and tightly against him. He rolled them over again, pushing faster now, his hips moving so quickly. "Aaaa!" he groaned; his face pressed hard against her cheek. Maggie squeezed him tight inside of her body, grabbing his ass and holding tight. "Mag you're the best I've ever had." He was growling more now, his body shaking, his arms strong and tight around her body holding her firmly.

"Billy, you're amazing," she moaned in his ear.

"Mag. Mag!" She felt him exploding inside her. "Ohhhhh Maag..." And his whole body shuddered, his hips still pushing in and out. She squeezed his ass, massaging firmly and holding him strong, deep inside. His head lifted, his eyes closing as he finished bursting inside her. Then he looked down at her for a moment before kissing her. Still growling and groaning with pleasure.

They lay tangled and trailing their hands over one another. Kissing and running their fingers through each other's hair. Looking into one another's eyes deeply, soft kisses turning to deeper ones, turning into heavy breathing, grabbing each other tightly, Billy sliding back inside her and rolling about the bed again. This time Billy sat on the bed and Maggie straddled him. She slid him in, halfway, sliding up and down, moving at a slower pace, holding his shoulders to help her control how far she took him in. Billy's hands squeezing her ass. His mouth sucking her breasts.

"Aw God, Mag," he groaned, Maggie so wet, she was dripping over him as she continued to rise and fall. She grabbed his face and kissed him hard. Billy held her hips firmly and moved her up, then right down, pushing himself all the way in, harder and quicker.

"Oh...Billy...Oh...You're so big," she breathed. That was all he needed, and he was bursting again.

"Mmmm," he groaned, moving her body tightly into his. They fell to the bed, kissing and laughing. Hardly able to catch their breath. "Damn, Mag. We might need to separate ourselves," he told her laughing as she started kissing his neck and running her fingers into his hair again.

"Mmm. Why would we want to do that, Lover?" she asked, still softly pressing her lips to his hot sweaty skin. "God, you smell good," she told him, sucking his earlobe.

"Ohh, Maag." And he rolled them, so he was on top again and kissed her deeply.

"Mmm." They both moaned, holding tight and kissing hard. Landing in a heap again and holding snug.

"Mag. I need a drink," he said, and they both laughed.

"Ok Lover, time out," she replied, grinning at him as he sat up.

"You coming, Mag?" he asked, getting up from the bed.

"Over and over!" she answered. Billy's head fell back with a chuckle, and he looked back at her and winked. "Yes, but I'll wait until I've watched you leave," she added, grinning saucily at him. Billy walked away, goofily walking extra sexy. "That is one fine ass, Sergeant Stanton!" she said and shrieked with surprise as he turned around, grinning with fire in his eyes and ran back to the bed and landed on top of her, kissing her all over.

"Might need to have a little role-play one night, Babe," he said with a twinkle in his eye.

"Sounds fun," she spoke. The two of them finally got out of bed, grabbed their robes, and headed for the washroom and the kitchen.

Maggie came out of the bathroom and found Billy at the kitchen sink. She ran up behind him and slid her arms under his, wrapping herself around him tight. His hands came up to hold hers, giving them a little squeeze.

"What's cooking, good-looking?" Maggie asked, giving his bum a firm two-handed squeeze. Billy laughed and turned to face Maggie.

"I was thinking of going fancy, Mag, and making sandwiches." He grinned cheekily at her.

"Mmm, I love you more everyday, Lover," she told him with a big grin, pulling him down for a kiss.

"And I love you, Babe!" he said, kissing her back. "Okay Babe, we don't have all the things for our usual sandwiches, so, let's just check what we have left and see what we can make?" Maggie followed him to the little fridge and taking things as he pulled them out and passed them to her, she sat them all down on the kitchen table.

"Okay," Maggie said looking down at the buffet. Half a loaf of frozen bread, cheese, pickles, patties, bacon, an onion and three eggs.

"Western, Babe?" Billy asked.

"Mmm, yes, sounds good." Kissing as they worked together, snuggling and full on make out attacks for a minute here and there. While eggs and bacon, cooked, Billy sat Maggie up on the counter so they could snuggle, and kissed sweetly, wrapped up together. Things soon got very hot and heavy again, but sizzling bacon and eggs brought them back. Maggie set the table while Billy finished with toast and building their westerns.

"Beer or bubbly, Babe?" Maggie asked Billy, her head in the fridge, to grab her bubbly.

"Bubbly, I think Mag, thanks." Maggie grinned to herself. *Mmm, guess he means business.* She stood up and walked over to give him a kiss. Then the two sat down and ate.

"When are we leaving, Lover?" Maggie asked, putting down her drink.

"Thinking fairly early in the morning, Babe. Might try to get a jog in before we go. I've been slack'n," he said with a grin. Maggie finished her drink, then leaned over and kissed his cheek.

"Okay gorgeous man," she replied. Billy smiled at her, and she felt his hand slide up her leg, just skimming past her center. She grinned at him and flashed him a seductive look. They sat for a little while before cleaning up together. Maggie popped the kettle on, and they took tea up and sat on deck watching the beginning of the sunset.

"Feel like a swim, Lover?" Maggie asked, reaching her hand out to hold his.

"Ya, for sure, Mag," he responded with a smile. They got ready and walked down to the beach for a sunset dip. Maggie had pulled her hair up into a bun, so it wasn't all wet for bed, and they swam until the last of the sun disappeared into the water. Billy wrapped his arm around Maggie and picked her up. Her legs up high, water dripping off her toes, as Billy walked them both out of the water and back onto the beach. She wrapped her arms around his shoulders and kissed him. One hand sliding up to hold his cheek. They could hear the beat of the music in the clubs and bars and all the lights were bright and flickering. They grinned at one another, both thinking about their naughty dance night.

"What happens in Montego, stays in Montego?" Billy said with a cheeky grin. Maggie laughed.

"Oh ya!" she responded with her big Maggie smile and planted another kiss on him. Setting her down, they grabbed their towels and shoes and headed back to the boat. They made their way into the boat cabin and locked up, their hands trailing over one another.

"Tired, Lover?" Maggie asked, giving his sweet cheeks a squeeze.

"No, napped today." His eyes twinkled enticingly as he looked at her.

"God, you send shivers right through me, Billy." His grin grew bigger.

"Never too tired to lay with you, Mag." Then he chuckled, "Or stand up." And she laughed with him. They walked down the hall to the bedroom and stood on their towels to take their bathing suits off. Then Billy moved closer to Maggie and held her face. Smiling at each other, Billy moved his face down to Maggie's, softly touching his lips to hers. He kissed her so gently, his hands reaching up, loosening her bun, then letting her hair fall down over her shoulders and her back. He looked at her again, such love and affection in his eyes, brushing her curls off her shoulders, sliding his hands and fingers up her neck and into her hair. Maggie's lips parting slightly, his hands supporting her head as he kissed her again. His thumbs softly sliding over her cheeks as they kissed tenderly. Maggie's hands slid up his body, over his shoulders and arms and held his hands.

"Mag," he said between kisses.

"Mmhmm?" she responded.

"Let's get it on," he sang, in his deep husky voice.

"Jelly legs, Lover," she told him, and he grinned, then he kissed her again. They undressed themselves from their wet clingy bathing suits, then stood looking at one another again.

"You are so beautiful, Billy," Maggie told him, her hands sliding up and over his chest, out over his shoulders and down his arms. Her eyes traced over his body as she touched him. Then her hands slid up his neck into his hair. Leaning forward, she kissed his chest, and his neck, then looked up into his kind and dancing blue eyes. His strong hands ran up and down her back, over her firm peach of a bottom and back up again, watching her closely.

"Mag, when we first met, I genuinely remember my heart skipping a beat," he told her, holding her head again and kissing her face, softly, all over, then her lips. "You have always been the most beautiful creature

I've ever seen, and one damn fine lover," he added with a grin. "The finest, Mag." She smiled at him. "God I'm glad we found each other again." He breathed deeply and kissed her harder and longer, wrapping his arms around her and pulling her close. He stopped kissing her and looked down into her green eyes again. Then reaching his hand down and taking hers, he led her to the bed. He climbed on and laid down; Maggie laid down beside him. They moved onto their sides, looking into each other's eyes as they ran their hands over one another's bodies, not talking, not kissing, just soaking it all in. Their fingers trailing over every inch, like they were memorizing every defined curve. Maggie moved her body closer and caressed his cheek, moving his hair gently and smiling at him. Their eyes locked and sparkled. And then, their lips pulled into one another. Pressing slowly and deeply. Hands holding each other's faces as they kissed, their bodies tightly pressed together.

* * * *

Maggie sat on deck with her second coffee, her eyes softly closed listening to the waves and the breeze, inhaling the smell of the Caribbean.

"Morning, Beautiful," came Billy's voice from behind her, as his hands held her shoulders.

"Morning, Handsome," she responded, watching him as he walked in front of her. His body glistened with sweat.

"Have a good run?" she asked as he sat across from her. Billy nodded.

"Love my beach runs," he told her. "Just going to hop in the shower, Babe," he added, getting up, kissing her forehead, then heading below. Maggie held her coffee close with both hands, smiling as she soaked up the peaceful beauty of the early morning. After she finished, she went back down and started making breakfast. They didn't have much left, but she had what she needed to make pancakes. She heard the bathroom door open and looked behind her, hoping to catch a glimpse of her sweet cheeked lover, and she did.

"Oh Lover boy!" she called. Billy grinned.

"Yes, Maggie?" he answered with a wink.

"Come'ere lover boy!" he chuckled as she walked over to him, slid her hand between his legs and cupped him softly. "Mmm, what a man!" she said, slightly growling. Billy grabbed her ass with both hands and pulled her against him hard.

"Hold that thought, Mag," He kissed her, then headed to the bedroom to get dressed. Maggie stood and watched him walk away with a big grin on her face.

* * * *

"Okay Mag, hoist the sail," Billy said as he came down from unclipping the mainsail. She started pulling up the jib and locked it, just as Billy joined her at the cockpit and started hoisting the mainsail beside her. They were headed to Falmouth today, docking at Port of Rio Bueno. Maggie and Billy had decided to sail past Runaway and St. Anne's and go right to Ocho Rios after Falmouth, then make their way back to visit with the Robinson's before heading home. They still had ten days before their flight.

Billy started up the engine just to get them out of port and into deeper waters. Maggie went below deck and started on the first of three loads of laundry. The little washer wasn't very big, but it did the trick. Then she took fresh coffee up with her and sat next to Billy. Loving the feeling of cutting through the water, Billy next to her sailing his vessel proudly, the breeze blowing her hair, the sun warm on her skin. She knew she'd miss this when they returned to their regular land life. The engine was off, and there was a strong wind moving them at a good twenty knots.

"We'll be there in no time, Mag," Billy told her, taking a sip of his coffee.

"Oh, I'm so looking forward to the Luminescent Lagoon!" Billy smiled at her, his eyes twinkling.

"Me too, Mag." The waves were stronger today than they had been the whole trip, and the clouds were looking a bit like they were threatening rain. Over their three weeks, they had been lucky enough to never have a day of rain. Maggie hoped their last week and a half would be as clear.

They drifted into the harbour around noon, and found they were the only boat needing to dock. They saw a sign reading "Tank Weld Limited Port", and Billy lowered the mainsail, then turned the engine on as Maggie lowered the jib. Docking, showing the usual paperwork, and going through the registration, then heading back to the boat and wrapping up the mainsail. They sat and relaxed, sitting down at the table on deck. Once again, Maggie found herself awestruck at how beautiful the scenery around them was. Bright blue sky, clear turquoise water, white sandy beach arching out of sight, buildings, trees, and green mountains in the distance.

"Billy, it's so beautiful here," she said to him, snuggling up close. He wrapped his arm around her and pulled her tight.

"Jamaica's like Heaven on Earth, Babe," he answered with a smile. "Feel like a bite to eat?" he asked, sliding off the bench seat and standing in front of Maggie, holding his hand out to her.

"Sure, Lover." She took his hand, following him below deck. They grabbed a couple things before locking up and leaving the boat. Billy knew the area a little. Enough to get them to a little place called Peppers. It had a number of cabana style seating areas outside, and a brightly painted red covered bar where they found an empty cabana table and sat down. The street was fairly busy with local shoppers, and the restaurant had a number of patrons as well.

"Hail friends, what ya would like to drink?" a loud smiley woman asked as she approached their table.

"Greetings," Billy answered, and the woman smiled at him.

"Oh, me brutha, yuh know de land yuh?" she said happily.

"I lived here for ten years," he answered her.

"Oh fine, where abouts?" she asked as she patted him on the shoulder.

"St. Ann," he told her, seeing Maggie's face and smiling at her as she listened with a grin.

"St. Ann eh. My cousin lives dar." The woman smiled at Maggie.

"Hi," Maggie said with a big smile.

"Hail luv." Billy's eyes twinkled watching Maggie.

"Who's your cousin?" Billy asked her.

"Alvita Baxter," she replied with a grin.

"Well, no, she be Alvita Robinson." Maggie and Billy looked at each other quickly.

"No?" Billy said. "Married to Delroy?" he asked. The woman smiled broadly, clapping him on the shoulder again.

"That's right!" she told him with a laugh. "Yuh know dem?" she asked him. Billy nodded with a chuckle.

"Know them? I lived on their property for almost ten years." She clapped her hands together and laughed.

"Oh, den yuh be Billay?" she asked.

"That's right," he answered with a grin.

"Oh, my Alvi and Deli, them luvs dem Billay!" She shook her head with a laugh. "Little world," she added. "An who might dis be?" she asked, smiling at Maggie. Maggie held out her hand and the woman took it, shaking it, then patting it when Maggie answered.

"I'm Maggie," she told her.

"Hail Maggay, names Jada." Maggie smiled at her.

"This is my wife," Billy added with a big smile.

"Oh my goodness, dats right, yuh just get married." And she put a hand on each of their shoulders. "Drinks be on de'ouse. What yuh like to drink?" Billy looked at Maggie, one eyebrow raised,

"Vanilla rum, Babe?" She smiled, then looked up at Jada.

"Yes, something with vanilla rum please."

"Okay, Maggay." Then she looked back at Billy.

"I'll have a rum and ginger," he answered.

"Yuh get it!" she announced with another big smile, then left them.

"Wow, fancy running into Alvita's cousin," Maggie said, smiling at Billy across the table.

"Ya, funny," he said, leaning over the table and stretching out his arms. Maggie reached for his hands and held them. "You look gorgeous, Babe!" he told her, his eyes crinkling into a smile.

"Thanks, Lover," she replied leaning closer and meeting him halfway for a kiss. Jada came back with their drinks and told them the lunch specials. They thanked her for the drinks and ordered the jerk chicken with rice and peas. While they waited and sipped their drinks, their feet rubbed and slid together as usual. Talking about their plans to swim in the lagoon that evening. They took their time enjoying their meal, surprised at the huge portions and in no hurry to go anywhere. Jada brought them over another drink halfway through and chatted a bit more with them. She and Billy were surprised they'd never met before, but Jada did say they didn't usually get to St. Ann because of their restaurant. So, any family gatherings that were organized, the Robinsons usually came to see them. They finished, paid their bill, visited with Jada and met her husband Thomas, then headed back to the Emerald Pearl.

"Oh, that was good, Babe!" Billy said, patting his stomach.

"It was also a lot of food," Maggie replied, rubbing hers. They went into the cabin and plunked themselves down on the bed. They didn't nap, but they laid together for quite a while before peeling themselves off the mattress.

Around 6:00 they got into their bathing suits, put their clothes over top and headed out to grab a taxi.

"Glistening Waters Marina, please," Billy told the driver.

"Ok," he replied. When they arrived, they joined a half dozen other people and boarded a small boat. Their guide told them about how the water was fresh, with a low percent of salt, that the blue glow was from the bioluminescent marine life and that it was completely safe to swim in it. They traveled out into the bay and then he dropped an anchor. Everyone had the option of swimming or staying in the boat. Only two people stayed on the boat watching the other's surrounded by light. Maggie and Billy peeled off their clothes then jumped in. The water was quite shallow, and they found they could touch the muddy bottom easily. The deepest part was only about six feet. It was beyond words, the most amazingly magical thing they'd seen. Well, actually, Maggie said to Billy that she felt like she was swimming in the Northern Lights, which had been an amazingly magical moment shared between them too. Every movement they made; the water glowed a brighter blue. Lifting their hands out of the water and watching blue sparkling drops drip from the tips of their fingers.

"Mag, this is unreal!" Billy said, swimming next to her.

"Billy, I want to live in this water!" she said, and Billy chuckled. After half an hour or so, their guide called them back to the boat, where everyone piled back in. With big smiles, and hearts full of wonder, some of the others chatted with Maggie and Billy about the experience. Another couple had visited bioluminescent lagoons in a few other parts of the world and said, this one was by far the brightest and most beautiful they'd experienced.

"Bless," said the cabby as Billy patted him on the shoulder and slipped him their fare and a tip.

"Walk good," Billy said, and he climbed out of the back of the taxi behind Maggie. He took her hand in his as they walked towards the dock.

"What a beautiful night," Maggie said quietly, looking up at the brightly lit starry night sky.

"That was so awesome to share with you, Mag," he said, squeezing her hand. They hopped onto the boat and headed inside.

"So, Ocho Rios tomorrow, Lover?" Maggie asked him, closing the door behind her and locking it.

"That's what I was thinking, unless you want to do something else, Babe?" Billy asked.

"No, that's fine, gorgeous husband." Billy grinned at her.

"We should maybe grab some groceries though. I know we're only a few days from stopping, but we've got next to nothing left," she added. They walked towards one another and pulled each other in for a hug. Looking at one another with smiles.

"That really was quite amazing wasn't it, Mag?" Billy asked, leaning down and giving her a kiss. Their bodies rocked as they hugged.

"Yes. Glad we got to do that together. This whole trip has been such an amazing experience, Billy." Billy kissed her again, holding her face gently, the two grinning at one another.

"Making up for lost time nicely," he said, his voice becoming more of a husky whisper. His eyes became darker and more seductive. He pulled her body tightly against his, his hands sliding all over her and up into her hair, holding her face and kissing her mouth with long, soft kisses. Then Billy looked into her eyes again and Maggie felt butterflies in her stomach.

"I love you, Mag," he whispered.

"I love you, Billy," she told him as he kissed her again.

"I want to tell you how much I love you, over and over," he

breathed in her ear. Maggie felt goosebumps all over her body, as his hands slid down and grabbed her ass, giving both cheeks a good squeeze and pressing his body into hers. He kissed her ear, her cheek, her mouth, his fingers back in her hair, massaging and tickling into her curls. Maggie slid her hands up to his chest and started to softly push him back, sticking close to him and walking them towards the bedroom. Billy stopped them and held her head, kissing her deeply, his tongue slipping into her mouth and moving slowly, circling hers and kissing her hard. Her legs hardly supported her, Billy turning her into putty in his hands as their energy built and ignited quickly. Then he stopped kissing her and moved his body down hers, grinning at her as he picked her up. Maggie wrapped her legs around him and smiled, her eyes bright and alluring. "You're all I've ever wanted," he told her. Maggie held him tight and kissed him deeply. He walked to the bedroom and sat her down on the bed. Maggie grinned as she pulled him by the shirt towards her, backing up to lay her head on the pillows. Billy sat straddled over her and looked at her with adoration.

"You're the only one I've truly loved," Maggie told him, and he leaned down and kissed her. His lips soft and hot on hers, pressing into her, his hands holding her face and sliding into her hair. The sound of his breath stoking the fire growing within her. So tenderly, they undressed one another. One piece of clothing at a time. Watching each other, eyes intense, sliding their hands softly over one another's bodies and kissing softly. Billy kissed down her neck, gently moving her hair and kissing to the other side. His lips pressed softly against her skin. "Your touch sends chills up and down my spine," Maggie whispered softly as he kissed down to her chest. She held his head softly and ran her fingers through his hair as he kissed each breast, then kissed his way back up to her lips again. Maggie's hands trailing over his back, down to his ass, back up to his arms. He laid down on top of her, then rolled them over.

"Damn, you're beautiful, Mag," he said, looking up at her with determination and desire. His hands moving her hair back from her face. She smiled softly at him and bent down to kiss him. Maggie started moving her body into his now, Billy's hands holding her ass and massaging.

"Mmm," she moaned, kissing him. Moving her face down to kiss his neck and chest, sweeping her hands softly over his chest and shoulders and kissing back up to his ears. "You're a beautiful lover," she whispered, and he held her tight as they kissed deeply, rolling them back over and looking down at her again. Keeping his gaze deep, within her emerald greens, he ran one hand down her shoulder, over her breast, squeezing gently, then sliding down her stomach and hip and down her leg, squeezing again. Then he made his way back up and softly swept his palm across her cheek before leaning down and kissing her again. They stared at one another deeply, trailing their hands over each other so tenderly. Kissing, then staring again. "I need you," Maggie said, and she saw that look of animal hunger building in his eyes. He slid his hand down and gently grasped her breast, moving his face down and sucking and kissing slowly. Squeezing as he licked. "Mmm," she moaned. Then she felt his legs moving hers apart, and looking right into her eyes, pushing himself slowly inside her, with a deep growling breath he said,

"I love you, Maggie." She held his face and lifted hers to kiss him. Then their gaze locked again, and he slid in and out so slowly. "I love you," he said again. Maggie's whole being was exploding. Her heart, body and soul were transported into ethereal waves of tenderness. He slid so long and slow, staring into her eyes.

"Billy, I love you," she said back to him, more waves of warmth rolling over her. Watching as he continued with his sensual thoughtful movements. "God, you turn me on Billy," Maggie groaned with tantalizing pleasure. He leaned closer and kissed her mouth gently. His nose brushing hers, then kissing her cheek, and as he moved closer to her ear he whispered,

"I love you, Mag." She felt herself hold him tight inside and release.

"Ohhh Billy... I love you," she breathed. His nose moving across her neck, his breath softly tickling her skin. Then he sat up and held both her breasts, squeezing slowly, still gliding in and out so slowly. Maggie felt herself cumming, so quietly, softly, wet and flowing as his body played hers with such beautiful patience.

"Maggie...oh gawd," Billy growled so deeply, bending Maggie's legs and holding them. Still making long slow glides and starting to pick up the pace.

"Ohhh God," Maggie moaned, holding the sheets beside her, her body moving and lifting into Billy's.

"Mag! Maag." Billy was moving faster and bursting, holding her bent legs against him and pushing deeper. "Gawd, Mag," he said, his body shuddering. Maggie cumming again.

"Oh Billy," she breathed, stretching her legs out and pulling him down towards her, and hugging him tight. Billy rested his face next to hers and whispered,

"I love you." Maggie squeezed him tight and whispered back.

"Billy, I love you." He looked at her and smiled. Maggie smiled back and he gave her a soft kiss.

CHAPTER 13

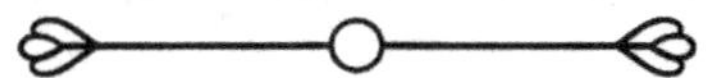

Side by side, pushing the grocery cart together, Maggie and Billy shopped for their last week aboard the Emerald Pearl.

"Oh, I'm really going to miss this," Maggie said, resting her head against his arm. Billy wrapped his arm around her, pushing the cart with the other hand. Squeezing her tight, he replied,

"So am I, Babe. I'm so glad you've enjoyed it though." They didn't get too much, just a few staples and some snacks and drinks. They took a short cab ride back to the marina, packed up and headed out for lunch.

"Only about an hour from Ocho Rios, Mag." Maggie stood beside Billy at the helm, her arm around his shoulder, looking out at the forever blue Caribbean. The sun was bright and high, hardly a cloud to be seen, the water crystal clear. Maggie kissed Billy's cheek, then sat in her chair next to his.

As they drifted into port, Maggie was reminded of Montego.

"This is a busy place," she said, dropping the sail.

"It is another popular vacation spot," Billy replied, slowly coming up to the dock. Maggie hopped out onto the dock with the rope and tied the Emerald securely. Then she jumped back in and joined Billy up top to finish with the sails.

"Hot today," Billy said, securing the rigging. Maggie thought she noticed him stagger slightly.

"You alright?" she asked, looking at him with concern.

"Sure thing Babe, just feeling the heat. Think we should have a lazy beach day," he suggested, smiling at her. Maggie watched him for a moment, trying to read him before answering.

"Billy, are you sure you're alright?" she asked again. Billy nodded and smiled, but she thought he looked a little off and knew he was hiding something.

"All good," he told her.

"Want me to go do the paperwork, Lover?" Maggie asked, running her hand down his arm.

"Oh, no, that's okay, thanks Beautiful. I need to arrange maintenance and pay to fill'er up too." He leaned down and kissed her. She kept looking at him and Billy chuckled. "Mag, I promise, I'm fine," he said and kissed her again. After he finished with registration, and paid for three nights, they put on their swimsuits, packed up a few things and headed for the beach. The beach was one of Maggie's favourites so far. All the others, a very close second. It was the usual white sands, turquoise water, heavenly beauty, but there were huge, lush trees scattered along the beach here, making it feel like home and heaven mixed together. They found a somewhat quiet patch of sand and laid down the blanket, put down their things and sat together ready to veg the day away. Maggie pulled her coral dress off, folded it and placed it next to her. Then she laid down on her back and soaked up the sun.

"Well, one thing I will miss immensely is seeing you lying in the sand in that bikini," Billy said, leaning over and kissing her stomach. Maggie giggled and looked up at him, lifting her sunglasses and grinning.

"Well, I'll just have to wear it at home once in a while for old times then won't I, Lover of mine?" she told him.

"Deal," he said, laying down next to her. They spent the day lounging and swimming. Wrapped up together in the water, kissing and carrying on. Laughing and swimming some more, then lounging in the sun again. The beach had filled up significantly by the time they decided to pack up and go back to the boat. On the way, they found a boardwalk, and decided to explore it. Enjoying the scenery and views across the marshlands as they walked along for half an hour before turning back. Once they were back at the beach, they went for a long cuddly swim, Maggie's legs wrapped around Billy, water up to their shoulders. Both caressing and holding each other, talking, and kissing, they gazed lovingly, and touched each other affectionately. Bodies gently bobbing in the water. The beauty of the scenery was beyond words. Creamy white beach stretched as far as you could see. Bright blue and turquoise water, becoming one with bright blue and white sky. White foamy waves washing up onto the beach, and lush green, rolling hills up into mountains. They took one another's hand, emerging from the water and drying off, then walked further along the beach. Eventually putting their clothes back on, and deciding to clean up and go for a bite to eat.

"Perfect lazy day, beautiful wife," Billy told her as they climbed back onto the boat.

"Always perfect with you, gorgeous husband," she replied.

They took turns having showers, then put on some dry clean clothes to go for dinner. The restaurant they went to was super clean and spacious. The walls, chairs and decor were all in green and yellow. There was a huge mural on one of the walls with a man doing the "To di World" pose, known around the world as the Lightning Pose. There were different sized records and collector type paraphernalia tacked up on the other walls. It felt like an oldies style diner mixed with a sports bar. Maggie and Billy both ordered a Bob Marley cocktail. Billy started with Red Stripe chicken wings, and Maggie had the red pea soup. The jerk pork dish was highly recommended, and they were not disappointed as they licked their fingers clean. Full but wanting to indulge, they shared a sweet tomato pudding for dessert with coffee, before leaving.

Hand in hand they walked the beach, enjoying the glorious sunset and the laid-back feeling that made Jamaica one of Billy's, and now one of Maggie's favourite places to be.

Back on the boat, ready for bed, they curled up together listening to the radio. Both softly singing, holding each other close, they fell asleep.

* * * *

"Good morning, Beautiful," Billy said, kissing Maggie's lips softly.

"Mmm. Good morning, Handsome," Maggie replied, opening her eyes and smiling up at him.

"I booked us for the whole day tomorrow with the Eco Tours, Mag," he told her.

"Excellent, can't wait." And she reached up and wrapped her arms around him. "You coming back to bed, Lover?" she asked hopefully.

"Well, I don't know. Why would I want to do a thing like that?" he asked teasingly. Maggie let go, rolled over, pulled the sheet up to her neck and closed her eyes. Billy stood there for a moment, then started laughing, climbing into bed under the covers, moving up behind her and wrapping his arms around her.

"Sleeping!" Maggie told him, trying her hardest not to laugh. Billy's hands sliding over her, one slipping under her tank top, the other moving down between her legs. His face nuzzling into her hair.

"Mmm. I love your smell," he breathed heavily and moved his body tightly against hers. Squeezing her breasts and sliding his fingers between her legs, trailing them back and forth over her underwear. Maggie lasted about three seconds before reaching up, moving her hair and turning her face to kiss him. He kissed her lips softly. Then Billy kissed her neck, sucking gently, breathing heavily. "I could eat you up!" he growled. His hand was now sliding down the front, inside of her underwear. Rubbing her softly, with gentle pressure, and sucking her neck. Maggie slid her hand down behind her and pulled her underwear down. Billy's hand moved from between her legs to help pull them down to her ankles. She heard his zipper come down and felt him wriggle out of his shorts. Then he was pressed tightly against her again with his very ready package pushing between her legs. With one arm under Maggie's upper body, holding her chest softly, he reached down with the other to move her legs apart. Then he slowly slid himself between her legs, sliding that hand down to hold her hip. Maggie held his arms as he pushed himself inside. His face was down at her neck again, kissing her as he slid in and out, only penetrating halfway.

"Ohhh," Maggie moaned happily, holding his arms snug to her body. She bent her legs slightly, so did Billy, their bodies spooned snugly, and as she became wetter, he slid all the way in.

"Maggie, you're beautiful," he whispered. She reached her arm up and ran her hand up his neck. Still holding her hip with one hand, he grabbed her breast with the other and started squeezing with the same steady rhythm of his glides. Pinching softly and squeezing again. Softly running his palm over her nipple. Maggie traced her fingers into his hair and over his skin, moving her body with pleasure and moaning her enjoyment.

"You feel amazing," Maggie groaned. Billy's tempo speeding up. "Ohh, God I love your body," she said with a deep purr, her hand sliding down and holding his ass and squeezing firmly. Billy made shorter, harder movements now, pulling her hip tight to his body.

"Damn Mag. You're too effing hot," he told her, sliding his tongue over her neck. "I'm not going to last." His face pressed against her neck, his hot breath making her skin tingle. Maggie was so turned on.

"You feel so good," she whispered. He licked and sucked, massaging her breast, pulling and twisting her nipple gently. "Ohhh," Maggie moaned. "I'm so close, Billy," she told him, and his body kept pumping steadily into hers.

"Maggie!" he yelled, his hips hitting her body hard. His release, strong and powerful, adding to her arousal. He sucked her neck and Maggie continued to move her body into his. Her legs shaking, her head tilted back as he pinched and pulled and squeezed.

"Ahhh," she moaned softly, her body releasing with a quiver. Billy's arms wrapped around her tightly again and she held him close. He kissed her neck softly, then rested his cheek against her skin. "Mmm, yummy," she said, and he hugged her tighter.

"Delicious," he replied.

"So, is it another stay in bed kinda day?" she asked him.

"If that means naked on the boat with you all day, then most definitely, yes." They both laughed and snuggled up.

* * * *

"I have to get up, Lover," Maggie whispered after they had held each other for some time.

"Noo. Don't go!" Billy said and hugged her tightly, kissing her neck.

"I promise I'll come...back," she said, sitting up and grinning at him. He gave a little growl and grinned back.

"Mmm, gorgeous goddess of mine!" his voice velvety, and his stare, just the same.

"Jelly legs!" Maggie said smiling, her face looking down slightly and her emerald, green eyes twinkling up at him desirously. She grabbed her housecoat and left, stopping at the door and looking back with her big Maggie smile.

"Don't make me wait too long, Beautiful." Maggie laughed to herself warmly. *God, I love that man.* She thought, *fully and unconditionally. And with excellent benefits too.* She smiled to herself again. After freshening up in the washroom, Maggie went back to the bedroom.

"Think you can handle joining me for a coffee, Lover of mine?" Maggie asked, crawling across the bed towards Billy. His eyes crinkling with sheer mischief and enjoyment in her enticing, seductive play. Her robe fell open as she made her way up to straddle him, wrapping her arms around his neck and kissing him deeply. Billy's hands rubbing her back, then up into her hair, cradling her neck and head.

"Mm!" Maggie, wanting to attach herself to him, but she pried herself away from Billy and smiled.

"Coffee?" He grabbed her fast and pulled her in for another deep kiss.

"Mmm," she moaned, then he moved and smiled at her.

"Okay Babe, coffee."

They spent the whole day, naked in bed, getting up for drinks and the odd snack. Mostly playing with one another's bodies, taking turns pleasing each other. Massages, foot rubs and lots of yummy foreplay, followed by oral satisfaction. They let the radio play in the other room, Maggie growing quite fond of the Reggae beats in the background. By nightfall, they had made a light dinner, and sat in the steadily brightening moonlight, snuggled up together. Thinking their naked fun was over for the day, but when they made their way back inside and got ready for bed, they found they still had one more romp left in them and finished their evening breathing heavy, sweaty and wrapped together ready to sleep.

* * * *

Billy and Maggie arrived at the meet up location, outside a shopping center about 15 minutes from Montego airport, around 8:30 am. There were a handful of other guests that arrived around the same time. After a beautiful scenic drive along the Northern Coast, the bus drove them through the rainforest, through the hills of St. Ann Parish and back into Ocho Rios. They were taken to the famous Mystic Mountain Adventure Park where they spent 45 minutes. Maggie and Billy made their way straight for the Jamaican Bobsled Rollercoaster. The five minute ride started off fast, then slowed and leveled out twisting and turning its way through the lush mountain scenery. After that, they boarded the bus again and stopped at a local farm where they had a guided tour informing them on how the community gardens started and how they continued to run today. After a break they headed back to the bus, and they were driven to the Blue Hole Waterfalls. Hiking through dense beautiful jungle then stopping, the travellers soon came upon the breath-taking Secret Falls, famous for its twelve waterfalls, one leading into another and nestled within the lush greenery of the island. They were able to swim, jump off the falls, swing and climb through hidden tunnels behind one of the bigger falls. It was like something from a movie. A hidden magical water paradise. They perused the many hidden wonders. Billy couldn't resist swinging from a rope and dropping into the fresh waterfall magic of Jamaica. Making their way up, Maggie and Billy climbed to the top falls and sat on the flat rocks together looking down at their progress in awe.

"Mag, this place is unbelievable," Billy said, smiling as he looked around at its wonder.

"I feel like I'm in a dream, Babe!" Maggie replied, grinning from ear to ear.

"Shit, we've seen some magical things, haven't we, Beautiful!" Billy said, shaking his head in disbelief. Maggie leaned over and Billy looked back at her. His hand held her face as they kissed, then they rubbed noses, smiling and looking into each other's eyes. They had paid for a tour photographer to take pictures of their day out and Maggie was thinking about how glad she was to be able to see this adventure again, once they were back home. It was one of the most beautiful once in a lifetime experiences she'd had and she wanted to capture it forever. Two hours later, they were back on the bus heading for the Hidden Beauty, a Rastafarian house run by a friendly older man and his family. After a late lunch the group enjoyed a walk on the property, saw gardens and beautiful swimming holes along the way. Then they hopped back onto the bus and after an hour and a half found themselves back at the shopping plaza. Maggie and Billy thanked their tour guide, and Billy gave him a nice tip before leaving. They said goodbye to the other guests and got themselves a cab.

"That was yet another amazing day, Lover," Maggie said as they neared Ocho Rios Port.

"It really was, Babe!" Billy agreed, pulling Maggie closer. It was dark when they were dropped off, and they were happily tired from their day long adventure. They brushed their teeth together, then climbed into bed and chatted a bit about their favourite parts from the day, which were many.

"I'd love to go back to Hidden Beauty," Maggie said as they snuggled cozily.

"We'll just have to plan to come back then, Babe," Billy promised, kissing Maggie's forehead and squeezing her tight.

* * * *

Finishing up their breakfast dishes, Maggie and Billy decided to go for a swim before sailing out towards the Robinson's just east of Runaway Bay. Then they went back to eat at Jada and Thomas's restaurant, having a nice visit over lunch.

"Yuh be sure tuh give our luv tuh Alvi an Deli for us Billay an Maggay," Jada told them, giving each other hugs before Maggie and Billy left hand in hand.

Back aboard the Emerald Pearl, Maggie and Billy got things ready, hoisting the sails and heading back into the blue waters of the Caribbean.

"What time do you think we'll get back to the Robinson's, Billy?" Maggie asked him as they sat in their spots at the helm. Billy looked down at the wind gauge.

"We're moving against the wind, so we should be there in a couple hours I'd say, Mag." And he looked back up and smiled at her.

Heading south towards the silver sand shores of St. Ann near 4:00 pm, Maggie stood next to Billy with her arm over his shoulder as he turned the engine off and moved them towards the familiar dock at the end of the Robinson's property.

"Hey Babe, can you lower the jib for us?" he asked as he brought them towards the dock with expert precision. Maggie brought it down, then waited in case he needed anything else. As they drew closer, Maggie climbed down to the main deck, ready to hop out and tie the Emerald securely. Billy lowered the mainsail as Maggie climbed back up to meet him, joining in on covering it and clipping everything into place. "Thanks, Babe," he said, following her back down to the main deck. She turned and hugged him tightly. Billy wrapped his arms around her and smiled at her. "Alright, Beautiful?" he asked, kissing her, and looking back into her eyes.

"Always." Maggie smiled at him, kissing him back.

"Ok Mag, let's go," he added, and they made their way up the dock and beach, towards the Rockhouse.

"I can't believe we left this spot almost a month ago!" Maggie said, walking hand in hand with Billy.

"Bittersweet eh, Babe!" Billy said, looking at her with a smile.

"Very." They could see Delroy out on the porch as they walked. He was waving and grinning as they approached.

"Hey Alvi, Billay an Maggay, our sweet 'oneymoonas are back luv!" they heard him hollering. They laughed as they made their way up the porch steps. Billy and Del grabbed hands, pulled each other in and hugged hard. "Wuh Gwaan, Billay?" Delroy asked.

"All gud my brutha," Billy replied. They clapped one another on their backs, both smiling broadly. Then Delroy came over to Maggie and pulled her in for a big hug. "Empress Maggay!" he exclaimed, squeezing her tight. "Yuh be more beautiful den eva!" he added, looking at her with a big grin. Just then Alvita came out.

"Uhh, yuh back!" She grabbed Billy and hugged him. Billy chuckled happily.

"Hiya Alvi," he said, hugging her.

"Our Billay an his Maggay," she chimed, walking towards Maggie now. Maggie and Alvita held their arms out and pulled each other in for a big hug. "Gorgeous gyal, how yuh doing?" she asked Maggie, beaming at her. "Yuh stunning gyal!" she told Maggie.

"I'm great Alvita, how are you?" Alvita, still with one arm around Maggie, walked them into the bar. Billy and Del close behind them.

"Oh, we di same as always. Everyting criss gyal, everyting criss!" she answered.

"Drinks?" Del asked as the four came inside.

"Water please, Delroy," Maggie answered.

"Billay?" he asked.

"Same, thanks Del." Delroy and Alvita looked at one another.

"Yuh two, okay?" Del asked. Billy and Maggie laughed.

"We're great!" Billy answered as he and Maggie sat at the bar.

"So, tell us all about yuh trip!" Alvita said, standing next to Delroy behind the bar. The four chatted for half an hour, barely scratching the surface of their adventures before opening up for the night and tending to their customers. Billy and Maggie hung out for the night, helping and visiting, heading back to the boat around 2:00 am. It had started to rain earlier on in the evening and hadn't let up yet. Maggie listened happily to the sound of the raindrops on the dock outside the boat, glad the weather had provided a month of sunshine. Again, happily tired, they snuggled under the blanket for the night, the rhythm of the rain pulling them into dreamland.

* * * *

Maggie and Billy spent the next day with Alvita and Delroy. They had a big lunch together out on the front porch and the two filled Alvita and Delroy in on all the places they'd visited. The four laughed and chatted for hours, enjoying each other's company over good food and good rum.

"Oh, almost forgot, Alvi." Billy said nearing the end of their adventure stories. "We ran into Jada and Thomas." Alvita sat up and clapped her hands.

"No yuh neva!" she said with a serious look, slapping Billy's arm.

"Yes, they send their love," Maggie added, grinning.

"We ate at their restaurant a couple of times, Alvi. Lovely, friendliest couple!" Billy said and Alvita gave him a look. Billy's eyes crinkled cheekily. "Not as lovely as you and Deli of course!" he said laughing. Delroy pushed playfully against Billy.

"Eh mon, no buddy call me dat except Jada an Tommy," he said grinning. Billy laughed. Again, Maggie and Billy stayed late, dancing and visiting with the Rockhouse regulars. They climbed aboard the Emerald close to 1:00 am, and when Maggie sat down on the couch, Billy stopped in front of her and grinned.

"Feel like a late-night adventure, Beautiful?" he asked, his eyes twinkling at her.

"Well, I'm definitely intrigued, Lover!" was her response.

"K, give me a few minutes, Babe." Maggie sat smiling for a moment, then decided to use the washroom and freshen up for whatever Billy might have planned. She sat down on the couch again and waited a few more minutes. "Okay Mag, let's go." he said, carrying a big blanket and stopping to grab a couple bottles of water.

"What are you up to?" Maggie asked him with a grin.

"Can you grab that other blanket, Babe?" he asked, nodding at the quilt on the back of the couch. Maggie grabbed it and followed him to the upper deck. He passed her the waters, then locked up. They climbed out onto the dock, and Billy took Maggie's hand and led her up towards his old shack, stopping on the beach and laying the big blanket down on the sand. He kicked his sandals off and stepped onto the blanket, then patted the spot beside him. "Come join me, Beautiful," he said with a smile. Maggie slid her sandals off and joined him, placing the other blanket and the water bottles down on the corner, smiling at him affectionately and sitting down next to him. The moon was full and bright, and its light glistened like diamonds over the water. It was absolutely beautiful and so romantic sitting there in the sand, in the dark under the glow of the moon. The trees in the distance were just dark shadowy shapes, casting shadows around them on the blanket and the sand. Maggie looked out at the sparkling diamond water, loving the smell of the Caribbean, and feeling the soft breeze on her skin. Watching and listening to the waves rolling up onto the sand. "Marvelous night for a moon dance, don't you think, Mag?" Billy said to her with a wink. Maggie looked back at him, and he was looking at her with such love. Reaching up and sliding his hand over her cheek, into her hair, then holding her face softly, he leaned in for a kiss. Maggie reached her hand up and held his. Billy kissed her softly, moving his body beside Maggie's and facing her, his legs crossed. Holding her face, kissing more purposefully, his hands sliding into her hair, then over her cheeks again tenderly.

"Mmm," Maggie made loving, enjoyable noises as he kissed her. Her hands were soon in his hair, holding his face too. The sound of the waves stirring an inner ebb and flow within her. Billy moved, and pulled Maggie's legs over his, moving his body closer to hers. Then he held her face again and looked into her eyes deeply.

"Absolutely beautiful," he told her, leaning in to kiss her softly. Maggie held his face again and they pulled each other in deeply, their movements like the waves moving back and forth on the sand. He held her face and looked at her again. His eyes crinkled into a grin. "My beautiful wife," he said softly. Maggie smiled at him, and he kissed her mouth so gently, cradling her head, he kissed her chin, then her neck, looking back up at her and smiling again, he kissed her mouth again. They pulled one another in tight, holding and squeezing as they kissed more deeply still. Maggie shivered as Billy's hands slid up her arms and neck, then down her arms again. Her fingers found their way to his shirt buttons and started to undo them, then she slid under his shirt and softly ran her hands over his chest and shoulders, slipping his shirt off. Billy's hands were pulling Maggie's dress up now and they stopped kissing for a moment while he pulled it over her head. Maggie slid her hands up to his neck, her fingers trailing along his skin, into his hair, pulling him tight. Billy's hands slid behind her and undid her bra, pulling her straps down and letting it drop to the blanket. Their half-naked bodies shivering in the breeze dancing off the water, their warm hands running over one another. Billy stood up and reached down to help Maggie stand. He looked into her eyes as he undid his shorts, dropping them and his boxers at his feet. Then he pulled her underwear down and she felt them land at her feet too. They pulled one another close, hugging and caressing as they began to kiss again. Billy slid his tongue in and out, slowly, kissing Maggie passionately. Then he held her face again and looked at her. Sliding his hands down her neck and shoulders, then back up to hold her face. Maggie slid hers up his back, over his shoulders and up his neck.

"I love you, Billy," Maggie told him, and he pulled her close again.

"I love you, Mag," he replied, as he leaned in to kiss her again. Their breathing becoming heavier, tongues sliding more frequently, Billy pulled them down, sitting first and then pulled Maggie on top of his lap. Holding each other in a tight, caressing embrace, they started kissing pressingly. Billy held her head and kissed her neck, his fingers tickling into her hair, Maggie's doing the same in his. Then his hands ran down her back and under her bottom, lifting her up and sliding her right on top of his hard awaiting dick.

"Ahhh!" they both gasped as her body slid down to his lap. Maggie moved her body towards his and over his lap, back and forth, as Billy held her lower back pulling her into his body tight, the other hand sliding up into her hair at the back of her head, squeezing into her curls. Kissing deeply as she moved her hips back and forth, their bodies moving with the rhythm of the waves. Then Billy's face and hands were down, sucking her skin, grabbing her breasts and Maggie began lifting her body up and down, riding him slowly.

"Mmmm," he moaned as he licked and sucked. Maggie pushed him back, and as Billy laid down flat, Maggie began rising and falling faster. Her hands were behind her on his legs as she rode him. "Gaawd, Maggie," he groaned, his hands holding her hips and helping her lift and fall. Watching one another in the shadowed moonlight, Maggie leaned forward, taking Billy's hands in hers, interlocking fingers as she laid his hands down either side of his head, holding them down, and moving back and forth into his body quickly. She was grinding side to side and back and forth now. Her head falling back, she looked up at the moon as she slid him in and out of her body with delightful enjoyment. Moving faster and harder, grinding sensually, her body leaning forward to kiss him, still holding his hands. Pushing herself in tightly and taking him in deeply. Then she let go of his hands, her pleasure-consumed body taking over completely, the moonlight pulling her out of herself, totally unencumbered. Her hands running up and over her own body, trailing over her stomach, her breasts, up her neck and into her hair and reaching up to the sky as she lifted up and down, hard and fast, Billy's hands back to helping her ride him. "Damn Mag. Oh Gawd!" he was yelling with the impact of her body into his.

"Ohhh Gaawd Billlllly..." she moaned, slow and long, back to grinding, her hands holding her hair up, looking into his eyes with animal-like hunger and radiant intensity. "I'm cumming," she breathed, looking right at Billy. She felt him shudder. "Oh Billy, I'm cumming," she breathed again, and his hips were pushing into her hard. "Cum with me," she moaned, her head falling back slightly, grinding in deep slow circles.

"Maag," his voice a moaning, growl, consumed with raw pleasure.

"I want to feel you cum, Billy," she told him, her eyes dark and sparkling in the moonlight. He lifted her up and down, short hard lifts.

"Oh, ohhh Maggie." And he was exploding. Maggie smiled watching him as he came. His eyes closed and his body moving and working hard as it released into hers, abundantly. He sat right up and embraced her tightly, Maggie still sitting on his lap, wrapping her arms around him as he kissed her with fierce hunger. "Mmmm. Damn, Mag!" he said between deep kisses and lashing tongues. Holding each other tight, skin pressed together, Billy looked up at the moon and gave a husky howl.

"Oowuuuu!"

Maggie grinned and held his face in her hands, then raised her face and howled too. Billy smiled at her, and both grinning, eyes twinkling at one another, they howled together before they were locked in a deep kiss again.

Wrapped under the small blanket, Maggie's head against Billy's chest, embraced in his arms, they lay on the beach still listening to the waves rolling over the shore and looking up at the full blue moon. Softly trailing their fingers over one another, contentedly peaceful on their blanket in the sand as they watched clouds float past the moon.

"I think we should howl at the moon every month, gorgeous lover," Maggie said, hugging Billy. Billy chuckled.

"Sounds like a great plan to me, Babe," he answered, hugging.. Maggie turned over to face him, moving her body up so she could kiss him. She reached up and held his face, softly caressing his cheek, looking at him with love. Then she leaned in and kissed him again. Pressing long and firmly. Billy held her face, kissing her back deeply. Then she snuggled back down in his arms and hugged him tight.

CHAPTER 14

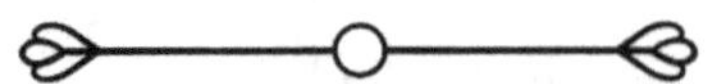

Maggie snuggled closely to Billy, smiling softly, her eyes still closed. The beginning light of a new day softly touched her eyelids. *Oh, that sounds so glorious,* she thought to herself, listening to the waves. She felt the breeze on her skin and then she heard birds chirping and opened her eyes, realizing they'd fallen asleep on the beach.

"Billy!" she said, moving his body.

"Mmm. What is it, Mag?" he asked sleepily. Then his eyes popped open, and he looked up at her. "Oh shit!" he said, and Maggie started laughing. He looked down at her and started laughing too.

"Oops!" Maggie said, with a giggle. He grabbed her face and kissed her, still grinning. They took turns holding the blanket up for one another as they got dressed, then gathered up the blankets and water and headed back to the boat.

"Hey, what are yuh two doing up so early?" came Delroy's voice as he came down the long staircase and headed for the Rockhouse. Maggie and Billy laughed again.

"Oh, just enjoying the birds," Billy said with a grin.

"Ok, den yuh two. Lata." Delroy yelled back as he headed up the porch steps. They looked at each other and laughed and walked back to the boat.

"Wow, am I ever stiff!" Maggie said as they made their way into the bedroom.

"Ya, me too Babe," Billy told her, stretching.

"Wanna do some yoga with me, Lover?" she asked him with a coy smile.

"Hmm, well ya, might not be a bad idea, Mag." Maggie was pleasantly surprised and once Billy found a padded blanket to use, they went up to the dock together. Maggie led them through a gentle yoga practice. As they lay in savasana, she smiled listening to Billy's deep inhalation and exhales. "Thanks Mag. That felt great," he told her, rolling over onto his side to face her.

"No problem, so glad you enjoyed it." He pushed himself up to sit and Maggie joined him.

"How bout some massage?" he said smiling at her. Maggie grinned at him.

"Like what kind?" she asked, and Billy's head fell back with a chuckle.

"Like turn around, Mag," he replied, grinning at her. She turned, sitting in front of him, looking out at the water and she instantly melted. His big warm strong hands started rubbing her shoulders and her back.

"Mmmm, that's nice, Babe," she purred as he softened her up. He finished off after about fifteen minutes, then Maggie returned the favour. Both of them felt like melted butter, making their way back on the Emerald. They each had a shower, then made something to eat. After lunch clean up, they headed up to see Alvita and Delroy. They were busily getting the bar ready for that evening and Maggie and Billy joined in.

"Say Maggay, can yuh help me with sum prep in da back, our gyal running late today?" Maggie followed Alvita to the kitchen.

"Of course," she told her. It was close to 3:00 when Alvita got Maggie busy at work, cutting lemons and limes, emptying, and filling the dishwasher and then giving the front tables and the bar a good wipe down. "Hey Del, where's Billy?" Maggie asked, once she had finished helping Alvita.

"Empress, him say tuh get yuh to meet'em on the boat." Delroy held up one of Maggie's dresses. She took it with a confused look. Alvita came out of the back.

"Yuh go change upstairs gyal," she grinned at Maggie. Maggie went up and changed and when she came back down Alvita thanked her for the help and they sent her on her way. "Yuh 'ave a good night gorgeous gyal!" Alvita called out as Maggie left the bar. The sun was starting to set and the sky darkened. Again, the moonlight was quite bright, lighting her way as she walked down the beach towards the boat. She could hear music playing as she stepped onto the dock. "6345789" was playing. Maggie smiled nostalgically, her thoughts drifting way back to loving glimpses of her parents dancing together in the kitchen when everyone had gone to bed. There was always music in her home growing up. She smiled reminiscently, as Billy came up from the lower cabin.

"Hello, Beautiful," he said with a grin.

"Hello, Gorgeous. What's going on?" she asked, looking at the upper deck table, lit up with a lantern in the center, dishes and glasses set, along with their last little bottle of champagne. There were fairy lights hanging above, and the CD player was sitting on the bench seat.

"Come aboard, my Love," Billy said, walking towards her and holding out his hands. Maggie took them and hopped down.

"You look really beautiful, Mag," he told her, giving her a kiss. Billy was in his khaki shorts and his white linen button T-shirt.

"Thanks, Handsome," She replied, her smile growing.

"Have a seat," he told her, untying the boat. Then he went up to the helm. Maggie hadn't realized the engine was on, until they started moving. Billy only drove about 100 feet out, shut the engine off, then dropped the anchor and joined her again. Maggie was sitting smiling at him, the lantern light twinkling in her eyes.

"Be right back, Beautiful," he said, going below deck. "My Girl" was playing and Maggie grinned, feeling quite happy at his choice of music. Oldies music was a deep threaded part of Maggie's tapestry, and she could hardly wait for him to come back so she could kiss him, hoping to be able to express her love more deeply with her lips, and her soul, rather than with words. She sat waiting and singing along. As Billy came back up, carrying dishes, "Georgia" was playing. Maggie was swaying gently, smiling at him as he sat the dishes down. She stood up and walked over to him, wrapping her arms around his shoulders, and pulling him down for a kiss. They grinned at one another, then Billy placed his hand on her lower back, softly guiding her back to the table.

"Have a seat, my Love," he said, and they sat down together. Billy lifted the lid of the casserole dish filled with rice and curry chicken.

"Mmm, smells delicious," she said as he dished out small servings for both of them. Maggie still singing along with the music. "You've Really Got A Hold On Me" making her rock in her seat. Billy opened the champagne and poured them each a glass.

"To my beautiful, beach babe lover," he said, raising his glass to hers.

"To my gorgeous, sweet cheeked man!" Maggie added and they clinked their glasses. They ate, and Billy stared and grinned at Maggie, their feet rubbing together as usual. Maggie grinned back, feeling her cheeks flush at the way he was looking at her. They finished their dinner and drank their champagne, making eyes at each other, holding and rubbing each other's hands, all through "What I Say," Maggie itching to dance. Then "You're The First, The Last, My Everything" made them both want to sing and dance. They smiled broadly at one another. Billy stood up and walked around the table in front of Maggie, just as "Ain't No Sunshine" started playing. He held out his hand, Maggie took it and he pulled her up into his arms, singing to her from his deep soulful heart. She wrapped her arms around his neck and rested her head on his chest. Billy's hands at the bottom of her back, swaying as he sang. Maggie closed her eyes, smiling, inhaling him deeply and softly running her hands up and down his neck, feeling nearly thirty years of love engulfing them. They danced to "Beautiful Brown Eyes," Billy singing "Beautiful green eyes" to her, then "He'll Have To Go," moving them in closer. Their bodies pressed tight, moving slower and deeper. Billy's hands moved lower, holding her firmly. Maggie looked up into his eyes and he kissed her as he danced her around the boat. Billy's deep voice singing in her ear. Then "Goodbye Baby, Baby Goodbye" started playing and Maggie was melting deeper into his embrace. He held her face again, and kissed her lips slowly, his fingers in her hair, still moving their bodies to the music. Maggie rested her head on his chest again. They were swaying in slow wave-like motion, looking into each other's eyes again, Billy kept singing to her as they danced, eyes locked. As he hit the deeper notes at the end of the song, her legs turned to jelly. His hands sliding over her face into her hair, kissing her and swaying them back and forth, hitting more low notes, and smiling as Maggie's body quivered in his arms. Their insatiable desire accelerated as "Bring It On Home" began. They were undressing each other, Maggie singing with him, their movements becoming a grinding seductive caressing dance as their clothes came off and fell to the floor. Softly sliding their hands over each other, kissing and dancing. Billy lifted her up and Maggie wrapped her body around him tight. Kissing deep, pressing into each other hard. Hands in one another's hair, rubbing and squeezing. Billy sat down on one of the bench seats, Maggie sitting on top of him. Still deeply kissing to "Nothing Can Change This Love." Stopping and holding one another's faces, staring with fire in their eyes, back to attacking each other breathlessly, Billy lifted her and Maggie sat down, taking him into her loving body. Their moans and groans mixing in with the music. "You Send Me" in the background as Maggie moved him in and out. Their kisses more ravenous, tongues circling, hands pulling and grabbing, Maggie sliding back and forth over Billy's lap. She stopped, kissing him hard again, holding his face, then climbing off of Billy, she walked backwards towards the table. She moved the food down to the seats,

Billy quickly helped her clear the table, then she hopped up and pulled him in towards her. Wrapping her legs around him as she perched on the edge of the table. "Lovable" started to play as he pushed himself back inside her. Mouths locked, Maggie squeezing and massaging his sweet cheeks, pulling him into her, Billy's hands in her hair, kissing her so passionately. Their pulses racing, hearts thumping, Billy sliding faster. They were back to staring at one another as he pumped in and out of her, Maggie squeezing him tight, then placing her hands on the table behind her, as Billy held her hips and kept his tempo. "I've Been Loving You Too Long" played as they reached climax together. Maggie's head fell back, Billy holding her tight as she shook, and the song, close to ending, as Billy's body shuddered. Maggie hugged him close, Billy still pushing deeply, as he came with her. Their moans mingled with the singer's voice. Falling into each other's arms as "Cry To Me" started. They smiled at each other, from the sheer pleasure they had just experienced, and from the memories of the last time they danced to this song. Billy pulled Maggie up and danced with her. Holding on to one another snugly, swaying and kissing softly. Swinging her body around easily, Maggie letting Billy guide her, and dancing her body into his. As the song ended, Billy took Maggie's hand, and they went into the cabin. They grabbed their robes and pulled them on, laying down on the bed holding one another tight.

"Great playlist, Lover." Maggie whispered, as Billy snuggled her closer.

* * * *

They spent the following day walking and lounging on the beach together. Soaking in their last moments in Jamaica. They grabbed wraps and ate them on the beach, sitting at the edge of the water, waves washing up over their legs. Then they walked back to the boat and got changed and went up to spend the rest of the day at the Rockhouse.

Their 4th night with the Robinsons was filled with laughter and music. Alvita and Maggie chatted more about all the places Maggie and Billy went to and all the things they did. Alvita smiled the whole time, happily listening as Maggie beamed, talking about Billy. Billy and Delroy hung out at the bar, laughing together. Mostly reminiscing about old times.

They had plans for Billy to sing and word spread quickly that he was back at the bar for one night. Maggie helped Alvita set up, clear, and set tables, get the stage ready and any other little things that needed doing. Billy and Delroy got the sound system ready and set it up for later. The four had a quick bite to eat together, before opening the bar. People piled in, and soon there was a good size crowd filling the Rockhouse, drinking, eating, and playing pool. Several people were visiting with Billy, meeting Maggie, and catching up on their honeymoon adventures. Somewhere close to 9:00, Delroy went up to the stage and spoke into the mic,

"Okay my friends, come an grab yuh drinks before our Billay be singing, in fifteen minutes." Then he headed back up to the bar where he and Alvita busily prepared orders for everyone. Billy took his guitar up front and grabbed a couple stools. Then he found Maggie and pulled her in for a big hug and kiss.

"You gonna sing with me tonight, Beautiful?" he asked, his eyes looking pleadingly into hers. She grinned at his attempt to coax her.

"Well, maybe one or two songs. But only because you're so delicious." He chuckled and gave her a big kiss before heading back to the stage. She found a spot to stand, already in dreamland watching him sitting with his guitar on his lap. Billy started with a number of house favourites, most of which were Reggae songs, then he sang some oldies and some rock. He took a break after about thirty minutes and sat at the bar with Maggie. She leaned close and whispered in his ear. "You look so sexy tonight!" She kissed his cheek before moving back and looking into his eyes. He grabbed her face and quickly pulled her close, pressing his lips firmly against hers. Then rubbing his nose against hers he smiled at her.

"Love you, Beautiful," he told her with a wink. Finishing his drink, he hopped off the bar stool and went back up to do his second half. Again, lots of Reggae mixed in with some of his favourites. Maggie was sitting with Alvita at the bar when she noticed Delroy and Alvita look at one another with what she could only assume was shock or concern on their faces.

"I be right back gyal." Alvita said, getting up and walking over to Delroy. The two whispered together and looked out at the crowd. Maggie looked out towards where their gaze was but wasn't really sure what they were looking at. Alvita came back over to Maggie.

"Something wrong, Alvita?" Maggie asked her as she stood next to her.

"Me hope not, Maggay!" she answered with a forced smile. "Come gyal, let us guh stand at de front." Maggie got up, Alvita linking arms with her, and they walked through the crowd to stand at the wall at the front of the group. Maggie noticed Alvita looking at the same spot in the crowd every once in a while. She looked towards the spot and noticed a woman she hadn't seen earlier standing in the crowd, close to the front and center. She was beautiful. Tall, dark, thin, and sultry. Long dreaded hair, hanging down to her round perky bottom. She looked to be in her thirties and carried herself almost regally. She was wearing a strapless, tight fitting floral top, tight jeans, and bright blue high heeled boots. Her eyes were locked on Billy, and Maggie had the strongest feeling of unease as she surveyed her.

"Alvita, who is that woman?" she asked, leaning close. Alvita hesitated, then pulled Maggie back to the bar.

"Maggay, gyal, 'ave our Billay eva tell yuh bout Taniyah?" Maggie's stomach knotted slightly.

"Um, not much, a man named Jo mentioned her when we ran into him in St. Elizabeth. Billy said they dated for a bit?" She didn't like the look on Alvita's face.

"Oh gyal. Maybe me nuh be de one telling yuh." Delroy leaned between them across the counter.

"Alvi, Luv, yuh'ave got tuh tell her." They stared at each other for a moment, then Alvita turned back to Maggie.

"Okay gyal. Taniyah use tuh work here for a couple years. She was massively in luv with our Billay, but him neva date anyone." She stopped and smiled at Del and he grinned at Maggie.

"An well, we all know why now don't we luv?" he said, patting Maggie's hand on the counter. Maggie grinned at him, then looked back at Alvita.

"Go on, Alvita," Maggie coaxed, looking out towards Billy, then Taniyah, then back at Alvita.

"Okay, so Billay, him lonely Maggay, an close tuh him leaving Jamaica, him finally give in. He and Taniyah dated for a month or so, before it ended badly." Maggie felt sicker by the second.

"So, what happened?" she asked urgently now.

"She wanted tuh marry him, gorgeous gyal. She was trying tuh ave'em babies." Maggie's stomach flipped. Delroy slid a drink across the bar at her.

"Drink up Maggay. No worries. Him neva wanted tuh marry her, even if dat mean him wud be alone, an so him broke tings off with Taniyah." Maggie took the shot glass, held it to her lips and downed it in one, surprising herself and the Robinsons.

"So, she get desperate an try tuh keep him. She tell him she was pregnant, but she neva was. Tings get kinda heated an him tell her he'd neva marry, especially after lying to him. She be angry an she leave before him move a couple weeks later. Our Billay smart an true though isn't him gyal, an him heart tell him he need to guh." Maggie smiled at Alvita.

"Yes and thank the high ones." Maggie replied as Alvita patted Maggie's arm warmly. Delroy spoke up,

"First we see him in two years when him come back here to marry yuh." Both Delroy and Alvita were smiling broadly at her.

"So, what's she doing here now?" Maggie asked, looking back out towards her.

"Guess she hear him back. Let us go back up to de front gyal." She and Alvita slid off the stools and headed back up towards the stage. Billy had just finished a song and was having a drink of water. He saw Maggie and smiled. She smiled back, then as he looked down at his guitar, she looked at Taniyah who had just looked away from Maggie and locked her eyes on Billy again. He started playing and Taniyah started moving closer to the front, dancing her body sensually. Alvita's voice suddenly whispered near Maggie's ear.

"Yuh watch her, Maggay." Maggie already knew that but nodded at Alvita. Billy looked up and saw Taniyah, his fingers faltered slightly as he played. But he kept going, and carried on with the intro. Then he looked back at Maggie and started singing, his eyes looking right into hers, clearly singing to her.

"Just Breathe" like liquid velvet, husky and deeply sexy, his voice pouring from his soul, he sang to her. The crowd almost held their breath as they watched the magic between them. Maggie walked up to the stage and sat on the stool next to him. Billy smiled adoringly as he turned to face her, his voice growing stronger and deeper. Maggie's hands over her heart, she softly sang harmony with him through some of the lines, and sweetly humming along. Their eyes deeply connected. Her body softly rocked back and forth, smiling back, lovingly. She knew his heart was hers. And she fell in love with him over and over, with each and every day they were blessed with waking up together. She sang the last lines with him, her heart bursting with love as they leaned towards one another and kissed. His hand reached up and held her cheek as they looked at one another and smiled. Everyone in the bar was cheering and clapping, and the lovebirds grinned at one another, before his fingers were making magic again. Billy sang "Wondering Why", again, looking at Maggie so soulfully, so lovingly and Maggie swayed next to him, watching and listening with ever-growing love. His eyes twinkling and crinkled, smiling at her, his salt and pepper hair softly moving over his jaw when he'd look down at his guitar. The expression on his face when he'd strum certain cords, his body shifting to hit the notes and the way his fingers moved with such strength and tender ability over the strings made Maggie's heart overflow. She leaned in and kissed his cheek as he finished the song.

"So sexy," she whispered in his ear. He grinned and winked at her, before he looked out at the room and spoke into the mic,

"Ok my friends, one more song." Of course, all the voices in the bar complained, Maggie watched with fondness as she saw his eyes twinkling with delight. "You singing the last one with me, Babe?" he asked looking back at Maggie. She grinned at him, waiting to hear what he had planned before deciding. She watched his fingers dancing over the strings, and felt the energy from his body, as he started strumming "Into The Mystic". She smiled and started rocking happily on her seat, singing along with him. Both smiling as their voices danced together effortlessly. She watched as couples danced together, others swayed on the spot, some people singing along with them, and feeling herself falling into the musical magic of Billy and his world. There were so many people packed into the bar now, they could hardly dance. She understood Billy's love for performing. The enjoyment was tangible from the people watching and listening happily. And the energy bouncing back and forth was beautiful. They finished the song, and everyone was yelling "Encore!" and clapping. Maggie smiled at Billy and shrugged. He winked at her and smiled back. Maggie went back into the crowd to watch Billy finish his set.

"Okay, *two* more," he told them all, and the crowd cheered. He played "Lime in the coconut" and of course, to finish off, he sang "Somethin' Bout A Boat", everyone roaring and hollering, all their voices joining with Billy's. The whole room dancing as one. Maggie stayed near the front, joining in the dance, swallowed up by the collective vibe. Alvita and Delroy were dancing next to Maggie, singing along with everyone. Then Billy finished and stood up. Of course, they all wanted him to keep singing, but he stepped off the stage and walked over to Maggie, Alvita and Delroy. The four made their way back to the bar, the stereo now going, playing a mix of Reggae. Then, as the four of them chatted, suddenly making her way through the crowd, walking with boldness, came Taniyah. She looked right at Billy as she approached them, smiling at him.

"Well, well, hail Billay." And she leaned in and kissed his mouth, her hands sliding from his shoulders down, off his chest.

"Taniyah," he said with an awkward greeting, pulling back. She kept her eyes only on Billy, moving towards him, her body pressed against his. From behind the bar, between Billy and Maggie, Alvita spoke up,

"What brings yuh back here, Taniyah?" she asked her with a sharp tone. Delroy looked mildly amused. Taniyah still staring at Billy intensely, took her time before looking up at Alvita, then with cool composure answered,

"Just in de area Alvita, hear a oldy was playing tonight." She looked back at Billy. Taniyah had her back turned to Maggie and Billy stretched out his hand to hold Maggie's. Taniyah stepped back slightly, acting like she hadn't noticed anyone was even there.

"This is Maggie," he said. "My wife," he added. "Maggie, this is Taniyah." Maggie smiled at Taniyah.

"Hello, Taniyah," she said to her politely. Maggie extended her hand to shake Taniyahs. Taniyah gave Maggie the once over, looking down at Maggie's hand but not taking it, before speaking again.

"Maggay, was it?" she asked her, then looked back at Billy. "Yuh wife yuh say, Billay? Well, isn't that nice." Maggie looked back and forth between the two of them, letting her hand drop back down at her side. Alvita mumbled something angrily to herself and headed into the back.

"What yuh drinking, Taniyah?" Delroy asked, trying to break the tension.

"Red stripe of course, Delroy," she answered, sitting down on the stool next to Billy. "In a glass mind. A clean one!" she told Delroy. Billy looked like he wanted the floor to swallow him up. He glanced at Maggie, and she smiled at him, trying not to roll her eyes. Then she leaned close and gave him a quick kiss. She looked at Taniyah and said,

"Nice to meet you, Taniyah." Then looked back at Billy, her hand on his knee. "I'll let you two catch up, Billy." She almost giggled at the look on his face. Then she went around the bar and joined Alvita in the kitchen.

"What yuh doing gyal?" Alvita asked when Maggie walked into the kitchen. Maggie smiled.

"Just letting them chat. They're at the bar with Delroy." Alvita shook her head.

"Not let yuh guard down, Maggay!" she told her, shaking her finger at her. "Dat Taniyah is on a mission." Maggie smiled again.

"I'm not too worried Alvita," she told her with a smile. Just then they heard a scream of pain from out front and ran out to see what had happened. Taniyah was on the floor holding her ankle. Billy and Delroy next to her.

"What happened?" Alvita asked, bending down next to Taniyah.

"Think I've broken my ankle!" Taniyah said back.

"Mag," Billy called. She bent down and looked at Taniyah's ankle, softly holding her foot and leg.

"Oww!" Taniyah yelled at her, glaring. Maggie moved it gently a couple different ways, all of which seemed to hurt immensely.

"What happened?" Maggie asked.

"My boot got stuck on this ridiculous stool," Taniyah told her with a pained and annoyed grimace, as Maggie felt around under her foot. Maggie slid her hand gently over Taniyah's ankle. She could feel the bone protruding slightly in one spot.

"It's definitely broken, Billy," she said, looking into his eyes. "She needs to get to a hospital." The bar was packed, which meant that Alvita and Delroy couldn't leave. Maggie didn't know the area or where the hospital was.

"Billay, I've got my car," Taniyah said to him.

"You still have the Coupe?" Billy asked Taniyah.

"Yea so, only room for two." Taniyah looked at Maggie with an air of contempt, then grinned slightly. Billy looked at Maggie. They stared at each other for a moment. No words, just feeling one another out. Maggie nodded at him, he looked at her like he was hoping she'd forbid him to go, knowing the thought would never cross her mind when someone needed help. Still looking at Maggie, he asked,

"Del, will you help me get her to the car?" The two of them pulled her up and supported her, Maggie grabbed Taniyah's purse for her and ran ahead to open the door. Then watched as they carried her off the porch and started to make their way up the long staircase to the street above, where Taniyah's car was parked.

"Yuh alright, Maggay?" Alvita asked as she sat down at the bar. Maggie smiled automatically.

"Oh ya, fine," she answered quickly. "Hope Taniyah is okay…" she added. Alvita laughed softly and shook her head.

"Gyal, you are a good one! Yuh made of de right stuff, Maggay." She told her, then walked off to take care of a customer. Maggie sat at the bar, feeling numb. She watched people coming and going, a few came over and complimented her on her singing, chatting a bit. Delroy came back and poured a shot for a regular. Then he leaned across the bar from her and patted her hand.

"Empress Maggay, can I get yuh something?" he asked. Maggie looked up at him and smiled.

"Oh, no thanks Delroy. Say, what time is it?" He looked at his watch.

"Nearly one." She smiled again, then got up and went to the kitchen.

"Alvita," she called.

"Yuh gyal?" She heard the reply from the back. Maggie went in a little further.

"Can I help in any way?" she asked. Alvita came from around the corner shaking her head.

"No gyal. We will not be closing for a couple hours." They were standing right in front of one another now.

"Okay, well I'm going to head back to the boat then," she told her. Then Maggie leaned close, and they hugged.

"Yuh Billay, he loves yuh, Maggay," she said with a smile. Maggie nodded.

"I know. Thanks Alvita." And she left the kitchen, gave Delroy a hug and left the bar. She walked down the beach towards the dock. It was dark, with a cloudy sky, but she could see the tiny lamp glowing in the back window of the cabin and used it to guide her, finding her way to the boat and climbing aboard. She didn't feel much like sleeping, so she had a shower, did some yoga, then went into the bathroom to start her nighttime routine, finishing and wandering about. Time ticked away slowly.

Maggie had been ready for bed for hours, but she couldn't drag herself from the big chair in the corner of the main cabin. Her thoughts bouncing back and forth between the sound of the waves splashing between the boat and the dock and the angst and worry she was feeling, and trying to ignore, causing her thoughts to fill with "what if's," and "I hope not's." She recognized that her thoughts were drifting to old stories of unfaithful ex's and tried to let them go, grabbing onto her time with Billy and how loyal he was, but it was difficult not to feel paranoid and worried. With her legs bent and her knees pulled tightly against her body, her robe falling open over her legs, she watched the flicker of the oil lamp. The room bouncing and blinking with the luminating glow, dancing over the dark wooden boat walls. Soft, orange beams of light stretching into the darkness. She hugged her knees tighter to her body and took a deep breath. A feeling of restlessness and unease filled her. They'd been gone for hours now. *Why are they taking so long?* She thought. Maggie wasn't really worried about Billy's actions, but she had felt the strong energy emitting from Taniyah towards him and knew what *her* intentions were. Recognizing she was a definite threat and trying not to think about any possible old feelings that might be stoked from within Billy. She stood up, pacing anxiously, unable to settle. "You're being ridiculous Maggie!" she told herself, walking over to the CD player and picking a random 90s "Women and Songs" disc. Popping the disc in and looking at the case, she remembered the first song being an old favourite. Maggie turned it up to maximum, hit repeat and let the music envelope her. As "Here With Me" started playing, she started moving her body. Slowly at first, barely moving. Softly rolling her shoulders and moving her body side to side. Coaxing herself into letting go and emptying her mind of all thought. Focusing on the bass and the drums, her natural intuitive desire to move and make music was awakened and she started to sing softly. Then the guitar started, adding more feeling and depth to her movements and Maggie's body swayed more deeply now. Sweeping her arms and hips in a flowing motion, her long caramel curls cascading and bouncing, sweeping across her shoulders and down her back. The silver highlights glinting in the lamp light. She closed her eyes. With each negative thought that surfaced, she moved the energy away from her body, swaying slowly, pulling white light and the healing power of the music inside of her. Maggie's voice grew louder. The beat becoming part of her. The drums and guitar pulling her further away from her worries. Feeling such a deep tug within her heart, calling out to Billy's. She could see him in her mind's eye, picturing him wrapped in a smoky pink glow, feeling herself engulfed by the same rose coloured energy. The deep steady drums rocked her without any conscious effort. Her head falling back, her arms reaching up, pulling down, gripping at the unseen vibrations and tempo, drawing the energy in, trailing her hands and fingers down towards her heart and into her very core. Nothing but the music and a hauntingly seductive energy, taking over her feelings and movements with fierce love and bewitching power. Singing from the depths of her soul, dancing and swaying, her movements becoming wilder with such emotional fluidity. Endlessly rhythmic. Exquisitely sensual. The song repeating. Again, and again. Maggie, dropped deeper into the entrancing spell, she'd let the music cast upon her. Sending and surrounding Billy with deep, unconditional love. Releasing herself from old pain and worry, letting go as she moved. Fumbling beautifully, deeper within herself, just being. She didn't know how many times she listened to the song when she first felt his energy around her. Keeping her eyes closed, still singing from her heart, her movements without conscious thought, she was suddenly surrounded by his warmth and love. She could feel an almost desperate ache and longing for her, calling out from his very soul. Envisioning his beautiful body, feeling his beautiful heart, imagining her hands holding his face softly. She could smell him, feel him, hear him from deep within.

"Billy..." the words barely escaped her mouth. A whisper floating out over her lips. Dancing with him in her mind, his arms wrapping around her, pulling her in. From deep within Maggie, she could feel their energy tangled, mingling like smoke licking a flame. Encircling them both completely. Then as the music started again, she really felt him. Still so deep inside herself, she wasn't sure it was actually him physically there with her until he leaned closer, and she felt his chest rise and fall. She could feel his breath on her neck as his face nestled into the curls at the back of her head. His hands on her waist, sliding together, and wrapping around her. His body closing the gap between them, pulling her tightly against him. Her hands reached up and slid behind his neck as he swayed with her, mimicking her movements. Billy nuzzled his face against her neck, and she felt his breath by her ear as their bodies moved together, hypnotically swaying. Unsure of where his body ended and where hers began, Maggie was still bewitched by the spell of her meditative dance. Billy quickly lost himself in Maggie's magic. Her scent and her sensuous energy captivated him. He ran one hand up her stomach, moving up between her breasts, up to her chest. His hand resting over her heart, the other still holding her waist. Maggie's fingers were in his hair and running up and down his neck. His deep voice soon joined with her luringly sensuous singing. His rich husky tone vibrating deeply from his body into hers. Hers tangling scintillatingly with his.

Angelically melodic, adding to the spell as they moved together like waves, pushing and pulling. So lost in one another's energy now, Maggie turned in his arms, her eyes still closed, still singing, Billy holding her lower back, the other hand sliding up her spine as her head fell back and she let her body softly fall back into his arms. Their bodies moving sensually, he pulled her back up and she felt his nose touching hers, her body almost limp, his strong hands supporting her as they moved together. One hand running up, sliding into her hair, and cradling the back of her head, Billy swept her body in a fluid half circle dip, Maggie's arms gently hanging down behind her, he pulled her back up, their faces resting nose to nose. Finally opening her eyes Maggie looked up into his deep blue stare. Their dance becoming more delightfully erotic with each movement. Keeping their gaze deep and strong. Billy took over, pulling Maggie's body tightly against his. She was still relaxed, fully trusting his hands supporting her body, letting him take complete control over her. Rocking, lifting, swaying, and pressing into her with such persuasive expression between their bodies and souls. The magic, the connection, the yearning, entangled in the gracefully salacious, unspoken language they shared. Then, still dancing as one, Billy's lips, softly and slowly kissing down her cheek, one hand on her lower back, the other cradling the back of her head, he kissed down to her neck. Pressing his warm lips against her skin, kissing deeply. She could feel his breath sweeping over her neck, as his fingers gently squeezed into her curls. Maggie's eyes closed, her lips parting slightly, she inhaled deeply, sliding her fingers into the hair at the back of his head, gently squeezing back, one hand sliding back down his back, resting at the bottom of his spine. Both pulling one another so close together. Maggie's breathing grew heavier as he kissed up and down her neck, taking his time, his open mouth trailing, his warm lips softly tracing over her skin. Supporting her again and dipping her, letting her head fall back so he could kiss his way down to her chest. As he pulled her back up, their eyes met and holding each other's faces they kissed deeply and passionately, their bodies swaying to the song. With their mouths almost touching, just slightly open and breathing with one another, they moved around the room. Lost in the seductive trance. Their hands were running all over one another, kissing, then staring, then kissing again. Billy ran his hands up her arms, over her shoulders, then pulled her robe down and leaned down to kiss each shoulder as he pulled it off her, letting it drop to the floor. Sliding his hands softly up either side of her neck, into her hair, he held her head as he kissed her lips long and hard.

Maggie began unbuttoning his shirt, taking her time, then slid it down his arms until it fell to the floor. Softly caressing his body, front to back, up and over his shoulders into his hair as he continued to move them to the beat still kissing her. She undid his pants and pulled them down far enough to drop them too. Together they pulled one another's underwear down and danced their way out of them. Hands sliding slowly over each other's bodies, staring deeply, still dancing, they continued to move seductively. As their gaze grew more intense, they began slowly grinding, grabbing one another's asses now and pulling into each other's bodies. Billy danced them towards the bedroom, stopping before they reached the bed, still moving to the music. He slid his hand down her hip, over and under her thigh and pulled her leg up, squeezing her tight. Maggie's center pressing into his body, slowly, subtly grinding against him. Their kisses becoming more intense, tongues sliding quickly together and around each other. Billy picked her up, walking them to the bed, sitting her down and crawling towards her as she backed up. Holding his face as he leaned close, they continued their slow, sensually hungry kisses, Billy's hand sliding from her hip, up her body and cupping her breast. He began to massage slowly, pressing his lips firmly to hers and pressing his body against hers tightly. Maggie reached down with one hand, squeezing his ass slowly and deeply. Billy moved his face down, sliding his tongue across the breast he was massaging, then he began to suck, rhythmically, still moving slowly, kissing, and sucking with pleasure. Maggie felt his hips lift right before he slowly pushed himself inside, her body rising and falling gently. They were still moving together as one, dancing, keeping rhythm with the steady beat of the song, his body almost flat, stretched out on top of her. Hardly leaving her, moving deep and slow. Pushing, and grinding together, back to kissing, tongues sliding so slowly, their hearts pounding together. Billy's hands slid up her body, pulling her arms above her head, and holding them down on the bed, their kissing deeper, tongues still dancing, he slid so very slowly. Moving deeply, in and out, not leaving her body. Maggie was moaning and writhing, her body felt like she was floating off the bed with such consuming tantalizing delight. After her deep meditative dance, their souls connecting, his body dancing as one with hers, and now Billy's steady, slow, deep glides, his heavy hot body pressing against hers, his hands holding hers down, and his tongue circling hers, all of it was taking her to places she'd never been before. Rolling into ecstasy, over and over. The slower he moved, the more she came. One beautifully stirring release after another. They kept eye contact, Billy continued to glide slowly, Maggie so wet, wrapping her legs around his body and holding him tight. She felt him growling deep within. Rocking her hips and pressing deeply against his body, he began to move a little quicker.

"You're amazing," she whispered, and Billy groaned, pushing harder. Letting go of her hands and pushing himself up to all fours. Maggie kept her hands above her head and grabbed onto the headboard. Looking deep into one another's eyes, into each other's souls, Maggie whispered the chorus as he slid back and forth. Her singing, as he moved inside her, awakening a deep, wild, hungered affection and desire within him. She watched as his gaze became more intense. Insatiably lustful. His dark blue eyes turning to the colour of midnight. His face contorting into intensely delicious elation. Then his eyes closed as he spoke her name,

"Maaggie..." he breathed. She was cumming again, shuddering. Still rocking her body gently back and forth, Billy still deep inside, the drums beating in the distance as their bodies pushed and pulled with the rhythm.

"Let go..." she coaxed him softly, and he held his breath, pressing deeper, making shorter, faster thrusts. "Billy," she whispered. He looked back at Maggie. Exhaling and inhaling deeply again, as he let himself fall completely into the magic of her sultry green eyes. Billy's breathing became heavier, Maggie's chest rising and falling. Her body and soul, lifting. Every cell dancing with exquisite euphoria as their skin pressed together, sparks dancing between them. She sang softly again, holding the headboard tightly. They kept their gaze. The climax building. Billy hitting a little harder with each drumbeat. Maggie squeezing him inside her, with each of Billy's glides in. Her heart almost aching with raw, tender emotion. Her energy flowing into him so deeply, his consuming her with such warmth.

"Ohhh Gawd, Maag." And his body started shaking as she felt him giving in to the sudden frenzied and explosive release. Still their hearts and bodies beating and moving as one, their lips pressed together, their hands holding one another's faces again, eyes open, slowly, and tenderly kissing all over each other's faces, holding tightly, still exploding together. Maggie lifted her head, her mouth opening, and she felt Billy's body quiver as he let out a long growling breath. They kept moving, uncontrollably dancing, unable to stop. Lips locked and pressing firmly, finishing their release in a harmonious full body shudder together. Still holding each other's faces, looking deeply and lovingly into each other's misty eyes, kissing so softly. Then Billy relaxed, his body lying on Maggie's, her arms hugging him tight, her fingers trailing over his back and arms. Billy's hand sweeping her hair from her face, playing with her curls, gently caressing her cheek, he looked into her eyes with astonished adoration.

"What have you done to me, Mag?" he asked, only able to whisper, and kissed her lips tenderly. Maggie smiled softly, her hand sweeping across his cheek lovingly, kissing him back.

"We're connected more deeply than we'll ever understand," she told him, hugging him tight. "We are one, Lover," she added, kissing his shoulder, her fingers tracing down his arm. He shivered and slipped his hands under her body to hug her tight. Whispering in her ear.

"I'll never be able to express just how much I love you Mag," he told her, and she smiled.

"Oh, but Billy, every time we *dance* together, you tell me, and it's absolutely beautiful," she whispered back. They laid together, holding on tight, looking at one another with unfathomable amazement. With soft kisses and caresses, the song still playing, holding them within their deep spell together for hours. They could still feel themselves dancing as they lay in stillness, their soul flames still mingling, soaking one another in from every corner of their being. Their breathing, slow and infrequent. Breathing softly together. The electricity still dancing, tantalizingly tip-toeing over every inch of skin pressed together. "Here, with me," Maggie whispered.

"Always," Billy breathed softly. Completely embraced in each other's arms. Neither one wanting to break the deep, beautiful connection they had somehow magnified in the dance their souls had shared. Unable to pull apart from one another. Billy whispered, "My heart beats for you. Always, forever, only for you my Maggie." She pulled him tighter.

"My Billy, my heart has always been yours." Hugging snugly. Billy lifted her face and moving so slowly, his eyes still so deep and dark, looking into her very depths, his lips gently found hers, and he pressed into her so softly.

"God, I love you!" he told her, brushing her hair off her face, and holding her cheek. She kissed him gently, her eyes smiling.

"And I love you," she breathed, his lips pressing to hers, and they both inhaled, their breath almost shuttering through their bodies together.

They never left each other the whole night. Drifting in and out of their enamored trance. Embraced, captivated, and deeply enchanted by the energy flowing so fiercely back and forth between them. Utterly spellbound. Awestruck, content, and completely charmed by one another. Connected by a deep inner pull. Their kisses, soft. The touch of their lips, their fingers, their breath, electric. Intensified. Relishing in each other's bodies over and over, softly, hypnotically. Their gaze, so deep. Their desire, unrelenting, and insatiable. They danced until the sun rose, engulfing them in a warm golden light as they held their bodies and their lips close, just breathing. Savouring the magic within and all around. As the sun shone on their feet and started making its way up their tangled bodies, Maggie and Billy felt a release. A beautiful new energy surrounded them. Looking into each other's eyes, they could feel one another's energy. Without words they had gone so deep together. Their connection surpassed their thirty years of togetherness.

* * * *

"Morning, Beautiful," Billy whispered to her. With loving, sleepy eyes, they gazed at each other.

"Morning, Handsome," she whispered back. Billy's hand softly brushed her cheek, and Maggie's trailed over his back. He kissed her gently, holding her face, his fingers in her hair.

"Something's different isn't it, Mag?" he asked, his eyes deep. Maggie's eyes sparkled as she smiled.

"Oh, yes. Fairly certain we've opened something deeper. I'm also certain this isn't our first life together, Lover." He chuckled softly.

"Just when I thought I couldn't love you more, Babe." They smiled at each other and kissed. Long and firmly, full of so much love. Holding tight.

CHAPTER 15

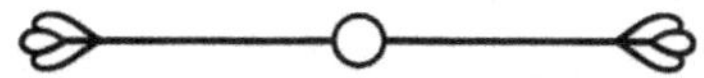

Billy came back to bed and crawled under the sheet.

"Be right back," Maggie whispered, kissing his forehead. She used the bathroom, then stepped back into the main cabin with a smile on her face and such warmth in her heart. Billy had already started the coffee maker, so she headed right back to bed and climbed in beside him. He held his arms open and pulled her in close, Maggie laying back onto his body and holding his arms around the front of her. They laid in silence for ages, feeling like they were conversing without speaking. Then Billy broke the silence.

"You're an amazing woman, Maggie," he told her. She pulled his arms tighter, hugging him in.

"Where did that come from?" she asked. Billy was quiet for a moment, then he spoke again.

"Your trust in me is not in vain, my Love," he said.

"I know that, Billy," she answered and turned over to look up at him, resting her chin on his chest. "How is Taniyah?" Maggie asked. Billy didn't answer for a moment.

"Her ankle is broken, babe, but she'll be fine." He looked at her seriously, his eyes worried. "Mag, Taniyah wanted to marry me. She'd been after me for years before we dated. When I realized she was trying to get pregnant I confronted her, and we fought. I told her I didn't want to marry her and then I ended things. Should I have told you all this before, Mag?" His eyes were soft and kind as he looked into hers. His hands were still sliding along her body softly.

"Billy, it's okay. No, you didn't *need* to tell me, but I'm glad you are telling me now. If you had been married and had children, yep, I'd say you would need to tell me that up front." She stopped and thought for a moment with a smile. Their eyes deep in their gaze with one another. They didn't need to say anything else. She trusted her heart with him completely and he trusted his with Maggie.

"I love you, Babe," he told her, pulling her up towards him. Maggie moved up and kissed his lips, running her hands over his face. Billy held her head and his eyes grinned looking at her.

"I love you," she replied quietly, and they kissed with pure love and trust for each other. They soon got out of bed and sat enjoying their pot of coffee. Billy had planned a surprise outing that they needed to get ready for, so after lazily lounging, he and Maggie got dressed and headed to Runaway Bay.

* * * *

"Dating back millions of years de Green Grotto Caves, one of de world's natural wonders an full of history, yuh will see de Runaway Caves used by our ancestors tuh flee from de plantations. It was also a frequently used hide out for pirates!" their tour guide told them dramatically as they looked around at everything he pointed out. Maggie, Billy, and the rest of the group put on their helmets and then started to make their way down into the caves. "De stalactites an stalagmites transporting us back in time. Notice de vibrant green colour of de cave walls are de result of de unique microorganisms dat are natural occurring here," he went on, leading them into a rock opening with many different tunnels. "Many believe there was a mystical spiritual veil in dem caves as well. If yuh look up yuh will see different sized openings; we call dem twilight zones an dem what de bats use tuh come an guh at night time. We 'ave nine different species of bats in here." Echoes and the sounds of bats could be heard as they walked through the stone halls, across bridges and into smaller caves. Some of the stalagmites were beautifully green in colour. "Dem caves did also be used as a nightclub for a while but due tuh safety reasons dem did shut dem down." They walked past the Runaway caves and came out into a clearing, then climbing down many stairs, they entered another series of caves leading them to a mixed salt and fresh pool of water. Continued sudden bursts of squeaking bats flying above them. Back out into the sunlight, then into more caves, a sign read "Wishing Well", and the guests were allowed to drop coins in and make wishes. Maggie and Billy waited then stepped up to the railing together. Grinning at one another, they threw their coins down and made their wishes. It took a while before they heard them hit the bottom.

"How deep is this well?" Billy asked their guide.

"Oh, bout forty feet," the man answered. Maggie and Billy stepped back and let the others take their turns with their wishes. It seemed unbelievable that there could be another forty feet below them. As they neared the end of the tour, their guide stopped to point out a large rock jetting out sideways and drummed on it so they could hear it was hollow. A marker for one of the exits that had been used during the club years. Walking past it, he led them back out into the light and thanked them for taking the tour.

"That was really interesting eh, Babe," Billy said as the cab pulled out of the parking lot and headed back towards the Robinsons.

"Very. Unreal to think of all the situations humanity has been in and how they've overcome them." Maggie was feeling very moved by the stories they'd heard walking through the caves and was feeling the spiritual energy from the experience strongly.

"Hey yuh two, how was yuh day?" Alvita asked as Billy and Maggie entered the bar hand in hand.

"Oh Alvita, it was so amazing!" Maggie answered quickly. The three sat at the bar and Maggie and Billy told Alvita all about it.

Joining Alvita in the kitchen, they made an early dinner together. Maggie, Billy and Alvita sat at the bar, Delroy joining in, and the four chatted and laughed as they ate. Then it was time to,

"Open for business!" As Delroy would say, and the Rockhouse was soon rocking. Maggie and Billy enjoyed yet another night of dancing with friends before saying goodnight.

"Goodnight lovebirds," Delroy said as they left. Alvita followed them to the door.

"Night, Alvi," Billy said, giving her a kiss on the cheek. Maggie and Alvita held and squeezed hands.

"Night, Alvita," Maggie said with a smile.

"Goodnight yuh gorgeous pair," she said back, then added with a playful snicker. "Mind yuh watch out for de wolves!" She turned and walked back into the bar, giggling to herself. Maggie and Billy looked at each other quickly, their eyes big.

"How did she know?" Maggie mouthed to Billy. He grinned cheekily, shaking his head with a chuckle.

"I don't know Babe. Alvi always knows. Everything!"

* * * *

Billy and Delroy spent the next day shutting down the Emerald Pearl. Maggie and Alvita cleaned the inside and took all the leftover food up to the Rockhouse.

"Thanks so much for your help, Alvita," Maggie told her, putting food into the fridge.

"No problem gyal. Everyting criss," she said with a big smile. "We are gonna miss yuh two!" she added, looking a bit sad. Maggie walked over to her and hugged her.

"Aw Alvita, we're going to miss you and Delroy so much!" Squeezing tight for a moment, then Alvita shook herself back to smiling.

"Ok, gyal, let us get tings ready for de night." They had spent the early morning getting things cooking for an early Christmas feast. It was only four days until Christmas and the Robinsons and the Stanton's wanted to enjoy the holiday together before Maggie and Billy flew home. Two big hams covered in pineapple, cherries and cloves were roasting in the oven along with three beautiful roasting jerk chickens. Maggie was stirring the massive pot of rice and peas while Alvita focused her efforts between her Jamaican Christmas cakes and goat soup.

"It smells amazing in here! I've missed your Christmas feast, Alvi!" came Billy's voice early that afternoon.

"Alvi Luv, we be hungry!" Delroy said, walking in behind Billy. Both men headed over to a tray covered in snacks and popped some into their mouths. Alvita ran over and started swatting their hands.

"Hey, yuh get outta here yuh naughty buoys!" she scolded. Maggie laughed as Alvita chased them out of the kitchen. "Guh an ave some crisps!" she said as she turned back and headed over to her cake. "Dem buoys!" she said, shaking her head. Grinning to herself, Maggie got back to work. She checked on the yampi and sweet yams.

"It does smell really good, Alvita!" Maggie exclaimed, taking a big sniff of the vegetables as she stirred them and recovered them. The outside of the Rockhouse already had an abundance of pepper lights hanging along the roof and the porch railing, but Alvita got Delroy and Billy working on decorating inside as well. Billy hung up more pepper lights and Delroy finished putting the decorations on the Christmas tree. Delroy had also gone out earlier and bought a dozen potted poinsettias and placed them around the bar. With traditional Christmas Reggae playing as they worked, the four danced around happily, setting up for the open feast. Every year they hosted their dinner for anyone who wanted to join or had nowhere to go for the holidays. They put all the food in warmers and lined them up on the tables that Delroy and Billy had moved to one side of the room. Delroy was setting up a huge punch bowl on the bar while Alvita worked at the stove in the back, slowly bringing water with sorrel, cloves, ginger, cinnamon and nutmeg to a simmering boil. Delroy would add the syrup and rum, orange and lime juice later and add the cut slices of oranges and limes then too. Billy got a half dozen Christmas CDs ready and put three into the player to start the night with. The stage was set as well, for a late-night carol jam, pepper lights strung all over the piano and drums, across the front window and down the walls.

Many guests, the Robinsons and Billy and Maggie enjoyed their Christmas feast together, drinking their punch and singing carols. They danced, drank, sang, and visited into the wee morning hours. Then after the bar was closed, Maggie and Billy helped pack up any food that was still left and cleaned up a little before saying goodnight to Delroy and Alvita. The Robinsons were taking Maggie and Billy to the airport for eleven the next morning, and they headed right up to bed after locking up behind Maggie and Billy.

"Come with me, Babe," Billy said as they headed towards the dock. Billy led Maggie down to the beach, holding her hand as they walked along in the moonlight. They walked for a while, then stopped and held one another tight, hugging and kissing, looking up at the moon and out into the Caribbean Sea. Billy squatted down and wrote their names in the sand. They watched as the waves rolled up over top and back down again. Maggie hugged him tight, and he leaned down and kissed her softly.

"Magical adventure, Lover," she said with a smile. Then hand in hand again, they walked back and crawled into the cozy cabin bed for the last time, hugging and drifting off to sleep.

＊ ＊ ＊ ＊

Packed up, sharing coffees with The Robinson's, they were all set and ready to go. The four were soon on their way to the airport, arriving an hour and a half later.

"Thanks for everything!" Maggie and Billy told Delroy and Alvita. Billy and Alvita hugging tight, talking into one another's ears and holding on. Delroy gave Maggie a big hug, squeezing her tight.

"Yuh walk good, Empress Maggay, an keep each other smiling!" he told her.

"We will Delroy. Thanks so much." She gave him a kiss on the cheek. Then they switched and Alvita and Maggie were holding on tight.

"Oh Alvita, I'm going to miss you. Thank you so much for everything." Maggie and Alvita hugged tighter.

"Yuh make sure yuh mind him gyal, an yuh better come back an see us soon!" she told Maggie. They pulled apart, both a bit teary. Maggie and Billy picked up their luggage and headed into the airport.

"Walk good, an happy Christmas!" Delroy called after them and they turned and waved at the Robinsons. Checking their luggage, they headed to their gate to wait out the next half hour. The terminal was very busy, and people were carrying all kinds of brightly wrapped parcels. Christmas decorations hung here and there, and Maggie realized how weird it was to hear Christmas Carols after a month of almost nothing but Reggae.

"Coffee, Babe?" Billy asked, getting up from his seat.

"Oh, yes please, Lover." Maggie answered smiling. Billy left and walked past the coffee shop and found a payphone.

"Yep?" came Frankie's perky voice answering the phone.

"Hey Frankie. Billy here," he said.

"Oh, hiya Billy, are you two on your way?" Frankie asked happily.

"Almost, waiting to board the plane. Say, were you able to get everything ready?" Billy asked him.

"Yes sir!" Frankie answered with a laugh. "I'll steer clear of the shed," Frankie added. Billy grinned.

"Thanks Frankie, we'll see you soon." And they hung up. Then Billy went to the coffee shop and grabbed two coffees and a couple carrot muffins and took them back to Maggie. Shortly after they finished their snack, they heard their boarding call. Sitting in their seats, hand in hand, both quiet.

"Thank you for the beautiful memories," Maggie said, looking at Billy with a warm smile. He reached out his hand and stroked her cheek.

"Thank you for being my wife," he said back leaning in and kissing her. "You know Mag, we'll still be over the Caribbean for a while." And he grinned cheekily at her.

"Mmhmm?" she said questioningly.

"Well, we could add one more thing to our list of memories of Jamaica." And he winked at her.

"We ask that you please fasten your seatbelts at this time and secure all baggage underneath your seat or in the overhead compartments. We also ask that your seats and table trays are in the upright position for takeoff. Thank you," came the announcement over the speaker. Maggie and Billy did up their seatbelts, Billy still grinning cheekily.

"What memory addition do you speak of?" she asked coyly.

"Mmmm. Meet me in the last washroom on the right when we get the 'all clear,' and I'll show you," Billy answered as they started down the runway and rose into the air. Maggie didn't want to leave Jamaica. Watching out the window as their paradise island grew smaller and smaller.

"You are now free to undo your seatbelts and move around the plane," came another announcement and Billy looked at Maggie and winked. He got up and made his way down to the washrooms. She sat still for a minute, then got up, and walked towards the washrooms too, passing the flight attendant and smiling. Maggie walked down to the last door and knocked softly. Billy opened the door and Maggie looked in. He was laughing.

"Damn Mag, not sure if this is going to work!" he said looking around at the 2-foot square space.

"Yikes, those washrooms are cramped even when you're alone!" she said disappointedly, leading the way back to their seats. The hours passed as they patiently waited for the lights to go dim, then they snuggled up under their blankets and tried to get some sleep.

* * * *

"Ladies and gentlemen, we have arrived at our destination. The local time is 12:03 am December 23rd. For your safety and the safety of those around you, please remain seated with your seat belt fastened and keep the aisle clear until we are parked at the gate." Waking from a not so comfy sleep, both Maggie and Billy sat up and stretched as much as they could. They waited until the plane was at the gate and the attendant worked her way down the aisle, indicating it was time for them to exit, before taking their carry-on luggage, and waiting for the rest at baggage claim. Then they headed for the washrooms to put their warmer, winter clothes, and boots on.

"Billy, it feels colder than I remember," Maggie told him as she joined him at a seating area.

"A month in the Caribbean will do that to you, Babe!" he said, laughing and rubbing her arms up and down, quickly warming her up. They sat and had a bite to eat and a hot coffee, then they both used the washrooms again, freshened up and brushed their teeth. Maggie pulled her hair back into a braid and Billy had a quick shave. Hailing a cab, they started their hours-long trek back to Tamarack. As much as Maggie was missing Jamaica, it was so wonderful to see homeland again.

Nothing like a view of nothing but trees, she thought to herself. Although, it was pretty strange to come back in the thick of winter when they'd just been walking sunny beaches. They both ended up nodding off for most of their journey, and the driver called out to Billy as they drove down the main street of town, announcing their arrival to Tamarack.

"Left after the b and b," he told the driver. The house looked so pretty nestled amongst the snow-covered trees. "Aw, Mag, it's good to be home," Billy said before they climbed out of the cab. She smiled and gave him a kiss.

"Home, with my husband," she said, smiling broadly. Billy paid the fare, then they unloaded their luggage and thanked the driver. The cabby gave a short beep and drove away. As they climbed the stairs of the porch, Billy stopped Maggie. Guiding her away from the front porch, Billy motioned for Maggie to follow him around the side of the house. He opened the back gate and headed for the shed.

"What are we doing?" Maggie asked him, plodding through a yard full of snow. He opened the shed door and let Maggie step inside, each of them setting down their things.

"Oh Billy!" she exclaimed, gasping. Christmas lights were hanging from the ceiling and strung all over the back wall. There were blankets and pillows in a cleared area on the floor and a blanket over the work bench along the wall. In the center of the blankets, was a bucket with a bottle of champagne sitting in it and Maggie's portable CD player sitting next to it. And hanging on the back of the door was a long black velvet dress and a blue shawl. "Billy, it's beautiful!" Maggie said, her eyes welling up. He turned her so she could see her dress. "Oh, my God..."

she said, her hands on her mouth. Billy was smiling at her, his eyes twinkling with delight.

"This crazy love of ours started in a shed Mrs. Stanton and isn't it only fitting we christen this marriage the same way?" he said winking at her. She laughed warmly and moved closer to hug him.

"Your crap pick up lines are getting better, Billy," Maggie said with a sultry look and pushing her body into his. He kissed her and smiled down at her with a chuckle.

"Well, here you go, Babe," he said, handing her the dress. It was just like the one she had worn all those years ago. *Well, maybe one or two sizes bigger,* she thought to herself. Billy walked over to the corner and took off his coat and boots. Then he watched her hungrily, as he looked through some CDs, picking one and putting it in the player. As Maggie undressed and pulled her new dress on, zipping it up and wrapping her shawl over her shoulders, "Sunshine" started playing softly. Then Billy stood up, and turned, and when he looked at her, he stopped dead, totally awe struck.

"Damn!" he said, his hand on his heart. "More breathtaking than I remembered, Mag." Maggie flashed her big smile, feeling her cheeks flush.

"Oh, Mr. Ashberry, I bet you say that to all the girls?!" she replied. He walked towards her with determined purpose.

"NEVA!" he yelled, both laughing, he picked her up and swung her around, kissing her hard and letting her feet touch down again. "No one but you, my Love," he told her. Billy held her close and began dancing her around the shed. They looked into each other's eyes dreamily, grinning as they relived old memories of each other from so long ago. Then, holding her hands he moved back to look at her again. He shook his head and gave a long exhale. "Damn, you're beautiful!" he said with a whistle. "You're good at looking beautiful, Maggie!" he added with a grin. Then he moved closer and pushed her back against the door. "What else are you good at, Mag?" he asked her with a wink. She felt her legs go weak. They smiled at one another knowingly, then they grabbed each other and started kissing deeply. "Mmm." Moaning and growling frantically, hands sliding all over, kissing hard. Billy lifted Maggie, her arms wrapped around his shoulders, legs wrapped around him. He walked them over to the work bench where he sat her down. They looked into each other's eyes, twinkling, smiling, then Billy reached out his hands and so very softly trailed his fingers over her shoulders, up her neck and into her hair, down her cheeks and neck again. Maggie's body was tingling, and she was suddenly aware of the music again.

"Listen To Your Heart" adding a reminiscent level to their embrace. Maggie's eyes closed, as he kissed her mouth, then her neck and back up. She slid her fingers up his neck and into his hair, their kisses deep and slow. Pulling each of her straps down and kissing her shoulders, then lifting her off the bench and standing her in front of him, he unzipped her, pulling her dress down, and kissing his way down her body. Maggie's hands still running through his hair as he squeezed and sucked her breasts, pulled down her underwear and kissed her center, then kissed his way back up her body and lifted her back up onto the bench. They looked at each other intensely, a smile playing on both their faces as Maggie undid his pants. Billy pulled them down, then Maggie held him firmly and licked the end of his nose.

"Why Mr. Ashberry, you are one fine man!" she told him and he growled at her, then grabbed her and pulled their bodies tight. "Angel" was playing as he began sucking her breasts again, before coming back up to gaze at her. She slid her fingers over his very eager cock, then wrapping her legs around him he pushed himself inside.

"Ohhh Gaawd," they both groaned. Hands running over one another, bodies moving fast and hard.

"Ohh Billy!" Maggie cried out. His face down and licking her neck, sucking, and kissing her as he pushed deeper and deeper.

"Maggie, you feel so damn good," he moaned, and she shuddered ecstatically. She lifted his face and held him in her hands, kissing him so deeply, sliding her tongue wildly into his mouth, playing with his tongue and sucking it, kissing him hard again. Billy's groans turned into deep growls as he glided with animalistic power. "With Or Without You" in the background. Billy held Maggie's face and looked into her eyes, their mouths open, inches away from one another, breathing deeply, he slid in so slowly, out, almost all the way, then in an inch, and back, almost out again. Maggie's eyes became darker and more seductive, and Billy continued to move so slowly, teasing her until she was growling with hunger.

"You're *so* hot, Billy," she moaned as he continued with long slow glides. Her body moving into his movements in sensual waves, squeezing him and *just* dragging her nails down his back, pulling him in.

"God you're sexy, Maggie," he groaned in her ear. Maggie grabbed his ass and pulled him in hard, squeezing his body tight with her legs. Keeping him deep inside, using her legs to pull him in tighter, her head falling back, she moved her body against his, her mouth opening slightly as she groaned with pleasure. Billy grabbed her breasts and squeezed again, sucking her neck and moving in and out quickly. Then he pulled her close, and they embraced each other completely, moving hard and fast. Kissing deeply and frantically. Their bodies pumping into one another. Moaning with delight.

"Ooooh Gaaawd..." Maggie's voice high, smiling as she let him take her away. Billy pumped faster, holding her tight. "Billy," she whispered his name and he bit and kissed her neck and shoulder. "Billy," she said a little deeper and louder and he moved faster still. "Ohhh Gawd Billy," she moaned and as he growled, his hips pushed forward hard, holding her ass and rocking his body into hers in smaller glides, pushing into her deeper still.

"Maaag…" he moaned, finishing with a full body shake. Their bodies shuddering and shaking as they kissed, pulling tightly into each other. Maggie continued orgasming as they kissed. The energy bursting between them. Then moving their faces around one another, mouths slightly open, brushing their cheeks over one another's faces and necks, Billy softly kissed Maggie's chest, then back to nuzzling and caressing each other's faces, rubbing one another's backs as they embraced so tenderly. "Forever Young" was playing and they held one another's faces and smiled, nose to nose. Billy kissed her and hugged her. Their bodies swayed with the music. Maggie wrapped her legs back around him and smiled. Sliding Maggie down to the floor, he kissed her again.

"Mmm mmm mmm. You are scrumptious, Mag." She smiled seeing his eyes crinkle with a grin.

"And my my my, you are lip smackingly tasty!" she said back. His head fell back with a chuckle, and he smiled at her.

"Hey, look what else is in here, Mag," he said, holding her hand and pulling her over to the blanket.

"Haa! Our pajamas and housecoats. How lovely!" Maggie said going over to pick her things up. It's nice and toasty in here too." she added. Billy winked.

"Ya, good call on the shed heater, babe." Maggie giggled, reaching for her things. They kissed and grinned as they put their cozy clothes on, and curled up together on the pillows, covered up with the blanket, they listened to the music and talked about the first time they christened a shed. They fell asleep listening to the nostalgic 80s music playing.

* * * *

Maggie kept her eyes closed, cuddling into Billy's warm body. She was transported back to their first naked morning together and smiled. Running her hand over his chest under the blanket and breathing him in.

"Mmm, morning, Mag," he whispered.

"Morning, my delicious lover," she purred back. Billy hugged her tightly.

"As much as I'd love to lay here with you, Beautiful, and greeting you with some morning wood, I need to beeline it into the house!" he told her with a laugh.

"Ya, me too, Babe!" she replied with a giggle. They pulled their coats and boots on, left the shed, and walked through the 2-foot-deep snow into the house. Loud barking from upstairs began as they closed the door and pulled their boots off. Billy ran upstairs first, and Maggie followed, waiting on their bed. Old Bill was sleeping down at the bottom where Maggie's feet would normally be. He looked up at her and meowed. As she bent down and picked him up, pulling him in for a cuddle, he started to purr, rubbing his head into her chin.

"Oh, Old Bill, I missed you so much!" Then a sleepy eyed, crazy haired Frankie poked his head out of his bedroom door.

"Magster?" he asked, looking towards her room.

"Hey Frankie, sorry we woke you." He scratched his belly as he walked towards her, Bojangles pushing past him and running for Maggie, barking like mad. Old Bill jumped out of her arms quickly and ran up to the head of the bed, clearly annoyed. Bo jumped up to lick Maggie's face as she fell backwards on the bed. "Bo!" she said laughing as he attacked her excitedly. Billy came out of the bathroom and Bo ran at him, almost knocking him down. Billy bent down and the two of them rolled about, Bo licking and barking happily. Maggie laughed, got up and gave Frankie a quick kiss on the cheek as she passed him, climbed over Billy and Bo and went into the bathroom.

"So, tell me everything!" Frankie said to Maggie as the three sat at the island with their coffees.

"Oh Frankie, it was so amazing!" Maggie said, her huge grin radiating, Billy's hand sliding over her back as he sipped at his coffee, Maggie's hand on his leg as their eyes twinkled looking at one another. Frankie was a great audience. A lover of travel himself, he was entranced by all their adventures. He asked questions and responded with excited enthusiasm in all the right places. They talked for hours and started on their second pot of coffee as they worked on the Christmas dinner prep together. Singing all their favourite Christmas carols as they worked. Billy ran out, taking Bojangles with him and grabbed a few things at the grocery store, then returned and joined in with dinner prep. They were having Carla and Stu over the next day for a family Christmas together. After washing, peeling, and chopping veggies, breaking bread for stuffing and doing a quick house cleanup they all lounged in the living room again, watching tv Christmas movies together. Maggie and Billy laid together on the couch, Bo on the floor beside them and Bill up on the back of the couch. Frankie was curled up under a blanket in Carla's favourite chair in the corner by the Christmas tree. Maggie had wrapped the few things she bought for the Myers and Frankie in Jamaica and put them under the tree. She hadn't bought Billy anything though, and wasn't sure what she would put under the tree for him. If Frankie wasn't with them, she'd have wrapped herself in a big bow and laid under the tree herself, but she'd have to think of something else this year. Billy made dinner for them, and they ate in front of the tv, watching "It's a Wonderful Life." Frankie went upstairs after dinner and showered. He and Carla had joined Stu's pool league, and they had a game that night.

"You two, sure you don't want to join us?" Frankie asked hopefully.

"Ah, thanks little brother but we're pretty tired from our travels," Maggie said. She and Billy glancing at one another, their eyes crinkling amorously. Frankie not missing the energy igniting between them and laughing.

"Okay, well, you too have a nice... relaxing evening then." He was still chuckling as he left, Billy close behind him.

As soon as Frankie was out the door, Billy locked it. He took Bo upstairs to Frankie's room and closed the door. Then he booted it back downstairs to Maggie. As Billy came down the hallway, he saw Maggie standing in the light of the Christmas tree, just enough light to see her eyes twinkling and her beautiful smile as she watched him approaching her. She pressed play on the stereo. Not taking into consideration Frankie's control of the music for the past month. Expecting to hear her own choice of favourites, she was a little surprised when the music started playing. Pleasantly surprised as the beat of "Fall In Deep" got her moving. Billy grinned at her hungrily and started dancing towards her. Snapping his fingers along with the song as he advanced on her. She turned the music up loud, and they danced in front of one another, seductively moving, letting the beat guide them. Softly running their hands over one another, moving around each other's bodies, they continued to dance, separately. Looking into each other's eyes fiercely. Saucily and playfully taunting one another. "Do You Remember" slowing down their movements, as they continued to dance around each other. Maggie moving deeply, swaying and almost belly dancing her way down to the floor and back up, her hair falling and swinging over her body. Billy watched her with intense desire. Hardly able to contain himself. They danced closer, still not holding one another, their bodies almost pressing together with their movements. "Play The Part" pulling them both into a sexier, more seductive dance with one another. Their movements suddenly becoming more like they were already tangled and devouring each other's bodies. Moving in and around each other, inches apart. Maggie's arms up above her head, down her body, her head dropping to one side, then looking back into Billy's eyes, her mouth slightly open. Billy's heart was pounding watching her provocative display as the music flowed through her, and into him. The bass carrying her into slower, sexier, grinding, hip rocking movements as they danced to "Put It On Me". Billy reached out and held her waist, moving with her. She looked at him with deep big hungry eyes, her mouth slightly open, almost pouting. With each deep drop of the bass, beating deep within them, their hips swayed sensually. Staring as they moved together, Billy's hand slid up the back of her neck, cradling the back of her head as they swayed more enticingly. He pulled her tight and kissed her passionately. His tongue slipping in instantly, Maggie kissed him back with an insatiable need. "On Our Knees" rocking their bodies in closer, and down deeper as they kissed. The song, softer than the last. Maggie's body moved so slowly as she undid her jeans and pulled her shirt off. Billy watched her with a grin as she danced out of her pants and kicked them to the couch. Maggie danced up to him again and pulled his shirt up and over his head as he undid his pants. Then they pulled one another in hard and close and started grinding together. Maggie's hand around his shoulder, her fingers tickling over the back of his neck. With her other arm hanging at her side, Billy held the back of her head again, his other hand sliding down her side and hip, holding her ass and they kissed and danced. They danced slowly and moved into one another's bodies. Their gaze, intense and thirsty. Then holding each other's faces, they pulled each other in, kissing more frantically. A steady deep rhythm from "Fault Lines" like a heartbeat, amping up their rising desire for one another. Fiercely ripping each other's underwear and Maggie's bra off, Billy pushed her backwards and pinned her against the patio door, kissing her neck, and squeezing her breasts. Maggie was beyond needing him, and she pulled him back up and looked into his eyes again, mouthing,

"I need you now!" With his eyes flashing, Billy lifted her up off the floor. Maggie wrapped her legs around him as her skin pressed harder against the cold glass door. Delicious shivers rippled throughout her body. He was inside her as the tempo of the song grew more intense. Pushing her, over and over against the glass, Maggie squeezing and clawing at his back and shoulders wanting him deeper. They couldn't hear each other, just the music, and feeling the steady beat. They could feel one another's energy and vibrating growls and groans as they pulled into each other. She sucked his neck and his ear, and he moved in and out faster and faster. Then as the CD switched and started playing "Apocalypse" Billy's movements slowed down, and he made long, purposeful glides, in and out. Their mouths opened as they watched each other. Maggie held Billy's face as they kept their gaze. She ran her tongue softly and slowly over his lips, staring seductively into his eyes. Her head fell back with pleasure as he kept moving inside her, so slowly. His face nuzzling into her curls, kissing her neck, she ran her fingers through his hair. Glides, slow and lasting. "Looking Too Closely" changed their pace, making their kisses more intense again. Billy was moving faster. The change in speed and movement made Maggie quiver from her head right down to her toes. She was shaking, her legs holding him tight, quivering, moaning with delight, over and over. The vibrations from the music coursing through her, louder than her cries of splendid release. She leaned her face down and sucked Billy's earlobe, sliding her tongue over his ear and she felt him shudder. He was pushing hard, her body squished against the glass door. Pumping steadily and holding her close. And then she felt him explode inside of her. He looked up into her eyes, as he released, their gaze deep and rapturous. Then his lips pressed into hers, hard and firm, and she held his face in her hands. Maggie holding on tight, from within. Embraced as one. Lips still pressing together, pushing her into glass.

"Mmm," Maggie moaned contentedly, and she felt Billy's body do the same as they inhaled deeply together. He walked them over to the couch, where they sat down on a blanket, with Maggie still wrapped around him, on his lap. They kissed, hugging tightly, and breathing hard. The unknown music was still playing and masking their sounds. Feeling each other breathing and kissing into each breath deeply. As the song slowed and quieted, their hands slid into the hair at the back of each other's heads, holding and squeezing softly, and they smiled at one another. As the song finished they heard Bo barking above them. Billy gave Maggie another kiss, then got up, shaking his hips at Maggie, as he left the room.

"Sweet, sweet cheeks, Sweet Cheeks!" she called out to him. She heard him chuckling from the hall.

"Coming boy," Maggie heard Billy call as he reached the upstairs landing, letting Bo out of Frankie's room. Bo's tongue lolled happily out the side of his smiley mouth as he followed Billy downstairs and out to the backyard. Maggie went up to the washroom, then put on her warm pajamas and headed back down. Grabbing a pair of boots and a sweater, she joined Billy and Bo outside. Billy smiled at her lovingly as he took her hand and kissed it, they walked together hand in hand, watching Bo jump through the snow happily, disappearing completely into the deeper drifts and popping back up with a big smile, tongue out as usual. Billy pulled Maggie in and hugged her, kissing her and grinning at her, his eyes smiling.

"That was hot, Mag," he said, then kissed her pressingly.

"Mmmm. "Always is, Lover," she replied, with a saucy grin. Bo's head popped up, his eyes wide, ears perked, then barking he ran back to the house. Maggie and Billy called after him and followed him to the patio doors where they saw Frankie open the door and step out.

"Hey you two!" he called. Maggie and Billy said hello and joined him. Frankie slid the door open enough to grab a towel off the stool by the door, then held Bo as they went inside and dried his paws and belly off.

"How was pool?" Maggie asked him. Frankie looked at her with a funny grin. "What?" she asked, unable to suppress a goofy grin back.

"Hmm, you guys have a good evening?" he asked, smiling broadly. Maggie and Billy looked at each other and smiled. Billy shrugged.

"Sure. You know, quiet." He winked at Maggie.

"Mmhmm. Quiet," Maggie added, nodding at Frankie. Frankie shook his head and laughed.

"Quiet, eh?" And he went to the fridge to grab a drink, Billy walked over and got himself and Maggie drinks too. The three sat down together in the living room and Frankie told them about his night, before Maggie and Billy headed to bed with Bo and Bill.

"Good night, Frankie," Maggie called as they climbed the stairs.

CHAPTER 16

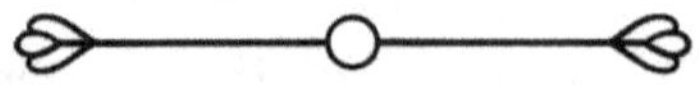

"Merry Christmas," Maggie whispered in Billy's ear, kissing his cheek softly and sliding her hand over it.

"Mmm, back atcha, Babe," he answered, grinning at her and turning to face her. His hands sliding over her body and hugging her tight. Bo jumped up onto the bed and put his front paws on top of them, leaning down and licking Billy's arm. Maggie and Billy laughed, patting him.

"Guess I better take him out," Billy said, giving Maggie a kiss, then sitting on the edge of the bed and stretching. Maggie watched as he stood up and pulled his pants and sweatshirt on. He sat back down and pulled his socks on, then turned his head and looked at Maggie again, smiling at her affectionately. Bo pushed his head under Billy's arm and licked him again. "Okay, boy, let's go," Billy said, leaving the room, Bo leading the way. Maggie snuggled up under the warm covers again and felt Old Bill hop up onto the bed then proceed to walk up her body. He sat down on her chest, looked at her and purred.

"Morning, Bill," Maggie said, sliding her hand out and patting his head. They snuggled for a few minutes, then Maggie got up and used the washroom before Billy came back up.

"All yours, gorgeous husband," she said, leaving the washroom, squeezing his ass and giving him a kiss.

"Mmm, let's just stay in bed for Christmas, Mag!" he suggested, pulling her back and kissing her deeply. Her legs turned to jelly.

"Merry Christmas to us!" she said with a grin. They parted and Maggie went down to feed Old Bill and grab a coffee.

With most of the prep ready, all Maggie had to do right away was get the turkey stuffed and put it in the oven on low for the day. Covering the pan and sliding it into the oven, she was just washing up when Billy came up behind her and held her tight. Moving his body against hers and rocking them gently, his face in her hair smelling her and kissing her neck. Maggie giggled as goosebumps spread over her body.

"You smell good," he breathed deeply. Maggie felt their fiery energy building as Billy growled his appetite for her.

"Morning, guys," came Frankie's voice and Billy and Maggie turned to see him walking over to the coffee pot, grinning at them impishly.

"Morning," Billy answered.

"Morning, Frankie. Merry Christmas!" Maggie said, smiling at him, and she and Frankie gave each other a quick hug as they passed one another. Maggie sat at the dining table, Billy joining her with his coffee. Looking out the patio doors, Maggie noticed big fluffy snowflakes softly falling and it made her smile. Filled with the magical wonder of Christmas, as she watched the beautiful white flakes landing on the deep snow in the yard.

"What time are Carla and Stu coming over, Magster?" Frankie asked.

"Planning on two-ish," she answered, then smirked at him. "Depending on Stu of course..." she added and Frankie and Billy both gave a laugh.

"So, Stu-ish o'clock, then?" Frankie said, laughing at his joke, then again as Maggie and Billy laughed at *him.*

"You need me to do anything right now, Babe?" Billy asked, finishing his coffee, and walking to the sink with his mug.

"Um, no, don't think so, thanks Lover," she answered.

"Kay, think I'll grab my shower now. You guys need the washroom?" he asked the two of them. Frankie went and sat with Maggie.

"No, all good," Frankie answered, and Maggie shook her head with a smile. Billy left for upstairs. Maggie waited a moment, then,

"Hey Frankie, I don't have anything for Billy for Christmas. I wasn't expecting to be gone for a month and didn't do any shopping. Got any brilliant ideas?" she asked. He smiled at her.

"Well, I can think of a couple things he might like, but it would probably be just another typical day's event for you two!" Maggie laughed and slapped his arm playfully.

"Sorry! Do we gross you out, little brother?" she asked him. He shook his head.

"God no, Mag. Love seeing you in love with such a great guy." Maggie beamed. "You might want to clean your ass prints off the sliding door though, Magster." he added with a laugh and his finger in his mouth pretending to gag.

"Oh my God, Frankie!" she replied, embarrassed and laughing. She bumped against him playfully, got up and grabbed her cleaning spray and a couple paper towels and laughed as she gave the glass a cleaning. "Well thanks," she said walking out of the kitchen as she continued to talk. "So, any other ideas for gifts?" Frankie had a mouthful of coffee and sat thinking about it for a few seconds, a bit of a smirk lingering on his face.

"I don't know sis, let me think on it a bit more." Maggie got up and took her empty cup to the sink.

"Wanna help me get some drinky things ready, Frankie?" she asked, and he joined her in the kitchen. "Oh, one sec," she told him, going over and filling the stereo turntable with her top five favourite Christmas CDs and turning it on. They washed oranges, and lemons, sliced some and wedged some, then got the cranberries boiling and were singing along to the carols when Billy came back down. Bo barked at him urgently, so he took him out back.

"Hey Magster, why don't you just wrap yourself up and sit under the Christmas tree?" Frankie suggested, giggling. Maggie shot him a quick look and grinned.

"Thought of that too Frankie but didn't think you'd appreciate it much." They both laughed.

"Ha, great minds think alike eh!" he added. Billy came back in and wiped Bo down.

"What are you two giggling about over there?" he asked as he walked towards them.

"Oh nothing," Maggie answered with a cheeky grin. Billy's eyes crinkled into a smile.

"Mmhmm," he responded. Maggie headed up for her shower shortly after, leaving the boys hanging out in the living room.

* * * *

"Merry Christmas!!" "Welcome home!" "Merry Christmas" "Come in, Merry Christmas" the five of them exchanged greetings, hugging and smiling. As Stu and Carla came in they quickly closed the door behind them, shutting out the storm that had just started on their way over.

"Should have brought our sleeping bags, Stu," Carla said, the snow on her head falling like icing sugar onto the mat at the front door. "Here ya go, Mags," she said, handing Maggie a dessert tray full of mixed squares.

"Thanks!" Maggie said, taking it from her. Once Carla had taken off her stuff the two friends walked into the kitchen together. Stu placed the gifts they'd brought under the tree, then joined Billy and Frankie at the island, sitting down on a stool.

"Beer, Stu?" Billy asked, getting up and walking over to the fridge.

"Ya, thanks," he answered.

"Frankie?" Billy asked, holding two beers.

"No, thanks. I'll wait for the Christmas punch," he replied.

"Oh ya!" Maggie said realizing she needed to finish making it.

With drinks in hand, the five gathered in the living room, the Christmas music still playing while they visited with one another. Carla coaxed Billy into playing his guitar and Frankie sent Maggie to her piano. He turned the stereo off, and they all sang Christmas carols together. Well, not so much Stu, but Bo joined in. Then they played Pictionary, laughing and carrying on merrily. Maggie and Billy against Carla and Frankie. Stu had a little nap in the chair in the corner, beer in hand.

"Let's open presents!" Carla yelled, moving over to the tree. Stu grumbled awake, but cheered up a bit when he saw it was time for presents. Maggie and Billy slid down off the couch to the floor, leaning against one another. Frankie came and sat on the other side of Maggie and leaned in too, making a cozy Maggie sandwich. Maggie happily snuggled between her two favourite men, grinning her big Maggie grin.

What a perfect Christmas this has been! She thought to herself. Carla started pulling gifts out from under the tree.

"To Frankie, from Mags and Billy boy," she teased and tossed Frankie a plush silver and gold wrapped gift. "To Mags and Sweet Cheeks," she said, smiling as she passed it to Maggie. "From me and Stu," she added. Stu laughed gruffly.

"I ain't giving nobody named Sweet Cheeks a gift!" Everyone laughed. Stu looked quite serious and rather confused.

"Thank you, Carla and Stu," Maggie said, taking the brightly wrapped box. She sat it on her lap and ripped it open. Inside was a beautiful white photo album covered in seashells, and inside were pictures from the girl's night at the Sunshine Villa, the guy's stag night and everyone's combined photos from the wedding. "Oh Carla, this is beautiful!" Maggie said, handing Billy the album and walking over to

Carla to give her a hug. "Thank you so much!" she said as they squeezed one another tight.

"No problemo, Mags!"

"This is really nice guys, thank you." Billy added smiling at Carla and Stu, then looking through the album again. Maggie walked over to Stu who was sitting in Carla's favourite chair and pulled him up for a hug too. He made a stink about it for a moment, then gave in, and hugged Maggie back.

"Merry Christmas, Stu," Maggie told him and he smiled at her.

"Ya, you too Maggie. Not hugging Sweet Cheeks though." And everyone laughed again.

"That's alright Stu, I'll get ya later!" Billy said, grinning cheekily as Stu shifted in his chair.

Maggie handed out the travel gifts she gathered over their honeymoon around Jamaica. Frankie loved his new Rastafarian hat Maggie found him. He always bought a new hat in every new country he went to and already had quite a collection. He was quite excited to receive a new addition. Stu was more than pleased with his mix of Jamaican rums from every port. And Carla couldn't stop thanking Maggie for her new fishing tackle box, brightly clad in yellow, green and red, with a few different hooks, lures and sinkers than she had ever had before.

After they opened gifts, they chatted for a bit while Maggie and Billy worked on food.

"Dinner's ready!" Billy called from the kitchen as he and Maggie finished putting food on the dining room table. "Get it while it's hot!" he added.

"Hells ya!" Carla hollered, pulling Stu out of the chair, and heading over to the table. Billy carved the turkey and Maggie passed out everyone's plates in turn. Billy gave them all a good size portion. Then passing their plates down the table, everyone helped themselves to potatoes, carrots and turnip, peas, stuffing, gravy, and cranberries.

"Mmm. Mags... this is effing delicious!" Carla said through a mouthful of stuffing. Maggie giggled, smiling her response,

"Thanks Carla,"

"Ya, well done Maggie!" Stu added. "Way better than your apple crisp!" he said with a pleased laugh at his own joke. Everyone except Maggie laughed. She grinned sheepishly as they all looked at her. They passed around Christmas crackers, reading their jokes and wearing their funny hats. As everyone laughed and chatted, Billy leaned in close to Maggie,

"Hey, Mag," he said quietly in her ear. "If I dress up like Santa Claus, will you sit on my lap?" Maggie almost choked on her mouthful, laughing. She looked at him with a grin and he winked at her. She leaned in close to his ear and with a very breathy whisper answered.

"Oh Billy, you don't have to dress up to get me to sit on *your* lap." Then she licked his ear lobe and added, "But if you did, it just might take us to our next level. Santa might get a nice Ho Ho Ho." She sat back up and grinned mischievously at him. She had out-aroused him. He kissed her and chuckled, sliding his feet together with hers. After everyone finished, they decided to relax for a bit before dessert, they took their egg nogs, rums, and punches over to the living room and flopped down to watch "A Christmas Carol." About halfway through, Maggie snuck away to use the washroom and as she came out Billy was waiting for her on the landing, holding the mistletoe.

"Happy Christmas, Mrs. Stanton," he said with a cheeky grin. He pulled her in, holding her close, holding the mistletoe above them, and looked down at her warmly.

"Happy Christmas, Mr. Ashberry," she said back. Then her eyes opened with surprise as he pulled her tighter. "Oh my! Is that a Christmas cracker Sergeant or are you just happy to see me?" she asked him flirtatiously. His eyebrows raising up and down, his eyes twinkling.

"Early Christmas present, Mag," he replied, giving her a kiss.

"Ohh, I wonder what it is?" she said giggling. Billy's head fell back with a loud chuckle.

"Mag, meet me out back with Bo, in ten," he said, winking at her. "Just Bo!" he said and went into the washroom. She grinned and made her way downstairs. Grabbing the rum, she brought it over to the living room and topped Frankie, Carla, and Stu's drinks up.

"Anyone need anything?" she asked.

"No, thank you!" was the consensus. Ten minutes later, she called Bo and took him out back. Billy was near the shed smiling at her.

"Why did you want me to bring Bo out, Lover?" she asked him curiously.

"Just give me one more minute, Babe," he replied and walked through the yard to the side gate and called out. "Come on, Bojangles." Bo came running. He let Bo finish his business, then he took him around to the front of the house, opened the door and let him in, closed it behind him and walked around the house to the backyard again. Maggie was shivering as she saw him walking back towards her. Big fluffy snowflakes in their hair and on their shoulders, still falling steadily making it look like they were in soft starlight with the added glow of the Christmas lights. "You look so beautiful, Mag," he told her, smiling at her lovingly.

* * * *

Nearing the last half hour of the Christmas movie, Frankie paused it so the three of them could take a bathroom break. They grabbed more drinks and sat down again, all ready to start the movie back up.

"Where's the horny honeymooners?" Stu asked, looking around. "When's dessert?" he added. Carla looked around, then she and Frankie made eye contact, and they knew the answer. Carla shook her head and Frankie smiled.

"Give you one guess, Stu!" Carla told him. It took Stu a second, then all three looked towards the back patio doors, the Christmas lights lighting up the path to the shed. Frankie walked over and opened the door slightly. All three stood silently for a moment then started grinning as they heard Billy singing, "Santa Claus Is Back In Town."

"So that's why they built it..." Frankie added laughing.

"Gawd, those two!" Carla said.

"Well, least they had the decency to take their randy formalities outside when there's guests about!" Stu said, and he walked to the island, grabbed the apple pie and three forks, came back, and sat down on the couch. Frankie and Carla sat on either side of him and looked down at the pie in his lap. "Roll the film!" he told Frankie, pointing to the TV with his fork. Frankie picked up the remote, shaking his head and laughing, pressed play and the three carried on with the movie.

* * * *

Looking lovingly into each other's eyes, embracing, and rocking gently together, standing inside the shed, Billy and Maggie grinned at one another. The Christmas lights twinkling in their eyes, as Billy leaned down and kissed her lips softly.

"Merry Christmas, Beautiful," he whispered.

"Merry Christmas, Handsome," she whispered back, and they hugged tightly, kissing deeply, looking at each other again and smiling.

"Always, my Love," Billy told her.

"Forever my Lover," she breathed back. Their lips pressing softly.

"Is it time for my present yet, Billy?" Maggie asked with a saucy grin.

"Damn straight!" he told her with a smile. "It's time for your Christmas Quicky," he said, winking. Maggie laughed.

"Quicky?" she repeated. "Mmm, really, just the one?" she purred and snuggled into him lovingly. Billy's eyes twinkled hungrily,

"NEVA!" he replied, and they pulled one another in for an epically merry shed worthy romp.

THE END

ABOUT THE AUTHOR

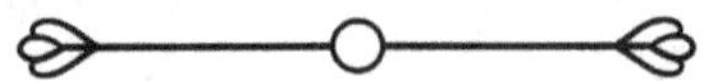

Katherine Waite-Gracie is a single, homeschooling Mom of two great kids, two fur babies, and a fish called Mr. Malory. Growing up in a small town in Ontario, loving community and nature, she spent most of her time in the water or taking long walks with friends, daydreaming of a life full of wooded, secluded comforts and spending her days and nights with a partner as loving and as passionate about life as herself. Before writing romance novels, Katherine attained degrees and certificates in Intervention, Reiki, and Animal Specialist Programs.

LinkedIn: www.linkedin.com/in/kat-waite-gracie-3681928a
Facebook: www.facebook.com/kat.waitegracie
Instagram: https://www.instagram.com/katsmyth/

Thank you to all those who continue to support my writing journey. As always, thank you to my two amazing kiddo's who have been such encouraging lights along the way. Thank you to those of you who just joined The Maggie Ashberry Series. I hope you find these stories hopeful, fun, delightfully intoxicating and full of all the love I've poured into them.
Remember, never stop following your dreams!
Love and Light Friends.

Come One Sweaty Pie

www.ingramcontent.com/pod-product-compliance
Lightning Source LLC
Chambersburg PA
CBHW072102300726
48975CB00003B/674